What Others Are [illegible] Omega Dragon

Similar to Merlin's final riddle, we know an author's true talent by the conclusion of the story he writes. Mr. Davis's thrilling saga has come to an end. *Omega Dragon* marks the last of a 12-book story that has captivated fans for the past 10 years. Dragons in our Midst, Oracles of Fire, and Children of the Bard have blessed more people than Bryan will ever know. In *Omega Dragon*, Bryan's ensemble cast of characters comes together for one final epic conclusion. A mysterious and captivating beginning grabs the reader till the last tear-stained page. Mr. Davis, congratulations, you have made your mark on the fantasy genre. Bryan Davis is one of the greats. When someone says C. S. Lewis and J. R. R. Tolkien, I say Bryan Davis. *Omega Dragon* is one of your finest works. Congratulations on creating a classic.

Alex Randazzo, Director and Actor of *Raising Dragons*,
a fan-made movie (Age 17)

Bryan Davis has concluded ten years of heart-pounding adventure with one fantastic novel!! Just when you thought our heroes had experienced it all, *Omega Dragon* unleashes one more faith-wrenching battle that drives them on a path of courage and sacrifice once again! But which of our heroes will end up sacrificing their all, even to the point of death? *Omega Dragon* is full of unexpected twists and turns, yet ends in a way that will leave you brimming with satisfaction! Bryan Davis has truly touched my heart throughout these three extraordinary series, and I am forever thankful for the ride he has bestowed on us all!

Ariel Johnson (Age 23)

Bryan Davis's writing never ceases to amaze me. *Omega Dragon* is no exception. This book took me on an emotional roller coaster, as his books always do. The relationships within the story are so complex, and I, as a reader, loved watching them develop and continue to grow. The journeys that the characters of *Omega Dragon* go on are very intense and keep you wanting more. The way this book ends the series was better than I could have hoped for. It does a beautiful job wrapping it up and even puts a bow on top. I loved this book, and I know you will too.

Megan Soucie (Age 13)

Trust. If I had to sum up the entire Dragons in our Midst story in one word I would say trust. Trust in God, trust in crazy statements, dragons, friends, family. It all required trust. Maybe that's what immersed me in this series. It conveyed trust that seemed supernatural, because a lot of times it was. However, it was also extremely human. In addition, Bryan Davis weaves a tale brand new in *Omega Dragon.* This book will have you grinning on one page, leave you in tears on the next, and cracking a joke in the first sentence of the following. Packed with action, humor, scripture, and amazing character development, *Omega Dragon* is truly a masterpiece and a fitting end to this fantastic series.

Josh Ryner (Age 15)

"We hope that what we have done will spark faith, hope, courage, and love in their hearts." A tale of faith, sacrifice and love, *Omega Dragon* is the spectacular conclusion to a world I have been blessed to be a part of for 10 years! Mr. Davis has once again captivated me with inspirational characters that display what it means to truly love the Lord and to love others.

Jessica Jones (Age 24)

This is it. Everything ends here. We've all spent countless hours poring over Dragons in our Midst, Oracles of Fire, and Children of the Bard for this final moment. Bryan Davis has built everything up for a spellbinding conclusion. Who will die? Who will live? I can't tell you how many times I cried out to the characters in the book, warning them of their coming challenges. Pardon the cliché, but I honestly had so much trouble putting this book down. This series is brilliant, and I am very satisfied with its closing installment.

Lana Aredhel Williams (Age 20)

All throughout the Dragons in our Midst, Oracles of Fire, and Children of the Bard series, I was taken on a journey of faith, hope, trust, and sacrificial love. I laughed and cried with the characters and even felt their pain. Mr. Davis has written a brilliant story that will not soon be forgotten. *Omega Dragon* is full of action, life, and adventure. It brings this wonderful journey to a conclusion, and I was very satisfied. Mr. Davis tied up all the loose ends quite beautifully. It is by far the best book I have read!

Amelia McClew (Age 16)

The final installment of the Children of the Bard series and the Dragons In Our Midst saga has climaxed in the most exhilarating book yet! The trials and victories of each character ignite a greater love for the Savior in the hearts of those who read it. This book has encouraged my faith in new ways by the tales of love, courage, sacrifice, humility, and tremendous faith of each beautifully written character. The ending of this story is one you will never forget! Thank you, Mr. Davis!

Emmaline Kempf (Age 22)

Omega Dragon is a great finale to a great series! Full of twists and turns, one moment you're laughing at Walter's sarcastic puns and next you're crying as Matt and Lauren face all manner of danger, both on Earth and in Second Eden. And all throughout the journey, you never forget that the Father of Lights has a plan to save the faithful from Satan.

Alahna Harrison (Age 15)

Thrilling! Jaw-dropping! Beautiful! These are the main words I would use to describe Mr. Davis's book *Omega Dragon.* It shows real truths without sugar coating them, and shows everything as it really is. It shows what can be accomplished with true sacrifice, true courage, and true love. Once this book starts and you have entered its magical performance, it is hard to put down (my family will attest to this). I wholeheartedly recommend that you add this book your reading lists. I also commend Mr. Davis on his wonderful books and the journey they have taken me on.

Micha-el Esslinger (Age 17)

Mr. Davis is a tremendous storyteller who knocks it out of the park in the amazing conclusion to the Children of the Bard series. I was torn between wanting to read to the end of the book and saying good-bye my friends—those characters who really have become like friends to me as we journeyed together over these last several years. My mom said anything that makes me excited to read the Bible and memorize verses is okay by her. Thank you for the cherished memories, Mr. Davis. Write more please!

Ian Primrose-Raines (Age 11)

I have one word: Wow. As someone who has been reading this story since I was 10 years old, I can truly say that this was a perfect ending to the journey Mr. Davis took us on. This was a finale that was needed, including wonderful character development, story pacing, and vivid images. *Omega Dragon* brought many emotions and ended with hope and curiosity. I can't wait to start my younger sister on these books!

Jessie Morrison (Age 18)

Omega Dragon was an amazing ending to a life-altering story. As this final chapter closes, you can't help but reminisce about past adventures, old friends, and the deep faith that runs throughout the pages. With both tragedy and love around each corner, it couldn't be more perfect.

Benjamin Steward (Age 16)

Mr. Davis has graced the Children of the Bard series with a truly spectacular conclusion that will leave readers content and thankful for the remarkable journey they have experienced.

Matthew Ammerman (Age 15)

From start to finish, I couldn't put the book down. Fiery battles, sacrifice, and a cast of returning characters doubled with plot twists around every corner kept me riveted until the final words.

Logan Farrington (Age 14)

Mr. Davis has done it again! *Omega Dragon* combines characters you know and love, nonstop action, and good vs. evil into one fast-paced adventure! You will stay up late at night reading this. (I did!) I think *Omega Dragon* is the best book in the series, bringing it to a satisfying and exhilarating conclusion. If I could rate this more than five stars, I would!

William Monin (Age 13)

Omega Dragon

Bryan Davis

Omega Dragon

Published by Living Ink Books, an imprint of AMG Publishers
6815 Shallowford Rd.
Chattanooga, Tennessee 37421

Print Edition ISBN 13: 978-0-89957-883-5
EPUB Edition ISBN 13: 978-1-61715-467-6
Mobi Edition ISBN 13: 978-1-61715-468-3
EPDF Edition ISBN 13: 978-1-61715-469-0

Omega Dragon is the fourth of four books in the youth fantasy fiction series, Children of the Bard. CHILDREN OF THE BARD is a registered trademark of AMG Publishers.

First printing—February 2015

Cover designed by Daryle Beam, Bright Boy Design, Chattanooga, Tennessee
Interior design and typesetting by Reider Publishing Services,
West Hollywood, California
Dedication page image on page ix created by James Art Ville
Edited and proofread by Susie Davis, Sharon Neal, and Rick Steele

Printed in the United States of America
19 18 17 16 15 –WO– 8 7 6 5 4 3 2

"Behold, I am coming quickly, and My reward is with Me, to render to every man according to what he has done. I am the Alpha and the Omega, the first and the last, the beginning and the end." Blessed are those who wash their robes, so that they may have the right to the tree of life, and may enter by the gates into the city. (Revelation 22:12-14 NASB)

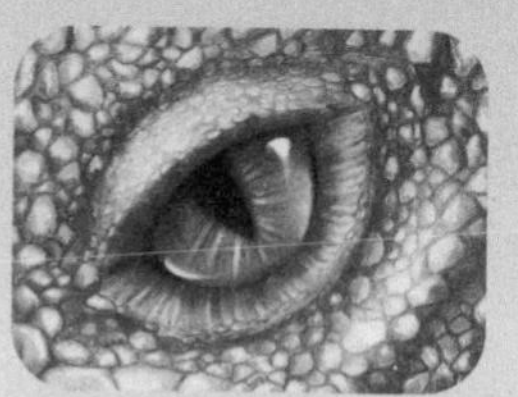

Author's Note

When *The Bones of Makaidos* came out, I thought the Dragons in our Midst story world had come to an end. After eight books, more than a million words, and a final chapter that provided a satisfying end, it seemed appropriate to wrap up the tales. Then a new idea developed, and it birthed a third four-book series that gave life to new characters and ignited fresh adventures. Children of the Bard proved to be more than a worthwhile addition.

When you read *Omega Dragon*, you will see that the tale has reached a conclusion. Of course, it is always possible to add more tales, and I might do so in short-story format, but I trust that this is the last novel that will feature Billy, Bonnie, Walter, Ashley, and the rest of gang.

I hope that these twelve novels have been a blessing to you. They certainly have been to me. I thank God for the opportunity to reach so many readers with themes that have touched their hearts in a lasting way.

It would be impossible to thank every person who provided help as these stories came to life, so please accept this blanket message of gratitude to all of you who offered a helpful hand. I would, however, like to single out a couple of people. First, I am thankful for my wife, Susie, who has been a tireless champion of my stories and me as a writer. Without her, I could never have persevered through this long writing journey.

Second, I am grateful for the late Dan Penwell of AMG Publishers who opened the door for these adventures. His foresight allowed many thousands of readers an opportunity to obtain a viewing portal into Heaven's glory.

May God bless each one of you with heavenly vision so that you may perceive the heart of God. Speak the truth, live the truth, and be the truth. Never let the faithless ones change any of those three principles. They are the means by which even the blind will be able to see the Light.

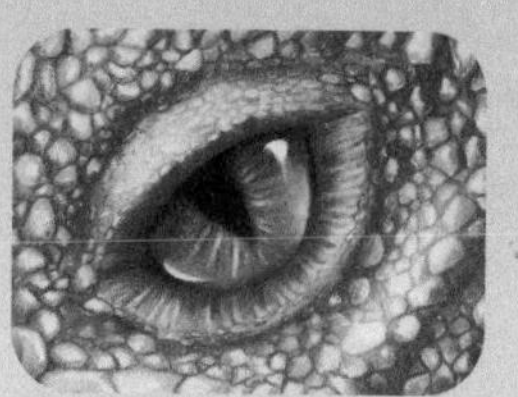

CONTENTS

CONTENTS

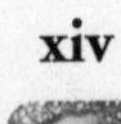

Merlin's Answer

I spoke a riddle long ago
Of dragons and their flight.
Are dragons vile or tame? I asked.
Are tricks concealed from sight?

And now at final eventide
I ask to those who've learned,
Did dragons set your hearts afire?
Or did your soul get burned?

The flame's design is not to harm,
To burn, to sear, to scorch;
A lantern shines, a candle glows.
The fire is a torch.

The pages turn; the words seep in.
The flame reveals our fears.
The puzzle pieces interlock
When minds explore frontiers.

We know why heroes charge to war
While cowards flee in haste;
A hero grasps for Heaven's flames
And asks for just a taste.

Then like a flood, infernos blaze;
A hero's heart is born.
He draws his sword, the light of truth,
And night melts into morn.

From tale to tale we felt the flames
Of dragons, girls, and kings.
They burned the chaff; they polished hearts;
They helped us spread our wings.

So reader friends, I tell you how
To solve the riddle's quest.
Entrust your heart to flames of those
Who pass this simple test.

They tear none down; their words uplift;
They set our wings to flight;
They blaze a trail, a holy path.
The shadows flee their light.

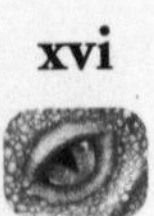

The greatest test of all is love
In sacrificial death.
We know a dragon's virtue by
A dragon's dying breath.

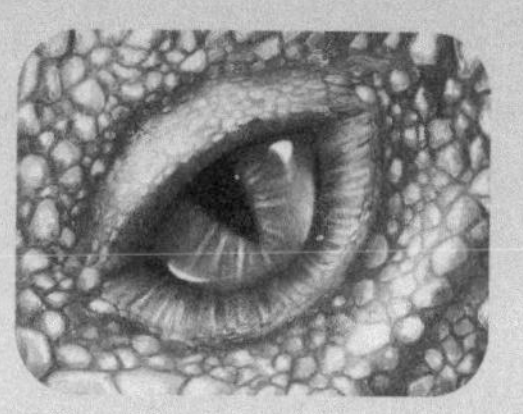

1

CHAPTER

The Life Reservoir

Frozen faces, pale and grim, lay sealed under a sheet of ice—lost … forlorn … without purpose.

Or so they seemed.

Standing at the edge of the reservoir, Merlin kept his stare on the nebulous faces, soulless phantasms that held no thoughts as they drifted in misty swirls under the icy surface. Mindless or not, they were a bit more animated than usual. Perhaps a newly slain martyr had recently infused a surge of energy into this sacred pool.

He pushed the bottom end of his walking staff into the thick ice. Radiance surrounded the smooth acacia wood and rode upward until it reached a candlestone wedged within a triple fork at the top. The candlestone, a crystalline gem about the size of his thumb, absorbed the light, made it spin around its dark core, and sent it out again in a dim yellow beam parallel to the floor.

He eyed the beam—still not white and far from bright enough. Even with the recent martyr's added life energy, the reservoir had

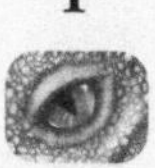

not yet collected a sufficient amount. The energy streams trapped below would need a significant injection as well as a resurrection to stir the frozen cauldron in order to keep the streams active. Until that time, the forlorn faces would have to stay in this frigid crucible. Releasing the energy prematurely would be a tragic waste, and it would be too late to fill the reservoir again since the time to deploy the energy might soon be at hand.

Merlin inhaled stinging cold air and let it out in a stream of white vapor. Troubling. Heartbreaking. More saints would die to bring about life. Yet wasn't that always the case? Without suffering, there is no sacrifice. Without sacrifice, there is no love. Without love, there is no purpose to life.

At the opposite side of the reservoir, a circle of red light glimmered about three feet from the ground. Merlin pulled the staff from the ice. What could it be? No red light existed anywhere else in this unworldly chamber. If only another source of illumination were available, something stronger than the weak radiance emitted by hundreds of glowbats hanging from the rocky ceiling or perched on the waist-high stalagmites that dotted the floor.

He set a foot on the ice. It seemed solid … so far. As he shifted his weight, a crackling sound rose. He leaned back and lifted his foot. A network of tiny white cracks appeared, as if his boot had imprinted a sparkling spiderweb. Strange. The ice was thick. Perhaps a thin top layer had grown weak.

He gazed at the red light again. Might the weakness in the ice be a sign of trouble on Earth or Second Eden and perhaps the reason for the appearance of the hovering beacon? Being charged with guarding this sanctuary meant that he had to investigate.

He stepped again on the ice. Although the crackling noise returned, it didn't seem as loud as before. He shifted forward and set his other boot ahead of the first. Then, sliding along, he glided toward the red light. Every move raised more cracks. Below the ice, the misty phantoms congregated. The usual ghostly faces appeared within the swirls as well as appendages brushing at his boots.

Shivering, Merlin slid a bit faster. Although only life energy abided below, the forlorn expressions never failed to raise an extra chill. For some reason, when people died at the hands of evil, death imprinted their faces within the energy, as if the souls inhabited the animated streams. Yet, of course, the souls themselves had moved on to a safe place, free at last from their tormentors.

Ahead, the red light grew clearer—a sphere that floated behind an icy, transparent boundary wall that reflected an image of himself drawing closer, his arms spread and jittery, like a feeble old man walking on a tightrope.

After several minutes, his foot reached the far edge of the frozen pool. Ahead, his reflection appeared to be cradling the red orb at waist level, now looking more egg-shaped than spherical. His face wore a smile, certainly out of place considering the gloom in this frigid chamber.

Merlin raised a hand and touched the wall of ice—cold and clear as crystal. His reflection's hand, however, stayed down. How odd! Surely his squinting examination should etch a deep furrow in his reflection's brow, yet the brow remained slack. Not only that, his hair was too neatly trimmed, and—

He touched his beard, full and scraggily from too many years guarding this chamber, but the man in the reflection was the picture of his freshly shaven self. How could this be?

The reflection's lips moved, and a muffled voice penetrated the curtain. "Merlin, you seem consternated. I assume you are surprised to see me."

Merlin drew his head back. "Charles Hamilton?"

"The very same." Charles ran a hand across his tunic, a perfect match to Merlin's, including a belt that slung low at the front of the dark leather material. "An angel suggested that I wear this in order to keep from startling you with the glory of heavenly attire." He tugged on a pant leg. "The trousers are a bit baggy, but they will do."

"The angel spoke wisely." Merlin eyed the red orb in Charles's hand. It appeared to be an ovulum, but why would he carry it to this realm? "What brings you here, my friend?"

"I bear this ovulum." Charles lifted it to chest level. "It is a communications device that should be quite useful, but I cannot enter where you are, so I will have to transport it through the barrier. Kindly be ready to catch it." He pushed the ovulum against the wall. A hole began to form in the ice, though no water dripped. Merlin propped his staff against the wall and set his hands just below the hole. Inch by inch, the ovulum appeared on his side and illuminated the area with red light.

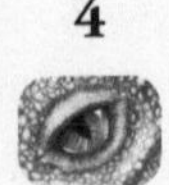

After several seconds, the ovulum popped through, and the hole sealed behind it. Merlin caught the ovulum and ran a thumb across its smooth, glassy surface. A core of red light pulsed deep inside. A bitter wind swirled, forcing him to draw his cloak closer. For a moment, he lost his balance and stepped back to regain it. The ovulum jostled in his grasp. A brighter light seeped out along a jagged crack around the perimeter.

"Are you all right, old chap?" Charles asked.

"Fine. Fine." Merlin peered at the ovulum closely. This had to be the one that fractured back in the days when Elam and Hannah lived in Scotland and narrowly escaped Devin.

Charles pointed at the ovulum. "With this you will be able to monitor events as they unfold on Earth. We had a recent martyr incident, and prophecies are culminating at a rapid pace, so it will be essential that you stay informed."

"I thought that might be the case. I noticed an infusion that stirred the pot a bit, but we need a new resurrection to activate the energy further. Or even better, the final surge that will deploy this reservoir to its prophesied use. Then I can finally leave this Siberian cell and go to Heaven. Having this creaking body restored reminded me of how old I am."

Charles folded his hands at his waist. "Well, I don't know if the newest martyr will meet that need. The young lady Karen Bannister, also known as Lauren, died in order to slay the foul demon Tamiel. She is still dead, but her brother, Charles, also known as Matt, will soon attempt to resurrect her in Abaddon's Lair. If he succeeds, at the very least, the reservoir will be stirred."

"Good. Good." Merlin probed the ovulum's depths. The red core slowly faded to white, revealing a tiny window. It wouldn't take long to become accustomed to this viewing screen. "Do you know if these new events signal that my time in this icebox is nearing an end?"

"That depends on how people respond. A flood of evil has reached Earth's shores, and it seems that it is overwhelming our remnant forces. Yet, we can hope for the best outcome."

Merlin let his shoulders sag. "The best outcome might be to let the final curtain fall. This generation cries out for judgment to come upon their heads. Perhaps we should rescue our remnant and open the fiery gates of retribution." He raised and lowered his feet in turn. "Let the grapes be trampled. Let the blood run high."

Charles cringed. "Well, yes, that is an option that is being considered, but our remnant loved ones are still on Earth. Forces are at work to guide them through the plan you and I discussed before you came here."

Merlin looked back at the frozen reservoir. "Will our plan really work? Arramos's strategy is a two-edged sword. If he is allowed to get to the reservoir …"

"I understand your point all too well." Charles's lips thinned out. "A sword can cut deeply and cares not which neck it severs, whether good or evil. My main concern is with those whom I have guided over the years—William, Bonnie, Walter, and their friends and families. For years they have overcome seemingly insurmountable obstacles, so they have come to expect victory in every battle and resurrection after death, which can make one take more risks than one ought. They have never experienced the finality of tragedy, of utter failure in the physical realm."

"I assume by your countenance that such failure is likely."

Charles looked down briefly, then met Merlin's gaze again, his voice low and somber. "In order for these final days to bring forth the necessary fruit, God has removed the usual protections from his remnant."

Merlin stroked his beard. "To put it succinctly, precious blood will spill, and resurrections to Earth will soon come to an end. Members of our remnant will die."

"True on all counts." Charles heaved a sigh. "Pray for their perseverance. Nothing will be more important than for William, Bonnie, and their loved ones to sustain their faith."

"To be sure." Merlin again caressed the ovulum. Its warm glow soothed his frigid fingers. "May God guide them all."

"Indeed." Charles clapped his hands as if to elevate the mood. "In any case, we expect that someone will soon make an attempt to join you there as a helper to release the energy."

Merlin straightened. "Excellent. Who is this person who has the wisdom to navigate Jade's puzzling path?"

"My sources are limited. I suspected that perhaps Joran and Selah would come, but then I saw them in Heaven and learned that their tasks on Earth have been completed, so that idea was dashed. I then heard that someone might come from Abaddon's Lair. We just have to hope for a quick learner."

"Ah! A dead person." Merlin shook his head. "With no physical body, how will he be able to accomplish the task?"

"Or she, perhaps. As you know, Heaven holds countless female warriors." Charles laid a hand over his heart. "Whether male or female, a resurrected person usually has bold faith and a sense of purpose."

"I wouldn't know from personal experience. The restored body I have now is not a truly resurrected one. I was supposed to go to Heaven with my wife, but when we faced the gates of Heaven, my wife entered, and I was turned away. Apparently I am not dead enough to qualify."

Charles laughed. "Merlin, even if you were dead enough to enter Heaven, you would have volunteered for this quest. You are too much of an adventurer to miss the opportunity."

Merlin allowed himself a smile. "Perhaps you're right. I've done something as insane as this before."

"Indeed. Your days in the candlestone numbered many more than those you have spent in this chamber."

Merlin glanced at one of the glowing bats hanging from the ceiling. "And the lighting is better here, though the food leaves much to be desired. Have you ever tasted a glowbat?"

"That is one delicacy that I have missed, thankfully." As Charles backed away, his body faded. "It is time for me to go. I don't know when your potential helper will try to solve Jade's puzzle, but I pray that it will be soon."

Merlin waved a hand. "Farewell, my friend. It seems that a full reunion is nearly at hand."

Charles disappeared, replaced by Merlin's real reflection. As expected, his hair had grown wild, and his beard was a matted mess. Such was one of the drawbacks of still being alive.

Cradling the ovulum, he retrieved his staff and slid his foot over the ice again. In the distance, a wavering light pierced the dimness, drawing closer. He squinted at the tiny glow. It appeared to be a bobbing flame, as if someone walked with a candle in hand, the flickering wick disturbed by the constant frigid breezes. Perhaps the ally from Abaddon's Lair had already arrived.

Merlin hurried his pace, keeping his stare on the approaching light. If he could reach the opposite shore in time, this helper wouldn't have to risk the danger of traveling over the slippery surface.

When he arrived at the edge, he halted. A glowbat took shape in the approaching light, flying in a haphazard line.

Merlin sat on the frozen floor and sighed. It was all right. He could wait. As Charles had indicated, his time in this place had been a blink of an eye compared to the centuries in the candlestone. And the glorious events that would take place once the helper arrived to release the energy in the reservoir … Ah! That would be worth the wait.

Arramos flew through a gap in the cocoon covering the church, then through a hole in the roof. After slowing his speed by orbiting the dim sanctuary, he landed on the stage at the front. Everything stood where it had been before—the pulpit, the piano, the clothing still strewn down the center aisle, and the pews, though the padded seats were now empty of the congregants who recently pledged their loyalty to him.

Arramos let out a throaty chuckle. Such a fitting monument to the fools' willingness to shed their trappings and reveal their dark hearts. By this time, every soul knew what reward their choices had earned, and they likely wept in darkness and gnashed their teeth without hope of rescue.

He extended his neck and searched the vaulted ceiling. "Vacule, are you here?"

"In the corner, Excellency." The huge spider skittered along a beam and lowered himself by a silk thread. When he descended to a level even with Arramos's snout, he blinked his humanoid eyes, his body the size of a grapefruit. "Has the time come to execute the plan?"

Arramos snorted a blast of hot breath, making the spider sway. "Is the trap in place?"

"Yes. It took a lot of doing, but our agents penetrated Jade's first barrier and planted the device. They were unable to pass to the second or third realm, so we will have to count on our Trojan Horse, if you will."

"That is an apt label. Tamiel was wise to make sure the man was removed from the house before the explosion." Arramos tried to focus on Vacule, but one eye kept wandering to the side, making the spider's humanlike face split into two. Arramos blinked to force the eye back to center. "I have taken care of penetrating the second realm, but the barrier to the third is impossible to breach. Yet, based on our enemy's previous actions, I think the plan will work."

Vacule squinted. "Are you in pain, Excellency? Is something wrong with your eye?"

"That wench, Darcy, shot me, and a pellet lodged in my eye. It has since come out, but the damage has not healed."

"Then you are vulnerable. What of your plan to strengthen your body? Did it fail?"

"My scales have been fortified and coated with the protective agent, so I am practically invulnerable, but I lack the ability to protect my eyes. They have no scales to toughen."

"Even with this handicap, I am confident that you will carry out your plan with stunning brilliance."

"I hope so. The vermin I bribed into service are a stupid lot. Their anger will make them anxious to kill, which is helpful to a point since I need them to slaughter children without flinching, but if they violate my wishes and kill either Sapphira or Bonnie, then all will be lost."

"Yes. Such curses are deadly." Vacule drew in some line and rose a few inches to Arramos's eye level. "Do you consider your portal-entry strategy as the primary plan, or is Tamiel's plan the primary one? Or should I even refer to it as Tamiel's since he is no longer with us?"

Arramos growled. "It is still Tamiel's plan even in his absence. His strategy once again relies on fragile stealth and the actions of our enemies while mine relies on brute strength. Perhaps both plans will work. Since I cannot allow failure, we will pursue both with relentless force. Clefspeare must be destroyed at all costs."

"One way or another, he will die." Vacule rose a few more inches. "While you are mustering your forces, I will monitor the progress of my agents and see if I can personally occupy our Trojan Horse. Your idea worked well to send my agents to the first pool."

"Yes, our attack against Heaven's portal provided that benefit."

"How so, Excellency? I was not in your service then, so I am unaware."

"While the fools defended Heaven, thinking that we actually believed we could win such a battle, we learned more about the substance of the portal and how it can be penetrated. The passage beetle experiment worked wonders, though, of course, the spy who passed into Heaven died immediately since he was not considered holy. The realm of the first pool has no such barriers to our kind."

"I have one beetle left, so it should be sufficient. I am ready to carry out the plan."

Arramos shifted his body under Vacule. "Then let us fly. We have no more use for this den of fools."

Vacule lowered himself to Arramos's back. When he had tied a silky thread around a spine and held on, Arramos vaulted into the air and began another orbit around the sanctuary. He blew a stream of flames at the discarded clothing, then at the pews. Soon, a blazing fire erupted and spread throughout the spacious room.

Arramos lifted through the hole in the ceiling and flew in a circle high above the church. Flames shot into the air and began melting the cocoon. Within seconds, an inferno engulfed the entire structure. The front portico collapsed, the roof caved in, and the building shrank into a fiery heap of rubble.

After a final orbit, Arramos flew away, laughing under his breath. Another conquest complete, another oasis transformed into a mirage. Soon this world would become a spiritual wasteland and Elohim's name a distant memory.

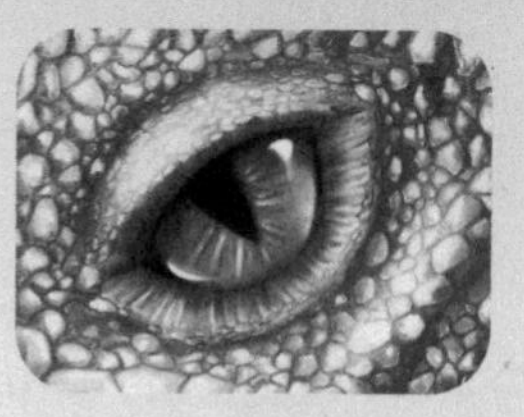

2

CHAPTER

Abaddon's Lair

Instructions for raising your sister from the dead. Matt leaned his elbows on one end of Abaddon's long stone table and held the phone's screen close to his eyes. The message title was so surreal, like a chapter heading from a miracle worker's secret handbook. Yet, with Lauren's corpse lying stretched out on the table's surface, the words delivered a cruel slap of reality.

Matt checked a foot-tall hourglass that stood a hand's breadth away from Lauren's hip. Sand trickled slowly to the pile in the lower glass. According to Abaddon, the sand counted the seconds until this chamber and the entire realm would be annihilated. Perhaps twenty minutes remained to resurrect Lauren and escape through a portal in a nearby window, currently shuttered to keep a stiff breeze from blowing through. That pathway led to Hades, and from there they could access Second Eden, where Semiramis had planted a lethal device—a second ticking time bomb.

Listener stood to his right in front of a pedestal that held Abaddon's resurrection book. Her eyes moved from side to side as she read something on a page near the beginning.

"What are you reading?" he asked.

"Oh." She looked up, her cheeks flushed. "A story. It's written in a language I understand, so I decided to read it."

"What's it about?"

"I shouldn't take the time to tell you." Firm lips matched a stern tone. Her egg-shaped companion hovered close to her ear, flashing red and painting a dim aura over her form-fitting beige tunic, roomy black trousers, and bare feet. "I apologize. I shouldn't be so terse. I haven't felt like myself lately."

"Don't worry about it. Probably just stress. With Valiant gone, too many people are relying on you."

"How well I know." She ran gentle fingers across the book's page. "But that's no excuse for impatient words. Please forgive me."

"No problem." Matt looked past a pair of humanlike statues that stood between him and an exit corridor. With vague features on both body and face, the statues lacked enough definition to be recognizable. Sir Barlow had positioned the more feminine statue closer than the other. He said that it had spoken to him, and the words indicated that Lauren's soul resided within, but it had stayed quiet ever since. A few minutes ago he left through the corridor to search for other statues, hoping that maybe a new one containing Darcy's soul might have materialized. "Do you think we should wait for Sir Barlow?"

Listener craned her neck. Matt joined her in listening. Complete silence reigned, save for the tiniest crackling from the candlewicks as they emitted a delicate, earthy aroma. "I don't hear him," she said. "We really have no idea when he'll return, so we should proceed without him."

"Maybe he'll show up while we're working."

"Of course. Trust the Father of Lights." With her signature pigtails beginning to unravel and her eyes wide and focused, Listener looked like a teenager on a dangerous mission, though she was probably nearly thirty Earth years old. Such was the blessing of living in Second Eden's slow-to-age environment. In contrast, the rips at the knees and elbows of her battle garments as well as a spyglass and sheathed dagger attached to her belt made her look like a fresh-from-combat warrior. "We can also trust Sir Barlow. He knows what he's doing."

"I believe that." Matt touched Lauren's pale face—cold and dry. Although she had been dead for a couple of hours, her limbs had stayed pliable. A pair of necklaces—a chain with a medallion and a string of beads—draped her motionless chest. Each bead glowed with a unique color, giving visibility to the seventh door's transparent key and its attached ring, which lay loose on her shirt.

"We don't want to lose this." He attached the ring to the medallion's chain. "Let's get started."

"First ..." Listener closed the book. "Do we have everything we need?"

Matt looked around the chamber. Three short candles sitting on the floor flickered, creating shifting shadows. Tall columns lined the chamber's walls and reached into darkness, leaving spaces between them for the shuttered window to his left, and straight ahead, a mirror on the wall that served as his entry from Jade's sanctum to this lair. "We have escape routes, and—"

"Sir Barlow's coming!" Listener's brow lifted. "I hear footsteps and heavy breathing."

Matt strained to hear. Nothing so far, but Listener's radar always picked up sounds before he could.

Seconds later, Sir Barlow tromped into the room. The scabbard at his hip slapped his beefy leg, the pistol on the opposite side of his belt hung low, and sweat clung to his bushy mustache.

"I am very sorry to report that I found no other statues, but I will be glad to go back and continue searching if you so desire. Obviously we cannot leave Darcy's soul behind."

Matt caressed a Cracker Jacks ring on his pinky finger. It seemed that Darcy's soul had flown to Heaven. Better for her to be at peace there than dealing with the dangers here. "No, Sir Barlow. Thanks for trying."

"Very well, lad." He pulled up his belt and stationed himself next to the statues in an at-ease position. His forest-green medieval tunic and dark trousers made him look like a movie prop. "I stand ready to help at your call."

As sand continued trickling in the hourglass, Matt's danger warning sounded a shrill alarm. Doom approached. They had to hurry. He surveyed the room again for the needed items. On the floor near a table leg, Listener had set a vial of liquid and a glass egg along with its wooden mount. Soon maybe their purposes would become clear.

He refocused on the phone and read Mom's note out loud. "At the back of Abaddon's book, look for a page with two columns. The column on the right lists souls who were to be resurrected to Second Eden, and the column on the left lists souls who went to Abaddon's Lair from Earth. The entries will be symbols, usually animals—birds and reptiles and the like. If Lauren is listed there, she will probably be the last entry in the column. Touch the symbol. It might take a second for it to recognize your dragon essence."

Listener flipped to the back of the book and set her finger on a page. "This must be it. The last entry in the left-hand column is a sitting cat."

"Since I have dragon essence, we should switch places." Matt gave her the phone and shifted over to the book. Sweat made his long sleeves stick to his arms and his camo pants to his legs, but it couldn't be helped. "Ready."

Listener cradled the phone as if it might crumble. "I've never used one of these, but I should be able to figure it out." She squinted at the screen and read quickly. "You should hear a voice speaking in a foreign language, but it will figure out your language and speak again. If it works like it did for me, the book will say the name of the person the symbol represents. With another touch, the book will turn itself to the correct page, so be sure to lift your finger."

"That's enough for now." Matt touched the cat symbol. Whispers rose from the page, distinct words but unfamiliar. "Anyone have a clue what the book just said?"

Sir Barlow cleared his throat. "I haven't heard that tongue in centuries. It is primitive Irish, a language my grandmother spoke. I'm not sure how to translate it precisely into modern words, but I believe this is a good approximation: 'Dragon nature confirmed. Language identified. Translation in progress.'"

The whispers returned, this time in English. "Lauren Bannister, also known as Lauren Hunt, also known as Karen Bannister. Died in sacrifice while attempting to stop the demon Tamiel from completing his destructive plans. When they came into contact, their opposing powers clashed, and the resulting burst killed them both. Since Lauren's power was bound up within her body, she was unable to use it against Tamiel without direct skin contact."

Matt's heart thumped. This crazy procedure was actually working. He touched the cat again and lifted his finger right away. The book's spine rose slightly, and the pages flipped toward the front by themselves. When they stopped, he turned to Listener. "What's next?"

She drew the phone closer and continued reading. "This is where Abaddon adds an entry in his handwriting about the person to be resurrected, but since Lauren died so recently, you might not find any words. Either way, touch one of the characters at the top of the page. If it's the right one, the book should give you a visual story. If Abaddon's entry is there, read it first. You might learn more from him."

"Okay. Stop again." Matt scanned the page. Animal characters filled the top half, and a handwritten note ran across the bottom. He read it silently while Listener looked on.

I have handled unusual cases in the past, but this one is the most puzzling. Lauren Bannister arrived fully aware of where she was, which is understandable since she has been here before when she acquired Joan of Arc as a companion, but she resisted encasement in stone more vigorously than do most souls. I suppose that Lauren's lucidity contributed to her desire for freedom. I explained that souls must be contained or they might get lost in this vast world because they lack a physical anchor, so she finally acquiesced and surrendered to my hypnotizing rhetoric.

When I consulted Elohim concerning her resurrection instructions, I received an unusual answer—that I should prepare my horde and be ready to fly up from the abyss to exact punishment on those who lacked his seal. This reply left me in a quandary. Besides Lauren, I had one other soul to process, whom I had placed in a statue that was once an empty monument. Yet Elohim had earlier told me to delay processing it, because Lauren might be coming, and she should be processed before the earlier one.

Therefore, without needed instructions for Lauren, I must leave her and the other soul behind and proceed with my final calling. I trust that Elohim will do whatever is necessary to resurrect these two remaining souls. Perhaps he will employ Jade to do his bidding, since only she knows how to access the life reservoir.

My remaining concern is what will become of my lair. If it is destroyed, as planned, the source for new life on Second Eden will end with it. Someone will have to activate the life reservoir and feed the soil of the birthing garden. Otherwise the sacrifices of many faithful ones will be for naught.

While Listener provided Sir Barlow with a quick summary of Abaddon's entry, Matt examined each colorful animal character on the page—a flying cardinal, a monkey with a long tail, several varieties of butterflies, a chameleon, and a glowing girl, each one about the size of a thumb.

He touched the girl. Misty light rose from the page and gathered into a hologram—representations of Lauren in Matt's embrace and Tamiel standing nearby. The semitransparent image animated. Lauren broke away from Matt and ran toward Tamiel. Arramos snatched Tamiel and lifted him into the air out of Lauren's reach. While they circled overhead, Lauren's stare followed their orbit. Barely audible voices emanated.

"Maybe you aren't gullible," Lauren said, her call like a whisper, "but a dragon who jumps to obey your every command certainly is. It looks like you're the master, and he's the slave."

Listener drew closer. "Is this how Lauren died?"

As tears crept into Matt's eyes, he nodded. "Any second now, but we don't have time to watch it."

"Then let the past stay in the past." Listener swiped her hand through the mist. The hologram dispersed. "My guess is fifteen minutes left."

Matt checked the hourglass. Sand continued to pour. "Right. Let's keep going."

She lifted the phone and read from the screen even more quickly. "When Abaddon prepared Timothy for resurrection, he breathed fire on the statue. The stone melted away like dark wax.

Timothy was covered in flames and started to slump, but Abaddon caught him, so it's clear that souls there are visible and physical while in the lair, which means that Lauren, if she's there, should also be in physical form. Then Abaddon poured a drop from a vial onto Timothy's head. Thick fog covered him, and after a minute or so, Abaddon blew the fog away, leaving a glass egg in his hand. He set the egg on a wooden mount at the center of the table and wrote something in the book."

Listener took a breath and continued. "When it came time to raise Timothy, because he had given up his right to resurrect, someone had to die before he could live again." She looked up, no longer reading. "I was a little girl at the time, and I wanted to be that sacrifice, but Acacia died instead."

"Mom told me that story while we were in prison." Matt nodded at the phone. "Is there more?"

"Quite a bit." Listener squinted at the screen once again. "In a few cases, someone on Second Eden had to call the person by name to bring about a resurrection, and it had to take place during an eclipse when the garden was energized. But babies sprout from the birthing garden without those conditions all the time. When Billy and I were resurrected, I assume someone called for us. I remember I called for Billy, at least in my mind, but I can't be sure if that was needed, because our bodies were available, and we resurrected to life on Earth instead of Second Eden. So the needed elements are not obvious. You might have to figure out this process as you go along.

"But I think one element is crucial. You must have faith. Just as Jesus called Lazarus from the tomb without doubting, so must you call Lauren. While I was training for four years in Abaddon's Lair, Joan of Arc said something profound. I don't remember the exact words, but they went something like this: Every call to life echoes the longing in the heart of the caller. It is like thunder within, a drum that beats without a rhythm. It searches for the power to infuse the thrumming of a new heartbeat in the loved one's dead body. It combines words of love with the music of sacrifice and the rhythm of a disciplined purpose. These blend in concert to create a song of passion, a heart set on fire, and without that fire no one can be reborn."

Listener glanced up briefly, as if checking for a reaction. "So, Matt," she continued, again reading the screen, "call for Lauren with all your heart, and I am confident that God will guide you through the steps on this uncertain path."

Listener laid the phone on the table and kept her gaze on it. Sir Barlow shifted uneasily in place.

"That's it?" Matt asked.

She nodded, her brow furrowed. "We don't have a dragon to melt the statue's shell, we don't know how to put a soul into an egg, and we don't know how to insert her soul back into her body." Her companion floated in front of her eyes and flashed red. "Oh, yes, of course. I'm not criticizing the instructions. I'm sure Bonnie did the best she could."

"That's all right. Don't worry about it." Matt exhaled heavily. "It's true, though. We'll be shooting in the dark, but we also learned a lot. I need to call Lauren to resurrect, and maybe the other steps aren't necessary."

Sir Barlow raised a hand. "If I may offer a suggestion. The dragon Karrick is in Second Eden. Perhaps he could melt the shell."

"Not enough time," Listener said. "Besides, according to Abaddon, the portal is safe to go through only in one direction—from here to the tree-of-life chamber in Hades. He did that so no one would return to his lair after Sir Barlow and I escorted everyone home to Second Eden."

Matt glanced at the floor where a flame-retardant cloak lay, the cloak they had used for protection when passing to this chamber from the bottomless pit. They could use it to return to Abaddon's Lair after finding Karrick, but, as Listener said, there was no time to search for him. The sand in the hourglass indicated about ten minutes left until the lair's destruction.

Sir Barlow gestured with his head toward the shuttered window. "We can take Lauren's body, her statue, and everything else with us to Second Eden."

"Can we?" Matt touched Lauren's lifeless hand. "I mean, I know we can bring her body, but isn't her soul supposed to stay here until she's resurrected?"

"Maybe not," Listener said. "Since her soul is encased in—"

A rumble shook the floor. Something cracked in the ceiling. Grit rained from above and pelted the table and their heads. Matt snatched up the cloak and draped it over Lauren's body. "Get everything through the portal!"

A louder crack echoed. Pebbles and larger stones cascaded from the ceiling. Matt slid his arms under Lauren's body and carried her and the cloak toward the window.

Sir Barlow ran ahead and threw open the shutters, revealing a low brick wall built above a waist-high sill. Wind rushed through the chamber and funneled out. His hair blowing askew, he intertwined his fingers and cupped his hands near Matt's knee. "Up you go!"

Still carrying Lauren, Matt set a foot in the cup. Sir Barlow boosted him over the bricks and launched him into a cylindrical room. Matt crashed onto a stone floor and slid headfirst with Lauren along a bed of fallen leaves.

A light flickered at the corner of his eye. The tree of life stood just a step or two away. The foliage burned vibrantly without consuming the leaves, warming the surrounding air. He rose to his knees and settled Lauren on her back, far enough from the fire to avoid contact and close enough to stay limber.

"Matthew!" Sir Barlow called from beyond the window. "We must hurry!"

Matt grabbed the cloak and draped it over his head. He leaped over the bricks and into the resurrection chamber. The cloak sizzled and popped, and a stabbing shock jolted his body. He toppled to the floor. His muscles twitched, and spots pulsed in his vision.

In near darkness, Sir Barlow dragged Lauren's statue toward the window. A huge slab dropped from the ceiling and crashed mere inches from him, raising clouds of debris. "Shout if you need help," he said with a grunt, "but if not, I suggest that you drag the second statue, and we can heave them together."

Matt struggled to his feet and walked on stiff legs toward the table. The only remaining lit candle lay sideways on the floor, its flame withering. Barely visible in the dimness, Listener carried Abaddon's book tucked under her arm, the glass egg in one hand, and the hourglass in the other. Loud cracks sounded along with a thunder-like rumble. "Hurry!" Listener shouted. "I hear a rush of water!"

The entire chamber rattled. The statue wobbled, now only a few steps away. Matt trudged toward it, his feet set wide apart as if he were walking on the deck of a storm-tossed ship. Listener walked in the same manner toward the portal window, the resurrection items now locked in one arm and her opposite hand reaching for the stone table for support.

As Matt passed by Listener, he draped the cloak over her shoulders. "In case you have to come back through."

"Thank you." She set the book and other items on the table and began fastening the cloak's clasp with hurried fingers. The ground quaked violently. The table lurched. The book tumbled to the floor next to a table leg. The binding snapped, and pages scattered. She dropped to her knees and began scooping the yellowed parchments. "I have to get these! Some might be important!"

"I'll be right there!" When Matt reached the statue, he wrapped his arms around it and dragged it toward the window. Water burst from a gaping hole in the ceiling, poured to the floor, and doused the last candle. Now the flaming tree beyond the portal acted as the only source of light. As more water gushed, a huge wave tore the statue from his grasp and sent him tumbling underwater.

He grabbed the top of the stone table and thrust his head into the clear. As he gasped for air, he scanned the roaring river. Sir Barlow stood in the chest-high flood, clutching Lauren's statue and the edge of the portal window. The rapid current tore at his body and splashed foam across his face. The wall turned the river to the right where it channeled into a corridor and disappeared from view.

"Listener is underwater!" Sir Barlow nodded toward a point near Matt. "Down there!"

Matt thrust his head back under. Listener swayed in the flow with the cloak caught under the stone table's leg, the clasp still fastened and her eyes closed.

He thrust himself downward, grabbed her around the waist, and wrenched the cloak free. As he held on, the flow sent them both hurtling toward the portal window.

Within seconds, Sir Barlow's lower body came into view. Matt latched onto his leg. Something caught hold of his collar and jerked him and Listener to the surface. He spat out a stream of water—warm and sweet. Barlow stared at him, his face only inches away. "You first, lad, and then I will hoist Listener to you. I already shoved the statue in there."

Matt twisted his body and, with a push from Barlow, climbed over the bricks and into the tree chamber. He spun and reached out his arms, but an electric shock burned his hands. He backpedaled and nearly tripped over Lauren's statue, which now lay next to her body.

Sir Barlow lifted Listener, wet and limp, until her shoulders crossed the portal plane. Matt grabbed her arms, hauled her through, and laid her on the floor as close to the fiery tree as he dared. He listened for respiration, but no sound emanated from her nose or mouth. He pushed once on her stomach. She coughed a stream of water and sucked in a gurgling breath.

Matt turned her to her side and repeatedly thumped her back with his hand. "Inhale through your nose. Exhale through your mouth." He turned toward the window. "Sir Barlow! Get in here before you get swept away!"

"Coming!" Sir Barlow sloshed to Matt's side and dropped to his knees. "It seems that the lass has narrowly escaped drowning."

"So far." As Listener coughed more water, the volume diminishing with each spasm, Matt continued thumping her back. "We just have to make sure she gets it all out and watch for secondary drowning symptoms."

"Yes, I have heard of that phenomenon."

When Listener's coughs settled, Matt helped her sit up. "Are you all right?"

"I will be." She coughed once more and smiled. "Thank you for saving my life." As she began shedding the saturated cloak, she turned to Sir Barlow. "Both of you."

"My pleasure, Miss."

Listener turned toward the portal. "Look. The water must be flowing out at least as fast as it's coming in."

Matt shifted and sat facing Abaddon's Lair. The water level still lapped close to the top of the brick wall. "I wonder how much time is left."

"Very little," Sir Barlow said as he set the hourglass at Matt's feet. "The timepiece floated up just before I climbed through, and it seems to have stayed upright, though I cannot be certain. I was unable to salvage anything else." He picked up Lauren and laid her between Matt and the portal. Her arms and legs barely shifted. Rigor mortis was setting in. "So we can keep an eye on her while we watch the demise of Abaddon's Lair." Sir Barlow sat next to Matt. "Perhaps we will be lucky enough to spot the book and snatch it out of the water."

"Not much chance of that." As Matt gazed at Lauren's corpse, his throat tightened. "Without the book or the instructions, we can't resurrect her."

Listener set the cloak next to Lauren, slid her arm around Matt's and intertwined their fingers. "We'll figure something out. Resurrection power does not abide in Abaddon's Lair or in a book or in potions. It is in the hands of the Father of Lights."

He looked into her eyes. Although sparkling with tears, they exuded assurance, determination. "Keep up that confident spirit. We're going to need it."

"I will. My companion will remind me." Listener pushed her fingers through her pigtails. "Matt, do you see her?"

He scanned the area around Listener's shoulders. With the braids wet but intact, the companion didn't have anywhere to hide. "No. Could the water have washed … uh … her away?"

"I had a vision while swimming in the flood." Listener's voice grew tense but stayed under control. "Maybe she really is gone."

"If I may," Sir Barlow said, "I noticed your companion near your ear when you ducked under the table, but when the wave hit you, you fell and disappeared underwater. I did not notice her afterward."

Listener's chin quivered. "Matt, if any Second Edener loses a companion, he or she dies within a day."

Matt searched the area again—the floor, near the tree, around the window. No luck. "How many times has someone lost a companion?"

"Just twice that I've heard about. And if you count me losing one when I was little, that makes a third time, but that companion was crippled, and I had one remaining."

Matt studied her face—bright eyes, rosy cheeks, slightly blue lips, probably from lack of oxygen. "Do you feel sick? Weak?"

"No. I feel ..." She touched her chest. "Filled?"

"Filled?" Sir Barlow touched his throat. "Well, Miss, this might sound insane, but could you have swallowed your companion?"

"She's too big to swallow, even by accident." Listener narrowed her eyes and ran her hands along her frame from neck to waist. "I feel fuller throughout my body. Calmer ... more ... rested, I suppose. I really can't explain it."

"That's great, Listener." Matt forced a hopeful tone. "Maybe it won't hurt you to lose your companion. You know, because it's happened before." He turned toward the portal. The flaming tree drew dancing yellow flickers across Lauren's body, massaging her with light. The fire also lit up the hourglass's trickling sand and made the grains sparkle as they dropped to the lower bowl. Every grain felt like a lost chance, hope dissolving. Only about a minute remained.

Inside the lair, the rest of the ceiling crashed into the flood and disappeared below the surface. A side wall toppled, sending a new wave that rolled up to the portal. Its crest splashed against the windowsill, and the spray washed over their faces. Water oozed onto the tree-room floor and seeped under Lauren's body.

When the final grains of sand fell to the bottom of the hourglass, Abaddon's Lair darkened. Without a sound, the shutters closed and faded, replaced by shelves where a few books and scrolls lay scattered in haphazard array.

A burst of light splashed across the wall. The shelves vanished. As if painted by radiant fingers, a vertical column took shape in the midst of a dark background, maybe five paces beyond the wall. From dozens of small holes in the column, crimson light emanated and created a surrounding aura in various shades of red.

The radiance dwindled, dispersed, and rained on Lauren's body like dying embers. Matt leaned forward and swept the sparks from her shirt. No harm done. Yet, his sense of danger spiked. Might something be lurking beyond the new portal?

When he settled back, he studied the glowing column. "That's Jade's sanctum, but it looks different."

Sir Barlow squinted. "Indeed. The room is darker than before. The mirrors are no longer—"

"Wait!" Listener craned her neck. "I hear crackling. Like fire."

"From the tree?" Matt asked.

"It's coming from ..." She rocked up to her knees and cocked her head. "From Lauren?"

"What?" Matt scooted closer. "How is that possible?"

Flames sprouted from under Lauren's back at both sides. "Fire!" Listener grabbed the cloak and threw it over her. "Smother it!" She and Matt shoved the edges of the wet material under Lauren's body. Sizzles erupted. Steam shot out in plumes, and foul-smelling smoke permeated the air.

Within seconds, the smoke dispersed. Matt heaved short breaths. "I think ... I think just her clothes got singed. No skin damage."

"That's wishful thinking." Listener set her ear closer. "I still hear fire, but it might be the tree. I'm not sure."

"We have to check." Matt lifted the cloak. Flames broke out anew across Lauren's body. Smoke billowed. He threw the cloak over her again and held it in place. The wet material sizzled. Heat radiated into his skin. Gasping, he looked at Listener. "Is she still burning?"

Listener's lips pressed together. "I think her body is burning on the inside while she's covered, and the flames ignite on the outside when you take the cloak off."

"We need water!" Matt searched the cylindrical chamber. A few puddles lay where the wave from Abaddon's Lair had sloshed in. He threw the cloak to the side and rolled Lauren's body into the water. New flames ignited. The puddles bubbled and popped. Steam shot upward and disappeared.

Now on his knees, Matt cupped his hands and desperately scooped water over her body. "Lauren! No! Don't burn!" He sucked in a breath and shouted, "God, help me!"

Listener and Sir Barlow added their own scoops, but the flames just grew higher. "Stop!" Matt shouted. "The water's like gasoline!"

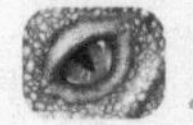

The fire burst into an inferno—a superheated blaze that towered over their heads. Matt fell to his bottom and slid back from the scorching heat. Listener and Barlow joined him. In less than a minute, the fire consumed flesh, bones, and clothing, leaving a pile of dark ashes.

Matt stared. Tears flowed. As his lips quivered, trembling words spilled out. "Lauren. My brave sister. Come back to me."

When the sizzles died away, the sound of a female clearing her throat interrupted the silence. Near the tree, Lauren sat cross-legged on the floor in the midst of a dark puddle. Not a fragment of the statue remained. "Well ..." She took in a deep breath. "*That* was a bizarre sight!"

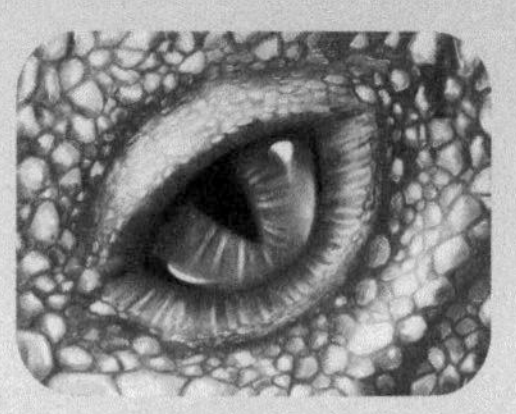

3

CHAPTER

New Wings

Billy stopped the rickety bus next to an airport hangar and turned off the headlights. Darkness shrouded the area. The lack of security flood lamps and runway lights indicated that the airport's generators had run out of fuel, which meant that the electricity grid might have collapsed some time ago. With no moon or stars visible above, darkness would rule for quite a while.

As the engine ran with a mild clatter, he twisted in his seat and looked back. Bonnie sat in the bus's first row, her eyes closed and her wings spread out over the side window and into the aisle. "Bonnie. Wake up."

She yawned and stretched her arms, her silhouette illuminated by the dashboard's weak glow. "My turn to drive again?"

"No. We're running out of fuel, so I made a detour. We're at an airport near St. Louis."

She blinked her bleary eyes. "Do they have fuel here?"

"Not that I know of. Even if they do, there's probably no power to pump it." Billy reached back and held her hand.

"Remember when Dad added a Learjet to his fleet? Mom and I came to this airport to get certified to pilot it."

"I remember." Bonnie rose, scooted forward next to the driver's seat, and crouched. "I couldn't come with you because the twins were so young."

Billy nodded toward the hangar, though it was no longer visible without the headlights. "Oscar Mendez was the main pilot. Locals hired him to fly bigwigs around the region. I'm hoping the jet's still here. If it is, Oscar's sure to have kept it flight ready."

"Definitely faster than this bus. We'd get to Castlewood in no time."

"And in style. Then we can pick up my parents and maybe Walter's family, turn around, and fly to the Second Eden portal. Everyone would be better off getting away from this planet."

"Perfect. But how many passengers will the jet carry?"

"Six, besides the two seats in the cockpit." Billy pulled a lever that opened the bus's swinging door. "Some can sit in the aisle if we pick up too many hitchhikers."

"That should work." Bonnie looked outside. "Have you seen anyone?"

"Not yet. I think the airport's closed."

"How did you get in?"

"The gate has a combination lock. It hasn't changed since I was here last—two, four, six, eight. I guess they're not too worried about people breaking in."

"No. I guess not." A tear trickled down Bonnie's cheek.

"Hey …" Billy brushed the tear away. "What's wrong?"

"I was remembering a dream I just had." Her voice cracked. "When you mentioned the lock … it came back to me." She sniffed. "I saw Lauren trying to break through some kind of barrier, but … but she couldn't. Then I saw Matt with his fingers inside a bleeding wound. Maybe Lauren's trapped somewhere. Maybe Matt was trying to heal his own wound."

She clutched Billy's hand and pressed it against her cheek. Her face contorted, and her voice pitched higher. "Billy, I … I have to know if they're alive. If I knew they were dead, at least … at least I would know they're in Heaven, but this … this silence is unbearable."

"Then we'll ask God to give you more information." He lifted her hand and kissed her fingers. "Maybe you're seeing Matt and Lauren in Second Eden, and they're fine. Maybe Matt is healing someone else, and Lauren isn't trapped. She's just trying to get to someone who's in trouble." He added a cheery edge to his tone. "And that would mean she's alive. She resurrected."

"Maybe." Bonnie sniffed again and looked at the floor of the bus. "I'll ask God for more dreams. Maybe he'll make it clear."

"In the meantime, we'll get to Second Eden as fast as we can."

"Then let's get started." Bonnie folded her wings tightly, descended the stairs, and squeezed through the open door.

"Right behind you." Billy turned the engine off, grabbed a flashlight from under the dash, and limped down the steps. His pair of broken toes still ached, but no crutches were available.

With the flashlight beam waving in front, they walked to the hangar's closed door, a garage-like entry, high and wide. Billy aimed the light at a numeric pad on the wall. "Electric. It won't work."

"Is there a manual override?"

"Maybe." Billy pointed the flashlight at a smaller side door. He tried the knob—locked.

"A locked door means something valuable's inside," Bonnie said. "The jet might be there."

"True." Billy rammed his shoulder against the door, but it didn't budge. The thrust sent a painful jolt to his toes. "It's solid."

"The bus might have a crowbar. I saw a lockbox in the back." Bonnie extended a hand and smiled. "The keys, please?"

"Good idea." Billy handed her the flashlight. "I left them in the ignition."

Bonnie ran that way, her wings flapping to boost her speed. Less than a minute later, the bus's engine rumbled to life. The headlights flashed on and turned toward the door.

Billy shielded his eyes with a hand. What was she up to?

The horn sounded a brief toot, and the twin beams darted toward him. He hobbled out of the way. Seconds later, the bus angled toward the smaller door. The corner of the bumper crashed into the door, ripped it from its hinges, and sent it flying inside. The bus backed away several feet with one headlight cracked and darkened.

Leaving the engine running, Bonnie hustled down the bus's stairs and flew to Billy's side. He crossed his arms and grinned. "Let me guess. You couldn't find the crowbar."

"The flashlight went out. Too dark in there." She winked, her smile evident in the headlight's glow. "I hope your father's company won't mind getting the repair bill."

"I think he'll get over it." Taking Bonnie's hand, he followed the headlight's beam through the doorway and into the hangar. A Learjet sat on a concrete expanse, its nose pointed toward the larger main door. Triangular chocks attached to ropes secured the wheels. "There she is."

Bonnie flapped her wings and glided to the jet. She ran a hand along a spot on the fuselage where paint had peeled away. "Looks pretty old."

"It still flies. If it didn't, they would've mothballed it by now." Billy scanned the main door's lifting mechanism. A wide strap on each side wrapped around a shaft near the ceiling. At waist-level, a lever protruded from a control box mounted on the wall.

"I'll crank it up." Billy grabbed the lever. "When I was here, Oscar kept the key to the jet's door on a hook near the back wall."

"I'll look for it." Bonnie walked toward the rear of the hangar and faded in the dimness.

Billy turned the crank. It was tough but manageable. While the door slowly lifted, more light filtered in underneath. "How's it going back there?"

"Nothing yet. I found a hook, but …"

"But what?"

"Someone's here."

"What?" Billy locked the sprocket in place and hurried to the back. Bonnie stood next to a man sitting on a folding chair. A cap covered his face, and his arms hung limply at his sides.

"I prodded his shoulder," Bonnie said, "but he didn't budge."

Billy removed the cap. As his eyes adjusted, the face clarified. Open sores covered both cheeks, his forehead, and much of his scalp. His mouth was wide open, and a fly perched on his lower lip.

"Oscar?" Bonnie asked.

"I think so. Hard to be sure." He checked for a pulse. Nothing. "He's dead."

"The poor guy!" Bonnie leaned closer. "Maybe—"

"Wait!" Billy pulled her back. "He might be contagious."

"Not to us." Bonnie lifted Oscar's arms and crossed them over his chest. "These are the end times, Billy. Those who don't follow God are suffering his wrath. We don't have to worry about it."

"Good thing, because we both touched him." Billy set the cap back in place and patted Oscar's pants pockets. Something jingled in the left one. He pushed his hand inside, withdrew a ring loaded with keys, and extended it to Bonnie. "See if you can find the right one. It should be narrow and silver. I'll work on the door."

She took the ring. "Will do."

Billy hurried back to the cranking mechanism, grabbed the lever, and began turning it again. "This might take a while."

"Let's make it quicker." Bonnie flew to the center of the door. Bending, she slid her hands underneath and beat her wings furiously.

Something clicked. The lever loosened. While Billy cranked, Bonnie pulled upward. The mechanism creaked, but it gave way. When the door lifted far enough to fit the jet underneath, Billy called out, "That's good!"

Bonnie swooped down and walked into an elegant two-step landing as she brushed her hands together. "Now we can see if the jet flies."

"It should, unless the tank hasn't been filled. Then we're out of luck."

Bonnie pulled the key ring from her jeans pocket. "How far will it fly on one tank?"

"About twenty-five hundred miles, depending on cargo and wind."

She flipped through the keys. "Twenty-five hundred? And we have to go to West Virginia and then to the portal?"

"Right, but I haven't checked the coordinates Elam gave me, so I won't know if we can make it until I plug them into the jet's GPS unit."

"But we know the portal is west of the Mississippi." Her eyes rolled upward in thought. "Not much room for error."

"We can make it." Billy looked toward the rear of the hangar. "I'm just wondering what to do about Oscar. We can't call anyone—tell them to pick him up. And we don't have time for a burial." He pulled a pair of ropes and slid the wheel chocks away. "We have to move on."

"I know." Bonnie lowered her gaze. "We have lives to save."

He set a finger under her chin and lifted her head. "Tell you what. I'll write a note and put it somewhere conspicuous in the bus.

With the headlight on, someone's bound to come along to check it out. They'll find him."

She kissed him on the cheek. "Thank you."

Billy searched a worktable that abutted a side wall and found a clipboard and pen. He jotted a note, speaking while writing. "To whom it may concern. I found Oscar Mendez dead in a chair near the back of the hangar. I had no way to call for help. Please take care of his body and contact his family. I took the Lear because of an emergency. It belongs to my father, Jared Bannister." Billy then added his signature.

Bonnie looked at the note. "I guess there's not much else to say."

"No time to write a book." Billy limped out the hangar door. "I'll be right back." He climbed into the bus's driver's seat, curled the note, and wedged it into the steering wheel. The bus chugged noisily, backfired, and died. The headlight dimmed. It wouldn't last much longer. Airport employees would have to find Oscar without a beacon.

He turned the headlight off and stepped outside. Darkness again enveloped the area, veiling the hangar. A cold breeze raised a chill. A vague sense of danger filtered in, like fog settling in a valley—nothing close or urgent, more like an encroaching influence, a corruption of the unguarded soul.

He looked up. The sky had cleared to the north, revealing a dazzling display of stars. Except for his thumping heart, all was quiet. The scene felt surreal … familiar … like a cold night in England when he and Professor Hamilton gazed at a star-filled sky while they waited for Bonnie to arrive from her transatlantic flight, a flight propelled by dragon wings.

The memory animated and added voices. The professor slid gloves over his aged fingers and said, "Much of what you have learned about faith, you have learned from me, but where you are soon going, I cannot come." After checking the time on his pocket watch, he enclosed it in his gloved hand and stared at the northern sky. "God always provides a guiding light, William. No matter how dark it seems or how terrible the situation, you can always count on finding a glimmer, a spark of light in the deepest blackness that will tell you which way to go."

As the memory faded, Billy searched the sky. The North Star twinkled in its usual place, never changing, always ready to provide a guiding light.

"Prof." Billy swallowed past a lump in his throat. "I wish you were here. The world has gone completely out of its mind. Arramos and the Enforcers are collecting children, even babies, and gassing them. And people aren't rising up to put a stop to the madness. It's like they don't care. I never dreamed that darkness like this could sweep across the world, but it's happening. It's really happening." A tear slid down his cheek. "I wish I could ask you for advice right now. While children are dying, I'm just a crippled man flailing in the darkness. I don't know what to do."

The professor's words returned to mind again. "God always provides a guiding light, William." The words echoed as if called from a distant valley. "Do you understand?"

Billy focused on the North Star and echoed his answer from that night. "Yes. I think I know exactly what you mean."

"Billy?" Bonnie called from the darkness. "Are you all right?"

"I'm fine." He whispered to himself, "Sort of."

"I got the jet door open and the stairs down. And the jet has snacks and water bottles."

"Good. Oscar must've been getting ready to fly somewhere." Limping again, he retraced his steps to the hangar, now visible in the glow of an emerging moon. As he passed Bonnie, he spoke through a narrowed throat. "Let's go."

He climbed the waist-high airstair and settled in the pilot's seat. Bonnie followed and stood in the aisle just behind the cockpit.

Billy nodded toward the copilot's chair. "This jet is supposed to have two operators, so I'll need a beautiful copilot to help me reach some controls."

"Assuming you mean me …" Bonnie folded her wings tightly and sat in the chair. "Thank you for the compliment."

Billy reached across and caressed her cheek. "We were separated for fifteen years. I'm not going to miss any chance to tell you. You're like a guiding light in the darkness, beautiful inside and out."

She grasped his hand and kissed it. "And so are you."

"You think so?" He grinned. "Even with broken toes? Bruised face? Smelly feet?"

Bonnie leaned across and kissed him. "More than ever."

"That does it. I am officially inspired." Billy flipped on the battery switch. The control panel lit up with various colors all across the front. As he read the instruments, memories of his training hours flowed easily to mind. "Okay. This shouldn't be a problem at all."

Bonnie touched a glowing screen near the center of the console. "GPS?"

"Yep. I hope the satellites are still functioning. With everything dark on the ground, we'll need the GPS to find a decent landing strip."

"Did Elam say what the terrain is like around the new portal?"

Billy picked up a map from the floor. "Just coordinates. No details. We'll have to check it out when we get there and put her down wherever we can. We might have to fly around a bit to find a spot."

Bonnie fastened her seat belt. "How long will it take to get to West Virginia?"

"Counting takeoff and landing time, a little extra to figure out where to land, maybe a couple of hours. We'll get there around dawn."

"Are you thinking about landing at the Castlewood airport? It's pretty far from your parents' house."

Billy shook his head. "We need to land close enough to walk and minimize exposure to fallout." He sketched a mental road map of his neighborhood including bridges and power lines. "I think I can put her down on the main highway near where it intersects Cordelle Road. I doubt anyone will be driving on it. But if the space to land is too short, I might have to deploy the drag chute to stop in time."

Bonnie nodded. "That's about a mile from your parents' house, so I'll just fly there from the highway. That's the best way to avoid much exposure time, especially since your toes are banged up."

"Good thinking." Billy fastened his seat belt. "Let's go to Castlewood."

4

CHAPTER

A Fork in the Road

Lauren!" Matt grabbed her hand. "How did you get here?"

"I don't know." She shook her head and blinked hard. "The last thing I remember is chasing Tamiel. I was wondering why he wasn't flying away. Then the dragon picked him up, and I said something that made the dragon drop him, so I just tackled him and held on as tight as I could." She furrowed her brow. "Did he die?"

"He burned to a crisp." Matt stood, helped Lauren to her feet, and pulled her into his arms. "You killed him. You sacrificed your life to save the world."

"Then are you dead, too?" She looked around, again blinking, as if in a daze. "This isn't Heaven."

"I'll try to explain." He drew himself back, leaving a wet imprint on her shirt. Her clothes still displayed rips in the fabric

from earlier struggles. How strange that she would be wearing the same clothes that perished in flames only moments ago. "Sorry. I got you wet. We went for an unscheduled swim while trying to resurrect you. I guess it worked anyway."

Lauren half closed an eye. "Did it really? I just saw my body burn to ashes."

"But you're solid now." He compressed her arm. "This must be your new body."

"Maybe." She touched a spot on her forehead, then on her wrist. "The stitches are gone, so that's an improvement."

After greeting Listener and Sir Barlow, Lauren set her hands on her hips and pivoted slowly. Flames from the tree highlighted her worried expression. "The portals to Earth and Heaven are closed."

"Portals? What do you mean?"

"This is the tree-of-life room in Hades. It had portals to Heaven and Earth." She stopped her rotation and looked at Matt. "How did I get here?"

"It's a complicated story." He glanced at the ashes that were once Lauren's body, but her presence seemed to make the human debris a nonissue. In any case, they had to hurry. Semiramis's deadly device still lay hidden somewhere in Second Eden.

He provided Lauren with a quick summary of events, including his harrowing descent into the abyss while carrying her body on his back, Darcy's sacrificial death in Jade's sanctum, Abaddon's written entry in his book, the destruction of his lair, and their need to find Semiramis's device. He also included his own failure—disbelieving Darcy's change of heart—and how he embraced the faith his mother had told him about, faith that helped him cast off the bitterness poisoning his mind.

When he finished, he gave a light shrug. "And now here we are, and apparently we have a new portal to Jade's sanctum."

Sir Barlow clapped Matt on the back. "Outstanding work, lad. You are a hero among heroes."

Listener folded her hands at her waist. "Thank you for baring your soul for us. I'm sure we will all benefit from your example of faith … especially me."

"Matt." Lauren took his hand. "I don't know what to say. You carried my body through all that … that torture?"

As a tear dripped to her cheek, Matt wiped it away with a thumb and cupped his palm under her chin. "You're worth suffering any torture."

Lauren pulled him into her arms, closer this time. As her lips brushed his ear, she whispered, "I love you, Matt. Thank you for everything."

"You'd do the same for me." Matt returned the embrace. Though her arms felt strong and comforting, something was wrong. Her body radiated no warmth.

Holding her wrists, he pushed back slowly and looked into her eyes. *Can you read my mind now?*

She nodded, her brow arched.

He felt for a pulse. No response. The resurrection hadn't worked after all. *You said you weren't so sure about being alive. Well … I don't feel a pulse.*

Lauren pressed two fingers on her wrist. Worry lines dug into her forehead. Reaching back, she slid a hand down her shirt. "My scales are tingling." She smacked her lips. "I have saliva, and I'm breathing. How can all of my body systems work without a heartbeat?"

"All systems?" Matt fixed his stare on her hand. "It's pretty dark in here, but you're not glowing."

"I didn't always glow before, pretty much only …" Her words trailed off. "When my scales tingle."

"And you say they're tingling now."

"Yeah … I know."

Sir Barlow laid a hand on his chest. "If I may offer my experience as a comparison, although my Earth body is merely light energy, my heart beats while I am here, and I have moisture in my mouth and eyes. I need no food, but I do thirst on rare occasions. The mystery regarding our bodies is mind-boggling."

Lauren's eyes widened. "My body!" She knelt next to the pile of ashes and blew a section away, revealing a beaded necklace and a medallion attached to a chain.

As she studied the items, Matt crouched next to her. "They're probably still hot."

She prodded a bead with a finger. "Not too bad." She picked the string up, draped it over her head, and straightened the beads. "Strange that this didn't burn."

"Or the metal stuff didn't melt. The fire was huge." Matt lifted the key ring, still connected to the chain. The attached key glittered for a split second before vanishing again. "Special materials, I suppose."

Curling a finger under the chain, Lauren lifted the medallion and pulled the key ring from Matt. "We'd better save everything." She slid the chain over her head and let the medallion and key dangle at her chest. "You mentioned a second statue. Do you know whose soul was in it?"

He shook his head. "Abaddon's book didn't give any clues except that the person died before you did. The flood took the statue away. I have no idea where it went."

"Interesting." She touched the medallion. "Eagle gave me this. He died not long before I did, so he might be the missing soul. We have to find the reservoir and resurrect him."

"And you." Matt looked through the portal at the column within Jade's sanctum. "Abaddon mentioned that Jade has access to the life reservoir, so we should ask for her help, but we also have to find Semiramis's device. We can't be two places at once."

Sir Barlow raised a hand. "May I suggest that Miss Bannister and I conduct a search for Jade and the reservoir? I already know that I am unable to safely enter Second Eden, and since Miss Bannister is, shall we say, without physical moorings, she is also likely unable to enter. This way, you and Listener can look for Semiramis's device while we search for the other answers we are seeking, including a way to raise Miss Bannister from the dead. I have already entered Jade's sanctum, so I assume I can enter again."

"Sir Barlow, that's perfect." Matt withdrew a wet scrap of paper from his pocket. "I have the coordinates of the device. Listener and I have to translate them to a physical location, find the device, and figure out how to disable it. If either team has a significant update, and if it's feasible, then come back here and leave a message. Spell it out with the leaves if you have to."

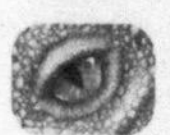

"Understood." Sir Barlow patted an empty holster on his belt. "It seems that I lost my pistol in the flood. I will have to rely on my sword."

"That'll probably be enough." Matt set his hands on Lauren's shoulders. "You be careful."

"Careful?" She smiled, though it seemed forced. "Matt, I'm already dead. You're the one who needs to be careful."

"Don't count on that. Everything I've done lately has been the opposite of careful." He looked into her eyes—dry and pale. "I'll help you with the resurrections as soon as I can."

She kissed his cheek. "I know you will."

"Then let's get going." Matt extended a hand through the new portal. A jolt sent him reeling backwards into Lauren's arms.

When she set him upright, she studied the portal. "The other ones the tree created never carried a charge."

Matt flexed his tingling fingers. "Well, this one does."

Sir Barlow picked up the cloak. "Fortunately, we have protection." He draped it over himself and Lauren. "Shall we go, Miss Bannister?"

She smiled. "Certainly, brave knight."

Covered by the cloak, the two walked through the portal. A flash of light framed the material, accompanied by pops and sizzles. Soon, they faded into the dimness beyond.

Listener checked the spyglass at her belt, then slid her hand into Matt's. "Are you ready?"

Matt looked at the clasped hands. Her cool skin and strong fingers felt good, though perplexing. What did her affectionate manner really mean? "I'm ready."

They walked around the tree, stepped up onto the lava field in Second Eden, and stood on a strip of grass—green and lush. A few feet ahead, the grass gave way to dark soil that stretched out at least a hundred yards forward and to each side. A birthing plant stood close to the near edge, and two others protruded from the soil farther away. A cool breeze blew across the field, making the plants bend slightly, though the stalks seemed strong enough to support the twin leaves even in a gale.

Matt touched his stomach. The danger sensation churned again. Something was wrong, but no obvious threat lay anywhere in sight. Yet, like Lauren's spontaneous combustion, a threat could pop up in an unexpected way.

"Our new birthing garden," Listener said, gesturing toward the rich soil. "The men finished plowing yesterday. We lost many people to the volcano, war, and disease, so we're hoping the Father of Lights will bring us a bountiful harvest."

"Babies, you mean."

"And possibly older children and adults. The garden has been known to produce them from time to time." She knelt and touched an undisturbed spot in the soil. "See these footprints?"

Matt edged closer. Near Listener's fingers two footprints interrupted the dark ground. They appeared to be reddish, as if whoever put them there had been bleeding. "Who walked here?"

"Your sister. Dr. Conner told me she did it when the lava field was still hot. There were six footprints, and the gardeners preserved these two as a memorial to her."

Matt touched one of the prints. "How could she do that without going up in flames?"

"A miracle." Listener swept an arm toward the village. "This entire place is a miracle."

Matt turned that way. In the distance, at least twenty wood-and-straw huts stood in the midst of an extensive meadow. With no trees or shrubs nearby due to the recent lava flow, they looked like lonely sentinels. A wooden tower loomed near the center of the cluster, maybe fifty feet tall, similar to a forest ranger's fire tower with a staircase winding to the top.

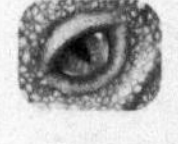

As they walked toward the tower, Matt's legs throbbed from carrying Lauren for so long. His danger sensation stayed constant—a cloud of doom over the area. And silence made it worse. Maybe starting a conversation would help ease the tension. "So, what else did Lauren do here that I might not know about?"

Listener looked at Mount Elijah to the north. "Have you heard how she tried to leap into the volcano?"

Matt studied the lofty mountain. Pale smoke rose from its ragged crater. "My mother mentioned it while we were crying over Lauren, but I didn't get any details."

"Then I'll tell you what I know." For the next minute, Listener told a thrilling tale about Lauren's attempt to save the original anthrozils from a parasitic disease and how Eagle sacrificially took her place. If not for him, Albatross, and those in the airborne hospital plane, she would have roasted in the lava field.

Matt glanced at Mount Elijah again. Lauren actually tried to leap into that crater. Not long after that, she intentionally gave her life to stop Tamiel. Could anyone match her selfless acts of courage? "Well … I'm not sure what to say about that. My sister is …" His throat narrowed. He couldn't go on.

"Your sister is a saint." Listener pressed a hand against her chest. "She has the heart of her mother and father, and after hearing about your sacrifices, I believe you have it as well."

"Thanks." Matt swallowed to loosen his throat. Listener's confidence in him was great, but living up to it would be hard.

He let out a silent sigh. Chatting hadn't eased the tension at all. Maybe another distraction would help. He pulled the scrap of paper from his pocket and carefully smoothed it out. "Any idea how we translate these coordinates into a physical location?"

Listener stopped and looked at the paper. "Valiant and I came up with the coordinate system, hoping to mimic Earth's, but since no one knows the size of our world or if its spherical shape has anomalies, we devised an alternative numbering algorithm. Instead of latitude and longitude, we use distances from the central hub in Founder's Village expressed in hundreds of paces." She pointed at the numbers on the paper. "Twenty point six nine equals two thousand sixty-nine paces to the east, and seventeen point four four equals one thousand seven hundred forty-four paces to the north. Negative numbers would indicate paces in the opposite directions."

"But paces are variable. They can be two or three feet or more, depending on who's walking."

"We call them SVPs—Standard Valiant Paces. They equal three feet in your measuring system." Lauren pointed at the numbers. "The extra zero three at the end is a code to verify that standard."

"How can you know if you're walking with SVPs?"

Listener gestured toward the tower, still about a hundred paces away. "Our central hub has multiple purposes. We have a handheld device that communicates with it and five other towers spread out across our explored boundaries. The combination of data allows a central computer to transmit location information to the device no matter where it is. It even has a map that shows where you are."

"Then it's like a GPS without the satellites."

"That's what Ashley said when she invented the system. Unfortunately, the central tower and two others were destroyed by the lava. According to Ashley, we need only three towers for the system to work, and although the men rebuilt the central one, we haven't tested the system yet for positioning, though we know it works for our version of tooth transmitters."

Listener began walking again. Matt folded the paper, slid it back into his pocket, and followed. "Where do we get the handheld device?"

"In the village." When they drew within ten yards of the closest hut, she stopped and pressed her palms together, fingers pointing upward. "Do this with your hands, and walk in front of me. I'll tell you which way to go."

He copied her hand position. "Wouldn't it be easier if you walk in front?"

"Only if you want people to think you're my suitor in a courting relationship."

"Well …" Matt glanced downward for a moment before looking at Listener again. "Would that be so terrible?"

She pursed her lips. "I see your point. Such a rumor would cause no great harm. In any case, I will lead until we come upon other villagers, and I can decide what to do at that time."

"Uh … sure. That'll work."

As they walked along a path between two rows of huts, she angled her head. "Strange. I don't hear any voices, not even the chatter of children."

Matt scanned the area. Unless people were hiding behind the huts, no one was around. "A meeting somewhere, maybe?"

"No one mentioned a meeting when I was here a few hours ago." She broke into a trot. "Come!"

He pushed his aching legs forward and matched her pace. They weaved around a few huts and stopped at the base of the tower. A clipboard hung on a nail protruding from one of the four wooden supports. The breeze rattled an attached page.

Listener snatched the page from the clipboard and read it out loud. "Listener, Karrick sensed grave danger in Founder's Village, so we have gone to Peace Village. If he does not sense danger there, we will stay. Otherwise, we will go to our enclave in the hills." She looked at Matt, concern etched in her expression. "It's from Candle, my older brother."

"Yeah, I felt the danger, too, but it's kind of … radio static, I guess. Not like someone's about to ambush us. More like something gathering in the distance."

Listener looked up. Matt did the same. The sky appeared hazy, as if smoke hung high in the air. She whispered, "Something gathering. Interesting."

"Maybe Semiramis's bomb or whatever it is." Matt pivoted in place, checking each horizon. "It might be ready to activate."

"I'll get the positioning device." Listener ran into a nearby hut and emerged seconds later carrying a red tablet that looked like an Etch A Sketch with two six-inch antennae. She glanced at the tower, then at a screen on the device. "It appears to be working. It says we are four point two SVPs north and two point seven east."

Matt leaned close. The screen appeared to be from an old mobile phone, wired to fit inside a kid's toy, but the blinking numbers proved that it worked. He pulled out the scrap of paper again and unfolded it. "So we head east northeast and correct our path based on what this device tells us."

She nodded. "By Earth measurements, the spot indicated by the coordinates should be a little more than a mile and a half away."

Matt whistled. "That's quick math."

"Well, I am not shy about saying that I am good at mental calculations, but ..." She pointed at one corner of the screen. "I entered the coordinates from memory. The computer displays the distance in Earth units right here. One point five four miles."

"Humble and confident at the same time. You really are amazing."

She dipped her head briefly. "Thank you, sir."

"You're welcome." Matt looked into her appreciative eyes. Not many girls could accept a compliment without a self-deprecating reply. "Well, we'd better hustle."

Listener pointed toward the birthing garden. "That way."

They jogged at a rapid pace, skirted the garden, and continued onto a verdant meadow—grass that extended for miles before ending to the north at a mountain range where Mount Elijah stood. To the east, a black expanse of rock interrupted the grassland, much farther away than they would have to travel.

As they hurried, Matt kept watch for visible signs of danger, but nothing appeared. The sense in his gut increased moment by moment—not a spike, just a gradual climb.

Every minute or so, Listener checked the numbers on the screen and adjusted their heading without slowing the pace. Yet, she neither gasped for breath nor perspired. As they closed in on the spot, Matt looked her over. Her stride, long and effortless, was perfect, even with a spyglass bouncing at her hip.

After a few minutes, Listener halted and studied the screen. "According to this, we should be standing right on the location. What does your danger sensation tell you?"

"It's higher than before but nothing drastic." Matt ran his foot along the ground—grass covering dark soil. "Semiramis said she hid the device, so it wouldn't be out in the open, but nothing's been buried here recently."

"True, but the lava flowed over everything, and this grass sprouted in a matter of hours. So did a few bushes and short trees. Much faster than normal. She could have buried it here, and now the lava is hiding any sign of her efforts."

Matt kicked at the hard soil with his heel. "Digging through lava rock might be impossible."

"It's probably hard on the surface and softer underneath, but we would still need picks and shovels to break through." Listener turned toward the village. "We could go back and get the proper tools."

"Maybe." Matt began pacing slowly. "The land is so barren, there really isn't anywhere to search, except for ..." He stopped and gazed at the smoke above, too thick to see beyond its lowest layer. "Could the device be hovering in the air? With all the smoke, no one could see it from down here."

Listener looked up. "Our hospital airplane is our only flying craft. Before we modified it, the hospital hovered, controlled by ground-based magnets, but they've been dismantled."

"A helium balloon could work, but it would need some kind of attachment line. Otherwise, the breeze would blow it away. And if the device weighs more than a few ounces, the balloon would have to be pretty big. It would need a tether that anyone could see, even from a distance."

"A tether!" Listener said. "That's it!"

"What's it?"

She gestured with her hands, reeling out a make-believe line. "Years ago, Semiramis used an invisible tether that Mardon attached to your mother. She could feel it sometimes, like an evasive spiderweb that she couldn't quite grab."

"I haven't heard that story."

"I'll have to tell it sometime, but if the device is really up there, we need to search from the air. Karrick will gladly volunteer. I assume Grackle will also, though his age might limit his ability to fly through the smoke."

Matt drew a mental picture of the dragons flying through the hazy sky. "Why doesn't the breeze carry the smoke away?"

"A local vortex." Listener twirled her arm over her head. "The air currents travel in a circle much of the time, though it's not perfectly consistent. Valiant told me that after one eruption, the volcanic ash stayed in the air over our villages for three weeks. This eruption was even bigger, so clearing the air might take longer."

"Do you know where the center of the vortex is?"

"I never asked." Listener lifted the spyglass to her eye and pivoted slowly. When she stopped, she pointed it upward. "The haze movements indicate that the center could be right where we're standing or at least nearby."

"More evidence we're in the right spot. Maybe Semiramis and Mardon want to use the wind pattern somehow. Spread something in the atmos—"

"I hear something." Listener lowered the spyglass. "Something high pitched. Like a squeal."

Matt's danger sense soared. "Trouble's about to pop."

Listener's eyes widened. "Now it's beeping."

"A countdown! Let's move!" Matt grabbed Listener's elbow, and the two dashed toward the village. Something shattered to their rear, like a thousand windows breaking. Sparkling shards, dark and spinning, flew past. Some pelted their heads and shoulders, stinging before bouncing off.

Listener stopped and crouched, her hands pressed against her ears. "Something's squealing!"

"Squealing?" Matt crouched with her, his head low. The shards continued raining down. "I don't hear anything."

"It's high pitched." Listener groaned. "It's drilling into my brain!"

"Let's find cover." Matt spied a short, bushy tree to the left, probably newly grown since the eruption. "This way!" He helped her up, and they ran to the tree, Listener with her hands still over her ears. As they bent low under its boughs, he pressed her head close to his chest and covered her hand over the other ear. "Is that better?"

She grimaced. "A little. It still feels like my skull is cracking."

"Maybe it'll be over soon. If not, we'll make a run for it to your village." The shards fell in torrential gray sheets. Like puzzle pieces coming together, they created a blanket of dark crystals that spread out and deepened as the ashy precipitation continued. "It looks like dirty ice. It must be collecting smoke from the air."

Listener moaned softly. "But why all the noise?"

"I have no idea." Some crystals fell through the leaves and drizzled onto their shoulders. Matt plucked a cold, wet crystal from Listener's hair and rubbed it with a thumb. "The ice is kind of oily. Like frozen soot. Volcanic debris, maybe. Add cold and moisture, and you get sooty ice."

Listener closed her eyes tightly. "Not enough moisture in the air for that much ice."

"What other source could there be?" Matt tossed the crystal to the ground and looked at the center of the vortex. A tornadic funnel protruded from above and extended at an angle toward the horizon. "Listener. What do you make of that?"

Keeping her ear pressed against his chest, she opened her eyes and looked that way. "A water spout. It's drawing from Twin Falls River."

"That explains the water and soot, but what about the cold?"

"Some kind of massive chemical reaction that absorbs heat." Listener shivered. "Mardon's smart enough to know how to do that. My concern is what his mother might have contributed to this scheme."

"Semiramis?"

"Right. Her potions."

Matt inhaled through his nose. "Garlic?"

Listener nodded, her facial lines still tight. "And camphor. The combination is her trademark. I also smell ammonia. One of her potions is definitely fouling the air."

"Any idea what it might do?"

She firmed her jaw. "Only that it will be something malevolent."

The crystalline blanket expanded along the ground and surrounded them, thickening every second. As the ice spread over Listener's bare feet, Matt reached for his laces. "I'll let you wear my boots."

"No." She grasped his wrist. "I have boots at home. Candle and I moved to a little hut at the edge of Founder's Village."

"How's the noise level?"

"Awful. Worse than ever."

"Then we should go." He slowly lifted his hand from her ear. "Can you stand it?"

She grimaced. "I'll have to."

"We'll hurry." Matt pried himself free from the ice and helped Listener break away. "We have to stay on top of this stuff."

While ice formed a gray crust on her head, she covered her ears again and marched in place. Her toes were already blue.

"Let's do it this way." Matt crouched low. "Up you go."

"Gladly." She mounted his shoulders and settled in place. "I'm ready."

Matt straightened and lifted her. His legs aching again, he grasped her toes—frigid and stiff—and high stepped over the slick ice toward the village. As the shards rained down, Listener brushed crystals from his hair and shoulders, in spite of the pain she had to be feeling in her ears. The sheet of ice rose an inch every minute, but constantly marching allowed him to stay above the rising mass.

Ahead, the swirling ash created a blinding curtain of gray. Even with Listener's guidance, finding their way back would be harrowing, especially without the locator device, which they must have dropped somewhere in their rush to escape the chaos.

Matt heaved a frosty breath and slogged on. After too many torturous minutes, a row of five huts came into view—hazy in the soot-strewn air. "I see the village!" Matt called, hoping his shout could overcome the squealing in Listener's ears.

She lowered a hand into his viewing field and pointed. "That way! The one in the middle!"

"I see it!" Matt tromped up a gentle rise—slick and treacherous. He halted next to the hut. Gray ice surrounded it and rose halfway up the only visible window, closed by wooden shutters. The angled roof, also covered by a dark, crystalline sheet, acted as an umbrella, keeping the pile of ice immediately around the hut down to a few inches and creating a gap between the hut and the surrounding wall of ice. The lower collection of ice blocked the base of the entry door.

Listener slid down from Matt's shoulders and looked at the window. She covered her ears, again grimacing. Her pigtails had frozen together, and an ashy sheen of ice coated her face and shoulders. "The shutters aren't too iced over, but we might get trapped if we go inside."

"And you'll be an icicle if we don't go in. Or your skull will crack from the noise." He hopped down into the gap and inserted his fingers into the crevice between the shutters. After pulling for a few seconds, he broke the seal and pried them open.

When Listener joined him in the gap, she climbed through the window. Matt followed and closed the shutters. "Does that help? With the noise, I mean."

She brushed ice from her shoulders. "It's better. At least my head isn't ready to explode."

Inside the square room, maybe four paces wide, an upholstered chair sat next to the closer of a pair of single beds positioned side by side, one against the wall with a narrow gap between them. A curtain cordoned off another room, and an overstuffed bookshelf stood against the wall next to it.

A potbellied woodstove sat in a corner with a small pile of kindling stacked nearby. From the stove's top, a black pipe led through the ceiling, but the exhaust vent outside was likely blocked by ice.

Matt gathered a handful of kindling and set it in the woodstove. "Can you build a fire while I clear the vent up top?"

"Let's see if the heat will melt it." Listener picked up a box of matches from a shelf attached to a wall. "Will you do the honors while I get us some water and a bite to eat?"

"Sure." Matt took the matches, struck one, and set the flame to the edge of the kindling. The dry wood caught, and fire slowly crawled along the fibers, spreading out as it moved. Smoke built up and swirled within the stove's belly, some leaking through the door's grating. Water dripped down inside the stovepipe and sizzled in the flames, though not enough to douse the fire. Soon, something popped, and the smoke shot upward through the pipe.

"That worked." Matt closed the woodstove's door. "We should have a good blaze going in a few minutes."

"Thank the Father of Lights." Listener handed him a hunk of dried meat and a glass jar filled with water. "If you need washroom facilities, there is a chamber pot and water basin behind the curtain."

"Thanks." Matt bit into the meat—beef with a peppery tang. Although dry and tough, with his inner furnace working so hard, it tasted like freshly grilled steak.

While he ate, Listener withdrew a pair of wool socks from a top drawer in a dresser within an alcove and disappeared behind the curtain to the adjoining room. She returned a few moments later, her face clean and her hair and clothes free of ice. He finished eating, took his turn in the washroom, and returned to find her sitting in the chair with her eyes closed and the socks on the floor.

An old book lay on a small table next to the chair. Matt picked it up and read the title—*Subterfuge in Warfare.* He flipped through the pages and scanned a few chapter headers: Silent Communications, The Art of Spying, Codes—Ancient and Modern, and The Ethics of Deception.

He set the book down and stooped close. Her deep, even respiration gave evidence of restful sleep. It was probably for the best. They were both exhausted, and the storm's fury seemed to go on and on. Traveling out there now would be treacherous, and the noise might injure Listener's ears permanently.

He slid one arm under her legs and another behind her back and lifted her in a cradle. She slept on, though she wrapped her arms around his neck, probably by instinct.

Moving slowly, he laid her on the outer bed, unbuckled her belt, and, lifting her hips, pulled it out from under her. He let the belt drop to the floor, weighed down by the spyglass and sheathed dagger. He then slid the covers back from underneath her body past her bare feet. Her toes, reddened by cold, would need more warmth than the thin sheet and spread could provide.

He retrieved the socks from the floor and slid them over her feet and halfway up her calves, then pulled the covers up to her shoulders, fluffed the pillow, and pushed it under her head.

Her eyes remaining closed, she nestled into the pillow and let out a contented sigh.

Matt stared at her. She was so strong. Fair of face and firm of body, she carried herself like a beauty queen for one moment and a powerful warrior the next.

He pushed a wet pigtail away from her cheek and whispered, "You really are amazing."

A barely perceptible smile bent the corners of her lips. Her deep breathing continued. She was still fast asleep.

Matt pulled off his boots and looked at the empty bed, inches away from Listener's. His aching body begged to lie there, to rest his tired limbs and sore muscles, but what would she think about such a close sleeping arrangement? Since it abutted the wall, he couldn't move it farther away without dragging it across the room.

He picked up the bed's pillow and blanket and carried them to the shuttered window. Since the door was blocked by ice, the window was the only possible access. He curled up on the floor, laid his head on the pillow, and draped the blanket over himself. Now no one could get in without him knowing it. Listener would be safe.

The pull of sleep washed over his mind. That was all right. He could let it come. The storm had to end eventually, and when it did, he and Listener would be ready.

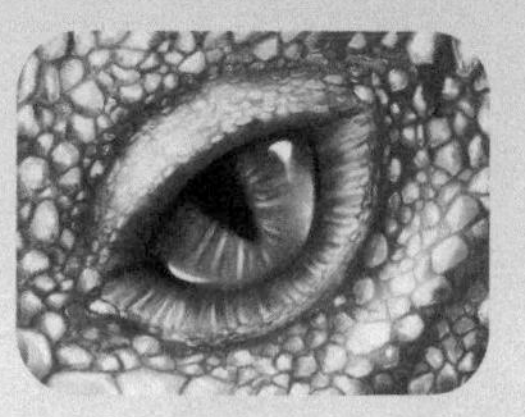

5

CHAPTER

Enforcers

Marilyn paced in front of Larry. Blinking lights from his control panel illuminated her short path—three steps from the desk chair to the window and back again.

Hugging a bowling-ball-sized pot filled with soil, she looked at the tiny plant rooted at the center, merely a stem, maybe an inch tall with a green leaflet on each side. Had it grown in the past hour? Maybe an eighth of an inch? Or was it wishful thinking? In any case, Jared's new form wasn't growing fast enough. At this rate, it might take months for him to regenerate into Clefspeare the dragon.

She looked at the room's worktable where Mardon had spilled the catalyst fluid that was supposed to make Jared grow faster. Near the fluid's remnant stain, Excalibur lay with its hilt near the edge of the table. Ever since Jared transluminated himself to start the transformation to his dragon state, the blade had remained dark. Without an heir to King Arthur grasping the hilt to energize its power, it would be nothing more than a cutting tool.

Using a finger, she petted one of the leaflets and whispered, "Jared, I'll do whatever it takes to turn you into Clefspeare. You will battle Arramos, you will defeat him, and you will rescue the children." She let out a sigh. "But what then? Larry knows how to transform you back to Jared, my husband, but what about the years that follow? Will you stay young while I grow old? Will your skin stay smooth when mine wrinkles? Will your hair be untouched by age while mine thins and turns white?"

She shook her head. "I'm sorry. I know we've talked about this many times. You'll still love me, of course, but that doesn't ease my turmoil. I want to be strong and vibrant for you. I want us to age together, side by side, facing the end of life in the same way, whether that takes thirty years or three hundred. I don't want you burdened with a crippled, senile old lady."

She laughed under her breath. "I'm worried about going senile, and here I am talking to a plant. I must be losing it already." After pacing through her circuit a few more times, she closed her eyes. "God in Heaven, I need a miracle. Either make Jared and me age in the same way or help me be content if it doesn't happen. But whatever you do, please keep Jared safe and whole, and make him ready to battle the Prince of Darkness. That's more important than anything."

Opening her eyes again, she turned toward Larry's main monitor. It displayed current atmospheric radiation levels for the region. As before, levels to the north and west were toxic, and in the immediate area they remained high enough to keep everyone inside their homes. To drive to the Second Eden portal, they could take a southern route, but with gas stations closed, they wouldn't get very far.

She pulled an elastic band from her pocket, tied her hair back, and grabbed a navy-blue baseball-style cap from Larry's control desk. As she put it on and adjusted her ponytail in the back, she called out, "Status report."

Larry's lights brightened. "Unchanged since my five a.m. report ten minutes ago."

She pinched the front bill and aligned the cap. "Have you been able to monitor any new communications channels?"

"Adding new channels would alter my status report. As I stated, it is unchanged." The display showed a scrolling list. "Ever since you shifted me to full power this morning, I have been listening to all emergency broadcast frequencies—Ham and shortwave, police bands, radio modulations, television stations, satellite transmissions, NORAD, and weather channels. The emergency broadcasts are providing safety alerts. Travel is banned in our region except for official government vehicles, which include police, fire, and … you will find this interesting … child-education agencies."

"So the Enforcers are still at work collecting children. Arramos isn't going to let a little event like a nuclear disaster stop him."

"That is a logical deduction."

Marilyn set a hand on her forehead. "Have you heard anything good on the airwaves?"

"There is a neighborhood radio hobbyist who is broadcasting himself playing violin—a soulful rendition of 'Jesus Loves Me.'"

"Perfect. Can you pipe that in? Maybe it'll calm my nerves."

"Of course." The gentle hum of violin strings emanated from Larry's speakers—soulful indeed, and quite good.

Marilyn sat in the chair and, with the pot in her lap, caressed Jared's leaflet again as she murmured along with the tune. "Little ones to him belong. They are weak, but he is strong."

"Children," she whispered as she looked toward the ceiling once more. "Jesus, we need you to be strong for them. And give them some of your strength. Arramos will not hesitate to torture and kill them."

Images of suffering children brought the words of Joan of Arc to mind, quoted by Jared as he lay near death in the Second Eden hospital. While in a coma-like state, he mumbled her message again and again until it branded itself in permanent memory. *Clefspeare, son of Goliath and Roxil, the children of your world cry for help. Arramos, the devil in a dragon's skin, is plotting to spill the blood of countless innocents, and you are the only dragon powerful enough to engage him in battle. I do not know if you will defeat him, but fight you must. Win or lose, you will be able to thwart his schemes and save the lives of children. And knowing your heart, the heart of the true Arramos, you will gladly sacrifice your life to save even one of those precious souls.*

Marilyn stroked Jared's stem. Somehow they had to get to Second Eden's birthing garden where Jared could blossom from this alpha stage to full-blown omega quickly, perhaps in mere seconds.

She glanced at the blinds-covered window. Dawn would arrive soon, along with the appearance of the eerie red sun that had presided over so many strange days of late. Would good news come with the morning for a change? They needed transportation, and Larry had managed to communicate the need to Ashley. Since there seemed to be no way to get to the portal by her own resources, all she could do was wait. Maybe a dragon would arrive—Makaidos, Thigocia, or Roxil. There seemed to be no other options.

Adam walked in from the hallway door, his dark T-shirt covered with white and yellow stains and his hair dusted with gray powder. "I filled the generator. Larry should be good to go for a while."

Marilyn lifted her brow. "I thought you used all the gas from your car. Where did you find more?"

"I didn't find more." He brushed his hands on his grimy jeans. "It's a home brew, but it should work."

"How are the solar batteries?"

"Fried. The pulse must've killed them. But the generator will be enough."

Marilyn swiveled the chair toward Larry. "How is your power level?"

"The generator's efficiency is running slightly below normal, but it can sustain me at full capacity for about two hours."

"Great!" She turned back to Adam. "What did you put in the brew?"

"A freakish combination." He grinned. "Let's just call it combustible hash. Mardon was the chef."

"Mardon?" Marilyn's cheeks grew warm. Even the sound of his name heated a firebrand within. "How is his eyesight?"

"Not great. He's sitting in the living room resting his eyes. He says they're still burning." Adam peeled a layer of scorched, dirty skin from his forearm, wincing as it came off. "I gotta hand it to him. He's a real genius. I mean, he knew exactly how every ingredient would react—rubbing alcohol, motor oil, spray paint, dirty socks, Epsom salts, and whiskey old man Nivitz across the street had thrown out. Amazing!"

Marilyn picked at a raised plastic nodule on the chair arm. "Well, good for Mardon. But I still don't trust him."

"Yeah, he might just be kissing up to us, but he's jumping all over anything I ask." Adam shrugged. "So it's all good, at least for now."

"He'll do anything to go to Second Eden. He's obsessed with being with Sapphira."

"By the way, I hauled that federal agent's body out like you asked. I don't know how he died. I didn't hit him that hard with the bat. Mardon thinks he might've popped a suicide pill."

"Alert!" Larry's monitor flashed, and new lines scrolled upward in a central text window. "I am displaying a transmission from Lois."

Marilyn rolled the chair closer. The lines ran by too quickly to read. "Larry, give me a summary."

"One moment, please."

Adam joined Marilyn at her side and whispered, "I wonder why Lois would risk a transmission. Is she thinking that the Feds are too busy trying to save their own hides?"

"Adam's suggestion is somewhat accurate," Larry said. "Yet, in order to safeguard the security of transmissions, Lois is sending data that any government monitor can decrypt. So if they are monitoring, they are receiving an innocuous update about Lois's battery status. The hope is that they will not suspect that the transmission includes a far more sophisticated string of data that I am collecting and will translate into a video stream. I will be able to show it to you when the transmission concludes."

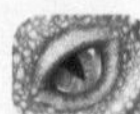

A few seconds later, a new window opened on the screen. A side view of Carly sitting in a driver's seat appeared. With both hands on the steering wheel, she kept her gaze forward, her dark hair flowing in the wind. As she turned the wheel to negotiate bounces, her arms, exposed by her black T-shirt's short sleeves, tightened and loosened. Her lips moved in a jerky fashion, as if the transmission skipped some of the frames. Her voice joined in, a half second out of sync.

"Mrs. B, Lois and I are on our way to Castlewood. We helped a woman get in touch with her son who is at a scouting camp for the week. She was worried about the radiation and the possibility that the Enforcers might take him. Turns out he's safe, at least for now. To thank us, she let us borrow this Jeep." Carly touched something on the dashboard. "The gas gauge is under a quarter, and Lois calculates we might make it to Castlewood, but it's impossible to be sure."

The scene bounced hard, then settled in a tilted pose. Carly's hand reached close and adjusted the view. "It's kind of bumpy, because I'm taking a back road—mostly loose gravel and a few potholes. Lois says the main highways are blocked. We'll lose some time this way, but it's better than running into some overly curious guys with guns, if you know what I mean."

She heaved a deep sigh. "One drawback. The Jeep is uncovered, so I'm exposed to fallout. But I had to take the risk. Lois reported that Ashley got through to her and said you're working on a secret project of some kind. Lois analyzed the possibilities and determined that it might have something to do with a genetic reconstruction involving Jared … or Clefspeare, I suppose. The trouble is that some of the information was transmitted to Lois's databanks after she was separated from Larry, supposedly for security reasons."

Another bump sent the camera off-kilter again, but Carly didn't bother to straighten it. "Lois doesn't know what the project is, but I assume it won't work if you try to complete it. Since it was important enough to offload a piece to ensure its security, and it was done without telling Lois what it is, we're guessing that it's critical, and we need to get Lois and Larry back together before you attempt it …" Her voice cracked. "If it's not already too late."

Carly brushed a tear from her eye. "I have to admit, Mrs. B. I'm pretty scared. I saw a woman carrying a child, and she threw herself into a bonfire. Both went up in flames, and I couldn't do anything to stop it. A guy stabbed another guy just for pushing into the line to watch the woman and child burn. Most of the people have terrible sores, I guess from the radiation, and dead bodies are lying in the streets of Morgantown."

She pointed at a dime-sized lesion on her cheek, raw but not bleeding. "And now *I* might be getting radiation poisoning, and they say it's a horrible way to die. If I run out of gas, I'll be out here alone, and no one will know where I am." She stared straight ahead and brushed another tear. Her lips quivered between a smile and a thin, horizontal line. After several seconds, she spoke in a shaking voice. "Well … never mind. This isn't about me." She reached close again, and the video ended.

Marilyn sat back in her chair. "Wow! It's getting rough out there."

"No kidding. And Carly's really scared."

"Can't blame her for that, especially since she has exposure symptoms."

Adam walked to the window and peeked between the blinds. "I wish I knew which road to take. My Mazda's not working, but I'd go looking for her on a bicycle."

"And risk your own life?"

"Well … yeah." He kept his gaze locked out the window, shifting from foot to foot and back again. "She's risking hers for us."

Marilyn focused on his nervous fingers as he held two slats apart. The new information about the offloaded data could wait a minute. "Adam, you're in your thirties, right?"

"Right." He let the blinds snap closed and turned toward her. "Why do you ask?"

She let the question float for a moment as she studied his inquisitive eyes. "You never married. Why is that?"

"Because I'm waiting for a certain girl. We kind of dated for a while years ago, but when I went to Bible school to learn about missions work, we drifted apart. She didn't want to be a missionary's wife." Adam slid a hand into his pocket. "It's for the best. Eight years in Afghanistan taught me that I was better off alone.

Besides, I could never marry someone who doesn't believe the same way I do."

"So this girl isn't a Christian?"

"I thought she was. But sometimes it's hard to tell. I guess fear removes a lot of masks."

"I know what you mean." Marilyn glanced at the screen where Carly's video was replaying, this time without the sound. "And she never married either?"

Adam shook his head and looked again between the blinds.

"So you're hoping she'll turn to faith in God. That's why you're waiting."

He stared silently for a moment before murmuring, "Something like that."

Marilyn rose and slid her arm around his shoulders. "Carly's worth waiting for, Adam."

He laughed softly. "Not hard to guess, huh?"

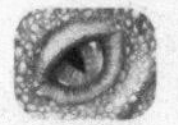

"Not at all. The day you two worked together to rebuild Apollo, I thought I saw a spark. You're both intelligent, passionate, and loving. You saw how scared she is. We need to pray for her now more than ever."

He nodded. "That's exactly what I've been doing. For years."

"Good. Keep it up. I'll pray for her, too." She patted him on the back and walked to Larry's control monitor. "All right, Larry. What did Carly mean about a piece of the project being missing? What piece could she be talking about?"

`"I do not know. Carly's transmission provided my first awareness of a missing piece."`

"But it couldn't be the genetic code. That has to be perfect, right? We wouldn't have a plant at all if there was something missing."

`"Although the data I have affirms your supposition, I believe that question would be better addressed by our genius scientist. A piece of the project could be` instructions on how to help the plant grow after implementing the genetic code, which Mardon might already know. Your concerns could be alleviated by simply asking."

Marilyn rolled her eyes. Talking to Mardon was like interrogating a snake. "I suppose you're right."

"I'll get him." Adam rushed to the hallway door and dashed out of the room.

Marilyn began pacing again. "Another question is who would have put in the procedure to offload part of the project to Lois? Obviously Carly didn't know about it, and Adam didn't speak up."

"Perhaps it happened while I was locked down. During that status, much could have taken place without my knowledge. Only a few people had access during that time, and only one person had sufficient programming skills to send data to Lois after we were separated."

Marilyn's ears turned fiery hot. "Mardon. That weasel!"

Adam hustled back into the room. "He's coming."

Still holding Jared's plant, Marilyn set a hand on her hip. "He doesn't need a guide?"

"He doesn't seem to." Adam looked toward the door. "I guess he's healing, trying to be independent."

Mardon walked into the computer room and stood in front of Marilyn, his eyes fully open behind his silver-dollar shaped glasses. With nervous hands, he brushed the sleeves of his tattered brown jacket. "Yes?"

She shot a hot scowl at him. "What do you know about sending a piece of Jared's transformation instructions to Lois and deleting it from Larry?"

Mardon wrung his hands. "I did that to … to …"

"To make sure no one else had all the pieces to the puzzle!" She jabbed a finger at the worktable. "The spill! The burning eyes! Was all of that an act?"

"Well ..."

"Was the catalyst liquid lacking what we needed all along?" She shoved Jared's pot close to his face and shouted, "You stunted his growth on purpose, didn't you? You did it to make sure we would have to go to Second Eden!"

Mardon folded his hands behind his back and straightened. "Yes. I admit that I did."

Marilyn slapped at his cheek, but her hand passed through his face, making her stumble with the momentum. When she righted herself, she stared at him. "You're a ghost!"

He nodded. "Which means that all portals to Second Eden have closed."

"Well, that's of no consequence to you. You're not coming with us." She handed the pot to Adam. "Please find a sturdy box for Jared. Maybe we can brew some more fuel and run a car engine. Then check the Foleys' house to see who's home. Last I heard, Shelly and her sons might be visiting."

"Just one of them," Adam said. "Ricky stayed in Morgantown with his dad. But Shelly might be heading back already. I'll check." Adam glanced at Mardon briefly before hurrying from the room.

Mardon smoothed out his shirt. "The fuel will work reasonably well in a car, but how will you enter Second Eden?"

"Sapphira can open a portal." Marilyn sat in the control chair, withdrew a memory stick from a drawer, and inserted it into an interface in Larry's front panel. "Larry, download Jared's project information and data to this drive. We'll take Lois to Second Eden and figure out how to grow Jared in the birthing garden ourselves."

An image of a padlock appeared on Larry's main monitor. "Encrypting data now. I will provide you with a key when the process is complete."

"Good."

Mardon edged closer. “I know why the portals have closed. You will not be able to open one without my help.”

She swiveled the chair toward him, a shout begging to erupt, but she kept her voice calm. “What did you do? How did you close them?”

“I did not close them. My mother planted a device in Second Eden, and I am assuming that it detonated, which created a sequence of events that sealed the portals. I am familiar with the device’s payload, so I am able to counter its effects.”

She rose and glared at him. “Then prove yourself. Tell me what to do.”

He lifted his head and sniffed. “You have already said I am not coming with you. Why should I give away the only leverage that might change your mind?”

“Then you *are* in this for yourself! You’re not trying to help anyone but Mardon.”

He looked her in the eye. “Guilty as charged. Yet, I realize that by helping Jared, I will be furthering the cause of destroying Arramos, which is another goal that we all cherish.”

“You’re such a snake!” She stalked to the table, grabbed Excalibur, and pointed it at him. “You intentionally hid a crucial step that would have helped my husband! Your selfishness endangered his life! Stop pretending that we have the same goals! It’s an insult!”

“Very well.” Mardon bowed his head. “I will rely only on your passion to restore your husband. Since you need me for that quest, I suggest that we work together in a cooperative manner, even if ours is a hostile relationship.”

She waved a hand at him. “Cut the hogwash. You’re making me sick.”

“Download complete,” Larry said. “You will find the remaining genetic material in a flask inside my cabinet.”

"Thank you." Marilyn jerked the memory stick out and slid it into her pocket. "I need to pack a bag."

Mardon spread his arms. "Are you taking me with you?"

"Only because I have to." She narrowed her eyes. His expression seemed too cocky, too self-assured for a ghost who could be sent away once the portal opened. "You have something else up your sleeve, don't you?" She lifted the blade close to his nose, though it couldn't hurt him. "What else did that device do to Second Eden?"

"You said to cut the hogwash." Mardon stared cross-eyed at Excalibur's tip. "Indeed, I do have more up my sleeve, as you say. My mother's device actually provided a benefit. It fertilized and hydrated the soil so that your husband will transform from alpha to omega dragon at an extraordinarily rapid rate. Yet only I know how to trigger the process. Although the information is in Lois's memory storage, you will not be able to interpret it without my help."

Marilyn squeezed the hilt, her lips tight. *Calm down.* Lashing out again wouldn't do any good. Mardon's leverage would eventually run dry, and then he could be expelled from Second Eden forever. Until then, altering her tone and playing along with this mad scientist's game was the best course to take.

"Okay." She set Excalibur back on the table. "You win. I'll take you with us. Anything for Jared."

"Excellent!" Mardon rubbed his hands together. "Adam told me about Carly's imminent arrival. I have a formula in mind that will work efficiently in a Jeep, and we can easily find the ingredients along the way. We will have no need for fueling stations."

"Good. That will be helpful."

"I will ask Adam to gather a few things." Mardon walked through the wall and disappeared.

Marilyn's heart thumped. Having a ghost around stirred this bizarre situation into a haunted whirlpool. Yet, his nonphysical state actually made one issue easier to deal with. He wouldn't take up any space in the Jeep.

She mentally counted. Adam, Carly, and herself—three. Carl and Catherine would make five. If Shelly and her son were still here, that would make seven. Did the Jeep have that many seats? And since it had no roof, what about the fallout risk? How well could a three-year-old boy tolerate—

Adam burst into the room. "Mrs. B! We've got trouble!"

"What kind of trouble?"

"Take a look." Adam pulled a string that drew the blinds up. Through the window, dawning light barely illuminated Cordelle Road. Down the street, two vehicles had parked in front of the Foleys' house.

"I can't make out who's there," Marilyn said.

"Enforcers. A police cruiser and a paddy wagon. I'll bet they're after Mark."

"How could they know he's here? Shelly lives in Morgantown."

"Tracked them down, I guess. Since they're your friends, the whole family is probably on a hit list."

"Then they'll kill Mark before the day is out." Marilyn jerked open a desk drawer, withdrew a pistol, and slid it into her pocket. "I'm not going to let that happen."

Adam grabbed Excalibur and hid it behind his back. "I'm with you."

"Larry, send an emergency signal to Lois. Hang the secrecy. Tell Carly to stay away." With Adam following, Marilyn rushed out of the room, ran down the hall, and opened the front door. She stopped and raised a hand. "Adam, stay here unless I need you. We don't want to spook them."

He nodded. "Got it."

With the reddish light of dawn growing stronger, Marilyn hurried to the street, then walked casually toward the Foleys' house. The paddy wagon had parked on the road, two wheels in the Foleys' lawn, while the police car sat in the middle of the street, its blue lights flashing.

An eerie silence blanketed the area. With dawn breaking, birds would normally be greeting the morning with a chorus of chirps and whistles. But that was before the days of the scarlet sun.

A loud flapping noise interrupted the calm, though the bird, maybe a vulture looking for an easy breakfast, stayed out of sight. With animals dying because of the fallout, the scavenger pickings had been easy lately, though probably not safe to eat, even for a carrion feeder.

Marilyn stopped at the rear of the paddy wagon and peered around it. Three officers wearing yellow hazmat suits and hoods stood at the Foleys' front door. One pounded with a fist and shouted, "Open up, or we'll break it down!"

A muffled voice emanated from inside. "Hang on. Hang on. I'm coming. I'm not as fast as I used to be."

Movement from the Foleys' backyard caught Marilyn's eye—a woman carrying a sleeping boy, his head against her shoulder, both barefoot and wearing long-sleeved pajamas. Marilyn stifled a gasp. Shelly and Mark!

While Shelly skulked toward the front, staying close to the house's stucco wall, the Foleys' door opened. Carl appeared, wearing a zippered West Virginia sweater and leaning on a cane. "What may I do for you officers?"

"Do you have a child here?" The officer looked at a notepad clutched by his thick glove. His voice was barely audible through his protective hood. "Markus Pastore?"

Carl shot him an annoyed look. "Of course not. Both of my children are grown and out of the house."

"Our information says that he's here." The officer unfolded a sheet and showed it to Carl. "We have a warrant to search the premises."

Carl gestured inside. "Be my guest."

The officer waved a hand at the other two. "Secure the perimeter."

One of the officers walked toward the wall where Shelly hid, while the other hurried in the opposite direction. Their thick suits and hoods made them look like yellow-skinned aliens stomping around in a hostile environment.

Marilyn ran toward the closer officer. "Wait! I saw a woman carrying a little boy! I'm so glad you came, because she's obviously exposing him to the fallout." She pointed down the street, away from Shelly. "They went that way."

"Impossible." The officer's eyes, visible through the hood's plastic shield, narrowed. "I've been watching the area. Besides, our drones would've spotted them."

"Drones?"

The officer looked up. Marilyn followed his line of sight. A winged beast sprang from a treetop and began flying in a circle above the road. With black scales, leathery wings, and hideous face, it looked like a cross between a dragon and a vulture.

Marilyn ventured a stealthy glance at Shelly as she pressed her back against the wall. "So that's a drone?"

The officer nodded. "There's more where that one came from. And you should get under cover before you get too much radiation." He pushed Marilyn to the side. "Now if you'll excuse me."

A shot rang out from inside the house. The officer spun and ran toward the front door. The third officer joined him, and they bustled inside.

Marilyn pulled out her gun and waved at Shelly, whisper shouting, "This way!"

Lowering her head, Shelly ran toward Marilyn. When she arrived, they hid together behind the paddy wagon. Mark's eyes were closed, and drool streamed onto Shelly's shoulder. "He's asleep," she whispered. "He's on Benadryl. He'll stay quiet."

"Good. We'll try to sneak—"

More shots erupted from the Foleys', too many to count. Marilyn pointed toward her house. "Go! Adam's there!"

Holding Mark close, Shelly ran. The drone swooped toward her. Marilyn aimed her pistol and fired at the beast—once, twice, three times. One bullet zinged past it, a second glanced off its scales, but the third plunked into its head.

The drone crashed to the street and toppled over Shelly. As it thrashed on top of her and Mark, Marilyn dashed toward them. Adam burst from the front yard and ran as well, Excalibur drawn. With a quick swing, he lopped off the drone's head. It fell limp, dark blood gushing from its neck.

Adam and Marilyn pulled Shelly from underneath the carcass. With Mark still in her embrace, she steadied herself. The boy wailed. Bleeding claw marks streaked across his cheeks and chin.

Marilyn pivoted toward the Foleys' house, her gun extended. More flapping noises drifted from the trees lining the street. Their branches rustled with veiled movements. "Adam …" Steeling her muscles, she glanced at him. "Get them inside."

"Let's go." Just as Adam reached for Shelly's arm, a second drone swooped. It latched on to Mark's shoulders, snatched him from Shelly's grasp, and zoomed upward.

Shelly screamed. Adam leaped but missed Mark's rising legs. Marilyn aimed her gun, then lowered it. With Mark swaying under the beast's talons, firing was out of the question.

"Shelly!" Carl shouted as he hobbled onto the street. Catherine supported him with a shoulder, blood on her long-sleeved blouse and denim pants.

As the second drone circled overhead, a third launched from a tree and dove toward Carl and Catherine. Adam took off toward them in a sprint, Excalibur still in his grasp.

A new shot rang out. Gun in hand, the first officer limped from the Foleys' house. Blood covered his hazmat vest. "Stop!" He lifted the plastic face shield and blew a whistle. The third drone flew up to the tree and perched on a limb.

Everyone stood motionless—Marilyn next to her driveway with Shelly, Carl and Catherine twenty paces closer to their house, and Adam halfway in between.

As the officer limped toward the Foleys, he pointed the gun at Carl. "This is for killing my partners." He pulled the trigger, but the gun just clicked.

Adam charged. The officer raised the whistle and shouted, "Stop, or I'll order the drone to drop the kid!"

Again Adam halted. He pointed Excalibur at the officer. "You'll kill him anyway."

"Ridiculous. He's being taken into protective custody." The officer backed to the paddy wagon and opened the rear door. "Everyone inside. You're all under arrest."

"In your dreams." Adam dashed toward him. The officer blew two short bleats with the whistle. The drone opened its talons, and Mark plunged toward the street.

A blur streaked by and snatched Mark out of the air. As the blur slowed and landed, its form clarified. A winged woman stood next to Carl and Catherine, Mark in her embrace. She patted him on the back as he sobbed.

Marilyn gasped. "Bonnie!"

Shelly staggered to Bonnie with outstretched arms. "Mark!" She took him and held him close as he sobbed. "Thank you, Bonnie! Oh, thank you! Thank you!"

Marilyn jogged over to them and grasped Bonnie's hand. "How did you get here? Where did you come from?"

"I'll tell you in a minute." She pointed upward. "First things first. Those monsters are deadly. Better check Mark for bites."

In the tree, a drone sat on the branch. Its head bobbed as if it were waiting for a command. Another flew directly above in a slow orbit.

Shelly pulled down on the collar of Mark's pajama top and searched his skin. "I don't see any bites. Just scratch marks. They're pretty deep, though."

Adam stood over the officer, who now lay on the road. He ripped the protective headgear away and set Excalibur's point at the officer's nose. "Tell the drones to get lost."

The officer held the whistle with a trembling hand and blew a series of short bursts. Seconds later, the pair of drones flew lazily away.

Adam pointed at the paddy wagon with the blade. "Now get in."

The officer struggled to his feet, groaning. "I'll bleed to death in there. My partners are already dead."

Marilyn focused on the officer's face. An ulcerated sore stretched across his forehead and down one cheek.

Adam jerked the whistle from him. "Then start walking. Maybe you can find someone to help you."

Holding a hand to his chest, the officer hobbled away.

When Adam joined the group, Carl patted him on the back. "Good work, son. But why did you risk attacking him?"

Adam winked at Bonnie. "I saw air support coming in. I knew she'd catch Mark."

With Mark crying softly on her shoulder, Shelly kissed Adam's cheek. "Thank you." She looked at the others. "Thanks, all of you."

"Something strange." Adam nodded toward the retreating officer. "Did you see the sores on that guy?" He dropped the whistle. "I don't want to catch whatever's eating him."

Bonnie nudged the whistle with her shoe. "Don't worry. I'll explain the sores after we get out of here." She spread her wings around Marilyn and Adam. "Billy's waiting with a jet on the highway next to the Shell station. Now that it's daylight, someone's bound to notice him soon."

"How is he doing?" Marilyn asked as she slid her gun into her pocket.

"He's banged up, but otherwise he's okay." Bonnie set her hands on her hips. "There's a lot more to tell, but basically we're going to fly to the Second Eden portal and get everyone we can out of this mess."

"That would be great, but Mardon says the portals are all closed and can't be opened till he gets there."

Bonnie drew her head back. "Mardon's here? How does he know?"

"Oh, he's here all right." Marilyn crossed her arms. "He's a ghost again, and that means the portals are closed. And wait till you hear about Jared, but I can tell you while we're hoofing it to the highway."

Catherine hugged Carl's arm. "Can you walk that far?"

He leaned to one side and grimaced. "I'm not sure. It's about a mile away, and there are a couple of mean hills between here and there. No use trying to start the car again. The nuclear pulse flat killed it."

"And my Mazda's cooked, too," Adam said.

"Then I'll get the wheelchair." Catherine jogged toward their house.

Adam handed Excalibur to Marilyn. "I'll get Larry's portable brain unit." He hurried toward the door.

"And bring Jared's pot!" Marilyn called.

Adam pivoted and walked backwards toward the house. "And Mardon?"

"Yes …" She let out a sigh. "And Mardon."

Carl set a hand on Bonnie's shoulder. "Can you tell us if Walter and Ashley are all right?"

Bonnie smiled, though her expression seemed to mask torture. "They're fine. At least they were when Billy and I left them last night. They were in a solar-powered car heading for the portal, so we might see them there if they haven't already gone through it."

"Bonnie?" Marilyn touched her arm. "What's wrong?"

"Well …" Tears crept to Bonnie's eyes. Biting her lip, she brushed the tears away with a knuckle. "I'll tell you while we're flying. I want Billy to be with us."

Marilyn's throat narrowed painfully. Something awful must have happened. "I understand."

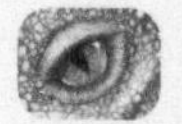

Catherine arrived pushing the wheelchair. A purse and a small suitcase lay in the seat. Carl slid the items to the side and squeezed into the chair. "Now …" He reached for Mark. "Let's give this big boy a ride."

Several shots rang out. Shelly crumpled to the street, Mark still in her arms. Catherine screamed and threw herself over them.

The officer stood next to the paddy wagon's open door, a rifle poised at his shoulder. "You should've listened! Now all of you get in the wagon!"

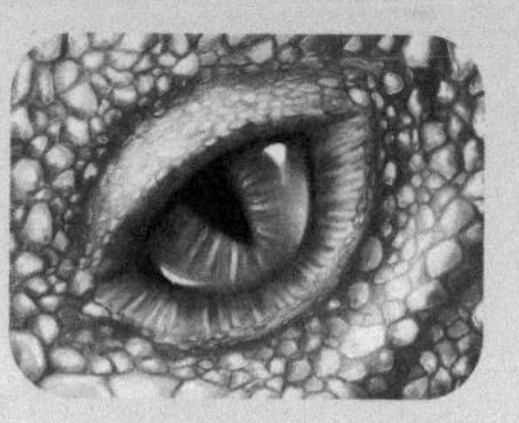

6

CHAPTER

Three Doors

Lauren walked with Sir Barlow into Jade's sanctum. From the rear, the flaming tree in Hades painted a thousand tiny flames on this room's surrounding wall. The flickers spun and danced; they seemed to fly back and forth—random and wild—radiant butterflies caught in a cyclone.

She snatched at a butterfly, but her hand passed through it. Was it a ghost? A hologram? In this chamber of mysteries, who could tell?

Sir Barlow pulled the cloak from their shoulders and tied it around his waist. "We are surrounded by a mirror, Miss. The lights are an optical illusion."

"A beautiful illusion." As her eyes adjusted to the carousel of lights, a glowing central column filled with tiny hexagonal holes came into view. A laser beam shot from four of the holes, each beam ending at a spot on the surrounding wall—a white one at the portal they had just passed through and three more spread equidistant around the perimeter, one white and two red. At each

beam's contact point on the wall, the light bled from the center and filled a window-like rectangle, its edges hazy.

"What is this?" Lauren reached for the chambers' central column, but Sir Barlow grabbed her wrist and pulled her back.

"Darcy met her tragic death by putting her finger into one of those holes."

"I'm already dead, but I'll be careful." Lauren waved a hand across one of the white laser beams. The light passed through without harming her skin or affecting the rectangle on the wall.

Sir Barlow pivoted slowly. "The four-armed lass is not in sight, but I assume she could appear at any moment. According to Matt, she can crawl along the ceiling or floor like a spider, so be watchful. She might be able to provide valuable information."

Lauren searched the floor. A glittering object lay near the base of the column. She picked it up and set it on her palm. The egg-sized stone cast a green glow over her skin. "A jade?"

"Ah!" Sir Barlow touched the gem. "The mistress of this chamber had this embedded in her chest, perhaps a symbol that matches her name." He touched his tunic several inches below his throat. "It was about right here on her."

"Embedded?" Lauren asked. "Through her bones?"

"I think so, though I failed to examine it closely." He cleared his throat. "Her four arms distracted me."

"Understandable." Lauren touched the gem with a fingertip. "It couldn't have accidentally fallen out of her chest."

"That much I am certain of." Sir Barlow dragged his boot along the spot where the gem had been. "Considering how Darcy died and the proximity of the stone to the column, perhaps Jade also inserted a finger into a hole and dissolved here."

"Or maybe she put a finger in each hole the beams are coming from. This column is narrow enough to reach around."

Sir Barlow again pivoted in place. "Agreed, Miss. Four arms, four beams, four portals. It all adds up."

"Which explains why the portal we came through was still charged. The tree didn't create it; Jade did." Lauren ran a finger along the gem's slick surface. "Why would Jade give her life to open them?"

Sir Barlow stopped his rotation. "Surely she knew that Abaddon's Lair was destroyed. Perhaps she is giving us passage to the life reservoir."

"Okay, but why four?" Lauren looked back at the tree room. "Well, one let us come in here, but why three unknown passages? We have no idea which one leads to the reservoir."

Sir Barlow tapped his chin with a finger. "Perhaps the way is guarded by a puzzle. Each portal leads to a puzzle piece, and once the three are joined, we can discern the proper path."

Lauren raised the gem and looked through it. The portal windows altered in color but otherwise remained unchanged. "I understand why the reservoir would be guarded by something, but if all you have to do is collect three puzzle pieces, anyone could solve it."

"Meaning that a scoundrel could also figure it out."

"Exactly."

"Then we will need an expert at puzzle solving. When I was trapped in the candlestone, my fellows and I concocted all sorts of mind-bending puzzles, so perhaps I can be of service." Sir Barlow passed his hand across a red beam. It also seemed to do no harm. "First, we confirm the purpose of the puzzle. Until now, Jade herself guarded against invaders, but once her duty had been fulfilled, she opened the portals for us because she knew you had not yet been resurrected. Such a sacrifice was both costly and risky, but it might have been the only way to bring you back to life."

Lauren lowered her head. Another death. Another tragedy. "So many people have sacrificed so much … for Matt … for me … for people they barely even knew."

"To be sure." Sir Barlow set a hand on her shoulder. "Sacrifice is the heartbeat of love, and those who love others sacrifice themselves willingly."

Lauren slowly closed her hand around the gem. Sacrifice *was* all about love. Darcy and Jade died willingly. Feeling guilty about it didn't make sense. "You're right."

"Now that we know the purpose, we can assume that each step of the puzzle will have the same theme—sacrificial love. Keeping this in mind will guide our steps." He gestured toward the laser pointing to the left. "I suggest that we try the portal with the white beam first, since it differs from the other two new ones."

Lauren slid the jade into her pocket and peered at the white splotch on the wall as it spread like oil across water. It vanished at the edges and created a ragged, door-sized window suspended two feet from the floor. Nothing but blackness lay beyond the boundary. "No time like the present."

Sir Barlow untied the cloak, spread it over himself and Lauren, and helped her vault to the window's lower border. As she stood with him in the portal plane, crackling light flashed in her peripheral vision. When they stepped through, the crackles ceased. She turned and looked back. The white beam faded until it vanished.

Arid heat blew across Lauren's face, drying her eyes. A dim land of cracked earth and sparse grass spread out in all directions, save for a long row of trees perhaps a hundred yards directly ahead. Near the horizon to the right, an enormous red sun illuminated the area. No clouds interrupted the purplish sky.

The hot breeze flapped the cloak. "Well, it is certainly too warm to keep this on." Sir Barlow whipped the cloak off and began tying it around his waist. "I suggest that we explore that stand of trees. Since it appears to be late afternoon, I wouldn't be surprised if night arrives soon, so we should not delay."

"It seems like the only choice. We just have to make sure we can find our way back. I suppose we'll leave footprints, but a breeze could cover them up."

"No problem, Miss." Sir Barlow withdrew his sword and pressed the point into the ground. "In this climate, I think it is appropriate to say that we will be hot on the trail."

"Good idea." A tremor ran along the ground, sending vibrations up Lauren's legs and spine. "An earthquake?"

"A minor one. Nothing to worry about unless another is ready to rumble. Such shocks often come in a series."

"Then we'd better hurry."

"Right." He marched toward the trees, holding the sword at his side as the tip scratched the ground along the way.

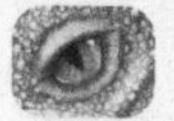

Lauren caught up and walked next to him. The blade's point dug an inch-deep trench that raised tiny plumes of dust. The breeze kicked up the gritty powder and swirled it, as if creating a slowly spinning tornado around the two newcomers to this realm.

The tremor continued, neither strengthening nor weakening. The vibrations made the scales on her back tingle, and whispers brushed by her ears.

"Help us."

"Save us."

"Water. We need water."

Lauren swiveled her head. No one was around. "Did you hear something, Sir Barlow?"

"Just the wind." He glanced at her. "What did you hear?"

"Voices. Thirsty people begging for water. But I can't see anyone."

"Mysteries abound in strange worlds." Sir Barlow marched on, still scratching a line on the ground. "Trees indicate a water source. Perhaps we can locate it, and then we'll try to find the thirsty souls who are crying out."

When they neared the stand, Sir Barlow stopped at the edge of a swath of lush grass that ran parallel to the tree line. The tremor stopped. He stared into the forest and whispered, "Do you hear anything now?"

Lauren peered between the trees. Fibrous vines hung from intertwined branches, some joining trees together to draw elongated arcs here and there, though nothing moved at all, as if the breeze were unable to affect anything beyond the grass line.

From somewhere in the forest, the sound of running water filtered through, like a shallow river spilling over rocks. "Water." She pointed at a narrow gap in the trees. "That way."

"We need a marker." Sir Barlow strode to the closest tree and hacked off a three-foot-long branch with his sword. Several large black birds leaped from the branches and flew to nearby trees.

"Crows?" Lauren asked.

"Ravens. It seems that this forest is filled with them." Sir Barlow pushed the branch vertically into the turf. "We will look for this when we come back."

The tremor returned with a violent shake. Sir Barlow teetered, but as the vibrations settled again, he regained his balance. "I am not one to shake in my boots, but we had better be on our way. As I mentioned before, I think it will be night soon."

They walked together through the gap and followed a barely visible trail. Vines and branches brushed against their arms and legs from both sides. With each touch, the tingle in Lauren's scales spiked. Above, the fluttering of wings increased. The ravens likely watched their every move. As the sky grew dimmer with approaching twilight, the ravens blended in with their surroundings and seemed to become invisible.

Soon, river sounds heightened, and new voices flooded the air.

"Water awaits. Refreshment. Life."

"No. Beware. It is death."

"The trees bear witness that the water is good. Drink your fill."

"The trees are dead where they stand. See for yourselves."

Lauren studied one of the trees as she passed by. With lush green leaves, sturdy limbs, and thick bark, it seemed perfectly healthy. "Sir Barlow, do these trees look healthy to you?"

"Strange that you should ask that." He stopped, hacked off the end of a low branch, and inserted a finger into the stub that remained. "Hollow. Just like the one I cut off earlier."

Lauren pushed against the trunk. It leaned, ripping up the surface roots. More ravens lifted into the air and migrated to other trees. "It wouldn't take much to knock the whole forest down."

"True, Miss. It is a house of cards."

She touched her ear. "I heard more voices. One told me that the water is life, and another said the water is death. Considering these trees, I think death is more likely."

"A fair deduction, though it takes more than water to nourish a tree." Sir Barlow gestured with a hand. "I hear the river now. We shall soon see for ourselves."

He hurried on, hacking freely at limbs and vines. Lauren followed and matched his brisk pace. They curved left, then right, then left again before breaking into a glade where they stopped at the forest's edge.

Several steps ahead and to the left, a stream perhaps ten feet wide ran to the right, poured over a head-high ledge, and tumbled into a circular pond about a hundred feet across. Although the running water appeared to be clear, dark scum covered the surface of the pond, and mucky-looking sludge bordered the entire circle. Bones lay strewn near the pond's edge, including several human skulls.

"Poisoned, I think." Sir Barlow inhaled through his nose. "And a foul odor hangs in the air. The pollutants in the water likely contain some kind of sewage."

"What could the source be? The water flowing in looks clean."

"Perhaps an upwelling at the bottom. Or rotting plant material. Or maybe someone comes here to dump refuse. In any case, it is strange that more than one human has partaken of the dirty water. If I were to come here in search of a drink and noticed skulls and bones, I would go elsewhere."

"Maybe they all drank at the same time."

"No, Miss. Trust me on this. The skulls differ greatly in age. If you wish, I can provide details on how to detect the amount of time a skull has been exposed to air."

"That's all right." An odd sound drifted into Lauren's ears—something squishing. She looked toward the right of the pond where the sound seemed to originate. A small hole opened at the top of a mound. Dark sludge spewed out, like a mouth vomiting sewage. The sludge rolled down a slope toward the pond and slid into the water. After the mouth erupted three more times, it closed to a barely detectable slit.

Lauren glanced from the clear stream to the sludge entry point and back again—clean water and filthy excrement entering the pond from opposite sides. Why would anyone create such an oasis? It seemed to defeat its own purpose.

Sir Barlow slid his sword into its scabbard. "Well, Miss, that is one mystery solved."

"But it creates even more mysteries." Lauren locked her stare on the incoming water. "The voices said the water is life. They must have been talking about the clear stream. We could take some to a parched area, pour it over some grass, and see what happens."

"We have no pail, but we do have a way to carry water. So in the interest of solving this puzzle before dark …" Sir Barlow untied the cloak from his waist. "Stay here, please." He walked up a rise to where the clean water toppled over the ridge and dipped the cloak into the stream. When he pulled it out, he let it drip freely. "This should be enough."

When he returned, he handed the cloak to Lauren and withdrew his sword again. "Shall we go to the parched area?"

Lauren held the cloak aloft and again stared at the pond. "Any idea why it doesn't overflow its banks? I don't see any outlets."

"Perhaps there are channels beneath the surface. If the soil is porous, water can create such outlets." Sir Barlow plunged his sword into the dirt at their feet. It penetrated easily up to the hilt. "See? Quite porous." Reddish water bubbled up from the cut. "Interesting. I am beginning to think that the land itself is—"

A vicious quake shook the ground. Sir Barlow dropped to his knees, and Lauren fell to her chest next to the sword. The ground tilted, making Sir Barlow slide toward the pond, which now swirled like a whirlpool.

Lauren grabbed the hilt of the still-upright sword. She extended her legs down the slope and shouted, "Grab my feet!"

Sir Barlow thrust out a hand and caught hold of her ankle. "Don't risk your life for me, Miss!"

"I'm already dead!" She clung to the hilt, but the blade sliced through the soft soil. Something screamed. The ground bucked and tossed. She tightened her grip and looked back. "Pull, Sir Barlow! I can't hold on much longer!"

"I am aware of your predicament." He peered at the swirling mass of dark water. "And that's why I must do what I must do." He let go and slid into the whirlpool.

The sudden release sent Lauren surging forward. Bracing against the undulating slope, she let go of the hilt, pushed to her knees, and spun toward the pond. Sir Barlow's hand stayed visible for a brief second before disappearing in the rapid spin.

"Sir Barlow!"

Only the rush of water replied. The ground straightened, alleviating the gravitational pull. The spin in the whirlpool slowed until barely a ripple disturbed the surface.

Lauren climbed to her feet and staggered to the edge, sidestepping a skull and a pile of bones. "Sir Barlow! Where are you?" She dashed back and forth and searched the water for any sign of movement. The murky water hid everything except a slow stirring of the floating scum.

"Sir Barlow!" she shouted again as she stepped into a shallow section. Her foot plunged into the muck. She fell to her bottom and tried to scramble back, but the fetid sludge held fast. Grabbing her leg with one hand, she pulled while scooting backwards. With every heave, she grunted, and her foot slid out an inch. Finally, it broke free to the sound of suction and a pop.

Gasping for breath, she sat with her arms wrapped around her knees and again scanned the area. As before, the incoming stream poured into the pond with no apparent outlet. Could the whirlpool have pulled Sir Barlow into a tunnel or some other kind of escape route, one of those channels he mentioned? Maybe he swam to safety at an outlet pool, and the dizzying spin disoriented him. And maybe she could guide him with her voice.

"Sir Barlow," she called, trying to keep her tone steady and confident. "I'm here. Where are you?"

"The waters of death have claimed him." The voice seemed to come from the air. "You should have heeded my warning."

She looked around. No sign of anyone, though with dusk arriving, it wouldn't be hard to hide. A gurgle sounded. The mouth opened and spat a ball of sludge that rolled slowly to the water.

Lauren directed her voice upward. "Heeded your warning? I heard opposite messages."

"Of course you did, though they were both truthful."

A second disgorging of dark muck erupted from the mouth.

She frowned. It seemed insane arguing with the wind. "That's nonsense. Two opposite messages can't both be true."

"By human logic, perhaps."

When a third vomiting episode ensued, Lauren narrowed her eyes as she watched the mouth. The pattern was becoming clear—ridiculous words before a surge of fecal matter. "It's not logical to talk to a human with any other kind of logic." She rose to her feet and backed away from the pond. "Listen. I'm not here to get into an argument. Just tell me how to help Sir Barlow."

"Remove the cursed weapon from my flesh, and I will consider your request."

Lauren looked back at the sword where the blade was still buried in the ground. She hurried to it, grasped the hilt, and pulled it out.

The ground shivered for an instant before settling. The voice returned. "Tree branches are painful enough, but a sword is torture."

She crouched at the wound and squeezed the bleeding soil together until it sealed. As she rose, the odor again assaulted her nose, the stench of urine and feces. She brushed her hand on her pants. "Does that feel better?"

"You do not care about my well-being. You ask in order to gain my favor."

"That's not true. I wasn't thinking that at all."

"Yet you do want to gain my favor."

"Well … yes. But I would've removed the sword anyway." Lauren glanced again at the pond. "I need to know where the whirlpool took my friend."

"Your *friend* is a man who stabbed me with his sword."

"He had no idea that the stab would inflict pain. In our world the soil has no feelings."

"Now *you* are speaking nonsense. There is no such world."

The mouth spewed another round of sludge.

Lauren walked toward the mouth. "On the contrary, in our world making holes in the soil is beneficial for aeration and plant growth."

"Plants are blood-sucking parasites. They all need to die."

More sludge erupted, now unceasing as the conversation continued.

"Without plants, erosion would—" She shook her head hard. "I don't have time to argue about this! I need to know where my friend is!"

"He is dead. Buried in the pond of purity. Never to return to life."

"The pond of purity?" Lauren bit her lip. Of course the pond wasn't pure, but arguing that point wouldn't help the situation. "How can you be sure? Maybe the whirlpool—"

"He is alive. Somewhere."

Lauren arrived at the mouth and drilled a stare at the spewing hole. "Wait a minute. You just said he's dead. Now you're saying he's alive. Which is true?"

"He is dead." After a short pause, the voice returned. "He is alive."

"Argh!" Lauren kicked a stray fragment of sludge. "Don't jerk me around! This is a matter of life and death!"

"That is exactly what I am saying."

"But you're contradicting yourself! Is he alive or dead?"

"Whichever you care to believe."

Lauren clenched a fist. "I can't make something true by believing it! It's either true or not true! My believing it makes no difference at all."

The voice sighed. "You are right. Of course you are right."

"Good. Finally." She relaxed her muscles. "Now tell me. Is my friend alive or—"

"And you are also wrong."

Lauren rolled her eyes. "All right. I'm done with you. I'm going to search for him without your help." Still clutching the sword, she stalked to the pond's edge and walked around the perimeter, but no clues appeared in the growing darkness—no footprints and no holes that might lead to a tunnel or cavern beneath the surface.

She stopped and listened. Although the waterfall dominated the soundscape, other noises filtered in, first crackling, then hissing in the cadence of language, like a radio station broadcasting from a great distance. With no other clues to guide the way to Sir Barlow, a thorough search seemed to be the only option, but what if she became lost when night's darkness fully arrived? Shouldn't she solve the puzzle first, just in case?

She scanned the area once more. This pond seemed to be the opposite of a life reservoir—dark, polluted, smelly, and deadly. The ground provided enough moisture to make the trees grow on the outside, but they were hollow and rotten on the inside, another apparent opposite. And, of course, the bones of humans lay around as if punctuating the proof of the poison.

This world displayed conflicting messages—images that belied reality, beauty that disguised ruin. Even the voice seemed deceived by the masks. How could anyone think this pond was one of purity?

"Purity," she whispered. The word raised a memory, something Abaddon said in his lair. *Like Bonnie who allowed me to melt her flesh rather than speak a lie about her purity, so Lauren must welcome her own flames of refinement.*

A lie about her purity—a claim that she wasn't pure when she really was. Lauren focused on the pond. The voice had spoken a lie about the pond's purity, claiming it was pure when it really wasn't—another bizarre opposite, especially since the claim was spoken by the source of the sludge that poisoned the pure water. With a puzzle of opposites, maybe the best way to solve it would be to separate them to see what would happen.

Sword in hand, Lauren hurried back to where the cloak lay. Sir Barlow had wanted to collect water to test it on some parched ground. She picked up the cloak, now dirty and merely damp. Maybe it would be a good idea to saturate it again.

After leaving the sword there, she carried the cloak to the stream well back from the waterfall and dipped it into the current. As dirt flowed away over a pebbly bed, she lifted a handful of water—hot, but not scalding. No odor. Crystal clear. And that raised a new question. Why would people drink from an obviously polluted pond when they could easily come to the source of the clean water?

She lifted her hand to her mouth and took a tiny sip. It carried a slightly sweet taste, as if someone had added a drop of honey. She slurped the rest. It flowed down her throat like warm cream. After drinking several more handfuls, she lifted the saturated cloak and tied it around her waist. Some of the water squeezed out and dripped down her pants, but it couldn't be helped.

She hurried to the sword and picked it up. Now feeling refreshed and invigorated, she looked once again at the mouth, the source of the poison. That orifice brought death to anyone who sought relief from thirst. It had to be stopped.

Yet she also had to keep searching for Sir Barlow. Both options seemed hopeless. How could she conduct a twilight search in a strange world for someone who disappeared without a trace? How could she alter the landscape to halt a polluting influence that had obviously been around for many years? And both options were urgent. Life and death hung in the balance.

She blew out a heavy sigh. Making a choice seemed impossible as well, but standing around and vacillating had to be the worst option of all.

With a tight grip on the sword's hilt, she marched to the mouth's mound. She rammed the blade into the mouth and sliced a gouge leading away from the pond and into a grassy area. Something screamed. The ground bucked. Lauren dropped to her knees and, tensing every muscle, continued cutting, sawing, and slicing as she shuffled backwards.

Sludge erupted from the mouth and flowed down her trench. Some spilled over into the grass. The blades instantly withered. When she reached a level area, she jerked the sword out. The ground settled. A final eruption of sludge poured forth and oozed into the lower elevation, drying as it spread out.

She rose and hurried back to the pond. As clear water poured in from the stream, the dark residue on the edges shrank. At this rate it wouldn't take long for the stream to cleanse every speck of sludge, and maybe as it cleared, any outlet channels beneath the surface might become visible.

The scum floating on top shriveled and vanished, and the water clarified, beginning at the top. As the cloudiness in the pool sank, something suspended in the water came into view. It looked like a gray patch of carpet with a lot of fibers missing.

After a few more seconds, the object's shape became clearer—a balding head with its hair remnants waving like grass in a breeze. Lauren stepped to the edge of the pool, now clear of muck. A corpse? It couldn't be Sir Barlow. He had more hair. Since skin still covered the scalp, this man couldn't have been there long, probably a recent victim of the poison. Either way, she couldn't leave the poor man in the pond.

She set the sword down and stepped into the water. Cringing, she slid her hands under the corpse's arms and walked backwards with him in tow. As the lean body rose above the surface, more details appeared. A wooden device lay over his shoulders, longer on one side of his neck than on the other. He wore a button-down shirt, jeans, and a belt with some kind of attached device, maybe a mobile phone.

When his bare feet dragged past the edge, she laid him down and knelt at his side. She used a wet sleeve to swipe some remnant sludge from his gray forehead and cheeks, revealing the familiar face of Gaston Hunt, her foster father.

Lauren blinked. She whispered, "Dad?" through her tightening throat. She wheezed shallow breaths. Who could have done this to him?

She studied the wooden device. It looked like a cattle yoke. One indentation rested over his neck, and another to his right was empty. An oxbow wrapped around his throat, fastened on the upper side of the yoke by a bolt. She grasped the oxbow and tried to force his head back through the opening, but it wouldn't fit. Using her fingers, she twisted the fastening bolt. It turned easily, a surprise considering the wet conditions.

When she pulled the yoke off and laid it at the pond's edge, the mental picture of his suspended body returned. Why was he upright underwater instead of horizontal on top or at the bottom? The yoke probably floated, so that acted to pull him upward, but what held him down?

She looked at his feet. A thin chain tied around his ankle led to the pond, the far end hidden below the surface. She grasped it and reeled it in. A pair of glasses dragged to shore. She picked them up and looked at the frames. A tiny screen extended in front of the right lens, a miniature computer monitor. He often wore these glasses to keep up with work-related projects after hours. He even wore them to the volleyball game, the last time …

She choked as she finished the thought out loud. "The last time I saw him alive."

After crying for a moment, she drew the glasses closer to her eyes. How could something so small weigh him down? It didn't make sense. Nothing made sense. Didn't he die in a house explosion? Shouldn't his body be torn to pieces or at least burned?

Her gaze drifted across the phone clipped to his belt. Maybe it held a clue. After laying the glasses on his motionless chest, she unfastened the phone and looked at the screen—wet and blank. She pushed the power button. The screen flashed. It worked! Another surprise.

While she waited for it to come on, a chorus of caws sounded from the forest. Dozens of ravens lifted from the trees and flew in a circle overhead, nearly invisible against the darkening sky. They probably wanted to get an easy meal as soon as she left him behind. Her back scales tingled. Might they attack? She eyed the sword where it lay a few paces away, then the yoke, which sat within reach. Either would be a suitable weapon should the ravens decide to get bold.

The phone sizzled, and sparks flew from the edges. She dropped it to the ground. Flames sprouted, and the frame melted within seconds. She sighed. So much for checking the phone for clues. Once again she had affected electronics in a damaging way.

She looked once more at the glasses. Might the computer screen hold answers to the mysteries? Maybe. But if she put them on, she might destroy them as well.

A raven landed a few feet away, followed by several others. As they formed a surrounding circle, they cawed and hopped closer, apparently testing their boundaries.

Lauren picked up the yoke and brandished it with both hands. "Don't you dare!" she growled.

As if emboldened by her challenge, the ravens closed the gap, swarmed over her foster father, and pecked at his flesh. Still on her knees, she swung the yoke and smashed the closest black bird. It squawked. Feathers flew. The yoke flashed blue and provided light for her counterattack.

With a backswing, she smacked another raven. The yoke's strobing light brightened. As more ravens flew down and joined the feasting, she rose to her feet and waded into the flock, her heart thumping. With every swing of the yoke, she crushed another raven and sent its limp body sailing away. The yoke grew brighter and brighter and warmed in her grasp.

She knocked away bird number nine, then number ten, but more and more joined in and covered the corpse. Her muscles ached, but she couldn't stop and let them strip his bones. He couldn't be just another skeleton among the dead masses.

After she had driven at least a dozen more ravens away, they scattered and flew toward the forest. Besides the glasses, only bones remained. She slumped to her knees. She had failed.

Night had fallen, leaving the yoke as the only light—now a steady blue glow. As she picked up the glasses, she wept. "I … I'm sorry. I tried to … to chase them away. But there were … too many."

Voices returned, chanting words, eerie and elongated.

I daily die,
Alone and lost;
I lived a lie;
I pay the cost.

Inhale the fires;
Exhale despair.
Each day expires
Without a prayer.

Lauren shuddered. She lifted the yoke and cast its glow, but it reached only a few feet into the darkness. The voices uttered the same words she had heard while in Hades. Had that realm somehow merged with this one? Did it mean the owners of the scattered bones had gone to that horrid place? How about her foster father? Did he go there as well?

New sounds entered her hypersensitive ears—her clothes rubbing against her skin, her own breathing, and … a heartbeat?

She laid a palm on her chest. Her heart *was* beating! And wasn't it beating hard while she battled the ravens? What could have caused it? Drinking the water? If so, did that signify one step closer to resurrection? Or had she already resurrected?

Inhaling deeply, she closed her eyes. This had to be the first puzzle piece. Water. Clean water that flowed into a poisoned pool, now cleansed by redirecting the flow of the poison. And the water restored her, at least partway, but what else could it do? "God," she whispered, "please help me think."

She opened her eyes and listened. Her scales tingled, and the static in the air returned. This time, however, it morphed into a voice that grew clearer every second.

"Lauren Bannister, I will keep talking in hopes that you can hear me. This is Sir Winston Barlow. I don't know where I am, but I can tell you that it is a nightmarish place. I don't suggest that you try to follow, because the pond sent me plummeting into an underground spout of sorts, and I nearly drowned. Since I can see Jade's sanctum through a portal, I assume you can come here if you retrace your steps to the sanctum and enter through one of the remaining portals. I would come to you, but I lack the protective cloak. When I tried to leap through the portal, the shock sent me flying backwards into … well, I suppose you should see it for yourself. Describing it would be rather difficult. In any case, I will wait for you here. I assume you will eventually give up looking for me in the other world." He heaved a long sigh. "Lauren Bannister, I will keep talking in hopes …"

Lauren slid the glasses into a shirt pocket and rose to her feet. Sir Barlow was alive. She had to find him. Besides, there was nothing left to do here in this gateway to the underworld.

Holding the glowing yoke in front, she picked up the sword, slid it behind the cloak tied at her waist, and hurried to the forest. After navigating the path, she emerged in the open area where they first arrived. She spotted Sir Barlow's marker and the sword's long trench. Following it, she hurried toward the portal, still listening to his speech.

As the rectangular door leading to the pulsing column took shape in the distance, his voice spiked. "Lauren! Wait! Don't come here yet. I see a—"

She halted. A clicking sound rattled in her ears. "Who are you?" Sir Barlow said, his voice agitated. "Get back, fiend!" A series of grunts followed, then a growl, then silence.

"Sir Barlow?" Lauren cupped her ears and faced the portal. Still no sound. She sprinted the rest of the way. When she arrived, she dropped to her knees and looked through the window. The column stood as before, still sending out beams, but nothing moved in the chamber.

She withdrew the sword and laid it down, then untied the cloak and threw it over her shoulders. With the sword and yoke in hand, she scrambled through the opening and hustled to the next portal. A red wash prevented a view of the other side. She listened for Sir Barlow's voice. Nothing. Not even static.

Still covered by the wet cloak, she ran to the next portal. Again, no sounds emanated, and another red veil blocked the view. She looked at the central column. Now only three beams emanated—one white and two red. The beam that pointed at the world with the strange pond had vanished.

The remaining white beam continued painting an opening leading to the tree of life, an escape route that seemed more attractive than ever, but taking it now would be cowardly.

A low growl trickled in from the first unvisited portal. She hurried back and set her ear close to the window. Silence ensued once again. Could the sound have come from the creature that attacked Sir Barlow? Or might Sir Barlow be groaning in pain?

She eyed the bottom of the portal—about three feet from the floor. After sliding the sword behind her belt, she backed up a few steps and tucked the yoke under her arm. Holding the cloak in place, she ran toward the window and jumped.

A jolt rattled her body. The portal bent and threw her back. She fell to the floor, rolled out of the cloak, and stopped at the sanctum's column.

Her skin tingling all over, she climbed slowly to her feet and staggered into the path of the laser beam. She looked at the portal and blinked to clear her vision. Between the portal and her body, the beam was now white. She swiveled her head. Between her body and the column, the beam was still red.

She looked down at the point where the beam intersected with her body. It struck the yoke, still tucked under her arm and glowing blue.

She stepped out of the way. The beam turned all red. After shaking her arms and legs to cast off the tingling sensation, she raised the yoke, now warm to the touch, into the beam's path. The section between the yoke and the portal turned white again. Did the white beam signal that the portal was open, that the beam had to pass through the yoke?

Her arms trembling, she picked up the cloak and draped it over herself, then set the yoke on her cloaked shoulders and slid her neck into one of the two indentations. After shifting to make sure the beam hit the yoke, she looked at the portal. The beam, now white again, struck the window and created an alabaster rectangle.

She walked to the portal, careful to keep the yoke in line with the beam. When she reached the opening, she leaped through.

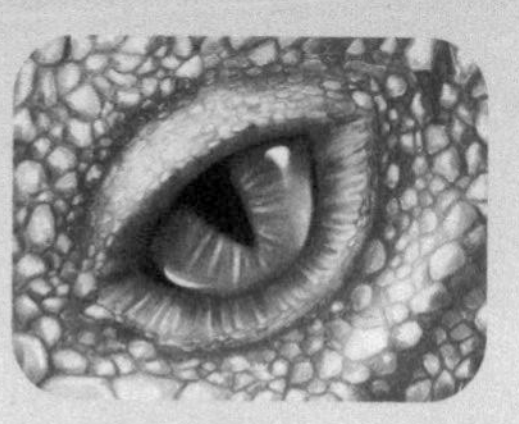

7

CHAPTER

FLIGHT

Bonnie snatched Excalibur from Marilyn, summoned its beam, and sliced it through the officer's head. A splash of sparks spewed from the hazmat suit's neck hole. His rifle dropped with a clatter, and his uniform collapsed in a yellow heap.

Marilyn sprinted toward him, shouting, "I'll be back!"

Shelly lay sprawled on top of Mark. Only his arm lay in view in a pool of blood. Crouching, Catherine held Shelly's wrist and cried out, "They're dead! Oh, dear God, they're both dead!"

Carl reached from the wheelchair and rubbed Catherine's back. His face knotting in grief, he sobbed with heavy spasms.

Adam burst out of the Bannister house lugging a large briefcase with an embedded monitor. In his other arm, he carried Jared's pot. "I heard shots! What happened?"

"The Enforcer murdered Shelly and Mark." Bonnie slid Excalibur behind her belt. As sobs threatened to burst forth, she sucked in a breath and held it. Her song had faded to a mere whisper.

Was anyone listening anymore? How could someone slaughter a mother and child in cold blood?

Mardon emerged from the house, his smile strangely proud. When he saw the carnage, he folded his hands at his waist and took on a sorrowful expression.

Seconds later, Marilyn returned clutching the officer's rifle in a tight fist. Redness streaked her watery eyes. "We might need this." A shaky growl ran through her voice. "In case more Enforcers come."

Bonnie rubbed Marilyn's shoulder. "We'd better get out of here before that happens."

Marilyn stooped and touched Shelly's motionless hand. "First we have to do something with their bodies."

"No time for that!" Adam pointed toward the sky. "More drones!"

Bonnie looked up. At least thirty of the beasts flew in a swirl. More streamed in as if they were gathering in formation about two hundred feet above. She gripped the wheelchair's handles and pushed. "I'll take Carl! Everyone run!"

Carl grabbed the wheels, stopping the chair. "What about Shelly and Mark? Those drones might … might …" His voice broke off in a sob.

"We can't carry them!" Bonnie imagined the drones landing on the corpses and feasting on the flesh. Yes, Shelly and Mark were dead, but how could she let those beasts desecrate their bodies?

She whipped out Excalibur and again called for the beam. When it sliced into the sky, the drones dodged the light. "Carl. Catherine." Bonnie took in a deep breath to settle her fractured voice. "Here are our options. Number one—stay here and fight using Excalibur, though the Enforcers are bound to send more armed officers soon. Number two—transluminate Shelly and

Mark so the drones can't violate their bodies. Then we run while I protect us with Excalibur." She inhaled again. "They're your family. Just say the word, and I'll go with what you decide. But we have to hurry."

Carl looked at the bodies, then at the drones, then at Catherine. "We don't have a candlestone to capture their light."

Catherine slid her hand into Carl's. "God will capture their light." Her lips firm, she gave Bonnie a nod. "Transluminate them."

"I'll cover you," Marilyn said as she aimed the rifle skyward. "It looks like the last of them are gathering. They might attack at any second."

Bonnie wrapped both hands around Excalibur's hilt and brushed the beam gently across Shelly and Mark. As the radiance spread, the bodies vanished, replaced by dancing sparkles that dispersed and disappeared.

Carl covered his mouth. Tears spilled from Catherine's eyes. Both appeared to be stifling new sobs.

"Now hurry!" Bonnie spread her wings and grabbed the wheelchair again. "Carl and I will stay at the rear in case they attack."

Adam set the briefcase on Carl's lap. "I hope you don't mind carrying Larry's brain unit."

"Sure." Carl set his hands on the case. "I'm ready."

Now carrying only Jared's pot, Adam took off in a rapid trot. Marilyn ran behind him, Catherine at her heels. Beating her wings, Bonnie lifted off the road and pushed the wheelchair. Above, the swirling drones drew nearer, looking like a black cyclone drifting lower and lower. They seemed to be waiting for something, as if they were being told what to do from a remote location.

Bonnie caught up with the others and pushed the chair alongside Marilyn. "Billy's just around that curve ahead. At this rate, we might get to the jet before the drones do."

Soon, the intersection with the highway came into view. A Learjet sat in the Shell station's empty parking lot. Billy stood a few steps away, his stare fixed on the sky.

"Billy!" Bonnie beat her wings and drove the wheelchair past the others. "Drones are coming!"

"I saw them!" When she arrived, Billy reached out and grabbed the wheelchair, stopping it. He helped Mr. Foley stand. "The engine's running! Let's go!"

Bonnie raised Excalibur. "I'll stand guard while you get everyone inside."

"Sounds good." After he helped Carl climb the stairs, he folded the wheelchair and slid it into the jet along with the potted plant, a suitcase, and a purse.

When Marilyn arrived, she hugged Billy with one arm while holding the rifle with the other. "I'm so glad to see you!"

"You, too, Mom." He gently pushed her away and grasped the rifle. "All right if I take it from here?"

"Gladly." She and Catherine hurried up the airstair.

Adam followed, Mardon close behind. "Sorry about the extra passenger," Adam said as he passed Billy. "Long story."

Billy rolled his eyes. "I can hardly wait."

After Adam and Mardon boarded, Bonnie folded her wings and scooted in. By the time she had settled into the copilot's seat with Excalibur in her lap, Billy was already climbing into the pilot's chair. He set the rifle on the floor between them. "Is everyone buckled?" he called. "We might run into some rough air."

"What about Carly?" Adam asked from the front passenger seat. "She's supposed to be on her way. We got a video message from Lois."

Billy looked out the side window. "The drones are closing in. We can't wait much longer."

"She'll be drone bait." Adam set the briefcase on his lap and flipped a switch. "Larry! Send another emergency beacon to Lois! Immediately!" He tossed a piece of metal to Bonnie and another to Marilyn. "Lapel clips. Built in microphone and speaker. Put it on your collar. Larry's mobile brain unit doesn't have speakers."

Bonnie fastened the clip to her collar. Larry's voice came through as if broadcast from far away. "I am receiving a video message from Lois that I am decrypting. I will play it in approximately three seconds."

Adam turned the case so everyone could see the screen. When the video started, Carly's strained face appeared. The image jostled as if she were limping at a hurried pace. "We ran out of gas. I'm carrying Lois, and I'm following the main highway, about five miles from your house." Her brow furrowed, now marred by a pair of new lesions. "I *think* I'm on the main highway. The only light I have is on Lois's brain unit, and she's pointing it at me so I'll show up on the video. I charged her battery in the Jeep's lighter, but I'm not sure how much juice she has. Right now I probably have more glow juice than she does. Maybe we should've equipped her with a radiation sensor. I might be getting cooked out here. Anyway, I'll see you soon … if I don't collapse first."

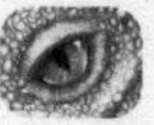

The video window faded to black.

Bonnie looked at Billy. "Can we wait?"

"Not sure." Billy stared out the front windshield. "Carrying that load, it'll probably take her about two hours to walk five miles."

"Based on the illumination level," Larry said through the lapel speaker, "that video was recorded roughly two hours ago. I assume Lois has been trying to send it for a while, but her battery is likely running low, and she is just now close enough to transmit it to me."

"Look!" Marilyn pointed forward. Far down the highway, a woman trudged toward them, carrying something in her arms.

A dark creature dropped from the sky and blocked the view with a hideous face. Black wings beat against the windshield, and loud squeals created a muffled clamor.

Adam set the briefcase in Marilyn's lap and snatched the rifle from the floor. "Billy. Ready to cook some drones?"

"Let's do it." Billy leaped up and grabbed Excalibur from Bonnie's lap. "Mom, can you take the controls?"

"With pleasure."

While Marilyn climbed into the pilot's seat, Billy inhaled deeply and gazed at Excalibur. The blade glowed brighter with every second. "Let's go."

Adam stationed himself at the side of the door and disengaged the latch. Billy stood directly in front and pointed Excalibur. As drones continued screaming and beating against the jet, he nodded. "Now!"

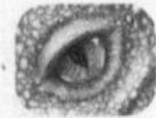

Adam pushed the door open. A brilliant beam shot from Excalibur and knifed through the opening. The radiance immediately struck a drone and disintegrated it. Billy leaped out. Adam followed and shoved the door closed.

Still sitting in the copilot's seat, Bonnie leaned forward and looked through the windshield. Billy limped past the jet toward Carly. After every few steps, he pivoted, swung the sword's beam, and sliced through an attacking drone.

Adam dashed ahead of him, rifle in hand. Two drones followed and swooped. He dropped, rolled, and shot at them. One fell and flailed on the ground, but the other attacked Adam with swiping claws.

While Billy ran to help Adam, Carly backed away, now about a hundred yards down the road.

Marilyn pushed a lever. "Let's get Carly."

The jet eased forward, faster and faster. They passed Billy and Adam and continued accelerating.

"I'll open the door." Bonnie got up and squeezed her way out of the cockpit.

Catherine joined her. "No time for the stairs. We'll lift her up."

"Right." Bonnie unlatched the door and looked at Marilyn. "Mom, tell me when you're almost even with Carly."

"Slowing down for pickup." As the jet decelerated, Marilyn kept her hands tight on the controls. "Three … two … one … Now!"

Bonnie shoved the door open. She and Catherine reached out, grabbed Carly's arms, and hauled her inside.

When they set her upright, Bonnie hugged her from the side. Her body shook hard as she ran trembling fingers along Lois, a metallic sphere the size of a basketball.

"You're safe," Bonnie whispered. "We've got you now."

"Thank you." Carly pulled away abruptly, slid to a rear-facing seat, and buckled in with Lois at her feet. As she stared straight ahead, her chin quivered. A drone smacked against her window and splattered blood. She gasped, then doubled over and sobbed. "When is it all going to end?"

"Just a few more seconds, Carly," Bonnie said as she leaned out the door and looked toward the rear. Billy and Adam ran alongside the jet, Billy clutching Excalibur, and Adam holding the rifle. From behind, at least five more drones drew closer.

"Billy!" Bonnie shouted. "Should we stop?"

He waved a hand. "Keep going! If we stop, they'll swarm us!"

Holding the door frame, Bonnie stretched out and extended a hand. Billy lunged, but his fingers merely brushed hers. She held the door with a wing and stretched farther. Barely a step in front of the jet's wing, Billy limped heavily. The gap between their hands grew wider.

A drone dropped from the sky and landed on Adam's shoulders. Just as it bared its fangs to bite, he twisted and whacked it with the rifle's barrel. It fell back, but its claws stuck in his shirt. He toppled backwards to the pavement. The other drones closed in, only seconds away.

Bonnie launched from the door. Beating her wings as she flew low, she grabbed the drone by the throat and ripped it away from Adam. She then clutched his shirt and zoomed back, passing Billy. The jet slowed. Bonnie flew alongside the door and thrust Adam into Catherine's outstretched hands.

Billy stopped, ducked under the jet's wing as it passed by, and waved Excalibur at the drones. One of them slipped past the beam and swooped toward him. Bonnie reversed course again and streaked to Billy. She collided with him head-on and slid her arms under his. With a loud oomph, she barreled under the drone's snatching jaws, then shot upward with Billy in her grasp, chest to chest.

As she flew toward the door, the drones gave chase. Excalibur's beam flashed. Guided by Billy, it sizzled through one drone, then another. Both burst into sparks and disappeared.

Billy grunted. "Two more, but they're flying at a higher angle. I can't shift the beam to get them."

"Just hang on." Bonnie beat her wings harder. Again Catherine waited at the door as the jet rolled along the pavement.

"Clear out!" Bonnie shouted. "Billy! Switch off the beam!"

Catherine retreated from the door. Bonnie shot in, folding her wings at the last second. She and Billy tumbled into a sea of hands and arms. While the hands steadied her, Adam jerked the door closed and latched it.

Billy shouted, "Punch it, Mom!"

The engine revved. The jet accelerated. Catherine leaped into a seat while Billy limped to the copilot's chair, his head low to avoid the ceiling.

Once everyone else had buckled, Bonnie slid into the seat that faced Carly's and fastened herself in. She reached to take Carly's hand, but the quick acceleration pushed her back and compressed her folded wings. Carly picked up Lois and held on, her expression blank, though her arms trembled as they hugged Lois's metallic sphere.

A drone landed on the jet's nose, its wings splayed against the windshield. It pecked at the glass with a pointed beak.

"Good-bye, buzzard," Marilyn said as she pushed the throttle. The jet took off and angled sharply upward. The drone peeled away and disappeared.

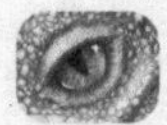

While everyone caught their breath, Bonnie looked around. Across the aisle, Catherine faced forward opposite Carl, who sat with the potted plant in his lap. Adam sat behind them, his face slashed with several bloody stripes, though his stoic expression gave no sign of pain. He held Larry's brain module in his lap. Blinking lights on the embedded monitor indicated that Larry was thinking about something.

As soon as the acceleration and angle eased a bit, Bonnie unbuckled and got up. Leaning over Lois, she embraced Carly. "It's so good to see you again."

Carly returned the hug. "Same to you. I'm sorry for my little outburst. It's really been—"

"No, no, don't worry about it." Bonnie sat, rebuckled her belt, and counted the lesions on Carly's face—one on each cheek and two on her forehead. They didn't look nearly as large or deep as Oscar's. Since they would soon be far away from the radiation, maybe she would be all right. "The crazy stuff we've been through is enough to make anyone—"

"Well, that was quite an adventure, wasn't it?" Mardon strolled up the aisle, apparently unaffected by the acceleration.

Billy twisted in the copilot's seat and pointed at Mardon. "Listen. You go as far back in the cabin as you can and sit in a corner. I don't want to see your face for the rest of the trip. If I do, I'll figure out some way to lasso your ghostly hide and throw you through the wall."

"Very well." Mardon put on a puppy-dog pout and walked backwards. "If you need my expertise, feel free to call on me." He lowered himself to the floor and sat in a shadow.

Billy turned toward the front and touched the dashboard's GPS. "We're on a course that'll take us fifty miles north of the portal."

"Why north of it?" Marilyn asked.

"In case we're being monitored. We don't want anyone to figure out our trajectory and locate it ahead of time. We'll adjust when we get close." Billy rose and limped into the passenger compartment, a first-aid kit in tow. "Who wants to be our nurse?"

Catherine raised a hand. "I'll start with Adam. He looks the worst off."

Billy grinned. "His face looks like he lost a fight with a deranged razor blade."

"Something like that." Adam unbuckled and stepped into the aisle. "That crazed buzzard also bit me on the back." He lifted his shirt and turned. Two red-ringed holes marred his skin about midway up his back. "Stings like crazy."

Billy glanced at Bonnie, then, keeping his expression upbeat, locked wrists with Adam. "You were amazing out there, like a human machine gun."

"Avoiding venomous fangs is good incentive." He staggered for a moment before grabbing the back of his seat. "I think … I think I feel sick."

Billy helped him sit. "I was afraid of that. The venom can cause paralysis. When I got bitten, I couldn't move a muscle."

Bonnie unbuckled and joined Billy in the aisle. She whispered into his ear, "Maybe Mardon knows how to counter the poison."

"I was thinking that, but asking him for help feels like choking down a pile of horse manure." He let out a sigh. "Mardon? Have you been listening?"

Mardon rose and walked forward, his hands wringing. "Yes. I hope you don't mind my eavesdropping."

"What do you know about the drones' venom?"

"I am unfamiliar with the chemical makeup of the venom in that particular species, but I am familiar with venom from two other demonic breeds. Since those two are similar to each other, it is fair to assume that this one has the same characteristics, especially since all three can cause paralysis."

"Do you know how to make an antidote?"

"Maybe." Mardon looked Billy over for a moment. "You say that you were bitten in the past?"

"Right here." Billy touched a spot on his neck. "Bonnie, too."

"Then you have antibodies, and with your dragon genetics, the antibodies should be able to survive the process of making an antidote." Mardon looked past Billy at the other passengers. "Does anyone have nail polish? Clear would be ideal, but any color will do."

"I have some." Catherine dug into her purse and withdrew a small bottle of pink nail polish.

Billy took it and laid it in his palm. "Okay. What else?"

"Does the label provide the ingredients? I assume it has a solvent like ethyl acetate or alcohol. I am hoping that it doesn't also have formaldehyde."

Billy held the bottle close and squinted. "I don't see formaldehyde listed."

"Good. We simply need to withdraw some blood from either you or Bonnie, add the precise amount of nail polish, and heat the solution to eighty-two degrees Celsius for thirty seconds. Then we wait for the impurities to precipitate and inject the serum into Adam."

"How long will that take?"

"Perhaps fifteen minutes to make the serum and thirty for Adam to begin healing. Of course I am assuming you have the proper equipment. If we have access to a glass syringe, we can heat the mixture in that, and we will need a source of heat."

"I can provide heat," Billy said, "but give me one good reason why I should trust you."

Marilyn called from the cockpit. "Because if he's lying, we'll drop him off in a radioactive wasteland, and he'll never get to Second Eden."

"I trust him," Adam said, his head back and his eyes closed. "He's been helpful so far. Besides, the venom is already pounding my skull, and my fingers and toes are numb." He licked his cracked lips. "Let's do it."

"Good enough for me." Billy rolled up his sleeve. "Let's get started."

Mardon set a finger on Billy's vein, but it passed right through. "I will need an assistant who is familiar with blood-drawing procedures."

"I can do it." Bonnie opened the first-aid kit. "I've seen it done to me enough times."

Billy tightened his fist, making his veins distend. "While we're doing this, let's get everyone up to date on what's going on."

For the next several minutes, Billy and Bonnie recounted their adventures—Billy getting captured by Tamiel's soldiers, Bonnie riding with Matt and Darcy until Arramos kidnapped her, and the rest of the details concerning the seven doors. When Bonnie told the story of Lauren's death and Matt's departure to search for a way to resurrect her, the cabin fell silent except for heavy sighs and gentle weeping.

During the tales, Bonnie found an antibiotic ointment in the first-aid box and applied some to Carly's lesions. She cringed during the application but offered no complaints.

After a few moments, Marilyn spoke up from the pilot's seat. She told how Jared sought transformation and became a tiny plant and explained their quest to root him in Second Eden's birthing garden. For Billy's sake, she added the most recent events—Bonnie catching Mark only to lose him and Shelly to the Enforcer's bullets.

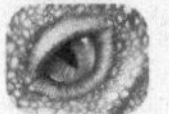

Again everyone grew quiet. The death of an innocent child and his mother felt like an anchor that weighed down every heart.

After Mardon guided Billy and Bonnie through the serum-creating procedure, Bonnie injected the final product into Adam's arm and attempted a perky tone as she swabbed the site with a gauze pad. "I transluminated Shelly and Mark to keep the drones from damaging their bodies. I hope it was the right decision. We didn't have a candlestone to collect their light."

"Like I said at the time ..." Catherine reached from her seat and stroked Bonnie's arm. "God will collect their light."

Billy clasped Adam's shoulder. "Just rest and let us know if you need anything."

He nodded weakly. "Maybe it's wishful thinking, but my toes aren't so numb anymore."

A hint of a smile crossed Mardon's face, but he quickly tightened his lips and backed away. "I will excuse myself. Kindly let me know if you need my help again."

"One question," Billy said, lifting a finger. "Do you know if Arramos has any idea where the portal is?"

Mardon nodded. "Tamiel forced me to aim the nuclear missile at a Midwest location, though the target later changed. I intentionally designed the navigation system to miss the original target by a considerable margin, just in case."

Billy looked at Bonnie. "That might be the old portal where the helicopters attacked and killed Legossi."

"We're not going there," Bonnie said. "So we should be safe."

"True, but we'll assume they're monitoring us. We'll be ready for hostile company."

"A wise strategy," Mardon said as he glided toward his corner. "Again, if you need further assistance, let me know."

Billy limped toward the cockpit, Excalibur in his grip. "I'd better get some rest."

"You need it." Bonnie capped the half-filled syringe and returned it to the first-aid kit. "I'm going to get some rest, too." She walked to her seat opposite Carly, partially spread her wings behind her, and buckled in.

Carly pulled an earbud from her ear that ran to Lois's spherical shell. Pale and bleary-eyed, she smiled. "So, to get back to our reunion … How are you doing?"

She gave Carly a weak smile of her own. "Tired. But that's my new normal."

"I have to admit you're not as perky as I remember."

"I've been through a lot. I would probably get exhausted just telling you about everything." Bonnie yawned. "I think I need a hundred-year rest."

Carly's smile brightened. "The last time I sat with you was on a train from Montana. Before that, on a school bus. Now we're on a jet together. What's next?"

"A dragon?" Bonnie yawned again. Her vision blurred. "Maybe when we get to the portal site, we'll ask Thigocia—"

"Bonnie. I'm sorry." Carly held up a hand. "Don't talk. Let's just sleep. I think we both need it. We'll talk more later. I've been thinking about a lot of things you wrote to me in your letters. I mean, before you went to jail. And I want to make sure we're both fresh when we talk about them."

"Perfect. I'd love that." Bonnie closed her eyes. As she drifted toward sleep, Carly's words echoed—*before you went to jail.* Images flashed to mind, troubling images—the prison cell that held her captive for so many years; Enforcers ripping her twins from her arms; Matt's determined face as he descended into the abyss; and, worst of all, Lauren's dead body, limp within a makeshift halter.

Sleep held sway. The images animated into a dream. Accompanied by Darcy, Matt carried Lauren into a cylindrical room illuminated by scarlet light pulsing from a column in the center. The scenes accelerated, at least three times normal speed. A dark-skinned woman with four arms opened a window in a wall, revealing Listener and Sir Barlow. Darcy suddenly vanished. Then Matt climbed through the opening, and the window closed.

The scene slowed. The four-armed woman walked toward another part of the curved wall. The pulses covered her in blood-red wash. She disappeared, then appeared again, instantly progressing a few feet with each reappearance. She looked like a scarlet-cloaked ghost filmed by a night-vision surveillance camera.

When she reached another wall, she touched it with a finger. A new window opened. A scarlet-veiled figure stood on the other side. The flashing redness kept his face obscured except for a scruffy beard lining his chin and cheeks. The man looked at an ovulum-like glass egg and spoke to it. "Jade? Do you have news?" His voice echoed as if originating in a deep canyon.

"I sent the boy to Abaddon's Lair." The four-armed woman, presumably Jade, crossed one set of arms over her chest. "All is proceeding as planned."

"Who sacrificed life energy to open the portal?"

"Darcy, the young woman who arrived with the boy. She died, and the winds of the abyss removed her remains."

The bearded man lowered his head, and his tone became solemn. "And will you now fulfill your part in our plan?"

"You need not worry." Jade set her four hands on the corners of the opening. "I always fulfill my agreements, no matter the cost."

"This is a perilous step. Opening the path to the reservoir is like unlocking the door for a burglar. You know who now stalks the netherworld."

"I know it all too well. It seems that your friends fell for his trap. He appears to have successfully taken the next step toward achieving his goals."

"This is unfortunate." The man's hands trembled—blood-red as they caressed the ovulum's glassy skin. "Do you know where he is now?"

"He tried to enter your realm, but your defense shield repelled him. He settled for the realm of martyrs. Since he was in a spiritual state, I was unable to prevent his transport."

"Then God's wisdom has been proven faultless once again. My efforts were successful in guarding the reservoir. That is gratifying."

"Indeed. And Tamiel is quite in a rage. The realm he chose forced him to take on his most ancient physical form, and being physical keeps him locked inside. He will not be able to escape without extraordinary cunning."

"Cunning is his trademark. We should not underestimate him. Besides his ability to create a dome of silence and knock people away as if he were a battering ram, he is also a master at deception. Everyone must beware of his craft."

"Let us hope that Lauren's wisdom grows as she learns the ways of an Oracle of Fire."

The man nodded. "She must unravel the mysteries on her own. An Oracle must gain the necessary wisdom from above. Otherwise, she will never be as powerful as Sapphira."

"Agreed. It was Sapphira's solitude and suffering that enabled her to become what she is." Jade let out a genial laugh. "And that is why I have kept the secrets from you, my old friend. You are not willing to see this new applicant suffer to earn her passage to the protected realm."

"I must admit that you are correct. God was wise to choose you as the guardian of these mysteries. You cannot be swayed from divine purposes."

"And with that, I must bid you good-bye." Jade drew her hands toward the center and collapsed the window. Spreading out all four arms, she walked to the central column—a rectangular, pedestal-like structure that stretched from its base on the floor to well over her head. As she drew near, a gemstone embedded in her sternum glittered, alternating between green and scarlet.

She sang softly. "He came by water, came by blood, O Son of God, the holy one. The Spirit speaks, and truth is known; the three agree, and all is shown. When Lauren calls to halls above, O let her see the hand in glove, that three lagoons complete a tale; the parched, the dead, the Holy Grail." Extending one finger on each hand, she reached to all four sides of the column and inserted the fingers into holes. The moment she pushed them in, her face tightened into a grimace, then blackness filled the scene.

Bonnie snapped her eyes open and tried to rise, but a seat belt held her in place. Carly sat just out of reach, her eyes closed and her chest rising and falling in a steady rhythm. Bonnie exhaled. Recent memories rushed to the forefront. She was in the jet, flying to the portal. But the dream—could it have been real? She had prayed for more oracle dreams. Maybe Matt did survive the abyss. Maybe he did make it to Abaddon's Lair with Lauren.

And what about Darcy? Bonnie bit her lip hard. After all the disrespect Matt had shown her, had she given her life for him and Lauren? And who was the man Jade was speaking to? His voice seemed familiar, but the dream warped it too much to be sure.

She took in a deep breath and brushed away tears. There was no way to know. She just had to keep walking her own path and trusting God to guide Matt's. What else could she do? Her song had already deteriorated to a weak hum. Dwelling on what couldn't be controlled would only make the situation worse.

She settled back and closed her eyes again. "Show us the way," she whispered. "In these last days I know we will be called to suffer. Just help us endure. No matter what happens, even if we die, I trust that you will carry us into your embrace. In that knowledge, I can rest."

8

CHAPTER

The Second Puzzle Piece

Lauren's cloak sizzled and flashed in a surrounding arc. She landed on her feet and took three braking steps to halt her momentum. With each footfall, something crunched under her shoes. She pulled the yoke and cloak off and held one of the items in each hand. The cloak material was still wet, and the yoke continued to glow with a blue aura.

Bones small and large littered the landscape—a flat expanse that stretched as far as the eye could see, interrupted only by a dark depression, perhaps a hole, about twenty yards away. In the sky, a reddish moon cast crimson light, making the bones look bloody.

Lauren tied the cloak around her waist and looked back. Through a window, the central column pulsed within the sanctum, a way of escape. But she couldn't take that route. Not yet. She had to figure out how this world might help her solve the reservoir puzzle, and she had to find Sir Barlow, wherever he might be.

Whatever had attacked him, the depression seemed to be the only possible hiding place. No sense letting the attacker know she was coming.

Still carrying the glowing yoke, she tiptoed forward, careful to step on the larger bones to avoid breaking the smaller ones, yet even careful steps raised crackling noises that sounded like thunderclaps in this quiet world.

As she drew close, the depression took shape—nearly perfectly round and about the same size as the pool Sir Barlow had fallen into. The moon appeared as a reflection within. Since the light cast everything in red, it seemed impossible to tell what the liquid might be. It looked like blood, but exposed blood would clot, and it wouldn't reflect the moon. Or would it?

She crouched at the edge and inhaled. A metallic odor rose from the motionless liquid. She leaned forward to see her own reflection, but only redness appeared.

She blinked. How odd. A pool that reflected some things but not others. And neither this pool nor the previous one could be considered a life reservoir. Both were polluted, void of life.

She extended the yoke. When the end touched the surface, circular ripples radiated in normal fashion, though the focal point grew in a strange way, swelling from a pinprick to a fist-sized hole.

A man's head erupted from the hole. Wet hair covering his face, he sucked in a gasping breath. His arm splashed forth, and he clawed at the brittle bones on the shoreline until he grabbed the yoke. It slipped from his grasp, and she fell to her bottom. The man began sliding back into the pool, still clawing as he gurgled, "Help me, lass!"

Lauren dropped the yoke, dove forward, and grabbed two fistfuls of his tunic at the shoulders. While he crawled, she pulled until he got his footing and surged from the pool. He fell on top of her, crunching the bed of bones and knocking the wind out of her lungs.

He braced with his arms and lifted his body. She sucked in a breath. Thick liquid dripped from his clothes and spattered on her shirt.

With a quick twist, she rolled out from underneath. He collapsed to his side and gasped, coughing and spitting between breaths. "I apologize … for the mess."

"Don't worry about that." Lauren sat up and patted his back. The liquid dripped from her arms, though it began hardening to a crust. Was it really blood after all?

When Sir Barlow's spasms eased, he climbed to his feet and helped Lauren rise to hers. He swiped caked blood from his face and scanned the area. "Where did the creature go?"

"What creature?" Lauren followed his gaze. As before, scarlet-shrouded bones covered the landscape from horizon to horizon. "There's nowhere to go except for that pool." She pointed at the portal. "Or the sanctum, but I didn't see any creature in there."

Sir Barlow inhaled deeply and relaxed his shoulders. "I call it a creature, because I have no name for it. It had a human head attached to an armored body with oddly jointed arms and legs, like a winged lobster that stands upright, perhaps a head taller than myself. When it attacked me, I had only my fists to counter with, so it defeated me in short order."

"Oh. Right. Your sword." Lauren slid it out and handed it to him. "How did you end up in the pool?"

"Well, I battled the creature hand to claw for a moment until it pierced my stomach with a spine or perhaps a claw, I can't be sure. In any case, blood poured from the wound and rushed to the pool like it was being suctioned. The suction carried my body with it, and a hole opened in the pool and swallowed me whole. I tried to swim out, but my hands struck a hard barrier. I couldn't see in the bloody place, so I assumed that the surface had become a wall. As I tried to break through with my fists, I held my breath for an intolerable amount of time. Then, moments ago, a tiny ray of light appeared, and I was able to break through, though without something to push my feet against, climbing out was still a struggle."

Lauren looked at the ground where the yoke now lay. "Weird!"

"Indeed. Now I have explored two unsavory pools. I hope to avoid investigating a third." Sir Barlow opened his shirt, revealing an inch-long vertical gash in his belly just below his solar plexus. Blood trickled from the wound toward his belt buckle. "It seems that I have made a significant contribution to this pool's contents, but the damage doesn't appear to be life-threatening."

Lauren eyed the wound. "No, but you'll need stitches."

"Not likely, Miss." He closed the shirt. "A stitch in time saves nine, but I have had worse wounds that were never stitched. Besides, I have doubts that this is my real body. Why repair a loaner when I am expecting a new model?"

Lauren laughed under her breath. "Trust me. I'm with you there. That's why we have to solve the puzzle and get restored."

"I realize that, but perhaps we should contemplate what we have learned while in the relative safety of Jade's sanctum, assuming it is still clear of lobsterlike creatures. We can return here after we collect our thoughts."

"That's fine with me. As long as the beam is still there, we should be able to come back." Lauren untied the cloak, now sticky from a mixture of blood and water. As it dripped, the blend of liquids streamed along the ground toward the pool as if drawn there. When the stream entered, the surface broke open again. Whispered voices rose—plaintive, mournful, though not as desperate as the ones that chanted the Hades poem.

"Do you hear that?" Lauren asked as she looked at the pool.

"I hear nothing." Sir Barlow brushed clotted blood from his ears. "Though I am sure that your hearing is far better than mine."

The voices continued, forming words in multiple languages—French, Spanish, something Oriental, and others that sounded Middle Eastern, African, and Slavic. Finally, an English speaker joined the chorus.

Lauren focused on his words and repeated them for Sir Barlow's sake. "How long, O Lord, holy and true, dost thou not judge and avenge our blood on them that dwell on the earth?"

The man spoke the words again, adding a melody that sounded like a Gregorian chant. When the phrase ended, she shook her head. "That's all. He keeps saying the same thing over and over."

"I recognize it," Sir Barlow said. "It's from the Revelation of St. John. Martyred souls say it from under an altar."

"Martyrs." Lauren stared at the bones near her feet. "People who die for a cause."

"That is one definition. The people who spoke those words in the Bible were described as souls who had been slain because of the word of God and the testimony they believed. I suppose any Christian who dies under an oppressive hand would be included in the definition."

Lauren touched a bloodstain on her shirt. "Martyrs' blood?"

"Perhaps so, Miss. Some of my blood is in there as well, so it could be any blood shed for the sake of others."

"Hmmm." She straightened and looked at Sir Barlow. "What else do you know about these martyrs?"

He brushed more blood from his sleeves. "Well, they are given white robes and told to wait until the fulfillment of the martyrdom of their fellows. White robes are a symbol of purity, complete cleansing."

"What do we have that relates to ..." Lauren lifted the cloak. "A robe." Something pulled against the material. The lower portion lifted, and the blood-and-water mixture streamed toward the pool. The cloak faded from black to white, beginning at the hem and moving toward Lauren's hand. Seconds later, the pull ended, and the cloak fell limp.

When the final drops entered the pool, the voices silenced. From the point of entry, a shimmer rippled outward. The pool transformed into crystal clear water from edge to edge.

"Incredible!" Sir Barlow touched the cloak. "It is as white as snow and dry as one of the bones."

Something crackled below. A clear swath ran from Lauren's feet to the pool, covering the path the water and blood had taken. The swath spread out to each side and dissolved the bones. The ground transformed into a crystalline floor that expanded out of sight in every direction. After a few seconds, it looked like an endless sea of glass. The moon reflected on the shiny surface as if buried deep within the floor. Red drops fell from the moon, and whiteness took its place from top to bottom until it shone like a fiery diamond above.

Wherever the red drops fell, they sizzled. Vapor rose and gathered into waist-level misty streams that flowed toward the pool. Human faces took shape within the lines of fog. At first, they wore frowns. Then the frowns transformed into smiles, as if the movement incited joy.

As a stream passed close to Lauren, a girl's face appeared, her smile dazzling. She looked so familiar. Could it be Micaela? Yes!

"Micaela!" Lauren called as she reached out, but the stream zipped by without a response.

At the tail end of the stream, a woman's face took shape as well as a young boy's. Fear in their expressions changed to delight, and they followed the others into the pool. The vaporous lines plunged through, raising no splash. Seconds later, they were gone.

"Well!" Sir Barlow stood as erect as a statue. "I have witnessed many strange events, but this, as they say, takes the cake."

"You're telling me." Lauren gave the pond another look. Why would mist that looks like Micaela go there? Because it's clean now?

"This is interesting." Sir Barlow ran a shoe along the glassy floor. "Names have been etched everywhere."

"Names?" Lauren stooped and ran a hand across an etching. Each letter was about a foot long and ran deep into the crystal. A gap of a foot or so separated each name. "This one says Justin Martyr. Isn't that where the word *martyr* comes from?"

"I believe so, Miss." Sir Barlow touched a nearby name. "And this one says Joan of Arc."

"Joan?" Lauren took in a quick breath. This floor had to be some kind of memorial, a tribute to those who had sacrificed themselves. She scanned the other names. Most were unfamiliar, some carved with odd letters or in foreign languages. Finally her gaze came upon Micaela's name near the portal window. She strode there and found another familiar etching next to it. A capital *E* began a single-word name.

"Eagle," she whispered.

Sir Barlow picked up the yoke. "Where did this come from?"

"I didn't get a chance to tell you my story." She quickly recounted the details of what happened after Sir Barlow fell into the other pool. When she finished, he ran a finger along one of the yoke's indentations.

"It seems strange that it had only one oxbow. They are needed to keep the yoke in place. A missing one would indicate that the partner carried his or her part of the burden willingly, unless, of course, someone unfastened or broke the other oxbow."

Lauren withdrew the glasses from her shirt pocket. "I also found these computer glasses that my foster father used to wear. They were attached by a chain to his ankle, like they were an anchor to hold him down, but they're too light to do that. Anyway, I kept them hoping they held a clue to what happened to him. But I was worried about putting them on, because I tend to mess up electronics."

"Allow me to look. I have often hoped to try one of these." Sir Barlow took the glasses and put them on. His eyes crossed for a moment, then he blinked, and a look of disgust pinched his face. He jerked the glasses off and threw them away.

"Sir Barlow!" Lauren watched the glasses slide along the crystalline floor. "What did you see?"

As his face reddened, he growled. "Miss, I dare not tell you the details." His voice spiked with anger. "Any chivalrous man should be outraged at such a display! Women are to be treasured! Honored! Not exposed as fleshly playthings!"

Lauren's own face heated up. Had her foster father been looking at pornography? With his wife suffering from cancer, had he resorted to …

She clenched her eyes shut. *No! Don't think that way!* She inhaled deeply and recalled Nashville memories, those days before this endless nightmare began—days when Fiona and Gaston Hunt were Mom and Dad, days that included croquet in the backyard with Mom while Dad, wearing a greasy chef's hat and apron, grilled hamburgers and hot dogs. He would sing silly songs as he drummed on the grill with the spatula.

Tears seeped past her closed eyelids. Dad was good and kind. He never spoke a cross word. Well, maybe a profanity when he hurt himself. But he always treated Mom with kindness. He wouldn't go on the Internet and look at … at that stuff, would he?

"I apologize for my tirade, Miss." Sir Barlow's tone grew calm. "Now I understand the symbolism of the fettered yoke. Perhaps he felt shackled—"

"No, Sir Barlow." A lump swelled in Lauren's throat. "Please . . . just don't. It's too painful."

He laid the yoke down and spread an arm over her shoulder. "Of course. I apologize."

Something splashed at the pool. A huge creature burst out, beating enormous wings and slinging shining droplets. Its head was that of a man, and it shouted with a human voice. "Cursed water!"

"The lobster!" Sir Barlow shielded Lauren and extended his sword. "Stand back, Miss. I will tackle it." Just as he bent to lunge, the creature shot out a pincer, grabbed Sir Barlow around his waist, and slung him away. He crashed to the floor and slid until he lay motionless on the glass, his sword still in hand.

Her heart thumping wildly, Lauren glanced at the portal window, her only escape, but how could she leave Sir Barlow? There had to be a way to elude this … this thing.

The creature stared at her and smiled. "Ah! I was wondering if you would come."

She squinted at the humanlike face. Although a pair of antennae protruded from a scaly cap on its head, those dark eyes were all too familiar. "Tamiel?"

He laughed. "I am glad you remember me. Our relationship has been, shall we say, strained, at best."

"But … but you're supposed to be dead."

"And you as well." Tamiel clicked his pincers together. "Snip, snip. Two lives snuffed, yours and mine. Yet here we are."

She glanced at Sir Barlow. As he lay on his back, his chest rose and fell with rhythmic breaths. "But what about the curse? Wasn't it true? I grabbed you. I sacrificed my life to kill you."

"Of course it was true. We both died. But you grabbed me only because I let you. My cowardly call for help from Arramos was merely part of an act. I could have flown away at any time."

She lowered her head. "I was wondering about that."

"Yet you proceeded with your insane plan to kill us both. I counted on the intensity of the moment to cloud your thinking."

She raised her brow. "You *wanted* to die?"

"Yes, you fool, but not until that moment." Tamiel's antennae quivered, and his tone altered to one of smug condescension. "I waited for Sapphira to bring the abyss to light so I could travel to Jade's sanctum. Of course, destroying Bonnie's song was a major goal, and we succeeded, but without securing this second goal, all would have been for naught."

"What is your second goal?"

He snorted. "I am no fool. I tell you only enough to shame you, to demonstrate that you and your deity are no match for my cunning. I want to bury you under an avalanche of reality. Your *heroic* sacrifice has played right into my hands, and every potential move you make has already been calculated and planned for. You cannot stop me."

She nodded toward the pool. "You seemed surprised by the cleansing of the water. I roused you from that pond."

Tamiel shook his armored tail. "I knew that was within the realm of possibilities, though I thought the risk to be low. It was the only place to hide in this barren land, and I was able to stay under for quite a while."

"Really?" Lauren scanned the area once more. With the moon now brighter, everything was clearer—an endless expanse of flat glass. As he said, there was no place to hide. Yet, why would he *want* to hide? Obviously he didn't hide from Sir Barlow when he first arrived. The only possibility left was fear of something … or someone. Maybe the curse was still in effect.

"Does it take so long to verify my explanation?" Tamiel waved a pincer. "Now take the knight and go. Since I can defeat him in the bat of an eye, I have no worries that he will be an obstacle to me. In fact, he is likely to be a hindrance to you."

Lauren studied his darting eyes. Yes, he was cunning, but now he seemed more transparent than before. He wanted her to leave, so her departure was part of his plan. He intended to follow, to wait for her to do something that would open a door, just as raising the abyss had opened one earlier.

"The Listener is not deaf, is she?" He opened and closed his pincers with twin snaps. "Now go! Or I will behead that fool of a knight!"

"All right. But it will take a while." Lauren walked toward Sir Barlow. With her back to Tamiel, a feeling of anxiety rode up her spine. Her scales tingled, and thoughts trickled into her ears.

I know you read thoughts, but you will not learn any secrets from my mind. I know how to guard against your futile power.

She resisted the urge to look back. Even his thoughts were a form of mocking, so acknowledging his stab from behind would give him a victory. She draped the cloak over her shoulders and pushed her arms through the sleeves. Flames ran along the material all the way to her hands, though the fire caused no pain.

Lauren stifled a gasp. Where did the flames come from?

"What is this trickery?" Tamiel asked. "How do you have fire on your cloak?"

Turning slightly to view him from the corner of her eye, she lifted the hood over her head. "I thought you planned for every possibility. Didn't this one come to mind?"

"It is of no consequence. You can do nothing to stop me unless you wish to die again." He waved a claw. "Be off with you now."

"You leave first. I don't want you to see where I go or what I do."

"Suit yourself, but there is no way to hide your actions. The moon is too bright, and the land is laid bare. " He turned and skittered away, his armored appendages clicking on the glass.

Lauren pivoted back to Sir Barlow and stared at her sleeve. Tiny firelets rippled across the lustrous white material. What could it all mean?

Bending her back, she laid Sir Barlow's sword on his chest and dragged him by the wrists across the glassy floor. After a few steps, she slipped on the slick surface and landed hard on her bottom. She kicked off her shoes and socks and continued on bare feet. Her sweaty soles adhered to the glass and provided traction.

When she arrived at the portal, she dropped to her knees at his side and listened. Shallow breaths wheezed through his narrowed throat, and his heart thumped erratically.

She patted his cheek. "Sir Barlow? Can you hear me?"

His eyelids twitched, but he stayed unconscious.

She looked at the pool again. Maybe it could help. She ran to the water, scooped some up in her hands, and tiptoed back. Kneeling again, she poured it over his face and let some dribble past his parted lips.

After a few seconds, his eyes shot open. "Where is that blasted creature?" He flexed to rise, but Lauren laid a hand on his shoulder and forced him down.

"He's gone. Don't worry."

A grimace knotted his face. "What happened?"

"He grabbed you and threw you over there." She gestured toward his landing spot. "Then he left, and I dragged you here."

"He left?" Sir Barlow lifted his head and looked around. His eyes stopped at his sword, still lying on his chest. "Did you chase him away with my blade?"

She smiled and shook her head. "Let's just say that I encouraged him to leave."

Sir Barlow blinked. "Well, lass, it seems that you are the valiant knight, and I am the skirted maiden."

"Nonsense." Lauren studied his eyes. They seemed clear and focused. "Are you dizzy at all?"

"Not in this position. I suggest that you allow me to test my feet."

She rose and extended her hand. He set the sword to the side, grasped her wrist, and rose with her pull, but his knees gave way, and he fell to a sitting position. A new grimace tightened his face. "Back spasms, Miss. Why this is happening to a body without substance, I can't say."

"Maybe there's more substance than we think." She lowered the hood and gazed into his eyes. "Sir Barlow, it's really strange. While I was in that place with the dirty pond, my heartbeat returned. And here ..." She lifted an arm and showed him the cloak's sleeve. "Somehow I'm creating fire."

"Amazing!" His eyes wide, Sir Barlow combed his fingers through her hair. "My dear girl, your locks are as white as snow."

"White?" She pulled some hair forward and looked at it. Every strand was indeed snow white. "The moon, maybe? It makes everything look white."

"Not your eyes. They are as blue as a summer sky."

"But they've always been blue." She touched her skin near her eyes. "Well, sort of hazel-blue, like my dad's."

"Ah, but now they're like bright gems, sparkling and vibrant. No one would call them hazel." He set a finger on her cheek. "And you are glowing, a soft, ivory glow—lovely to behold."

"So that's returned, too." She looked at her hand but, as usual, couldn't see her own glow. "I wonder what it all means."

Sir Barlow shifted and winced with the movement. "It means that the changes we have both experienced point to an astonishing conclusion."

"And that is?"

He laid a hand on his back and stretched. "That we have been restored. You are now alive, and I have my body again, such that it is."

Lauren compressed his shoulder—solid and muscular, but he was that way earlier. "How can we be sure?"

"Well, as they say, the proof is in the pudding. We can travel through the portals to Second Eden and see if we enter in a physical state." He gestured toward the portal. "Shall we?"

"But you can't walk."

"I can crawl."

"Wait. Let me see if more water will help." She hurried to the pond and brought another double handful of water. Along the way, she spotted the yoke on the crystalline floor, still glowing blue.

After Sir Barlow slurped the water from her hands, she walked toward the yoke. "I have to get something." She picked it up and returned to him. "This might be part of the puzzle."

He rubbed the surface with a finger. "Perhaps you have already solved it."

"How so?"

"Betrayal is the most painful experience of all, but those who survive it gain much wisdom."

"Betrayal? You mean my foster father?"

He nodded. "I am beginning to think that our quest is more of a line of stepping-stones of experience than a physical puzzle. It is you who are changing rather than our environment."

Lauren touched her fiery sleeve. "I think I see what you mean."

"In any case, I don't think more water is helping, so …" He turned to his hands and knees and grasped his sword. "Lay the cloak over me. I will crawl through and throw it back to you."

"Just a second." Lauren studied the portal. The beam from the column appeared to be white now, so Sir Barlow probably didn't need the yoke. She stripped off the cloak and draped it over him. With a quick glance, she checked the area. No sign of Tamiel. "Go ahead."

As Sir Barlow crawled through the portal, the cloak sparked and sizzled more than ever. His knee caught on the material, making it slip from his head. In a splash of sparks, he fell to the sanctum's floor with a loud thud, and the sword clattered at his side.

Lauren dropped the yoke and lunged to the window. Sir Barlow lay motionless on his back, the cloak pinned underneath as the column's white light pulsed over his body. Blood soaked his tunic where Tamiel had speared him.

"Sir Barlow?" She set her ear as close to the portal as she dared. The sound of breathing drifted in as well as a regular heartbeat and a slight gurgle. The portal's jolt and the fall must have knocked him out.

After glancing again to check for Tamiel, she ventured a louder call. "Sir Barlow!"

He stayed motionless and quiet.

Lauren touched the portal plane with a fingertip. A jolt shot up her arm. She jerked her hand back and shook it. This one seemed more electrified than the others.

She sat down hard and pulled her knees to her chest, the portal to the right and the pool to the left. Every few seconds, she glanced to one side then the other to check for movement. What could she do but wait? Sir Barlow might wake up soon, so wandering around looking for another way out wasn't a good idea, especially with Tamiel lurking somewhere.

She gazed into the sanctum again, leaning forward to get a different angle. Three beams remained—a white one aimed at the tree room, another white one at the portal where she sat, and a red one at the opening of the last unvisited portal.

Lauren sighed. Too many mysteries—the martyrs' voices, the cloak and her hair turning white, her eye color changing, a new ability to generate flames. What did it all mean? Now that she was transforming into a … a whatever, had she really completed the second portion of the puzzle? It was all so confusing!

She lowered her head between her knees. So tired. So sore. Maybe exhaustion was another proof of resurrection and certainly proof that she needed help.

"God," she whispered. "I know you're not used to hearing much from me, but I hope you're listening now." She lifted her head and gazed at the silvery moon. "I don't have Sir Barlow. I don't have Matt or Joan. Or Mom, Dad, Walter, Ashley, or anyone else. I don't understand what's happening. I'm in way over my head. I feel like a sparrow flying in a hurricane."

She took in a deep breath and let it out slowly. "So if you'll please wake up Sir Barlow, and get rid of Tamiel, and help me find the life reservoir and figure out what to do when I get there …" She let herself smile. "That sounds like I'm asking a lot, like I want you to do everything for me. So how about if you just give me the wisdom to know what to do and the strength to do it, and I'll leave the rest up to you. Is that all right?"

Her back scales tingled. Whispers drifted into her ears—voice after voice saying Amen—men, women, and children in chorus as if sung by angels. Echoes followed in Spanish, an Oriental language, several indistinguishable tongues, and finally French.

"Ainsi soit-il, mon ami."

"Joan?" Lauren searched for a companion around her shoulders, but none appeared.

A sense of warmth washed in—peace and comfort. Surely God was in this place. Someone was watching, guarding, caring.

Her hands for a pillow, she lay on her side over Eagle's name and closed her eyes. Peace descended. Tamiel's lurking presence no longer mattered. Touching her meant death to him, and Sir Barlow was safe from his pincers.

As sleep approached, the voices returned—Joan's lovely affirmation, the chorus of martyrs, and finally Sir Barlow's resonant bass. "We have been restored. You are now alive, and I have my body again."

She drew her body into a tight curl and listened to her heart as it beat with a slow, steady rhythm. Within seconds, she drifted off to sleep.

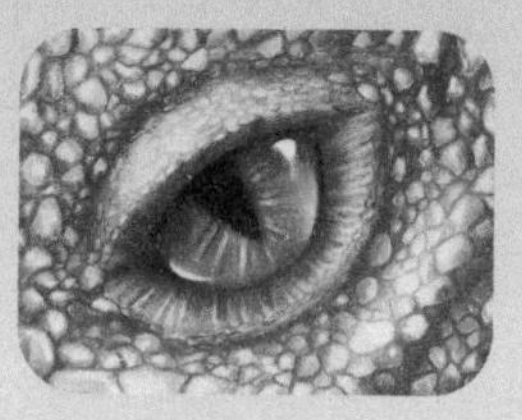

9

CHAPTER

The First Assault

Bonnie?"

She turned toward the voice. Adam approached from the rear of the jet, carrying Larry's brain-unit case and walking with stiff legs.

Bonnie suppressed a yawn. How long did that nap last? An hour, maybe? "I see you're feeling better."

"I feel like I got body slammed by the Incredible Hulk." Adam stretched his neck, raising a few pops. "But it looks like Mardon's serum worked." He set Larry's case on the floor. "Our digital friend wants to hook up with his chip mate. He's picking up some radio chatter. Heavily encrypted. He says Lois is better at decrypting than he is."

"An excuse to reunite with his wife?" Bonnie winked. "Or is Larry humble all of a sudden?"

"I am realistic," Larry said through the lapel speaker. "Lois and I have to combine our data regarding the plant's growth. She still has a piece of it."

"Right." Bonnie looked at Carly as she slept in the facing seat. Her earlier lesions had doubled in size, and new ones had erupted on her cheeks and chin. Might the reason for her illness be the curse instead of radiation exposure? If so, did that mean her soul was also in danger?

Bonnie leaned forward and prodded Carly's knee. "Sorry to bother you."

Carly's eyes fluttered open. "Are we descending?"

"Not yet," Adam said as he slid Larry closer. "Can we hook the spousal circuits together?"

"Sure." Carly lifted Lois's spherical unit and set it next to Larry.

Adam sat on the floor, pulled a cord from Larry's control panel, and plugged it into Lois's shell. "All right, you two, you'll have time to get reacquainted later. Just confer on the chatter and Mardon's plant-growth secrets and let us know what's going on."

Bonnie touched Adam's arm. "Why don't you get some rest? Carly and I can handle it from here."

"No argument from me." Adam slid his hand into Carly's and smiled. "It's good to see you again."

"You, too, Adam." She compressed his hand, her own smile wavering. "We'll talk later. Okay?"

"I'll look forward to it." He rose and hobbled to his seat.

Lois's voice emanated from her sphere. "The chatter uses a blend of encrypted code, military jargon, and street lingo. I suspect that those engaging in the conversation are young, perhaps newly trained recruits. The haphazard nature of their communications makes the decryption more difficult. This will take a good deal of time, especially since the chatter is intermittent."

Bonnie leaned closer to Carly. "Since Lois is running on batteries, doesn't that mean her reception power is low? That the chatter must be close by?"

"Did we fly over a military base?" Carly asked. "That's close enough, I think."

Marilyn called from the cockpit. "That's a negative. I'm steering clear of all airports and anything remotely military."

Seated in the copilot's chair, Billy turned toward them. "We'd better be on the lookout for fighter jets. They might be talking to each other."

"I can't evade military fighters." Marilyn pointed at the dashboard map. "We're coming up on a big forest. We could land and hide under trees."

Billy rose and limped down the aisle, his head low. "If we hide because something might hurt us, we'll never stop hiding."

"How far from here to the portal?" Bonnie asked.

Marilyn touched the GPS. "Forty-three miles. We'll be there in a few minutes."

Bonnie looked out the window. Reddish clouds floated in towering formations, rising from a floor of lower clouds—plenty of hiding places for other aircraft. "Maybe they're just staying out of sight till we get there."

"Let them." Billy took an adhesive bandage from the first-aid kit on a vacant seat and returned to the copilot's chair. "If they're tracking us, we'll have to face them eventually." He peeled a bloody bandage from his forehead and applied the new one. "Besides, we're cutting it close on fuel."

"You got that right." Marilyn leaned back in the pilot's chair. "Just keep me up to date."

While they continued flying, Lois and Larry provided updates. The amount of chatter elevated, though their decryption efforts had not yet succeeded. They also combined the plant data and concluded that the offloaded piece needed a decryption key. Everyone agreed that Mardon likely had it, and there was no use asking him for it.

Moments later, the jet descended through the lower clouds and broke into the clear. Far below, houses and lawns snaked around schools, parks, and playgrounds. The suburban area soon gave way to a rural landscape where a two-lane road ran alongside a stadium.

"What was the city we passed?" Bonnie asked.

Billy turned from his seat in the cockpit. "St. Louis. We're west of it now."

"So we flew a round-trip."

"Pretty much. I just had coordinates. I didn't know we'd come right back here until I plugged them in." Billy pointed at the jet's GPS screen. "It looks like we're supposed to go to that football stadium."

"Does the highway look long enough to land on?" Marilyn asked.

Billy leaned forward. "I think so. We need four thousand feet, but we have a drag chute, so let's go for it. We'll taxi to the stadium's parking lot."

"Will do." Marilyn began a wide turn. "I'll circle back to get enough highway space. Fortunately, no one's on the road, but there's a neighborhood close by. We'll be seen."

"I thought the portal would be in an uninhabited area," Bonnie said. "If it's open, anyone could just walk through it, couldn't they?"

Lois spoke through the lapel speaker. "It is not normally open. Elam and Sapphira planned their portals carefully. As you might know, it takes great effort to move a portal from one place to another, and it is exceedingly difficult to create a new one. Elam brought warriors through one portal that led to a remote mesa, which they kept open by a fire in Second Eden, but an event occurred that caused the fire to go out."

Bonnie looked at Carly. "The event Lois is talking about was Mount Elijah's eruption."

"Got it." Carly tapped Lois's sphere with a finger. "Please continue. I need to get up to speed on this."

"Certainly. That portal's closure and Elam's inability to return to Second Eden through it led to government authorities finding the portal, killing Legossi, and capturing Sapphira. The closure also prevented those authorities from exploiting the portal for their purposes, but they are certain to be monitoring it."

"Which is why we're not flying to that one," Carly said.

"Correct. Elam has always had a secret portal that he has never used. Since adversaries expect portals to be located in remote areas on Earth, it stands to reason that the most secret one would be somewhere they do not expect. Elam never stored the coordinates anywhere. He provided them verbally when needed."

"That sounds like Elam," Bonnie said. "He'll do anything to keep Second Eden safe."

Carly gazed out the window. "It looks … deserted."

Bonnie joined Carly, the sides of their heads touching. The stadium appeared to be significantly smaller than a professional-league complex, though the parking lot was big enough to hold hundreds of vehicles. A set of high-rise bleachers made of concrete and metal ran along one sideline, and collapsed bleachers lay piled along the other. With no goalposts on the field, it looked like it had been abandoned long ago, though some of the lines and a faded logo were still visible on the grass.

At field level, a human figure ran through an open gate that led to a passage within the undamaged bleachers. "I saw someone," Bonnie said. "Whoever it was took off like a shot."

Billy turned toward her. "Could you tell who it was?"

"No." Bonnie looked toward the field again, now out of sight as the jet banked sharply. "It was too far away. I couldn't even tell if the person was male or female."

"White hair or wings?" Billy asked, playfulness in his tone.

Keeping her gaze through the window, she smiled. "I would recognize Sapphira or Gabriel even from this far."

"Let's hope we're being watched by friendly eyes," Billy said. "Soon we should have dragon allies to counter whoever's tracking us."

Bonnie leaned back in her seat. Makaidos, Thigocia, and Roxil. Maybe the stadium included an overhang or some other shelter under the concrete section that prevented an aerial view of dragons hiding underneath.

As they descended to within a few hundred feet of the ground, the line of flight paralleled a straight portion of highway. The painted stripes down the middle zipped by faster and faster, and the stadium came back into view about a mile ahead.

"We might shoot past it," Marilyn said.

Billy pointed forward. "See where the pavement turns darker? Let's touch down there and brake hard. A curve is coming up."

"Deploy the chute?"

"No. We have room."

Marilyn set a hand on one of the controls. "Everyone check your belts."

Carly unplugged Lois from Larry and set her in her lap. Bonnie tightened her belt and braced Larry between her feet.

The jet descended sharply, then leveled out and touched down. The screech of tires skidding on pavement filled the cabin along with a whoosh of air. Bonnie's waist pressed against her belt until the momentum eased.

"The parking lot's gate looks wide enough," Billy said as he pointed out his side window. "Let's take her right in."

Bonnie looked through her window. The stadium lay in an east-west configuration parallel to and north of the highway with a parking lot in between. A side road and open gate led to the lot where two cars sat near the perimeter fence—Ashley's solar-powered car and the Mustang that transported Elam, Sapphira, Thomas, and Mariel here. Grass grew through cracks in the pothole-scarred pavement, and faded white paint marked parking-space lines here and there.

The jet bounced on the bumpy road, jostling everyone. After a few seconds, Billy called out, "That's good." When the wheels stopped, he threw off his buckle and leaped into the aisle, Excalibur glowing in his grip. "Okay, let's try to get out as fast as possible."

Bonnie unbuckled, grabbed Larry, and stepped into the aisle behind Billy, a hand on his shoulder as she followed him toward the door.

"Carl," Marilyn called from the cockpit, "I'll get Jared."

Billy opened the door, deployed the airstair, and hobbled down to the pavement. He spun back and extended his free hand to Bonnie. "Let's go, everyone. Careful on the steps."

When Bonnie reached the bottom, she set Larry on the pavement and whispered to Billy, "I'll be the lookout." She leaped and flew toward a tall lighting pole. At the top, four square lamp shields protruded outward from the central pole, the shields' protective glass parallel to the ground. She alighted with each foot on a shield and crouched. Her perch provided a westward view of the highway, a forest to the north beyond the stadium's wrecked bleachers, and a partly cloudy sky, reddened by the scarlet sun.

The overhang at the closer set of bleachers shadowed a perimeter walkway that ran parallel to a pair of restrooms and a concession stand embedded in a concrete wall. A crinkled square of greasy paper blew by one of the restrooms, the only movement in the stadium.

Bonnie searched every visible nook and cranny. Maybe Elam, Gabriel, and company were hiding and would soon send someone to greet the new arrivals. Below, the other passengers continued disembarking. Billy, still holding Excalibur, scanned the area while Catherine helped Carl descend the steps and Adam followed with the wheelchair. Then Mardon glided down and marched away from the jet. Within seconds, he faded and disappeared.

Bonnie scanned the path the ghostly scientist seemed to be taking, a course to her right that led to the stadium. There, a human-shaped shadow moved behind a column supporting the bleachers. The person who cast the shadow remained out of view, too far away to contact by voice.

"Bonnie!" Billy shouted as he looked up at her. "I sense danger! Do you see anything?"

She pointed toward the stadium. "I saw a shadow over there. Mardon went that way, but I don't think he's had time to get there." She turned her head and looked down the highway to the east. Above the city skyline, a tiny object appeared, growing larger as it followed the highway. The distinctive whipping hum of helicopter blades rode the air.

With one hand braced on the light pole, she cupped her other hand around her mouth and called, "A helicopter is coming!" She pointed to the rear. "From that direction!"

Three people ran from the bleachers—a man, a woman, and a petite, white-haired female dressed in a Second Eden battle uniform. Bonnie blinked. Sapphira! And who were the others? Yes! Walter and Ashley!

The whipping blades grew louder. The helicopter's frame took shape, growing as it zoomed closer.

Walter, Ashley, and Sapphira stopped at Billy's side and watched the helicopter's flight. Bonnie strained to listen over the growing din. "It's been patrolling," Ashley said, "but we've kept out of sight."

Billy squinted toward the east. "Any idea what it's capable of?"

Walter pulled a handgun from behind his belt. "It's a Cobra. Rapid-fire guns and missiles. I don't know if they're air-to-air or air-to-surface. Maybe both. Either way, Elam and Gabriel are keeping the dragons out of target range. They'll attack if they have to, but Elam has them on a tight rein. You know. After what happened to Legossi."

"Just so you're aware," Ashley said to Billy. "I haven't had a chance to check the blood you collected in the abyss. I need a lab to do a DNA match."

"No worries. Bonnie and I are pretty confident Matt survived."

"Good. Keep the faith."

The helicopter slowed somewhat, now less than a mile away. Bonnie hunkered low. Would she be more valuable here as a lookout, or might it be better to join the others?

Sapphira extended a hand. A small fireball sizzled in her palm. "I came in the dragons' place. I won't be an obvious target like they would, and they don't know what I'm capable of doing."

Billy raised Excalibur. "Any idea if that bird has organic components?"

Walter's eyes widened. "Cool! Excalibur's back!"

"Yeah. Long story. And I don't know the half of it."

"Whatever. We can sure use it." Walter gave the helicopter another look. "The military knows what Excalibur can do.

They probably protected all their equipment and the uniforms, but it won't hurt to send them a laser love letter to light their fire."

Ashley stared at the oncoming chopper. "I'm reading thoughts. Two crew members. They sound inexperienced. They plan to fly close to indentify targets and then destroy anything they believe to be the enemy."

The chopper accelerated, now only seconds away. The blades sounded like rapid gunfire.

"Here we go." Billy set his feet. A laser beam emanated from Excalibur's tip and shot into the sky. "Bonnie! Take cover!"

She launched from the pole and flew down to Billy's side. The moment she landed, Billy swiped the beam across the helicopter, now only a hundred feet away. The armor sizzled. Sparks flew, but the chopper continued forward, though much more slowly. It halted and hovered within fifty feet. The nearly invisible blades sent windy pulses that beat against hair and clothes. Inside, the forward pilot wore metallic-looking gloves and a helmet with a dark visor, making him look like a faceless robot. A second pilot sat behind him, visible only when the helicopter turned a bit. He wore the same robotic uniform.

"The pilot radioed a count of the targets," Ashley said as she pulled her denim jacket closed. "They want to kill us all."

"Everyone duck!" Billy waved Excalibur around. "Now!"

Sapphira crouched low. Walter grabbed Ashley, and they dropped to their knees. Bonnie spread her wings over Carl and Catherine. Adam pulled Carly down and hunkered with his arms over her back while Marilyn stooped with the plant tucked under her body.

The beam expanded overhead and created a radiant shield. Bullets fired. Sounding like a thumping buzz, they slammed against the shield and ricocheted off at a hundred angles. A few bounced backwards and clanked against the chopper. It ceased firing and reeled in reverse. When it stopped, it hovered, as if contemplating its next move.

"The pilots are getting ready to fire a missile," Ashley called over the noise, "but they're arguing over the target. I can't figure out what their options are, but they're saying that they know the dragons are around here somewhere. They're the real trophies. We're small potatoes."

Billy kept swirling the beam. "They're probably threatening us to bring the dragons out of hiding."

"Uh-oh," Ashley said. "They're tired of waiting."

The helicopter turned toward the football field. A missile shot out from the underside and blasted toward the stadium. A storage building exploded in a ball of flames. The metal roof flew away in a rapid spin, while strips of aluminum siding peeled out and scattered all around.

"Oh, they're so proud of themselves," Ashley said with a huff. "These guys aren't soldiers. They're show-off punks out for a joy ride."

"Any idea what their next move might be?" Billy asked.

Ashley gulped. "We're the target. Another missile."

The helicopter turned toward them and slowly backed away.

Ashley's eyes narrowed. "Now they're radioing our descriptions. Apparently someone wants to make sure one or more of us doesn't get killed, so they have to get approval to fire."

Billy nudged Walter with a knee. "Get everyone ready to run. I don't want to test this shield against a missile."

Walter shot to his feet. "I have an idea." He whispered to Sapphira. When she nodded, he grasped Billy's wrist. "Turn this bubble off for a split second and give Excalibur to Bonnie. You, Sapphira, and I will run out, and Bonnie'll fire the shield back up."

"What do you have in mind? A distraction?"

"Yep. Your jet is a Lear model thirty-five, right?"

"Yeah. So?"

"Just trust me."

Billy rolled his eyes. "Then it must be dangerous."

"And standing here isn't?"

"Good point." Billy turned toward Bonnie. "Can you take over?"

"Sure." Bonnie lifted away from the Foleys and set her hands next to Billy's. "Ready."

"Okay. Here goes." Billy stilled his arms. The shield vanished. He pushed the hilt into Bonnie's hands and ran with Walter and Sapphira outside the shield's range.

The chopper approached again. Bonnie waved Excalibur above her head. The shield formed in front and spread to each side. Bullets strafed the surface again. The target point shifted, following the shield's expanding edge faster than it could congeal. Bullets zinged past it and ripped into the pavement next to Adam and Carly.

Adam pulled her away and rolled with her on the pavement. The shield grew to block the new attack and coalesced into a full, protective bubble. The strafing ceased, and the chopper backed away again.

Still waving her arms, Bonnie blew out a sigh. "I'm sorry. I'm not as fast at shield making as Billy is."

"Fast enough." Adam sat up with Carly. "No harm done."

"They wanted to keep Sapphira alive," Ashley said. "The pilot's asking for the go-ahead to fire a missile at us now that she's gone, but they're still arguing about one of us, something about telling Bonnie apart from Shiloh."

Bonnie folded in her wings. "It's pretty obvious that I'm not Shiloh."

Ashley huffed. "And it's pretty obvious that these guys are as dumb as dirt."

"That could be good or bad." Bonnie looked around. Billy and Walter leaped into the Learjet. Seconds later, the airstair disappeared, and the door closed. "C'mon, Billy," she whispered. "We need that distraction."

Sapphira halted at the center of the highway and stood facing eastward. Her white hair tied back in a ponytail, she raised her hands high.

The jet taxied to the road, accelerated, and took off westward at a sharp upward angle.

"Missile strike countermanded," Ashley said. "They're going after the jet. They don't want anyone to have an escape aircraft."

The helicopter banked to the side and zoomed away in pursuit.

Bonnie shut off the beam and lowered Excalibur. The shield vanished in a shower of sparks. "Now's our chance! Get under cover!"

Ashley waved an arm. "Everyone follow me!"

"I'll guard your backs!" Bonnie set her feet and lifted Excalibur again. "Go!"

In a mad rush, Ashley guided everyone toward the stadium. Marilyn carried the plant, Catherine pushed Carl in his wheelchair, and Adam and Carly carried the computers.

Bonnie raised a hand to shield her eyes from the crimson sun and searched for the jet and helicopter. The distinctive sounds throttled the air, but neither craft was in sight. Still carrying Excalibur, she flew to the top of the pole and scanned the sky. Two splotches moved north to south far away to the west, maintaining a consistent gap as they drifted.

Bonnie furrowed her brow. The jet had to be faster than that helicopter. Why wouldn't Billy get out of range? It could shoot him down.

She looked at the highway and shouted to Sapphira, "What's the plan?"

"Billy's going to lead the helicopter past me." Sapphira kept her hands lifted. Her palms sizzled with sparks. "I'll try to set it on fire."

"But even Excalibur couldn't penetrate it. How can you?"

"Billy's going to—" She craned her neck. "Look! They're getting closer!"

The jet zoomed by going eastward, a mere twenty feet above ground. The chopper followed at the same altitude, maybe a quarter of a mile behind.

A voice crackled in Bonnie's lapel clip. "Do you have me patched through?"

Bonnie sucked in a breath. Billy!

"Affirmative," Larry said through the clip. "Everyone can hear you."

"Good. Got a status?"

"The pilot is ready to fire an air-to-air missile. I advise evasive maneuvers."

"No kidding."

Now far in the distance again, the Learjet banked hard and turned a 180. It lined up with the highway and flew toward Sapphira. The helicopter veered and pursued.

"The pilots are planning to shoot bullets close to Sapphira," Larry said. "They hope the scare will get you to surrender."

Walter's voice came through as if spoken from a tunnel. "Try it, macho man. If you pick on that girl, she'll burn your britches."

"Larry!" Billy shouted. "Do they have a lock on me?"

"Affirmative. The commander called the payload unconventional. He wants the pilot to shoot you down while you are close to the stadium, in order to deliver, as he put it, 'A second dose to the scaly devils.' I assume, therefore, that the missile carries something that is toxic to the dragons."

"Then I'll have to lead them away. I can outrun that hunk of junk."

"Negative. If you evade, the pilot will likely break off pursuit and again attack the stadium directly. You will no longer be a distraction."

"So we'll keep playing cat and mouse." The Learjet ascended and descended in rapid fashion, as if following a hilly course. Not far behind, the helicopter flew in a beeline and slowly closed the gap.

Both engines roared. Chopper blades riddled the air. Bonnie put her fingers in her ears. Billy was taking a terrible risk, but it seemed that he had no choice.

"The pilot is ready to fire," Larry said. "He is astonished that you returned to the stadium and are putting your friends in danger."

"That's because he can't think past his cocky trigger finger." Billy's voice lowered. "Walter, the switch is right there. Get ready."

Just as the Learjet passed Sapphira, the drag chute sprang out. The chute snapped off, flew back, and draped the chopper's windshield. The moment the chopper buzzed over Sapphira's head, she pointed at it and shouted, "Ignite!" The drag chute burst into flames.

The chopper banked hard. The flaming chute flew up into the blades. As it ripped to shreds, the helicopter spun wildly and hurtled toward Sapphira.

She dove for a ditch next to the road. Clutching Excalibur, Bonnie leaped and flew toward her. The helicopter skidded upright along the highway. It then flipped forward, bent the propeller as it cartwheeled, and rolled upright again.

The pilots leaped out, handguns drawn, and stalked toward Sapphira. Bonnie landed between the pilots and Sapphira and summoned Excalibur's beam. She swiped it across the men, but their dark uniforms merely glowed.

One of the men scowled. "I don't care what the boss says. The dragon girl tried to kill us. Let's take her down."

The moment they aimed their guns, Bonnie lunged and sliced the blade across their wrists. Their gun hands dropped to the road. The men crumpled in place, writhing and moaning as they clutched their bleeding stumps.

Bonnie searched the sky. The Learjet zoomed toward her. As it approached at a low altitude, its landing gear descended. The engine coughed and sputtered. Seconds later, the jet dropped and landed hard. The tires popped. Sparks flew. Metallic squeals pierced the air until the jet stopped about a half mile away.

When Billy and Walter jumped out, Bonnie exhaled. Good. They made it. She used the tip of the sword to lift the visors on the chopper pilots' helmets. As with Oscar and the Enforcer, sores covered the skin around their eyes.

"Who sent you here?" Bonnie demanded. "Who is your commanding officer?"

"You gotta be kidding me!" one pilot groaned as he pressed his stub against his chest. "Just kill us and get it over with!"

Lying on his back, the other pilot breathed in heavy gasps. "We get our orders … from Washington. … We don't know his name. … We do what … we're told because … they offered us … a cure for the disease."

"Are any more of you coming?" Bonnie asked.

He closed his eyes tightly and nodded.

"How many?"

"Don't tell her!" the first pilot shouted. "She cut your hand off, you idiot!"

The second pilot turned to his side and curled into a fetal position. "Too many." He then closed his eyes and moved no more.

The first pilot propped himself with his good arm and sneered. "I know who you are, dragon girl! You're the cause of all the curses—the nuke, the fallout, and the disease. My wife is dying because of you and your *merciful* God, and now she'll die alone." He spat at Bonnie's shoes. "Well, curse you, you winged freak. And curse your God, too. If we have to kill a million children to get the job done, we will."

"Get the job done?" Bonnie set the tip of the blade at his throat. "Take one more breath and tell me. Why the children? What have they done that deserves death?"

"We all deserve death." The pilot lunged past the blade and dove for his gun. Just as Bonnie raised the sword to strike, he set the barrel to his own head, his finger on the trigger.

Bonnie averted her eyes. A shot rang out, and a thud followed. She peeked at the two pilots. They lay motionless in pools of blood.

Her feet feeling like dead weights, she hurried to the ditch where Sapphira had leaped. She sat upright at the bottom, shaking her head as if trying to recover from a daze.

Bonnie extended a hand. "Think you can get up?"

"Probably." Sapphira grasped Bonnie's hand and pulled to her feet. "I hit my head but not really that hard, so it shouldn't hurt this much. I think age is catching up with me."

"Well, you still look like a teenager to me." Bonnie brushed off the back of Sapphira's tunic. After living for multiple millennia, maybe the inside of her body really did feel all of those years.

But since she ate fruit from the tree of life, supposedly she couldn't die a natural death. For some people, that might feel like a curse. "Are you all right now?"

"A little better." Sapphira looked up, her eyes not quite as sparkling blue as usual. "I'm going to tell Elam what happened. I'll see you at the stadium." She walked away, a slight limp in her gait.

"I could fly you there."

"I can manage. Thanks anyway." Sapphira continued walking, her head low.

Bonnie kept her stare on the great Oracle of Fire. Something was wrong. Maybe the age issue was real. Who else but Elam could relate to thousands of years of life, much of it locked in solitary confinement under miles of stone.

A moment later, Billy and Walter arrived. "We ran out of fuel." Billy glanced at the dead pilots. "Looks like you got the job done."

"Please don't say it that way." Bonnie pushed Excalibur into his hand. "That wasn't a job I wanted."

He pulled her close and wrapped her in a tight embrace. After a few seconds of silence, he whispered, "You're an amazing woman. Do you know that?"

"Well . . ." She nestled into his chest. Somehow the odor of dirt and sweat brought comfort. It meant he was close. "Keep telling me. After what one of the pilots said, I need a confidence boost."

"Really?" He rubbed her back. "What did he say?"

"They're killing children. Lots of them. And he called it 'getting the job done.'" Bonnie pulled back and looked into his eyes. "I asked him why, but he wouldn't give me an answer that made any sense, just that everyone deserves to die and the curses are all my fault. Then he shot himself."

Walter winced. "That must've been hard to handle."

Billy took Bonnie's hand. "Let's talk on the way to the stadium."

As they walked, Walter piped up again. "I saw the sores on the chopper pilots. They had the disease. Billy told me about it. You know, finding Oscar dead."

Bonnie looked back, but the pilots were too far away now for their sores to be in view. "I'm wondering if Carly has it. Her sores look similar."

"If so," Walter said, "there's probably no cure."

"I think there's a cure. I'll have to watch for a chance to talk to Carly about faith." Bonnie gazed at the city skyline. "I wonder what percentage of the population it's affecting."

"I'll bet the children don't have it," Billy said. "Why else would anyone try to kill them? If the kids had the disease, no one would bother. They'd die anyway."

Bonnie repeated the awful words in her mind. *To get the job done.* "Killing children is a goal. But why?"

Walter shrugged. "Some kind of sick, twisted idea that we're all supposed to die because we're evil? Some kind of retribution madness?"

Billy laid a hand on his stomach. "I sense danger."

"I smell danger." Walter inhaled through his nose. "Garlic. Just like what we smelled when the nuke blew up."

"The missile payload. I'll bet the first missile knocked out the dragons. Otherwise Elam would've sent them to help us."

"And more soldiers are coming," Bonnie said. "Probably a lot. One of the pilots told me."

"No surprise." Billy looked skyward. "Arramos knows where we are now, and he knows where the portal is, so he's bound to send muscle this way."

Walter kicked a pebble. "That was just one helicopter, and now we don't have a jet. Imagine what it will be like if they send an armada."

Billy heaved a sigh. "So we regroup, put our heads together, and figure out how to open the portal."

"That's the big puzzle," Walter said. "We'd be long gone in Second Eden if we could've opened it. We weren't going to wait for you. Sapphira was planning to keep watching through the portal till you got here."

"I don't blame you for that." Billy released Bonnie's hand. "Let's kick it in gear. We have to warn the others."

They accelerated to a jog. While Billy limped, Bonnie stayed close to his side, ready to help if necessary. If he wanted a ride, he would ask. She touched Walter's shoulder. "Did you see that we brought your parents?"

"I did. Thanks." Walter gave her a glance. "I can't remember the date, but Shelly and Mark were supposed to visit. This week, I think. Did they come?"

"Um ..." A vision of Shelly's and Mark's dead bodies invaded, clamping her throat shut. Billy didn't tell him. "I ... ah ..."

Walter stopped. When Billy and Bonnie stopped as well, Walter grasped her elbow. "Just tell me ... Dead or alive?"

"Shelly's dead, Walter." She curled her arm around his. "So is Mark. An Enforcer shot them both. No word on her husband or other son."

His lips tightened. "Okay." He cleared his throat and let out a soft laugh that sounded like a stifled sob. "You know ... I ... well . . . it's not so bad. I mean, it looks like this world is about to blow up, so they'll skip the torture and go straight to Heaven, right?"

"Right." Bonnie tightened her grip on his arm. "Heaven is better than you can imagine. It's perfect."

"I'm sure it is." He pulled away and took off in a trot, calling back, "I'd better talk to my parents."

As they watched Walter rush across the parking lot, Billy took Bonnie's hand and whispered, "Poor Walter. He really got close to Shelly after … you know."

"The incident with Morgan."

"Yeah." Billy used a thumb to brush a tear from each eye. "I wanted to tell him I know how it feels to lose someone you love, but it sounded pretty lame. So …" He shrugged. "You know."

"Not lame. Painful." Bonnie laid a hand over his heart. "You didn't want to reopen your own wounds."

"Yeah. Something like that."

"Billy …" She intertwined their fingers. "I think Matt made it to Abaddon's Lair with Lauren's body. I had another dream like I prayed for. I didn't want to tell you, because I wasn't sure. Actually, I'm still not sure. But now … well … I thought you'd like to know. Maybe it'll help you to share that hope with me."

"We'll hope together." Billy lifted her hand and kissed her fingers. "After all we've been through, I learned one lesson that I'll never forget. There's always a light, no matter how dark it gets."

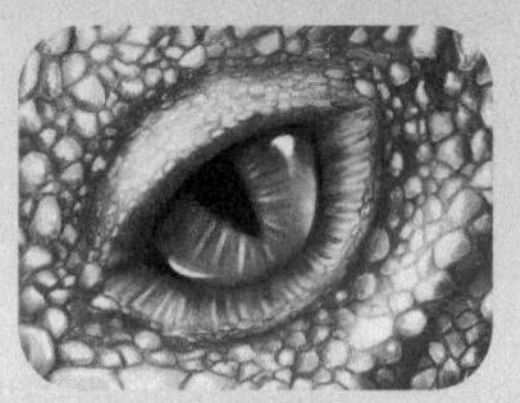

10

CHAPTER

Back from the Dead

Lauren walked in a dense fog. Moonlight cut through the mist just enough to allow slow, cautious steps. A humanlike statue appeared out of nowhere. She stopped and reached to touch its vague, masculine face, but her hand passed through. She blinked. How could that be? A phantom statue?

Memories flowed in—the bloody pool turned clear, Tamiel's emergence from the water, the etched names on the floor, and Sir Barlow's tumble into the sanctum. How had she transported from the realm of the blood pool to this foggy place?

She looked back. A copy of herself lay sleeping on the floor near the glowing yoke. Might she be dreaming?

"You seem perplexed."

Lauren spun. The voice was light and feminine, unexpected from a masculine-looking statue. She set a hand close to its face. "Did you say that?"

A dark-skinned woman stepped out from behind the statue. "I did." Long black hair ran from the top of her girlish head, along her arms, and down to her knees. Wearing a skin-tight body suit that showed off womanly curves, she crossed four arms over her chest, one pair on top of the other. "As I said, you seem perplexed."

Lauren looked at the girl's chest. A shallow hole had been gouged in her sternum, exposed by her V-neck garment. "Are you Jade?"

She nodded.

"I found your gem." Lauren reached into her pants pocket, withdrew the green stone, and extended it.

"You cannot give it to me, because what you hold is not real. You are dreaming, so you and everything on your person is a phantasm." Jade began walking around Lauren, keeping her stare fixed as she orbited. "Yet, since you are a dream oracle, your mind has manifested a body as you walk in a realm of prophetic mystery."

Rotating to watch the strange woman, Lauren slid the gem into her pocket. The slick feel of the stone and the texture of her pants certainly felt real. "So are *you* a phantasm?"

"I am the angel of the sanctum, and I am real. Although my body has perished, I am able to enter this realm in a spiritual state that resembles my former appearance." When she completed the orbit, she returned to the statue and stroked its head as if petting a dog. "This statue is also real. It exists as the only remnant from Abaddon's Lair. It contains a soul that has not yet been resurrected, and with the exception of the souls already growing in Second Eden's garden, it will be the last one to resurrect until you find the life reservoir."

"Whose soul is in there?"

"That mystery remains unsolved." Jade waved a hand toward Lauren's sleeping body. "Your work in this realm has loosed the shackles of the soul who dwells in this stony abode. You have also released the sacrificial energy of many martyrs, and that energy has flowed into the life reservoir."

Lauren pointed at her. "Did you leave those portals in the sanctum open? Is it a puzzle of some sort?"

"I did open the portals, but it is not really a puzzle. You see, a clever villain might be able to solve even the most complex puzzle I could design, so I made it more of a journey that no villain is able to complete." Jade smiled. "And to answer the next question you will want to ask, no, I will not tell you what to do now. Part of the preparation is the act of seeking."

Lauren gave her a tight-lipped nod. "I think I understand."

"Do you?" Jade touched the top of the statue's head with all four hands and ran them down its body on the sides, front, and back. As her hands descended, the statue quivered, and grit fell from the surface. When her hands reached the floor, the statue lifted its legs in turn and stretched out its arms as if testing them. With so much weight on its limbs, every movement seemed to be in slow motion.

Jade stepped between Lauren and the statue and laid two hands on each of them. "I brought the statue here for two reasons. One, to show you, Lauren, the power you have as a dream oracle. You already know that you are able to learn truth from your dreams, but you are also able to communicate with those who are in this realm. Two, to give the resurrected soul instructions regarding a sacred task."

Jade spoke directly to the statue. "You must find Lauren's brother, Matt Bannister, and Listener. I know only that they are in Second Eden, so you will have to search. Let wisdom guide you. I do not yet know what help you will be able to bring, because many decisions are yet to be made that can alter the course of events."

The statue's head melted, sending dense rivulets running down its body. As the melting continued from the shoulders to the arms, mist rose from the hole at the top of the torso and streamed away. Soon, the statue was gone, and the pool of molten liquid on the ground vanished.

Lauren drew her head back. "What happened to him?"

"Him?" Jade lifted her brow. "What makes you think the soul is male?"

"Well, it kind of looked masculine to me. And I was hoping for Eagle to resurrect." Lauren lowered her head. "I guess it might have been wishful thinking."

"Wishful thinking is not always false thinking." Jade again crossed her arms over her chest. "In any case, I truly do not know the soul's identity, only that the person has a good heart. I assume such a person will want to help Matt and Listener."

"Okay. That's good." Lauren rolled her eyes upward. Since this dream might be over soon, she had to get as much information as possible. As she looked again at Jade, she attempted an upbeat expression. "So now my goal is to get out of this realm and go through the third portal. That's the next step, right?"

Jade chuckled. "I admire your ingenuity, but revealing secrets will only slow your journey. The path is before you. Simply follow it." The fog thickened and covered her body. The moonlight dimmed. Seconds later, the mist blew away, and Jade was gone.

A voice trickled into Lauren's ears as if spoken from far away. "Lauren? Is that you?"

She opened her eyes. In the light of the brilliant moon, a girl knelt inches away. Her short dark hair dripped water as she loomed close, her eyes wide and excited.

"It *is* you!" the girl squealed. "I almost didn't recognize you with that white hair. When did you fade it? What did you use? Peroxide? Bleach? And what else?"

Lauren fluttered her eyelids, still lying down and half asleep. "Micaela?"

"Yes, of course." She took Lauren's hand and helped her rise to a sitting position. Wearing a jacket over a volleyball jersey, sweat pants, and gloves, she dripped from every extremity. "Do you have any idea where we are?" She twisted her neck as she looked around. "'Cause I'm lost."

"We're in …" Lauren squinted. "You mean you don't remember how you got here?"

"Not a clue." Micaela pointed at the pool. "I woke up half drowning in that water, so I crawled out and found you here. The last thing I remember was us winning the game that sent us to state. I got in my car to go home, and then—" She clapped her hands. "Swim party!"

Lauren looked at the pool. Could it be the life reservoir? Now that the blood had turned clear, did it resurrect Micaela somehow?

"Look." Micaela pulled at the bottom of her shirt, exposed by her unzipped jacket. "I'm still wearing my uniform, so I haven't changed clothes since the game. But you …" She pinched Lauren's sleeve. "You had time to change, bleach your hair, and take a nap. What's going on? And what happened with that creepy guy who was stalking you at the game? Did you lose him?"

"No. I … I kind of gave him a ride. But it's a long, long story." Lauren climbed to her feet and pulled Micaela up. "Listen. Trust me on this. If I told you the whole story, it would freak you out. Just let me help you get out of here."

"Okay." Micaela set her gloved hands on her hips and glanced from side to side. "But where is here?"

"It's kind of like a … a …" Lauren winced. "An alternate universe?"

Micaela stared wide-eyed for a moment, then laughed. "Good one, Lauren. You had me going there for a minute. You bleached your hair for some kind of sci-fi convention, and you're staying in character, right? What are you, an alien? A goddess?"

Lauren suppressed an exasperated sigh. Maybe going along with Micaela's idea was the best option for now. "Right. That's it. A convention. And I'm what we call an Oracle of Fire." She gestured toward the portal. Beyond it, Sir Barlow still lay on the floor with the cloak underneath him. "We're role playing, and I have to get to that knight, but the door between us is electrified, so I have to come up with a way to get through to rescue him."

"Wow! Cool idea." Micaela stooped in front of the portal and extended a finger. "So does it buzz, or do you just pretend that—"

"Don't touch that!"

The portal zapped. Micaela flew backwards and slid on her bottom several feet. When she stopped, she shook her head hard. "Wow! What a jolt! This is some serious game you're into."

"Yeah." Lauren helped Micaela up. "Now you see why I haven't figured out how to get through."

Micaela looked at her glove's fingertip, torn and smoking. "Well, in role-playing games I've been in, you always have to be aware of your character's powers." She touched Lauren's hair. "So you said you're a … an oracle of some kind?"

"An Oracle of Fire."

"So what are your powers? Besides glowing in the dark, I mean." Micaela scanned Lauren's body. "Obviously you can still do that."

"Well, I have super hearing, but you knew about that, too." Lauren extended a hand, palm up. "And supposedly an Oracle of Fire can create—

A flaming ball blossomed on her palm. Lauren gasped and shook her hand. The ball dropped to the glassy floor and dwindled until it disappeared.

Micaela backed away. “Lauren …” She stretched out the name. “What’s going on here?”

“I … I don’t know.” Lauren brought her hand close and stared at her palm. The cloak catching fire was crazy enough, but this? Insane. What did it all mean?

She extended her hand again and whispered, “Give me light.” A new fireball sprouted in her palm. She extended her other hand and raised her voice. “Give me light.” A second fireball grew in that hand. Now she held flaming spheres the size of baseballs. Heat washed over her fingers and wrists, uncomfortable but tolerable.

Micaela trembled. “Lauren … um … is this some kind of magic trick?”

“Don’t worry. It’s all right.” She raised her hands high and walked to a spot a foot or so in front of the portal. “Get close to me, and we’ll get out of here.”

Micaela stayed put. “You’re kidding, right?”

“No. This is serious. Get over here.”

Micaela scooted next to Lauren, her arms pressed to her sides. “Okay. What now?”

“Let me think.” Lauren closed her eyes. While at the prison, Mom told stories about how Sapphira created a flaming curtain that protected her and everyone nearby from a portal’s jolt. After seeing something similar when Sapphira moved a portal, maybe she could do it herself.

Lauren waved her arms in circles above her head, releasing the flaming balls and stirring them in midair. The flames swelled into fiery cyclones that combined and expanded downward like a spinning curtain around their heads.

Soon, the swirling flames descended to their feet and crackled all around. Air blew with the swirls and rippled through their clothes, hot but not quite scalding.

Micaela hunched her shoulders and shook. "Well ..." She laughed nervously. "This is one way to get dry."

"Now that the fire is protecting us, we should be able to jump through the portal."

"Should?" Micaela shook harder. "Is this your first time trying this?"

"There's a first time for everything." Lauren nodded at the yoke. "Carry that for me."

"The glowing blue thing?"

"Right."

"Whatever you say, boss." Micaela picked it up and pressed it close to her chest. "What next?"

"This." Keeping one hand up to spin the fire, Lauren grabbed Micaela's arm with the other and leaped.

The flames' crackles spiked for an instant. The moment their feet touched down, their momentum sent them stumbling into the fiery curtain. Scorching heat engulfed Lauren's face. As she batted the flames from her hair and shirt, the curtain collapsed and vanished. Her forehead and cheeks throbbed, hot and stinging.

Micaela dropped the yoke, lifted her shirt's tail, and pressed it against her cheeks. "I think you burned my face off!"

"Let me see." Lauren pulled Micaela's wet shirt down. The central column's pulsing light shone on her reddened cheeks. "Looks like a bad sunburn. I'll bet it hurts."

"Like crazy." Micaela eyed Lauren. "You look kind of roasted yourself."

Lauren dabbed at her cheek with a finger. Heat pulsed painfully. Apparently an Oracle of Fire could be burned by her own flames, or maybe after many years she might develop an immunity. "I'll be all right." She looked at the spot on the wall they had just jumped through. The beam and the portal were gone.

Now only two beams remained, the one leading to the tree room and the other to the yet unexplored world, both white.

"Okay," Micaela said, "what's next in this sicko game?"

"Check on my friend." Lauren knelt at his side and patted his cheek. "Sir Barlow? Can you hear me?" A blister reddened his other cheek, and his beard and hair appeared singed. "Sir Barlow?"

Micaela walked to his other side and knelt. "By the way, I found these near that crazy swimming pool." She extended the computer glasses. "Just like the ones your father wears."

"Right. Thanks." Lauren took the glasses and slid them into her shirt pocket.

"Hey! Look! A sword!" Micaela picked it up and eyed the reflective blade. "Looks authentic."

"It is." Lauren reached across Sir Barlow and grabbed the bottom of Micaela's shirt. "Lean over his face."

"What? Why?"

"Just do it."

When Micaela leaned, Lauren squeezed the shirt and wrung a few drops onto Sir Barlow's eyes, then his swollen cheek and dry lips. She released the shirt and watched for any movement.

His eyelids twitched, and his lips absorbed the drops. After a few seconds, he groaned and turned to his side, but his eyes stayed closed.

Micaela lifted the cloak and pulled it free from under him. "What's this?"

"A protective cloak. It shields you when you go through a portal."

She touched the material to her cheek. "Interesting."

"We'll see if the water helps. He took quite a jolt from that electrical field."

"So the cloak didn't protect him very well." Micaela looked back at the portal, skepticism in her expression. "You sure play some dangerous games."

"This isn't a game, and the cloak slipped off as he went through." Lauren exhaled in a huff. "Okay, Micaela, I have to tell you what's really going on here."

"Good, 'cause I have to admit, your believability is wearing pretty thin right now."

Lauren framed her hands in a sphere. "Look. There are multiple worlds—Earth, Hades, Second Eden, and probably a lot more. The place we're in right now is like a central hub that leads to all of them. We just came out of one, and now I need to get you to a safer world."

"Okay ..." Micaela gave her a condescending smile. "Supposing I believe that, tell me how I got into that world we just came from."

"The volleyball game. You said you remember that. And I texted you while you were going to your car, something like, 'weird stuff happening.'"

"I remember. We called that guy the mutant."

"Right. And you told me to meet you at your car in the usual parking space. But then the mutant texted me and told me he put a bomb in your car. So I tried to text you to warn you about the bomb."

Micaela's mouth dropped open. "Don't start your car," she whispered. "Get out now. I remember."

"Do you remember anything after that?"

"Just a flash of light." Her eyes seemed to drift away with her softening voice. "And then ... and then ... stillness. Peace."

Lauren reached over and took Micaela's hand, still covered by a moist glove. "You died in the explosion." She nodded at the portal. "I think the pool in there is some kind of life reservoir, and it resurrected you."

She drew her hand back and pointed at herself. "Why me?"

"I guess because you're my friend. I saw your face in a foggy stream, so I was thinking about you."

"You can resurrect someone by just thinking about them?" Micaela's skeptical look deepened. "Well, Lauren, this game is getting a little too intense for me. You almost had me convinced with that bomb story, but I'm guessing it was really all a dream, and I told you about it."

"A dream? No. It really hap—"

"Good-bye, Lauren. I'll call your parents and tell them where you are, if I can ever figure out where this place is." Micaela rose, the sword and cloak still in hand. "I'd better take these."

"Micaela!" Lauren shot to her feet. "Those are ours! We need them!"

"I have to get out of here." She draped the cloak over her shoulders. "And I don't want you to hurt yourself … or someone else."

"You don't understand!" Lauren lunged and grabbed the cloak.

Micaela pulled but couldn't free herself. "Lauren, this is for your own—"

"Don't say it!" Lauren retightened her grip on the cloak and peered into Micaela's eyes. Her scales tingling wildly, she probed her friend's mind, but nothing came through. "You're blocking your thoughts."

"Blocking my—" Micaela frowned. "Girl, you really have lost your mind."

"You wouldn't block your thoughts if you didn't know I could read them." Lauren narrowed her eyes. "Who are you really?"

"Like I said. You've lost your mind." Micaela jerked away, this time pulling free. She covered her head with the cloak, ran to the tree-of-life portal, and leaped through in a splash of sparks.

Lauren hustled to the portal. On the other side, Micaela skirted the tree and disappeared beyond it. Lauren lifted her hands and created a new firestorm. She jumped into the tree room, extinguished her flames, and ran around the tree.

She stopped at the opposite portal and looked into Second Eden. Dirty ice covered every inch of the land. A blizzard of sparkling particles fell in swirling sheets and cast a dark shadow over that world. A line of footprints interrupted the filthy expanse and led away from the portal window. A whistle sounded from within the storm, annoying but not too bad.

Lauren bent her knees, ready to jump. In seconds the reality of her resurrection might be proven. Or she might blow away as a fog of twinkling energy.

She leaped and landed with a crunch. Cold air blasted her face. Needlelike ice pricked her skin. The whistle squealed—shrill, painful, mind-numbing—much worse on this side of the portal.

Lowering her head and lifting a shielding arm, she pushed against the wind and followed the footprints. Icy shards fell across her path and masked the prints. Ahead, the trail led into a fog of swirling gray—no sign of Micaela anywhere.

Soon, the footprints vanished, covered by ice. Lauren scanned the path to the rear. Her own footprints were already fading. If she continued following Micaela, the way back might be impossible to find.

She trudged toward the portal, her head splitting from the squeals. Scrambled thoughts tumbled in a vortex—images of Micaela as she left with the cloak and sword. She had two open portals to choose from. Yet, she didn't hesitate. She ran straight to the one that would take her to the tree room, and she chose to dash into an ice storm that covered the world in gray.

With the frenetic noise pounding, Lauren picked up her pace. The real Micaela wouldn't do that. Was she really Tamiel in disguise? Tamiel was the only other person in that world of etched names and crystalline pool, but how could he disguise himself so perfectly—her face, her uniform, her memories, her voice and mannerisms?

And what about the curse? Their hands touched. She grabbed Micaela's arm when they jumped. As the mental images replayed, Micaela's body appeared. She was wearing gloves and a jacket, normal for the cold evening when she died, and perfect for Tamiel's scheme to avoid skin contact. Everything made sense now.

When she reached the portal window, she leaped through, walked straight to the tree of life, and set her hands close to the flames. Warmth bathed her skin. An icy coat melted, and water dripped from her hair, nose, and chin. The whistle eased to a background hum, still annoying, like a teacher scolding from far away.

How stupid she had been! Tamiel had played her like a toy banjo, preying on her hope for a resurrected friend. He, himself, had killed Micaela, and he knew of their friendship, so picking her as a disguise was an easy choice.

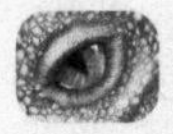

When her clothes had dried somewhat, she hurried back to the sanctum portal, created another fire shield, and passed through. After the flames cleared, she walked with long strides toward the portal they last entered.

Sir Barlow stood there with the yoke on his neck, a hand resting on each side. The steady blue glow washed over his serene face. "Ah! It's you! When I saw the swirl of fire, I thought Sapphira had entered. I didn't realize that you had gained all of her powers."

"Apparently not her wisdom." Lauren stopped and exhaled heavily. "I'm such an idiot!"

"No, lass. Don't say such a thing! You are far wiser than most your age. Trust me on that."

"But you didn't see how Tamiel tricked me. I fell for his disguise." She let out a huff. "I unleashed a demon in Second Eden."

Sir Barlow gave a thoughtful nod. "That is troubling. He'll get into mischief, to be sure."

Heat surged into her cheeks, spiking the pain. "And I couldn't chase him. A strange storm is raging there—dirty ice flying in all directions. It's covering everything, including the birthing garden."

"Ah! Mardon's device, I'll wager. Perhaps Tamiel plans to exploit this storm somehow. Arramos has longed to destroy Second Eden for centuries."

"And now it's happening." Lauren clenched a fist. "It's my fault Tamiel's out there, Sir Barlow. He impersonated a friend of mine, and I didn't figure it out until it was too late." Tears flooded her vision. "I wanted so badly for it to really be Micaela, to believe God raised her from the dead. It would mean … it would mean . . ." She wrapped her arms around Sir Barlow and sobbed into his chest.

"It would mean that the people you care about really do rise from the dead." He patted her gently on the back. "Besides Micaela, whose resurrection are you yearning to see?"

She spoke into his cool, damp tunic, muffling her words. "My foster parents … and Darcy … and me, I guess. I was able to go to Second Eden, so I might be resurrected already. I'm not sure. It's all so confusing."

"Well, my dear, I think once we get to Heaven, we will have a splendid reunion, complete with all manner of holy revelry." He took in a deep breath. "Considering the circumstances, I think it is reasonable to take some time to tell a story. That is, if you're willing."

"Definitely. I need to settle my nerves." Lauren raised a new fireball in her hand. "And we both need to dry off."

"Very well. And this story is relevant, because I yearn to see my own parents." Pulling Lauren, he lowered himself to a sitting position on the floor. Once they sat comfortably side by side, he set the yoke over her neck as well. "I found it warm and soothing, but if you don't like it, please say so."

Heat radiated down Lauren's spine and out to her feet. After the cold journey through the ice storm, it definitely felt good. "It's wonderful, Sir Barlow. Thank you."

"You are quite welcome." He folded his hands in his lap while Lauren used the fireball to radiate drying heat across their hair and clothes. "My father was a fine gentleman who died when I was fourteen, and my mother passed the very next day. Heartbroken, she was, she loved him so. I am pleased to say that a cross word never passed between them, though they cast quite a number my way. Deservedly so, I assure you. I was a wretched lad."

"You don't have to tell me about that, Sir Barlow. Lots of people were rebellious at that age. They grew out of it."

"Ah, but I do need to tell you so you'll understand why I commiserate with your heavenly hope. You see, my father died because I cursed at him while he was carrying an exceedingly heavy load of logs. I was embittered that it would be my duty to split all the logs, and he had decided to give me more work than I cared to undertake.

"Well, my curse startled him. He stumbled, fell, and rolled down a hill. The logs rolled after him and pummeled him one by one. His crushed body was a heartbreaking sight, exceeded only by my mother's face as she watched it happen." Sir Barlow's eyes took on a faraway look. "Grief, disappointment, shame, horror. All expressed on my mother's anguished face. And it was my fault. Every emotion that ripped her heart in half was my fault."

"So what did you do?"

Anger flitted across his face. "The same thing any little beast would do. I ran away and hid in the woods for two days until the constable found me and told me about my mother's death."

Lauren touched his arm with her free hand. "Oh, Sir Barlow, that must have been awful."

He offered a sad sort of smile. "It was, to be sure, but the shock set me on a better course. I enlisted as a soldier and learned the ways of a gentleman. When I became of age, I inherited my father's manor. I did, as you say, grow out of my wretched phase, yet, the image of my mother's face haunted me night after night. I would often wake up in a cold sweat, and the only way I could go back to sleep was to utter a certain prayer."

Closing his eyes, he tilted his head upward. "God in Heaven, forgive me of all my horrible sins, and please tell my folks about how I have changed." He opened his eyes and looked at her. "It took me years to stop kicking my own backside, and I still long for that great reunion day when I will see my mother's face once again, a happy face, a proud and pleased face. And I want to ..." A tear dripped to his cheek. "To hug my father ... and beg for his forgiveness. He was a good man. I should have treated him like one."

Lauren leaned her head against his shoulder. "I'm sorry, Sir Barlow."

"As am I, Miss." He heaved a deep sigh. "As am I."

After sitting silently with him for a moment, she touched her shirt. It seemed dry enough. She extinguished the fireball and slid a hand over Sir Barlow's. This gallant knight had opened an old wound to teach a valuable lesson. "Thank you for the story. I'll stop kicking myself for getting fooled by Tamiel."

"Of course you will. Like I said, you are wise beyond your years."

Lauren looked at the final portal. A white beam from the central column painted a ragged hole that expanded and contracted with the beam's pulses. The white likely meant that they didn't need the yoke to allow passage. "Are you ready to go?"

"I am." Sir Barlow lifted the yoke and rose. "Though my old bones are creaking a bit."

Taking his hand, Lauren climbed to her feet. "We won't have a weapon this time, so we'll have to be more careful than ever."

"If you have Sapphira's powers, then you *are* a weapon." Sir Barlow balled a fist and punched the air. "And I'm not bad in a fight, as long as my opponent isn't stronger than the average ox … or lobster."

Lauren laughed. "Let's hope we don't run into any more seafood." They walked together to the portal. "Ready for a little heat?"

He straightened his tunic and tucked the yoke under an arm. "I am with you every step of the way, no matter what."

"Then let's go." She lifted her hands and, as before, created a flaming shield that swirled around with a crackling wind. When the bottom edge reached the floor, she shouted, "Jump!"

They leaped through the last portal. Lauren touched down on something hard. Her feet slipped and shot forward, but Sir Barlow caught her and set her upright.

She breathed a quiet, "Thanks."

A cold breeze cut through her clothes and raised a chill. Blackness dominated the landscape in every direction, including to the rear. The portal window should have provided a view of the central column and its pulsing light, but even it was invisible.

Lauren tested her traction on the floor. Her bare foot slid easily over the icy surface. Since the soles of her feet were practically immune to extreme temperatures, the cold wouldn't harm her skin, but it might get uncomfortable after a while.

Sir Barlow whispered, "Well, Miss, it seems that we have entered a cold world this time. In my experience, enemies rarely strike when the temperature is this low."

"That's some comfort." She shivered. "It's strange. My fire shield snuffed out immediately. I didn't do anything to extinguish it."

"Perhaps the breeze blew it out. You could test it. We do need light."

Lauren raised a hand and stared at the spot where it had to be. "Give me light!"

Darkness prevailed. Not even a spark ignited.

"Give me light!" Lauren squinted. Still nothing. "What could be wrong? Is it too cold?"

"I have no idea, Miss. I have lit many a campfire on bitterly cold days, so I think temperature is not a factor."

"Well, we can't explore this place in the dark. Who knows what we might run into?"

"Indeed. If this realm is similar to the other two, there is likely a pool of some kind out there, and, as I said before, I don't relish the thought of falling into one for the third time."

"I can't blame you for that."

"And since you are unable to create fire, we cannot safely return to the sanctum."

"So we're stuck."

"It seems so." Sir Barlow let out a grunting sound.

"What are you doing?" Lauren asked.

"I am sitting down and putting the yoke back on. I suggest that we wait here for the time being. If you will join me, I am sure you will be more comfortable. Perhaps it is merely nighttime in a world without moon or stars. Dawn will come soon. The landscape will brighten, and we will see the new quest that lies before us."

"That sounds like a good idea." His strong hands guided her down to a cross-legged sitting position. The floor radiated cold through her pants, but when he placed the yoke over her neck, heat surged through her body and warmed every inch of skin.

"While we are settling, perhaps we can share stories. I have told you some of my history, a darker portion of my life, to be sure, but it's not all so gloomy. And I would love to hear more of the life story of one of the bravest lasses I have ever met. I trust that it will be fascinating."

She let out a soft laugh. "Not as fascinating as yours, I'm sure. You were alive in King Arthur's time. I can't match that."

"Perhaps not, but I still want to hear your story. Start with your earliest memory. Then whenever your voice tires, I will interject with a story of my own."

"My earliest memory?" Lauren took a deep breath. "All right. Here goes."

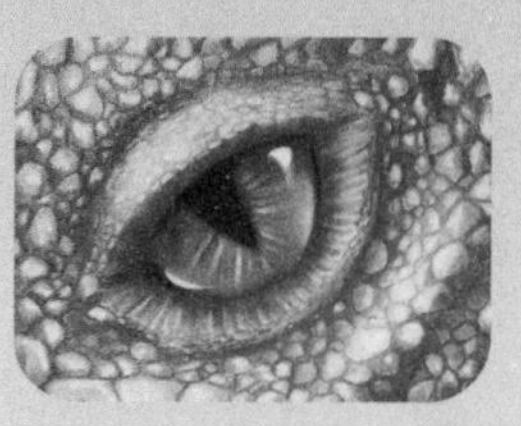

11

CHAPTER

First Strike

Beating wings sounded from above. Bonnie looked up. Gabriel appeared in the sky, flying from the direction of the stadium. Seconds later, he landed and walked alongside Billy and Bonnie with a powerful stride. Although he had to be more than eighty years old, he looked to be in his forties. "I've been doing some recon. No other aircraft around."

Bonnie gave him a brief hug. "How are the dragons?"

"Weak as kittens." Gabriel folded in his wings. "A missile blasted one of the buildings, and it spewed something that knocked them for a loop."

Billy propped Excalibur on his shoulder. "Smart strategy. Weaken the opponent's most powerful weapons, bring in reinforcements, and attack."

"Any news on the portal?" Bonnie asked. "If we could open it, it wouldn't matter what Arramos's army does."

Gabriel kept his gaze straight ahead. "Sapphira senses that it's still there, but it's locked tight. We heard from Marilyn that

Mardon knows why, so Sapphira will confront him when everyone gets together. She says she's known him for a long time and can tell when he's lying."

"Thanks for the update," Billy said, "but you don't have to hang with us. My broken toes won't let me go much faster."

"I could carry you, give you the aerial view. It's not far. I can carry even a big lug like you that distance."

Billy smiled and waved a hand. "No need. Like you said, it's not far."

"All right. I'll see you there." Gabriel flapped his wings and took off.

After he flew out of earshot, Bonnie looked at Billy. "Why didn't you want a ride?"

"This way I get more alone time with you."

"I'm all for that, but is there something you want to talk about?"

"Nothing concrete. Your dream got me thinking." He met her gaze. "Suppose Matt made it to Abaddon's Lair and resurrected Lauren. That means they're probably with Listener by now, and they're working on finding that device Semiramis planted."

"Maybe. Is something wrong with that?"

"Only that I'm worried about Listener. When she was little, we were like this." Billy crossed his fingers and showed them to Bonnie. "I mean, really close. But when I last saw her at the chasm, she acted … well … aloof. Almost like we were strangers. I was hoping we would pick up where we left off."

"That was when her companion was ailing because of the corruption here. She was out of sorts."

"True, but is that enough of a reason for her behavior? Aloof is one thing, but you told me she killed a man who might have been surrendering."

Bonnie sighed. "I know. She claimed that he pointed the gun at her, but it didn't look that way to me."

"So that's been bugging me. If losing a companion can cause such a change, what does it mean? Is her heart really as pure as it ought to be?"

"That's worth being concerned about." Bonnie slid her hand around his arm. "I assume you noticed how Matt looked at her."

"I noticed." He smiled. "That's why I brought it up. Just trying to be a dad to a teenager I barely know."

"A teenager who has a good head on his shoulders. If he can work out his animosity toward Darcy, he'll be fine. I think that's his only roadblock to faith."

"Let's hope so. I can't help but be concerned."

"Of course you can't." Bonnie patted him on the chest. "You're a good father, Billy Bannister."

They walked on in silence. After another minute, they arrived at the stadium and followed a concrete path under the bleachers to a gate that opened to the playing field. Near the opposite sideline Elam and Sapphira spoke privately in a huddle while everyone else milled about closer to the center. Marilyn embraced the pot in both arms, Catherine and Walter stood behind Carl as he sat in his wheelchair, Carly and Adam tinkered with the computers' brain units, and Gabriel stood over Thomas and Mariel who sat in the shade of his outstretched wings.

Several yards from the humans, Thigocia lay over Makaidos with her wings spread while Roxil blew a weak stream of fire over her scales. Apparently the healer was the first to recover from the potion's effects, and she was working on restoring the other two. Ashley sat in the midst of them and stroked Makaidos's head as if petting a cat.

Bonnie smiled. It would probably seem strange to most humans to see a woman doting on three dragons, but this woman happened to be a daughter to two of these dragons and a sister to a third. To anthrozils, such a scene was normal.

Closer to the end zone, Mardon sat alone, as if ostracized for bad behavior. Who would want a conniving ghost hanging around to listen to secret plans?

Once on the field, Billy and Bonnie walked along a faded white stripe that led past the numeral 50. Jagged-blade weeds and crabgrass dominated the greenery, a disguise that had made the lawn look healthy from far away.

When Sapphira noticed their arrival, she marched to the center of the field over a bluish logo of a rearing horse and stopped near its nose. She rotated her body slowly, her hands open, palms up. "The portal is still here, but the sensation is weak. I'm wondering if my power is diminishing with age."

"You're probably just tired," Bonnie said. "Nothing to worry about."

Mardon walked toward her, a boyish smile on his face. "You still look young and beautiful, in spite of your thousands of years of life."

Sapphira glared at him but offered no reply.

"I remember," he continued as he drew closer, "when I put your tiny body, barely more than an embryo, into the soil. Even then your beauty was—"

"Stop it, Mardon." Sapphira glared at him. "I can tell when you've rehearsed a speech. What do you want?"

Mardon wrung his hands. "I want to help you open the portal."

He reached for her, but she leaned back. "Don't touch me."

Elam stepped between them. "What is all this drivel leading up to?"

"You need not fear. I cannot touch her. Yet, I can feel her energy field if you allow me to get close enough."

Elam held his ground. "Why would that help?"

"The device my mother planted in Second Eden closed the portal by raining ice and employing a magnetic disruption in the atmosphere. I created the device against my will, knowing that I could eventually repair the damage as I am trying to do now. You see, the disruption keeps Sapphira from opening the portal, and the ice doused the fire, which would have stabilized the immediate area, including the portal, and allowed her to open it." Mardon leaned to the side and addressed Sapphira. "I can teach you how to maneuver the magnetic field to overcome the disruption and the lack of fire."

Sapphira set a fist on her hip. "Once you teach me to open the portal, you'll lose your leverage. You'll become physical again, and we could leave you behind." Her eyes sparkled, more vivid than earlier. "What else do you have up your sleeve to make sure we'll bring you along?"

Mardon pulled on his shirt to straighten it, though it wasn't wrinkled. "I should have known not to underestimate your intelligence."

"And you should know better than to try to flatter me." Tiny flames sprouted in Sapphira's hair. "Just tell me your plan."

"Very well." Mardon folded his hands at his waist. "First, do you know which kind of portal this is? Is it a walk-through portal?"

"Yes. Walk-through and materialization, though protection is needed for either option." Sapphira turned to the others. "With some portals, I surround people with fire, then we dissolve and rematerialize somewhere else. With some, we walk through. With a few, I grab the energy within the portal and pull, like I'm pulling a rope, but I haven't seen one of those since my time in Hades. Most portals need some kind of protection to pass through, though there have been a few exceptions."

Mardon rubbed his hands together. "A walk-through portal is perfect for my technique. Once you use it, the portal will not open for physical passage, because the disruption will continue to be in effect until a fire is restored on the other side. Yet, the opening will be enough for a nonphysical entity such as myself to pass through. According to my theory, I will regain a body in Second Eden, as I always had while there. I will rebuild the fire for you, and you will be able to fully open the portal for physical passage."

Elam crossed his arms. "Assuming you do start the fire, then you would run away like a dog with its tail between its legs to keep us from throwing you back through the portal."

Mardon wrung his hands again. "Your illustration is unsavory, but the essence of your conclusion is accurate. I will, indeed, take advantage of my leverage and leave for the time being. Yet, rest assured that I will rebuild the fire first. I want Clefspeare to be restored so that he can kill Arramos, and I realize that Second Eden will be an uninhabitable wasteland without you and your company there to restore it."

"It's for the best," Sapphira said. "We'll let him go to Second Eden. At least he won't be able to get into any more mischief here."

"Speaking of mischief." Ashley strode from the dragons' resting area. "Trusting the guy who built the device that's keeping us in Arramos's crosshairs doesn't sound like a good idea to me."

Walter joined them. "Right. If not for Mardon, we'd be dancing in daisies by now."

"Trust me or don't trust me," Mardon said, "but as it stands, you have a closed portal. Feel free to wait for the reinforcements to arrive. They can't hurt me."

Elam moved out of the way. "It feels like trusting the devil himself, but we don't have much of a choice. Let's get started."

Mardon took a hesitant step toward Sapphira, a hand raised. As his fingers drew nearer, he closed his eyes. "The energy field around you is orbiting from your right to your left, and it is concentrated in a dense ring around your waist. In order to counter the magnetism that is blocking the portal, you will have to raise the field to head level so that you can perceive it with your mind. Only then will you be able to manipulate it in a way that affects the magnetic orientation beyond the portal."

"How do I raise it?" Sapphira asked.

Mardon opened his eyes and set his hands around her waist, as if ready to lift her, though his immaterial fingers merely floated inches away. "Put your hands where mine are, your palms open and against your body. Summon fire and run your hands up your sides as if you were trying to slide an invisible film that is clinging tightly to your frame." He took a step back. "Try it now."

Sapphira pressed her palms against her waist. As flames shot out from the edges of her hands, she slid them upward across her battle tunic. If not for the flame-retardant material, the tunic would probably have ignited. "Like this?"

"Yes. Yes. The energy field is already redistributing." Mardon lifted his hands as if helping Sapphira with the effort. "Repeat the motion until I tell you to stop."

While Sapphira continued massaging her sides in an upward motion, Ashley kept her eyes trained on Mardon, her brow deeply furrowed. Bonnie slid close to Ashley and whispered, "Are you trying to read his mind?"

Without shifting her stare, she nodded. "I'm not getting anything. His ghost status might make it harder, or his powerful intellect might be blocking me. I'll keep trying."

"Is his idea reasonable?"

"Definitely. I've studied the spectral trails of portal passages in depth. Nonphysical transport to another realm is possible. Walter and I proved it in the Circles of Seven."

Bonnie nodded. "So that gives more evidence that Mardon might be telling the truth. Sapphira can open the portal this way."

Ashley shifted her stare to Bonnie. "Open it? Most likely. But going through it might be dangerous."

"Will Mardon feel a jolt?"

"I'm not sure, but I think he's willing to risk it." Ashley crossed her arms. "It's no use. I can't read his mind, but maybe Thomas can sense something."

"On my way." Bonnie walked to Thomas and Mariel and crouched in front of them, both still shaded by Gabriel's wings. Thomas stared toward Mardon, his eyes completely white and unblinking. "Thomas," Bonnie whispered. "It's me, Bonnie. Can you sense if Mardon is telling the truth?"

Thomas's eyelids twitched. "He believes in his theory, so he is not lying. He desperately wants to get to Second Eden, so we can rely on his passion. But can we trust him to rebuild the fire?" He shrugged. "The motivation he provided is suspect. Once he is in Second Eden, why should he care about what will happen to Arramos?"

Mariel's red eyes flashed. "You're just parroting what I whispered to you a few seconds ago."

Thomas jabbed a finger at Mariel. "I was thinking it before you said it. But to prove my worth, I will add counsel." He reached up toward Bonnie. When she grasped his hand, he whispered, "Mardon's words are drenched with lovesick sentiment. He loves being with Sapphira. He sees her as his greatest achievement, the crown jewel of his scientific prowess. When he is near her, he feels a sense of accomplishment. His failure to draw Earth and Heaven together fades. The pain of his disfigurement vanishes.

I think we can trust him to do what is necessary to bring Sapphira to Second Eden. Let him go without hesitation."

"I understand," Bonnie said, "but should we tell Sapphira what you told me?"

"There is no need. She already knows. I sense that she has compassion for Mardon as a daughter has for an errant father. She is wise. We should trust her to sort out her feelings."

Bonnie patted his hand. "Thank you for your insight."

"You are quite welcome." Thomas nudged Mariel with an elbow. "See? I'm more than a parrot."

Mariel frowned. "You certainly squawk more than a parrot."

When Bonnie turned to leave, an engine hummed somewhere. She looked up, as did nearly everyone else, but nothing appeared in the sky.

"No!" Mardon snapped at Sapphira. "Keep concentrating. You're almost ready!"

"Does anyone see a jet?" Elam asked as he pivoted, his gaze upward.

"Nothing." Billy set a hand on his stomach, the other hand still holding Excalibur. "I don't sense danger. Maybe it's just a passing plane."

"With a transportation lockdown going on? I doubt it." Elam looked toward the resting dragons. "Do any of you sense danger?"

Makaidos rose to his haunches, Thigocia now at his side. "I sense background danger. It does not feel imminent."

Gabriel beat his wings and launched straight up. After ascending about a hundred feet, he flew in a slow orbit and called out, "I hear an engine to the east, but it's getting cloudy in that direction. Can't see anything."

At the middle of the field, Sapphira continued sliding her hands upward against her body. Fire splashed from her palms.

It seemed that she was stripping flaming layers from her slender frame and throwing them into the sky. An aura emanated from her hair, as if the whiteness in her locks were spreading out in an alabaster glow.

"That's it!" Mardon shouted. "The energy field is swirling around your head now. Do you sense it?"

Sapphira's eyes widened. "Yes! I see a wall of rock with a painted compass design." She blinked rapidly. "I see … I see sparkling ash swirling within a walled-in shelter."

"That's my ice storm." Mardon lifted his hands. "Now use your arms to spin the energy in the opposite direction, from your left to your right. Use the same motion you use when you spin fire to create a portal."

Sapphira raised her arms and stirred the air. The surrounding aura expanded into a flat, vertical ellipse about four feet across and six feet high. The whiteness faded to transparency. Sparks flew from the edges in a rhythmic pulse.

Bonnie took a step closer. Beyond Sapphira, dirty ice whirled in a frenzy, visible only within the aura. A red compass appeared on a far wall, similar to the one on the floor in Sir Patrick's mansion, though with far less detail.

"You've done it!" Mardon edged closer to the portal. "A superb effort!"

"I see an aircraft!" Gabriel shouted from high above. "It just appeared from behind a cloud to the east."

"A fighter?" Elam asked.

"Bigger. A transport of some kind. Four propellers. Maybe an A-Four-hundred. It looks like it's descending toward us. And now I see two more behind it."

"Likely military transports," Mardon said, once again wringing his hands. "Soon hundreds of soldiers will arrive with machine guns and heavy armor. I hope I have time to build the fire to allow for transport for the rest of you."

Gabriel flew down to ground level, breathless. "It's landing on the highway next to the field. Definitely military. The rear compartment could easily carry fifty troops." He took off toward the parking lot and called back, "I'll spy on them from the top of the bleachers."

Makaidos extended his wings. "Weak or not, we have to force ourselves to be ready."

Thigocia snorted twin flaming streams. "The three of us should be able to keep them at bay until Mardon builds a fire."

Roxil raised her head and nodded in agreement. Her flattened ears made her look angry, or perhaps tired.

"Then I will go now." Mardon turned toward the portal and leaped through the aura to Sapphira's left. The barrier sizzled for a moment before settling.

On the Second Eden side, Mardon tumbled to a floor of dark ice. He rose and brushed dirty crystals from his clothes, proving that he had transformed to a physical body. He looked back into the Earth realm. His lips moved but no words came through.

Ashley leaned close to the portal. "I can't hear him, but I can read his thoughts now. He says there is wood, though much of it is cold and damp."

Mardon's lips continued moving while Ashley provided the audio. "A few embers have survived the storm, so I will try to revive them. Although I see Earth, the view is extremely blurry, so I will not be able to tell how you are faring against Arramos's forces. In order to keep them from seeing through the portal, you might want to close it for now and reopen after I have had time to build the fire." He disappeared from view.

Elam waved a hand at Sapphira. "Let's shut it down."

"Will do." Sapphira lowered her arms. The aura contracted around her as if her body absorbed the whiteness.

Gabriel flew back from the bleachers and landed next to Elam. "Only about ten troops were on the plane, and they're carrying automatic weapons. One had an antitank gun, the shoulder-mounted kind. Four more planes and at least three helicopters are on the way, and a red dragon is flying with them. Arramos, I assume. It looks like the first ten troops are waiting for the others to arrive."

Elam heaved a sigh. "An entire legion to battle a few dragons and several outnumbered humans."

"Arramos is taking no chances. My guess is he's staying back until he gets word that the air is clear, because the anti-dragon potion affects him, too." Gabriel looked toward the parking lot again, skepticism in his eyes. "They're an undisciplined crew, probably hastily trained."

Elam looked at Adam and Carly as they knelt on the grass, still working on the computers. "Any chatter on the airwaves?" Elam asked.

Carly shook her head. "Nothing. It's as quiet as a graveyard."

"Same with Larry." Adam touched his lapel clip. "But he'll let us know if the chatter picks up again."

Billy clasped Walter's shoulder. "Walter, Gabriel, Elam. Are you ready to go into guerilla mode?"

"You bet," Walter said.

The other two men nodded.

"And me." Adam rose to his feet. "Just tell me what to do."

"We need a spy." Billy winked. "You have experience."

"I can't deny it." Adam nodded. "Go on."

"We'll strike immediately. With so many troops coming, they won't expect it, especially since they probably think our dragons are still too weak to fight. Once we take the soldiers out, you'll put on one of their uniforms, pose as the only survivor when the others show up, and infiltrate. If they're as untrained as Gabriel thinks, we should be able to pull it off."

"Makaidos," Elam said, "will you join us in a raid? The three of you should be able to take out ten of their thugs."

"With pleasure." Makaidos snorted a weak spray of sparks. "Say the word."

"The word is given. Fly ahead of us. If the soldiers begin shooting, then you have permission to strike with deadly force. We'll be right behind you. And don't forget that they might have candlestone bullets. Even Thigocia isn't immune to penetration, and they might also have the weakening potion."

Billy grasped Walter's arm. "Go on ahead. I can't keep up, so don't slow down for me."

"We'll wait for you before the final attack. First we'll check out their positions and make our plans." Walter took off toward the bleachers in a quick trot, followed by Elam and Adam. Makaidos, Thigocia, and Roxil vaulted into the air. Their wing beats sent buffeting breezes in their wakes.

Billy handed Excalibur to Bonnie. "They probably have uniforms to protect them from Excalibur, so you take it." He kissed her tenderly. "I love you. I'll see you in one world or the other."

"I love you, too." Bonnie grasped his hand. As he pulled away, her fingers caressed his until they broke contact. He turned and jogged with a heavy limp, his fists tight.

Bonnie turned toward the portal. Ashley stood near Sapphira, her arms again crossed. "Isn't it strange that Arramos is coming? We thought he was rounding up children as a way to bring God's wrath, but now he's coming here to battle a hopelessly outnumbered little band."

"The portal," Bonnie said. "He wants to get his forces into Second Eden."

"But why is that important to him?"

Bonnie gestured toward the pot in Marilyn's grasp. "I'm not sure if he knows Clefspeare is just a plant right now, but he might suspect that we have a plan to regenerate him, so Second Eden is his only real vulnerability."

Ashley looked at the plant with a skeptical frown. "I know Clefspeare is the only dragon powerful enough to defeat Arramos in single combat, but it took only an airborne potion to neutralize three dragons who could defeat him if they battled together. Since Arramos has anti-dragon firepower, what is he worried about?"

"The unknown. Secrets he can't control. Second Eden is a world of resurrection power, and Arramos doesn't know what it might generate. Destroy Second Eden, and he can't lose."

Ashley's brow slackened. "True, but he has to know that we'd die before opening the portal for him. He's too smart to come here without extra leverage. There's more to his plan than meets the eye. Remember, we're matching wits with the craftiest being on the planet."

"Well, you keep chewing on it. I'm going to watch Billy and the others, but I'll stay in sight. Shout if you need me."

With Excalibur gripped in both hands, Bonnie took wing, flew to the bleachers, and landed on the top row where a shoulder-high chain-link fence allowed a view of the parking lot and highway. The three dragons were nowhere in sight, maybe on the ground planning an angle of attack.

The ten soldiers stood near the airplane, now on the parking lot. Wearing helmets that masked their faces, they shifted nervously as they watched the sky, weapons at the ready. One held a missile launcher on his shoulder, and a soldier next to him crouched near a bag, perhaps filled with the launcher's ammunition.

To the east, the other aircraft flew at a low altitude. Still pretty far away, their engines droned at a low pitch. They seemed to be traveling at a slow speed, but they would probably arrive in a few minutes. Surely they would see the coming battle, and if so, Adam wouldn't be able to pull off the planned charade. Maybe a distraction would turn the eyes of the enemy away.

Bonnie raised Excalibur and summoned the beam. It shot straight into the cloudy red sky. Aiming carefully, she angled the beam and ran it across the closest airplane. Sparks flew. The plane wobbled in flight, though it seemed that no damage resulted. She whipped the beam from one aircraft to another and back again. Each plane and helicopter glowed with sparks, but they flew on, apparently unaffected. Still, the sparks had to be creating a distraction.

She kept waving the beam back and forth as she whispered, "Keep looking at me."

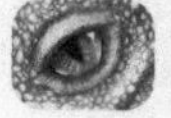

At the parking lot, Walter, Elam, and Adam ran onto the pavement at the near side, Billy trailing by a few steps. The soldiers aimed rifles and fired. Billy and the others dove low and rolled. The dragons appeared out of nowhere and swooped toward the soldiers. The soldiers shifted their aim to the sky. While bullets pinged off the dragons' scales, Billy and company stayed low and watched.

One man readied the missile launcher while another helped him load it. The dragons blew balls of fire. The first ball blasted the missile carrier, the second flattened the ammo man. The third bowled into the legs of several soldiers. When the flames struck, their uniforms and helmets glowed red, but most of the soldiers stayed upright and continued firing. The dragons swerved in midair, slashed their tails into the attackers, and sent them tumbling across the pavement.

Walter, Elam, Adam, and Billy leaped to their feet and ran into the sea of writhing bodies. They snatched the weapons away, tore the soldiers' helmets off, and smacked their heads with the butts of rifles. When they all lay unconscious or dead, Walter grabbed a soldier by the ankle and, with help from Billy, Elam, and Adam, dragged him toward the bleachers until they were out of sight.

The three dragons flew toward the football field again. Bonnie swiveled in place and watched their smooth flight. Apparently the soldiers had not been equipped with candlestone bullets or a weakening potion. Maybe Arramos's forces had finally run out of their supply. Yet, the fireproof uniforms proved that they had come prepared to battle dragons.

The buzz of engines grew louder. To the east, four planes lined up to land on the highway, and three helicopters led the parade. At ground level, a uniformed man belly crawled across the parking lot to the airplane that had carried the first ten soldiers.

Bonnie shut off the beam. That man had to be Adam, though with a dark helmet on, no one could see his face. Soon everyone would learn if the distraction worked.

Like alighting dragonflies, the trio of helicopters settled onto the parking lot, their blades sending gusts across Adam's body. His uniform rippled as he crawled closer to the airplane's open passenger door. Noise from engines and propellers created an ear-splitting din.

Just as Adam reached the door, a soldier leaped out of a helicopter and ran toward him. With a burst of energy, Adam climbed into the plane's passenger compartment and disappeared in the dimness. The pursuing soldier stopped at the door and shouted something into the void. He then nodded and walked away.

Once the other airplanes landed and taxied to the lot, a hatch door opened at the side of the rear compartment of each one.

Armed soldiers filed out and gathered, maybe forty in all, far fewer than the planes' capacity.

Several seconds later, Arramos landed nearby. His neck swaying, he shifted his head from side to side, perhaps looking for the source of Excalibur's earlier burst of light. Bonnie crouched low and peered through the gaps in the fence.

Ashley bounded up the bleacher steps and stooped next to Bonnie. "I'm getting confused thoughts from our men and the dragons. They are considering striking immediately because of the lower-than-expected number of soldiers. Three dragons could probably win a battle easily. The soldiers have been warned to guard their minds, but a few are leaking superficial thoughts. They have a secret defense. No details except that it would be a disaster for us to attack. Thomas verified the warning."

"The soldiers are wearing fireproof uniforms," Bonnie said. "Could that be it?"

Ashley shook her head. "Something more sinister, at least that's what Thomas indicated."

"Where did the dragons go? We have to warn them."

"Behind the equipment room rubble, under the roof that got torn away."

Bonnie spread out her wings, but Ashley caught her arm. "Wait! I'm picking up Adam's thoughts. He's begging for a distraction."

"Adam?" Bonnie looked at the plane Adam had boarded. It sat beyond the gathered forces, the hatch open. "Why is he still in the plane? I thought he would've tried to infiltrate the soldiers."

"He doesn't want to leave. He's …" Ashley licked her lips, her eyes sparkling with tears. "He's crying. I mean, really crying."

"I'll handle the distraction. You go tell the dragons and the men what you know."

"On my way." Ashley dashed down the bleacher steps.

Bonnie leaped up and raised Excalibur. The beam shot out and rocketed into the sky. "Hey, Arramos! Look up here!"

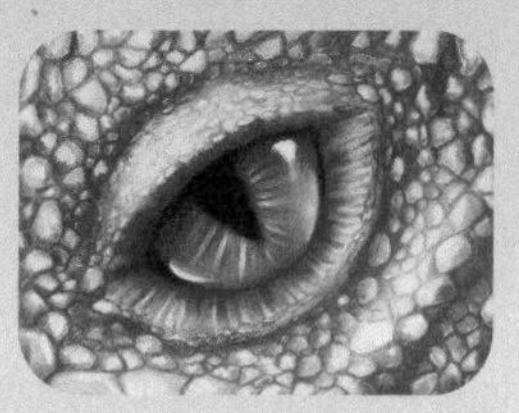

12

CHAPTER

A Portal Jump

At the parking lot, every head turned toward Bonnie. Arramos laughed, his voice audible now that the engines had silenced. "Bonnie Silver, I should have known that you would make your way here." His red eyes flashed, easily visible though he stood at least a hundred feet away. "How is your song? I'm sure after all you have seen, you have been singing praises to God for how well he has been protecting his created beings."

Though the words pierced deeply, Bonnie kept her face slack. Leave it to Arramos to strike at the heart and try to raise doubts. "I didn't know you were so concerned about my singing. Would you like to hear a song now?"

"Spare me the annoyance." Arramos scanned the sky again. "I recognize your stealth. What are you planning? Where are the dragons I saw earlier?"

"You tell me your plan, and I'll tell you mine." While Arramos laughed at her reply, she kept a furtive eye on the first airplane.

Adam stepped out, carrying a small child in his arms. He helped another drop down to the pavement in complete silence, then another.

Bonnie hid a tight swallow. So that was the defense! Child hostages!

"I will play along with your rhetorical game and speak as the fools do." Arramos stamped a rear claw on the pavement. "I asked you first."

"Very well." She trained her stare on Arramos. How could she make enough of a scene to allow Adam time to get away with the children? "I'm planning this!" She leaped into the air and beat her wings furiously to hover in place. She aimed Excalibur's beam at Arramos and swept it across him. Sparks erupted from his scales, but the beam did no damage. Without hesitating, she slashed the beam into the soldiers. Their uniforms absorbed the energy and glowed red.

Bonnie doused the beam, landed on top of the chain-link fence, and flapped her wings to maintain balance. Taking in deep breaths, she stared at the soldiers. Helmets shielded their faces and kept their eyes hidden from sight. Had the world's corruption turned them into mindless automatons?

Arramos's brow bent double. He scanned the area once more until his gaze came across Adam racing away with at least ten children chasing after him.

"Stop them!" Arramos roared.

Someone shouted, "Now!" Walter, Elam, and Billy charged into the parking lot. Makaidos zoomed into the soldiers. He thrashed with his wings and slung bodies with his tail. Thigocia and Roxil followed and blasted fire. The soldiers' uniforms deflected the flames, but the fiery splashes held them back.

Arramos bellowed, "Kill the children!" then joined the fray.

Her grip tight on Excalibur, Bonnie leaped from her perch and zoomed toward the closest airplane, one of the recent arrivals. A soldier broke away from the battle and rushed at its open door, a handgun raised.

Bonnie flew over him, snatched his gun, and shoved him down. His chin struck the base of the door, making a sickening crack, and he crumpled to the pavement. She zoomed into the airplane and spun toward the battle. She extended the gun out the door with one hand and pointed Excalibur with the other. In the midst of swirling flames and smoke, fists flew, scaly wings and tails whipped back and forth, and gunshots fired.

"Who are you?" someone asked, the voice barely audible over the plane's engines.

Bonnie swiveled her head. A little boy no more than six years old sat against the opposite wall, his hands and feet tied and a gag pulled down to his chin. Several other children about the same age sat around the perimeter, all gagged. Some leaned back against the cargo wall, apparently asleep or unconscious, while the rest stared at her with wide eyes. The odor of urine hung in the air, sharp and stinging.

She forced a smile and a gentle tone. "I'm Bonnie. I'm here to protect you."

"You're the dragon woman." His face took on a pleading expression. "Are you going to take us home?"

"I'm going to try ..." She swallowed down a sob. "With all my might."

He smiled, though the effort looked painful. "I think your wings are awesome."

"Thanks, I—"

"Bonnie!" Walter broke away from the chaos and leaped into the plane. "Get back to the portal and protect the others. Arramos sent some men that way."

"What are you going to do?"

"Fly this bird out of here." He reached for a door handle over his head. "The dragons are keeping them busy. Billy's taxiing another plane, and Gabriel's heading for a third. Adam cleared the kids from a fourth."

"What about the fifth?"

"God will have to take care of that one." His foot knocked over a tubular canister. Handwritten letters on the metal surface spelled out Dragon Gas.

"Walter! Look!"

"I see it." He gave her a nudge. "No time to worry about it. Just go."

Bonnie leaped out and shot straight up. As she ascended, she counted the planes. The first one, which arrived well before the others, sat motionless, presumably empty because of Adam's efforts. Two others rolled toward the highway. Walter's began taxiing. The fifth one sat on a section of the lot well away from the battle, its door open but too far away to see what lay inside. More children? Probably.

Now a hundred feet in the air, she looked down at the football field. Five armed soldiers stalked around the corner of the bleachers. Bonnie glanced at the fifth plane, then at the portal where Marilyn, Ashley, and the others stood exposed without protection.

Bonnie bit her lip hard. Which way to go? The plane or the field? Walter's words replayed in her mind. *God will have to take care of that one.* Without looking again at the plane, she beat her wings and flew toward the portal, gripping both Excalibur and the handgun.

As she drew close, the soldiers ran onto the field. Sapphira hurled a fireball with each hand, but the men sidestepped them, stopped within fifty feet, and raised rifles to their shoulders. "Surrender!" the lead man called. "Or we'll pick you off one by one until you do!"

Bonnie landed next to Sapphira in a flurry and shouted, "Come around me! Now!" She tossed the gun to Ashley and raised Excalibur. The beam shot out. She waved it furiously, begging for the shield to take shape. Catherine rolled Carl into the shield's range, while Marilyn and Carly guided Thomas and Mariel into the fold, Thomas carrying the plant.

One of the soldiers fired. The bullet slammed into Thomas's back. He slumped and fell on his face, and the plant toppled from his grasp.

"You pigs!" Ashley shot at the soldiers again and again. One dropped, then a second and a third. The shield formed, deflecting another of Ashley's shots as well as a hail of bullets fired by the remaining two soldiers.

Ashley shoved the gun into Marilyn's hand, tipped the plant upright, and knelt next to Thomas. "I'll see what I can do!"

While Bonnie kept the shield in place, she looked toward the parking lot, blocked from view by the bleachers. Out there, Billy and his men, along with the dragons, were the children's only hope. Although Arramos was powerful, he couldn't stand against three dragons, could he? And what did that canister mean? At least Walter took it with him, but were there more? Would the attackers deploy the gas? Probably not while Arramos was there.

The two remaining soldiers kept their rifles aimed, but they stood in uneasy postures, as if unsure about what to do next. Their indecisiveness reflected Gabriel's assumption that they lacked training.

"He's alive," Ashley shouted as she pressed on Thomas's back with the palm of her hand, "but he's hemorrhaging badly. He won't last long."

Bonnie kept the beam swirling above. "What can we do?"

"A healing blast from Excalibur!" Ashley sat on the ground and grabbed Thomas's hand. "Help me get him into my arms!"

"I'll need to take one of the gems out," Bonnie said as she fingered a rubellite in the hilt. "The beam is too powerful on Earth with all of them in place."

Catherine and Carly pulled Thomas onto Ashley's lap. She wrapped her arms around him tightly. "Now lower the shield for just a second and shoot the beam through the ground at me! Sapphira and Mrs. B will cover us."

Marilyn held the gun at her thigh. "I'm ready."

"So am I." Sapphira stood with a fireball swirling in each hand. "At least I can distract them for a second."

Bonnie shut off the beam and lowered Excalibur. The shield collapsed. Sapphira threw her fireballs. Marilyn fired at the soldiers. One man dropped. The other yelped and limped away.

Ashley threw a pocketknife toward Bonnie. "Let's do it!"

Bonnie caught the knife, opened the blade, and pried a rubellite from the hilt. After stowing the knife and gem in her pocket, she pointed the blade at the ground and again summoned the beam. It slammed into the grass. Flashes lit up the blades in a lightning-fast path to Ashley. The grass vanished, leaving a streak of dirt.

The energy rocketed into her. Her fists clenched. Light radiated from her body, and beams shot out of her eyes. She turned the twin beams toward Thomas. The energy stabbed into his shoulders and streamed down his back. Her teeth chattering, Ashley called out, "Just … a few … more seconds!"

An explosion rocked the ground. Bonnie fell to her bottom and dropped Excalibur. The beam wavered, disintegrating more grass in a zigzag path before it shut off.

Bonnie leaped up and grabbed the sword. A second explosion shook the field, followed by a third. She sucked in a breath. Had a helicopter fired missiles at the three dragons? Or maybe the escaping airplanes? She glanced at the sky. Plumes of smoke rose into the air, but at this angle it was impossible to tell what happened on the ground.

Turning her gaze back to the others, Bonnie called out, "Is everyone all right? Does Thomas need more healing?"

"I'll check him." Mariel pulled Thomas away, laid him on his stomach, and lifted his shirt. "He's still unconscious, but the bleeding's stopped. He probably just needs time to restore his blood supply."

Ashley rose to her knees and shook her head slowly. "I feel … terrible."

Marilyn laid a hand on Ashley's forehead. "She's red hot!"

"I'm all right. I'm all right." Ashley pushed her hand away. "It's been worse."

"No. You need to cool down. You know that."

Sapphira jumped to the portal plane and waved her arms over her head. "I'll see if it will open now. We can get Ashley into the ice storm." Within seconds, a cyclone of flames formed around her hands.

"How does it look?" Bonnie asked.

Sapphira narrowed her eyes. "I see a blazing fire and two dragons—Karrick and Grackle. No sign of Mardon."

"Maybe Karrick helped Mardon build the fire, and Mardon took off."

"I think I can open it." Sapphira gestured with her head. "Everyone stand next to me. I'm going to get you all out of here."

Bonnie slid Excalibur behind her belt, grabbed Ashley, and scooted her close to Sapphira. Marilyn, Carly, and Mariel dragged Thomas within range while Catherine pushed Carl and his wheelchair into the formation, the plant now in Carl's lap. Bonnie eyed their position. Was the wheelchair close enough? Sapphira would have to decide.

Sapphira began lowering the flames in a cylindrical curtain until it descended to head level. Helicopter blades whipped somewhere close. A Cobra rose from behind the bleachers, all but one of its missiles missing. Arramos flew up from the parking lot, sailed erratically over the bleachers, and landed at the edge of the field. He coughed and hacked as he struggled to keep his balance. "Surrender!" he called with a gravelly voice. "Or I will order my helicopters to open fire."

A second helicopter joined the first, and the two hovered side by side. The new arrival carried a full complement of missiles under its wings.

"Sapphira!" Bonnie hissed. "Is it open?"

"Yes. Just now."

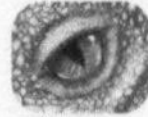

"Then let's go!"

Sapphira lowered the flames, but the fiery wall dropped between her and the Foleys. She raised it again to sweep it farther out, but could she do it in time?

Arramos shouted from beyond the crackling curtain, "Fire!"

Billy stopped the plane on the highway just before a bridge overpass. Without enough knowledge to fly this bird, taxiing it for a few miles had been his only option. Fortunately, Makaidos, Thigocia, and Roxil battled furiously to keep the helicopters from giving chase, but how long could they last?

He rose from the pilot's seat and limped back into the rear compartment. Twenty children sitting on benches stared at him, most with sleepy eyes. The gags and ropes that had bound them earlier lay on the floor at their feet. Since they had no toilets or cleaning supplies available, the place reeked of urine.

Billy put on the biggest smile his pain would allow. "You'll be safe here. They're not chasing us."

A girl wearing a pink backpack raised her hand. "Do you have anything to eat? I'm hungry."

"Me, too." A boy said while several others nodded.

Billy scanned the compartment. A foot locker sat against the wall opposite the side hatch. He knelt and opened the lid. Inside lay water bottles and MREs in foil pouches. He turned to the girl. "Can you pass these around?"

She nodded.

"What's your name, sweetheart?"

"Jillian."

"That's a pretty name." Billy gathered a few pouches into his arms. "How old are you?"

She leaned closer, her hungry eyes locked on the pouches. "Five and a half."

"Then you're old enough to be our waitress." He transferred the pouches to her arms, picked up another, and tore off the top. "Pass them around and show everyone how to open them. One pouch and one bottle for each. All right?"

"Sure!"

While Jillian handed out the supplies, Billy grabbed a bottle of water, opened the plane's hatch, and stepped out onto the highway. In the distance to the rear, two more planes drew closer, one descending in flight and the other rolling well back. Soon, the first one landed and stopped a hundred or so feet away. In a flash, Walter hopped out and ran toward Billy.

When he arrived, Billy nodded at his plane. "I thought Adam had cleared out that one."

"He did, but he couldn't find a safe place to put the kids. So I commandeered it and picked him and the kids up. He was kind of in a panic, because one of the girls was dead. The other kids say a soldier got sick of hearing her cry, so he just shot her in the head."

Nausea churned in Billy's stomach. "Shot her for crying?"

"Yeah. Disgusting. Pure evil. One of the other kids said the girl was autistic. Poor kid probably couldn't help it."

Billy swallowed erupting bile. "I think I'm going to be sick."

"I know what you mean. When Adam told me, I almost hurled my guts." Walter rolled a hand into a fist. "We have to fight back. Strike hard."

"We'll fight back but with what?" Billy picked up his water bottle and drank the entire contents to wash down the bile. When he finished, he swiped a sleeve across his lips. "Got any weapons or ammo in your plane?"

"Clean as a whistle except for a canister of anti-dragon gas, but we don't have a way to deploy it. Adam's still combing the interior while keeping the kids calm, but I don't think he'll find anything."

"Maybe we can grab a rifle or two in the parking lot. Some of them got thrown pretty far."

When the trailing plane stopped behind Walter's, the door popped open. Gabriel flew out, zoomed toward Billy and Walter, and landed on the run. With bruises on his face and rips in his jeans and shirt, he looked pretty banged up. "What's going on?"

"Just resting a minute," Billy said. "But we need to check on the plane that's still in the lot. The kids in there are probably bound and gagged."

"Walter can fly us back, but who'll stay with these kids?"

"Adam, probably." Billy looked down the highway to the east. Nothing in sight but the city skyline and dark clouds forming over the buildings. "Where's Elam and the other plane?"

Walter squinted in the same direction. "I showed him how to taxi, but he had some trouble. He ended up going the other way, but I think he escaped."

"We'll have to find him and make sure his kids have food and water."

"Mister?" Jillian leaned out from the plane. "Can we have two bags? We're all hungry."

"Jillian!" Gabriel beat his wings, leaped through the plane's doorway, and scooped her into his arms. As he glided out, he kissed her cheek and spoke in a cheery tone that belied his reddened eyes. "Where are Mommy and your brother?"

"I don't know. A big ugly bird took me away from them."

Billy laid a hand on Gabriel's shoulder. "I had no idea Jillian was your daughter. I would've told you sooner."

"No problem." As he hiked Jillian higher in his arms, something rustled in her backpack.

Billy grinned. So another little girl had sprouted wings. Very cool.

Gabriel put Jillian down and held her hand. "Isaiah was probably too old for them to take. If Shiloh followed our plans, she should have contacted Ruth for help."

"Patrick's wife?" Billy asked.

Gabriel nodded. "Before Patrick died, he and Ruth created a secret network that allowed communications to flow among our allies in Europe. It was a dangerous business sometimes. In fact, their son was captured and killed during a raid."

"That's terrible!"

"It was, and the tragedy made Ruth more determined than ever to keep the network going. So when Jillian was taken, you can bet that a lot of messages flew around. No telling what they're working on to rescue her, but knowing Shiloh and Ruth, they'll pull out all the stops."

"Listen," Walter said, his brow knitted. "We're kind of in dawdle mode. Let's get all the kids together in the first plane, and Gabriel can stay with them while we haul our fannies back to the field."

“Sounds perfect.” Gabriel picked up Jillian, flapped his wings, and lifted off the ground a few inches. “While you two are risking your lives, I’ll be entertaining the kids. Free rides from a dragon man!”

Jillian giggled. “Higher, Daddy! Higher!”

“Okay, winged wonder.” Billy jerked his thumb toward his plane. “We need to shove off, so we’ll leave it to you to gather the kids.”

“Sure thing.” While Gabriel flew toward the last plane in the line, Billy and Walter marched as quickly as Billy’s toes would allow.

Billy nudged Walter’s elbow. “When did you learn how to pilot one of these rust buckets?”

“While you were cooling your heels in prison for fifteen years, I learned to fly just about anything that could take off. Compared to hot-air balloons and jetpacks, the rust buckets were easy.”

A flash erupted from the football field. As rising smoke followed, an explosion sounded, then another, followed by a third.

“Trouble!” Walter broke into a sprint.

Billy followed with a limping trot. By the time he arrived, Walter and Adam had already herded the children onto the highway.

Carrying Jillian, Gabriel zoomed close and called out as he circled back toward the first airplane, “Follow me, kids! I have food and water!”

While the kids chased after him, Walter and Adam climbed aboard the plane. “Get your aching toes in here!” Walter called to Billy. “We haven’t got all day!”

Something flashed in the air toward the stadium. A beam of light streaked into the sky and waved in a circle.

“Excalibur!” Billy leaped into the plane and climbed into the cockpit. Walter slid into the pilot’s seat and grabbed the control yoke. With a loud slam, Adam closed the passenger hatch, slid into a seat, and called, "All clear!"

"Let's scram!" Walter turned the plane toward the stadium and taxied off the highway to get around Gabriel's plane. When he returned to the pavement, he set the flaps and pushed the throttle. "Don't bother buckling. We'll be there in no time." The plane lifted into the air and stayed at a low altitude just above the highway. "They'll hear the engine, but we don't have to give them an easy target."

Soon, Walter landed the plane in front of the parking lot gate. Billy jumped out first. Within the lot, three dragons sprawled motionless in the midst of dozens of dead soldiers and scattered rifles. The remains of a helicopter lay nearby, smoke rising from its wreckage. The fifth airplane still sat parked on a far end of the lot near the Mustang and solar-powered car, a safe distance from the battle scene. The buzz of helicopter props rose from the field, blocked from view by the bleachers.

Walter and Adam leaped out and joined Billy. "Okay," Walter said, "we've got kids trapped in a plane, three dragons down, and our wives in trouble on the field. Who's got what?"

Billy pointed at Walter. "You check on the kids. I'll see about our wives. Adam's got the dragons."

As they ran across the lot, each man picked up a rifle along the way. Walter angled toward the plane in a wild sprint. Billy pushed hard in spite of the pain that shot from his toes, through his spine, and into his skull. With every breath, the odor of garlic, thick and pungent, singed his nostrils. Semiramis's poison had again done its dirty work.

Adam passed Billy and dashed toward the dragons. He stopped at Makaidos. From this distance, it appeared that blood streamed down his flank.

Still fighting pain, Billy dashed onto the bleachers' walkway leading to the field. Slowing to a furtive jog, he bent low and drew close to the front railing. Ahead, two helicopters hovered over the nearer sideline. A gap between them revealed Arramos sitting on the ground. His outstretched wings blocked a view of the portal and anyone who might be close to it.

Flames shot out from the portal area and into the sky. Shouts erupted. Arramos roared, "Fire!"

The Foleys!" Carly ducked under the flames and disappeared from view. Rapid pops rattled the air, followed by cries of pain.

Carly fell. Bonnie bent low, latched on to Carly's wrist, and dragged her under the curtain just before it dropped to the ground. Tucked under an arm, Carly held Jared's pot.

"We don't have the Foleys!" Ashley shouted.

"It's too late! We're already through the portal!" Sapphira spun her flames furiously. After a few seconds, she lowered her arms and shouted, "Extinguish!"

The flames vanished. Bonnie dropped to an icy floor. A whistling breeze swept through. Wet, bone-chilling air slapped her face, though heat nearly scalded her wings. Something stung her scalp, but why? It seemed that fog veiled the last few minutes from memory.

She crawled away from the heat, a hand clutching Excalibur. Ahead, a wall displayed the upper half of a compass design, the lower portion obscured by a mound of dirty ice. She pivoted. A bonfire blazed—a towering fire that feasted on a pyramid of logs. A red dragon lay nearby, his neck draped over a pile of wood and a wing over his face. Next to him, a purple dragon sat on his haunches.

"Grackle?" Bonnie said.

Grackle whistled a low note, concern obvious in his tone.

As Bonnie turned, her head throbbed on one side. It seemed that a dirty film coated the world. Less than an arm's reach to her left, Ashley sat upright. Her eyes darted as she appeared to be taking in the new scene.

Beyond Ashley, Marilyn brushed dirty ice from Thomas and Mariel as she helped them move closer to the fire. To Bonnie's right, Carly sat hugging herself, her head low as she wept, Jared's pot sitting next to her. Sobs punctuated her words. "I tried … to get the Foleys … but the fire … the guns. He pushed the pot … into my hands. … And I fell. … I'm sorry! … I'm so, so sorry!"

"These two are fine," Marilyn called. "I'll check on Carly." She rose and bustled past Bonnie.

Her head dizzied, Bonnie looked beyond the fire at a head-high wall of bricks that partially enclosed them within a crevice in a mountain. A gap at each side of the wall allowed escape from the sheltered area. She held out her hand. In seconds, sooty ice crystals piled up on her palm and spread across her skin in a sheet. She rubbed a finger against her thumb. The slippery stuff felt infused with oil. "Where's Sapphira? Did she already go back to get the Foleys?"

"I'm here." As if growing out of the icy floor, Sapphira rose to her knees in front of the blaze. Her white hair whipped in the chamber's swirling breeze. She pressed a hand against her side and cringed as she looked around. "I'll try to go back and get them." With every word, her pained expression seemed to worsen. "I closed the portal to keep Arramos and the helicopters out. But now that this fire has settled the atmosphere in Second Eden, I think I can reopen it whenever I want to."

Still holding a hand against her side, she climbed to a standing position and grimaced tightly. Pain streaked her voice. "You have

Excalibur … so I assume you'll be able to … to guard everyone on your journey … to the birthing garden."

Bonnie took a moment to decipher Sapphira's words. They seemed warped and interrupted by static. "Sure. I can do that."

Sapphira lifted a leg and stood on one foot. The strain in her face eased. "Going back to Earth so soon is dangerous. They will be ready to fight, but I don't have any choice. I have to try to save the Foleys."

"I understand," Bonnie said. "But it looks like you need a healer."

"Something in the air is affecting me, but healing can wait." Sapphira looked toward the portal plane. "You should probably move out of here as soon as you can in case Arramos somehow manages to get through. If you find it too difficult to transport Thomas to the birthing garden, there is a cave just a few hundred feet upslope. Build a fire there, and he should be fine." She raised her arms and spun a new curtain of flames over her head. A dark, wet spot appeared where she had been pressing her side with her hand. Seconds later, the flames vanished in a plume of smoke. When the breeze whisked the smoke away, Sapphira was gone.

Bonnie felt her mouth drop open. Sapphira's injury had to be much worse than she was letting on. But they couldn't do anything about it now. They had to take care of business here.

"Bonnie? Are you all right? You look like you're in a daze."

She swiveled her head toward the voice. Ashley sat on the icy ground. A glittering dark crust lay on her head, like a cap of sparkling coal.

"I am kind of dazed. I think I banged my head somehow."

"A concussion, maybe." Ashley crawled to Bonnie and ran two fingers along her scalp until she reached a sore spot. "You have a bleeding lump. I'll bet a bullet grazed you."

"I think Sapphira got hit, too. She was still able to create fire, so maybe it's not too serious."

"I saw that. Waist area, close to the side. Maybe just soft-tissue damage. Blood loss could be a problem, though. She also seemed to favor a leg, but that could be a sprain from falling." Ashley swiveled her head toward Marilyn. "How's Carly?"

"Looks like a bullet grazed her hand," Marilyn said as she picked up Jared's pot. "She's in pain in other places, though."

"I'll be over to check her in a second. I don't know how much healing power I have left, but I'll do what I can." As Ashley's touch performed its magic, images flew back to Bonnie's mind—Thomas getting shot, the robotic soldiers, Arramos's evil eyes, Carly's heroic attempt to bring the Foleys into Sapphira's flaming coil. Although she failed to do so, she did manage to save Clefspeare's plant. Leaving that within Arramos's reach would have been a disaster.

Grimacing at the pain, Bonnie looked at the gray sky. When would God execute justice against that foul serpent? When would the suffering of the innocent cease? With all the corruption on Earth, maybe the only way to solve every problem would be to cleanse the world and start over.

Tears blurring her vision, Bonnie whispered, "Ashley?"

She continued the massage. "Yes?"

"I think we're coming to the end."

"The end?"

"The end of all things. The curtain on this creation is closing."

"But is that a good thing or a bad thing?" Ashley pulled her hand away. "Your eyes aren't so glassy anymore. I'm going to see about Carly. Then we need to get out of here."

Bonnie climbed to her feet and gazed at Excalibur's blade. The etching of two dragons in battle seemed clear. Her vision had returned to normal. "I'll see if I can wake Karrick. We'll gather some wood, find that cave, and start a fire for Thomas and Mariel, then the rest of us can head to the birthing garden."

Sheltering the pot with her body, Marilyn rose and joined Bonnie. "Carly says her left leg hurts the worst."

"I'm on it." Ashley turned to Bonnie. "I need my pocketknife."

Bonnie fished it out and handed it to Ashley.

While Ashley examined Carly, Bonnie and Marilyn walked over to Karrick. After setting Jared's pot at a point that would keep the plant warm, Marilyn pushed a foot against Karrick's foreleg. "Karrick," she called. "Wake up."

He groaned and kept his face hidden under a wing.

Bonnie set Excalibur down, gathered a few small logs into her arms, and looked at Grackle. "Can you blow some ice on his face?"

Grackle bobbed his head. Using a foreleg, he pushed Karrick's wing to the side and breathed a jet of ice over his closed eyes.

Karrick jerked up and shook his head, flinging ice crystals. "What? Who did that?"

Marilyn patted Karrick's neck. "We need your help."

His head swayed as if tossed by waves. "Kindly forgive my appearance. I succumbed to noxious fumes in the air, and I am still under their influence."

"Was Grackle exposed to it?"

"Not for as long as I was, and perhaps his subspecies is more resistant. In any case, Grackle and I had to come here to escape the fumes, which were more concentrated at lower elevations. They seem to have diminished now."

"Bonnie!" Ashley called. "Marilyn! Carly's in bad shape. I found a bullet wound in her thigh. It's bleeding profusely." She held a hand over Carly's inner thigh through a slice in her pants. Blood oozed between Ashley's fingers. Carly looked ashen and gaunt. Raw lesions now covered more than half of her face. "We have to do a healing! Now!"

While Marilyn hurried to Ashley, Bonnie threw the logs down and grabbed Excalibur. "I'll fire it up!"

"Are you sure?" Marilyn laid a hand on Ashley's forehead. "You're still hot as a rocket."

"If we don't, Carly will bleed out." Ashley shivered hard in spite of her heated body. "Sometimes cold temperatures will affect a beam like Excalibur's. Its power might not be stable."

"And it doesn't work in Second Eden without all the gems." Bonnie retrieved the rubellite and slid it in place on the hilt. "Ready."

Ashley nodded at her. "Go ahead."

After stepping back a few paces, Bonnie gripped Excalibur with both hands, pointed it at the ground toward Ashley, and summoned the beam. It ripped through the ice, splitting it in a jagged line and raising a series of resounding cracks.

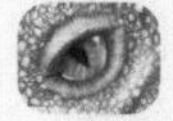

Light burst into Ashley and radiated from her body like thin sunrays. She stiffened, her hand still on Carly's wound. Twin beams shot from her eyes and penetrated Carly's thigh, though with far less brightness than usual. After a few seconds, Ashley closed her eyes and collapsed.

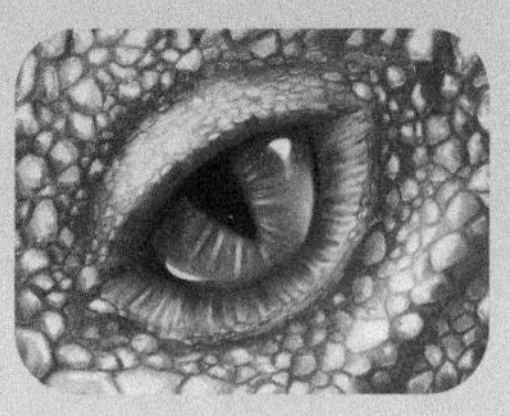

13

CHAPTER

A Wounded Oracle

Bullets buzzed from both choppers. Billy pressed the rifle to his shoulder, squeezed the trigger, and waved the barrel from side to side, riddling both choppers with bullets of his own.

Arramos beat his wings and zoomed toward the portal. “You fools!” he shouted. “You hit the Oracle!”

One chopper banked to the left, tumbled along the sideline, and shattered. The other dropped straight down and crashed in a plume of billowing smoke.

Billy lowered the rifle and stared at the wreckage. How did that happen? The choppers went down far too easily.

At midfield, grass burned in a ring around the portal site. Arramos picked up a body with his rear claws and flew toward the end zone. A few steps to the right of the portal, another body lay near a wheelchair. Carl Foley? Yes. It had to be. Nearby, a briefcase computer and a metallic sphere lay dented and ripped. Larry and Lois had also met their ends.

Billy dashed through the bleachers' gateway and ran onto the field, again favoring the aching foot. He glanced at Arramos who now stood with his head high near the goal line, apparently unafraid of retaliation, his scales likely impervious to bullets. The first body lay pinned under a rear claw, its identity impossible to determine.

Billy halted in front of the wheelchair and knelt at Carl's side. He lay motionless on his stomach. Billy checked for a pulse. Nothing. Bullet holes marred his blood-spattered shirt from his shoulders to his waist.

"Argh!" Billy sucked in a deep breath. Those murderers! Rising to his feet, he slid his finger around the rifle's trigger. It was time to test that monster's scales.

Fire flashed at the portal site. Sapphira toppled out of the flames and fell to her knees on the grass. With a powerful beat of his wings, Arramos flew toward her. Billy took aim and fired. A bullet pinged off his neck scales. He fired again and again. More bullets bounced and deflected at sharp angles.

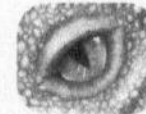

Arramos blasted a stream of fire. Billy dove out of the way. Still flying, Arramos picked Sapphira up with his foreclaws, banked a hard turn, and flew again toward the goal line.

Billy scrambled to his feet. When Arramos landed next to the other body, he lifted Sapphira and dangled her by her battle tunic. Blood trickled from her waist and dripped to the ground. "Put down your weapon," he growled.

Billy lowered the rifle to the turf and edged as close to Arramos as he dared. Now twenty yards away, he looked at the second captive woman—Catherine Foley. Her body appeared to be moving, perhaps from respiration. "What are you going to do with them?"

"Whatever I please." Arramos set Sapphira on the ground next to Catherine. "I did not intend for the Oracle to be injured, so I will allow you to take her for healing purposes, but I will keep the other woman as a hostage to ensure Sapphira's compliance with my wishes. We have already killed your dragon friends, so that should let you know that I will not hesitate to kill your human friends."

Billy forced himself to stay calm. He gave the grass a furtive scan. Excalibur was nowhere in sight. It wouldn't have burned in Arramos's flames. Maybe Sapphira had taken the others through the portal and returned by herself. "All right. I'll take Sapphira and—"

Gunshots ripped through the air, sounding like jackhammers pounding on metal. Arramos beat his wings and flew backwards. His head swayed as he searched for the gunman. Three men wearing army fatigues stood on the bleachers firing automatic weapons. They aimed high, apparently to avoid hitting the hostages.

Billy ran toward the fallen women, his speed hampered by pain. Walter sprinted onto the field. As bullets pelted Arramos's scales, Billy scooped up Sapphira, and Walter reached under Catherine to lift her. Arramos swung his tail and swept it under Walter's legs, upending him.

While Billy hobbled away with all of his might, Arramos pounced on Catherine and reared his head back as if to blast Walter with flames. Gunfire popped even faster. Bullets zinged into Arramos's face and open mouth. He backpedaled and dragged Catherine facedown across the grass.

"Walter!" Billy shouted from his knees as he laid Sapphira on the turf. "Get back! We'll regroup!"

"No way!" Walter ran and dove for his mother, but Arramos jerked her away. Walter slid across the grass with empty hands.

Beating his wings, Arramos lifted into the air and began flying in a tight orbit. Walter leaped to his feet and lunged for his mother's dangling legs as they passed by, but they were inches out of reach.

Billy jumped up and waved his arms. "Whoever is shooting, cease fire! You might hit Catherine!"

The gunfire stopped. When the echoes died, Arramos called from his orbit. "I will return in two hours at which time I will expect you to have mended Sapphira." He blinked hard, as if suffering an eye injury. "She will open the portal for me, or I will kill my hostage!" He angled away and flew toward the city. Seconds later, he disappeared behind a line of trees.

Walter ran to Billy's side and sat next to Sapphira. Gasping for breath, he glared in the direction Arramos had flown. "That snake has my mother. But we can't open the portal for him." He turned back to Billy, his face creased with worry. "Right? I mean, what options do we have?"

"We'll get together with Elam and decide what to do." Billy knelt next to Sapphira. Blood smeared her clothes all across her waist. He unbuckled her belt and pulled up her sticky, wet tunic. Blood trickled from a slice in her side at her waist, as if something had bitten off a chunk of flesh. He had to concentrate on helping her, but with Carl's bullet-riddled body lying not far away, it seemed that a hundred-ton weight pulled every thought toward the carnage. Since Walter's thoughts likely focused on his mom's capture, he hadn't even noticed his father's corpse. Someone would have to tell him soon. "Walter," Billy said, "what do you think of this wound?"

Walter knelt with him and peered at Sapphira. "No vital organs hit, but she might lose a lot of blood. Probably has already. Maybe she also has head trauma from a fall." He laid a hand over the slice and compressed it. "I saw a first-aid kit in the airplane. I should've thought to bring it."

"Don't worry about that." Billy took in a deep breath. This wouldn't be easy. "Listen, I have to tell you some—"

"Just a second." Walter turned toward the bleachers and shouted at the gunmen. "Can one of you guys go to the airplane and fetch a first-aid kit? The other two can cover us. Keep an eye out for Arramos. He said two hours, but he's the world's biggest liar."

One of the gunmen waved. "Will do, old chap!"

Billy squinted at the man. His voice sounded familiar, flavored with an English accent, but that wasn't important now. He grasped Walter's arm, barely able to speak the horrible news. "Walter, your father is dead." He gestured with his head toward the wheelchair.

"Dead?" Walter looked that way. His mouth dropped open. He rose and walked toward the chair in slow, shaking steps. When he reached it, he knelt and touched his father's face, then combed his fingers through the corpse's scant hair. Finally, he lifted his head toward the sky and screamed, "Nooo!"

Billy stayed with Sapphira and pressed a hand against her wound. Tears welled as his throat clamped shut. If only he could comfort Walter, but the poor guy had to grieve alone. Now he had lost his father as well as his sister and nephew, and Satan himself held his mother.

Walter staggered back to Billy. "What happened? Did Arramos kill him?"

Billy nodded. "Well, Arramos's orders. The helicopters got him."

"What about Ashley?" Walter's features twisted into a misshapen mask as he spoke in a rattling growl. "Where … is … my . . . wife?"

"I think she went through the portal. Sapphira just came back."

Walter sank to his knees, his voice still fractured. "So … she and Bonnie … must be safe … right?"

"I assume so. I'm guessing my mother, Thomas and Mariel, and Carly, too."

"I'm going to kill that lizard!" Walter rolled his hand into a trembling fist. "I'll gut him and feed his bowels to the birds!"

Billy compressed Walter's shoulder. "We'll gut the snake together, but we have to be patient. Keep the faith. Sapphira first. Then your mom. Then our wives. One step at a time."

"Right." As tears streamed down his dirty cheeks, his fingers loosened. "I'll take another turn." He nudged Billy's bloody hand away and reapplied pressure to Sapphira's wound. "Gotta take my mind off things."

"Let's see what we can figure out." Billy pushed his clean hand into Sapphira's and spoke in a loud tone. "Sapphira? If you can hear me, squeeze my hand."

Her fingers compressed his weakly. Then her eyes opened. "Billy?"

"Yes. Yes." He bent lower. "What happened?"

"So … so much to tell." She rasped through rapid, shallow breaths. "So weak."

Keeping his hand on her waist, Walter leaned close to her ear. "Can you at least tell us what happened to Ashley and Bonnie?"

She licked her dry lips and spoke in a halting whisper. "Through the portal … Bonnie … Billy's mother … Clefspeare's plant … Ashley … Thomas … Mariel … and Carly. … They are in … Second Eden."

New tears joined the others on Walter's cheeks. "Thank God for that."

Billy ran a thumb across Sapphira's knuckles. "Try to relax. We'll get that wound in your side stitched up."

"My … my leg hurts more. … Left leg."

Billy slid her pant leg up. Blood flowed freely from a hole just above her ankle.

Walter wrapped his free hand around her leg. When it shifted, Sapphira moaned. "It's broken," Walter said. "Probably a bullet cracked it. Maybe we can stop the bleeding and give her a splint." He winked at Sapphira. "You getting shot is a weapon in itself. Anyone who makes an Oracle of Fire bleed dies, right?"

Billy looked at the helicopter wreckage near the sideline. "I forgot about that. I was wondering why those two choppers crashed so easily when I shot at them."

At the bleachers, the two remaining gunmen opened the gate and trooped onto the field, rifles at their hips. The third ran from the bleachers passageway, carrying his rifle as well as a white box.

"Here comes the cavalry." Walter scanned the sky, his voice now steady. "Keep an eye out for more incoming aircraft. Arramos has something up his scaly sleeve. At the very least he'll bring someone who'll go through the portal for him—maybe more helicopters, probably enough force to kill everyone in Second Eden."

When the gunmen arrived, the trailing one set the box on the turf next to Sapphira. Marked on top with a red cross, it looked much bigger than a typical first-aid kit. The gunman tapped the top with his rifle barrel. "An excellent selection of supplies, my good man."

Billy opened the box. "She'll need stitches in her side and a splint for a broken left leg."

The leader of the newcomers, a bald man with short white whiskers, knelt and withdrew a pair of scissors from the box. "Stitches are not a problem. The splint will depend on the severity of the break, but I suppose I will be able to rig something for her. We have some pain medications here as well."

"Great," Billy said. "Thanks, but … who are you?"

"Ah! I was wondering if you would recognize me now that age has hooked my hide. My name is Standish." He gestured with his head to the rear. "My fellows are Edmund and Newman. They have aged better than I have."

Billy nodded at the other two men. "It's good to see you again." He looked at the bleachers. "Where are Sirs Fiske and Woodrow?"

"They have passed away, I'm afraid." Standish picked up a small bottle of alcohol and a packet of gauze. "Woodrow was already up in years when we entered the candlestone, and Fiske met with an automobile accident about a year ago. Struck by a drunk driver. Such a tragedy."

"Sorry to hear that," Billy said.

"Yes. Well, we all have to die at some point, don't we?" Standish pulled on Walter's wrist and eased his hand away from Sapphira's side wound. "What do we have here?" Blood immediately trickled again and dripped to the ground. "Oh, my! This will require many stitches, and I will need assistance. Newman, sterilize your hands with the alcohol, then mine, and we'll mend the lass's injury. I believe we have a topical anesthetic here somewhere, so the pain should be tolerable with regard to the stitches, but the broken bone is another issue entirely. She might have to bite a bullet while I set it."

Billy knelt close to Sapphira. Her blue eyes stared up at him, pain evident. "While our gallant knights are working on you," he whispered. "I'll find Elam and let him know what's going on."

She nodded, the motion hindered by the ground beneath her head. "We can't let … let Arramos go through the portal … no matter what. Second Eden … is too precious."

"Definitely. He'll go there only over my dead body."

"And mine." She slid her hand into his and offered a weak smile. "Thank you, Billy. You're a hero among heroes."

"That's quite an honor coming from one of the bravest hearts I have ever known." He kissed her forehead and rose to his feet. "I'll be back as soon as I can."

While Standish and Newman worked on Sapphira, Edmund walked to Billy and extended a rifle. "It seems that these weapons are no match for the dragon, though I think one of us put a bullet in his eye."

"I noticed. It might help." Billy grasped Edmund's shoulder. "How did you get here? What's going on?"

"We were summoned by Ruth, Sir Patrick's widow. At the airport in London, a splendid mother-daughter duo accompanied Ruth, and all three joined us. With the expertise of the duo, we were able to locate a plane that transported some UK children to the States. We became stowaways, and once we were in the air, we hijacked the plane. Since our destination had been entered in the onboard computer, we simply flew to that location where we joined other transports that eventually flew here. When we landed, we opted to stay out of the battle and protect the children."

"How did you pull off the hijack? There were at least ten soldiers in each plane."

Edmund smiled. "It would be better to ask them." He nodded toward the bleachers.

A woman and a female teenager walked onto the field. Both wore army fatigues that fit close to their trim bodies, boots that looked two sizes too big, and camo caps that squirreled their hair up in the back. When they arrived, the woman grasped Billy's hand with a firm grip. "You must be William Bannister. I am Elizabeth Hamilton."

Billy looked into her deeply set gray eyes. Hamilton? Yes, she looked a lot like Prof. "Charles Hamilton's daughter?"

"The same." She set a hand on the teenager's shoulder. "This is my daughter, Jennifer."

"I'm pleased to meet both of—"

"You're probably wondering about my last name," Elizabeth said. "When Jennifer was born, my husband decided to go his own way, so Jennifer and I changed our names to Hamilton to honor my father."

Billy smothered a grin. She was so much like Prof! "I'm sure he'd be pleased."

"It is hard to be certain, since he is dead, but we hope so." She pulled off her cap and let her ponytailed hair fall down, black without a hint of gray in the thick tresses. Although she looked to be in her thirties, she had to be in her fifties. "It is a superficial salute to my father's legacy, but we are glad to do it."

Jennifer kept her hair hidden. The few strands that appeared at the edges looked blonde, nearly white. She pulled out a mobile phone and took a photo of Sapphira as she lay on the ground.

Billy gave her a questioning look, but she just smiled in return and slid her phone away.

"William, let's discuss the narrative." Elizabeth removed her ponytail band and shook out her hair. "Kindly tell me what happened. I have surmised a good deal, but it is better to hear the facts from the proverbial horse's mouth."

"Sure." Billy extended an arm toward the bleachers. "While Walter and Edmund stand guard over the surgeons, how about if we go to the parking lot? I want to check on everyone out there."

"Yes, of course." Elizabeth withdrew a handheld computer tablet from her shirt pocket and tapped on the screen as she walked with Billy toward the sideline. Jennifer tagged along behind them. "If I understand the circumstances correctly, Arramos desires to keep Sapphira alive. If Satan were ever to pray, he is likely praying for her survival."

"Good analysis. Arramos wants access to Second Eden, and only Sapphira can give it to him." Billy opened the gate to the bleachers and held it for her.

"Ah!" She smiled as she walked through the opening. "My father was right about you. You are quite the gentleman."

"Thank you." Billy closed the gate behind them. "I left Adam with our dragon friends. Do you know if they survived? Arramos said they're dead."

Jennifer tugged on Elizabeth's sleeve. "I win, Mother. You owe me a milkshake."

"Predicting a lie from the devil isn't exactly rocket science." Elizabeth pulled the bill of Jennifer's cap down. "My father used to say, 'Never trust the word of Satan, a politician, or a liar, but, I repeat myself.'"

Billy tried to smile, but his lips stiffened. "So they *are* alive?"

"They are. They sustained wounds. Nothing life-threatening." Elizabeth led the way along the path toward the parking lot. "We have eyewitnesses to the donnybrook, and we surmised that the soldiers delivered an insalubrious agent at close range."

Billy narrowed his eyes. "Insalubrious?"

"What my mother means," Jennifer said as she tagged along at Billy's side, "is that the dragons have been drugged by something that drained their energy, and the dose they received was very high. It looks like they took a few bullets, but nothing penetrated deeply." She pulled a handkerchief from her pocket and spread it out over her palm. A yellow smudge covered the center. "I have a sample of the drug, but without a lab, I won't be able to analyze it to formulate an antidote."

"It seems," Elizabeth said, "that waiting for the drug to take its course is our only option. My understanding is that Thigocia will likely revive first and help with restoring the others, but she has not given us any reason to believe she will do so soon." She slid her computer back to her pocket and picked up the pace. "We are lollygagging. Jennifer, William has long-term friends waiting for him. While he gets reacquainted, you and I will go to our plane to see if we can find some replacement parts for Larry and Lois. I assume you saw their remains."

"I did, Mother." Jennifer copied her mother's arm-swinging gait. "Ghastly amount of damage."

As they closed in on the parking lot, Billy scanned the scene. A woman knelt next to Makaidos, poured water from a cup onto a cloth, and swabbed his face. A male teenager did the same with Thigocia, while an older woman, presumably Ruth, worked on Roxil. Adam was nowhere in sight.

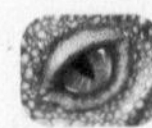

The younger woman looked up. "Billy?" With blue eyes and lovely face, she looked like a wingless Bonnie, perhaps a few years older, though she was now a senior citizen.

Billy smiled. "Shiloh!"

She extended her arms, a finger missing from one of her hands. "It's been so long!"

Billy limped to her and gave her a hug. When he drew back, he looked into her eyes. It seemed that Bonnie returned the gaze. His heart ached, but he forced a smile as he let her go. "It's great to see you."

"You, too." She touched the teenager's shoulder. "This is my son, Isaiah. I also have a daughter, but …" She bit her lip hard. "But the Enforcers kidnapped her."

"Well, I have some awesome news for you." Billy pointed toward the highway. "Gabriel is with Jillian at one of the transport planes. They're both fine."

Tears welled in her eyes. She looked upward for a moment and whispered, "Thank you," then threw her arms around Billy and laid her head on his chest. "Oh, Billy! We've been through so much! Years and years of trials. When will it all end?"

He rubbed her back. "I'm afraid the light's pretty far down the tunnel. We have to hang on."

"I know. I know." She pulled away, a trembling smile on her face. "We'll hang on. We always do."

Billy scanned the lot again. "Where's Adam? I thought he would have told you about Jillian."

"He hopped into a car, a Mustang I think, and took off. He said something about checking on Elam and some other kids. We haven't seen him since."

Billy looked at the highway toward the east. "So Elam's still with the other kids he rescued."

Ruth walked up, her cloth gripped tightly. "Billy, I have a suggestion for you."

"Sure, Ruth." He smiled. "By the way, it's good to see you again."

"And you as well, but further greetings will have to wait." Her eyes darted from the dragons to the stadium and back again. "Arramos wants Sapphira to open the portal to Second Eden so his forces can enter. None of us wants this to happen, so the key is to move Sapphira so he will be unable to force her to do it. I suggest that we take her to the portal at the chasm, the one that leads to the tree of life. Even if it's closed, she can probably open it, and once inside the tree-of-life room, we'll be just a few steps away from the birthing garden in Second Eden."

"That's an idea to consider. With all the children to transport, it would be difficult, but we could work it out." Billy looked at the dragons. "Two huge problems. There's no way we can take the dragons. If we leave them here alone, Arramos will kill them all. And what about Walter's mom? Arramos is holding her hostage."

"A hostage, you say?" Ruth bent her brow. "That certainly complicates the situation."

"Right. It kind of paralyzes us."

She raised a finger. "There is another option. While we planned our mission, we discussed the possibility of creating a Sapphira look-alike. Since Arramos covets a way to open the portal, we could offer to trade the look-alike for the hostage."

Billy rubbed an ache at the base of his skull. "I don't know. Arramos won't be fooled easily. And if he has more troops, we might not be in a position to bargain."

"I agree that the troops issue is uncertain. But regarding fooling Arramos, don't underestimate the brainpower we have here. Elizabeth and Jennifer can send Sapphira's voiceprint to a program Elizabeth has on her little computer. Type anything in, and it will speak the words in Sapphira's voice. If you have a photograph, the computer can render a holographic projection." Ruth nodded toward a plane. "The voice replicator is how we got into that cargo plane. Elizabeth called up central command and recorded the voice of a captain, then used it to get us on board as soldiers in disguise."

"That sounds good on paper, but who could be a Sapphira clone? She still looks so young. Pardon me saying this, but you're too old. So are Shiloh and Elizabeth. That leaves only Jennifer, and she's what? Fifteen? We can't send a teenager to do such a dangerous job."

"You haven't seen her in action. She'll jump all over it. When we discussed the possibility, Elizabeth suggested that we go ahead and prepare for it, so many of the steps have already been taken, including gathering what we need to fake a portal-opening fire."

"No surprise. Elizabeth is just like her father. Really forward thinking." Billy looked toward the airplane where Elizabeth and Jennifer had gone. "But leaving Jennifer behind? Alone? Just her and Arramos?"

"And our three knights and three dragons."

"I know. They're good men, but they'll be outnumbered if Arramos brings reinforcements. And the dragons are still out cold." Billy bent his brow. "And Jennifer's just a young girl. She doesn't know how to fight Satan."

"Ruth?" Shiloh touched her arm. "Allow me, please."

"Certainly." Ruth stepped out of the way.

"Billy ..." Shiloh pushed a hand into her pants pocket. "Do you remember when Morgan activated the poisonous gas and it looked like we would all die?"

"I wasn't there, but Walter told me about it. A plant sprouted out of nowhere, and you fed it to everyone and made them immune. You saved a lot of lives."

"The plant didn't sprout out of nowhere." She withdrew her hand and opened it. An orange bead lay in her palm. "I saved some of the seeds, and I pushed one into the wet soil. The plant grew as fast as it always did in the sixth circle of Hades. That's what saved our lives."

"So God prepared the rescue long beforehand."

"Exactly my point." Shiloh slid the bead away and touched a smear of blood on Billy's hand. "What's this from?"

"Well ..." He dabbed a stinging spot on the top of his head. "Maybe this cut when one of the soldiers whacked me with a rifle butt." He lifted his shirt, exposing a gash in his ribcage. "Or this one. I got it when I was fighting the drone buzzards. One of them clawed me."

"From the way you walk, I think you have other wounds as well." Shiloh shook her head sadly. "You've made so many sacrifices, Billy. You gave your life for others. Wasted away in jail for years. Suffered so many injuries."

"Well … I had to. Lives were at stake."

"Of course you had to, but don't you think it's time to allow others to do the same?" Shiloh raised a hand, displaying the gap in her fingers. "Sometimes even a fifteen-year-old girl is called to make sacrifices, even if it means spending forty years in misery. God saves lives in ways we can't even imagine."

Billy looked at the stump of a finger for a moment, then turned away. "Touché. I surrender."

"Let's talk to Jennifer." Shiloh took Billy's hand and walked with him toward the airplane. When they arrived, they hopped into the rear compartment where Elizabeth and Jennifer sat on benches and tinkered with a radio, apparently pulled out of the plane's dashboard. Jennifer still wore her cap, but now she also wore a dark cloak that hid the clothing underneath.

Elizabeth looked up at Shiloh. "Has William authorized our plan?"

Shiloh nodded. "It's a go."

"Now you're talking!" Jennifer pulled off her cap. White hair dropped to her shoulders, and she shook her head to fan it out. She then shed her cloak, revealing a Second Eden battle uniform complete with belt and boots. "I'll be ready as soon as I put in my blue contacts and we distress this uniform to match Sapphira's rips and burns. I snapped her photo on my phone so I can copy it."

Elizabeth withdrew her computer tablet and looked at the screen. "We'll also need a recording of Sapphira's voice. I already have one for Arramos. He is quite a blustery dragon."

Billy allowed himself a smile. These women were amazing. "I have a question. Do you have an escape plan? I mean, suppose everything falls apart. Maybe Arramos will figure out Jennifer's a decoy. What if he doesn't let his hostage go until someone proves that the portal is open? What if you can't get away with Catherine before he figures out he's been duped?"

"Then we will probably die." Elizabeth rose and set her hand on Billy's shoulder. "William, when my father jumped onto a dragon's back to save lives, he likely had no escape plan. He died, and I still miss him terribly. We ..." She gestured toward Shiloh and Jennifer. "All of us here ... hope to save Second Eden, and we are willing to die to do so."

Warmth rose into Billy's cheeks. How could anyone argue with that? "I understand. And you're right."

"Very well." Elizabeth turned to Jennifer. "Let's make you look like Sapphira."

14

CHAPTER

A New Train Ticket

"Ashley!" Bonnie shut off the beam, dropped the sword, and ran to her. Marilyn leaped to Carly and clamped a hand over her thigh wound.

Bonnie laid a palm on Ashley's reddened cheek. Heat knifed into her skin. She jerked her hand away. "I've never felt her this hot before."

"And Carly's still bleeding," Marilyn said. "Ashley might have slowed the flow a little bit, but I'm not sure."

Mariel shuffled toward them. "Pour ice over Ashley! And make a tourniquet for Carly!"

Bonnie scooped ice from the ground and rubbed it on Ashley's forehead. The ice began melting immediately. "What can we use for a tourniquet?"

"Ashley's shirt, of course." Mariel knelt and began unfastening Ashley's buttons, revealing a saturated T-shirt underneath. Vapor rose from the wetness in thin white strings. "Help me get this off

her, and then we'll ask Grackle to spray ice directly on her torso instead of using the nasty stuff on the ground. And don't worry about hurting her skin. Frostbite is the least of her concerns. We have to cool her down at all costs."

While Bonnie and Mariel worked on getting Ashley's shirt off, Marilyn spoke softly to Carly. "How are you feeling?"

"Kind of light-headed," she murmured, her eyes closed. "The pain's not as bad as before."

"Then Ashley's treatment helped." Marilyn repositioned her hand on the wound. "Hang on. We just need to slow the blood flow a little more."

Mariel pulled the shirt free, twisted it into a rope, and slid it around Carly's thigh. "I have to make this tight. It's going to hurt."

Carly gritted her teeth. "I'm ready."

As Mariel tied the shirt, Carly grimaced. She let out a soft moan, then bit her lip. Thin liquid oozed from a deep lesion on her cheek, but that problem paled in comparison to her thigh's hemorrhaging wound.

"Grackle!" Bonnie called as she lifted Ashley's T-shirt up to her ribcage. "Come here and spray her with ice."

Grackle shuffled over and blew a misty spray of ice crystals over Ashley. As the crystals fell, Bonnie spread them across Ashley's stomach and, reaching under her T-shirt, rubbed some over her chest. The ice melted on contact and raised new strings of vapor. She stayed unconscious, apparently unaffected by the treatment. "Keep it up, Grackle. This might take a while."

Grackle heaved in a breath and continued, his spray weaker this time. After several seconds, he coughed and let his head droop. Icy spittle dribbled as he whistled a long, low note.

"All out of ice?" Bonnie asked.

Grackle's neck sagged as he bobbed his head.

"Thank you. Let me know if you can give more later." She released Ashley's shirt, leaving her torso exposed from her ribs down to her hips. Cooling from evaporation would have to take over now.

When Mariel finished tying the tourniquet, she rose and brushed her hands together. "The bleeding hasn't stopped, but I think it slowed a little more."

Marilyn laid her hand on the wound again and applied pressure. "Thank you."

"I wish I could do more." Mariel walked toward Thomas. "I'd better check up on my favorite old coot. He's looking rather antsy."

Bonnie wrapped a wing around Carly and whispered, "How are you doing?"

"Not too good." Carly leaned her head against Bonnie's and shivered.

"Do you want us to move you closer to the fire?"

"I'm not cold." A tear spilled to her cheek. "I guess I'm …"

"Scared?"

Carly nodded.

"It's no wonder she's scared," Thomas said as Mariel led him closer, their arms hooked at the elbows. "Number one, Sapphira just left to face a vicious dragon and two attack helicopters. For some, such a move would be madness, but because she's the only one who can open the portal for our allies, she had to go. She certainly wouldn't be able to help them from here. Number two, the villains might break through the portal at any second, and we will be at their mercy. Number three, bleeding from the femoral artery can cause death in a matter of minutes, so we can't risk moving Carly to a safer place."

Mariel swatted his shoulder. "I told you not to mention the artery."

Thomas lifted his chin. "I am merely stating the facts so we can plan our next move judiciously."

"Our next move is to pray," Bonnie said as she motioned for everyone to come closer. "Dragons included."

Mariel picked up Jared's plant and sat with Thomas across from Bonnie, while Marilyn knelt to Carly's right, a hand still on the wound. Karrick sat behind Thomas and Mariel and spread his wings to protect them from the falling ice. Grackle did the same over the others. Ashley lay on her back a step away. Vapor still rose from her body. It was probably best to leave her away from the warmth of the others.

Silence descended, interrupted by intermittent crackles of fire, a sniffle or two, and the whistling wind. It seemed that the walled-in chamber had become a cathedral, complete with a fiery altar.

"Before we pray …" Bonnie rubbed her cold, tingling hands together. "Is everyone warm enough?"

Mariel nodded. "It'll take more than a sorceress and a scientist to keep us down. Right, Thomas?"

"Well …" A grim countenance bent Thomas's features. He stared straight ahead, though his dead eyes could see nothing. "I sense darkness … deeper than I have ever felt. I fear that we have come to the final precipice."

"Oh, don't be such a …" Mariel's shoulders drooped. "Never mind. Go on."

He grasped her hand. "Did you listen carefully to Arramos? Did you hear the tremor in his voice? He is fearful. He has lost his swagger. His brutal murders are desperate attempts to boost his own confidence in his power, and he is enraged that Second Eden is still forbidden to him. Something in this realm haunts his every step, and it has shaken him to the center of his darkened heart."

"His doom is on the horizon," Bonnie said. "He knows the prophecies."

"And his fear indicates that he believes them." Thomas sighed. "Yet, he will continue to do battle. Perhaps he believes he can thwart what is written. Perhaps he simply wants to plunge a dagger into the heart of his enemy and shed blood out of spite. In any case, he has never been more dangerous. So we must be on our guard, both to avoid his wrath and to remain steady in our faith. Remember, he can do no more than destroy our bodies. He cannot touch our souls."

Bonnie nodded firmly. "Right, Thomas. We'll be fine. We just have to keep trusting."

"And praying, as you suggested. Let us be about that crucial business." Thomas angled his head upward, his eyes closed as ice collected on his face. "Our Father in Heaven, my first request is that you heal Carly. Seal the wound in her thigh. Replenish her blood supply and restore her and Ashley to health. My second request is that you watch over Billy, Walter, Elam, Gabriel, and Adam as they fight against the forces of evil. And finally, I ask that you protect your precious Oracle of Fire. Although Sapphira is a formidable warrior, the odds against her are overwhelming. Yet, you are able to muster an army of angels against her enemies. We ask you to rain justice down on the heads of the wicked and peace upon those who call on your name. And we here call on that name, the name of our savior, Jesus Christ our Lord. Amen."

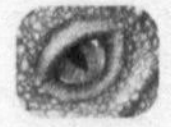

Bonnie echoed the *Amen* along with the others.

"So …" Marilyn shivered, her hand still in place over the wound. "What now? We can't move Carly, and I need to plant Jared in the birthing garden."

"Then we'll have to split up." Bonnie pointed at her. "You and the dragons can find the cave Sapphira talked about. Take Ashley, Thomas, and Mariel there and build a fire with some of the spare wood."

"I know where the cave is," Karrick said. "It is within easy walking distance."

"Perfect. Then you can go back and forth between here and the cave to make sure the fires stay burning." Bonnie shifted her focus back to Marilyn. "You can ride on Grackle to the birthing garden. I'm sure he knows how to find it."

Grackle let out a sharp whistle and bobbed his head.

"And you'll stay with Carly?" Marilyn asked. "Remember what Sapphira said about clearing out of here."

"I remember." Bonnie slid her hand into Carly's. "She's my friend. I'll stay with her for as long as it takes. I'm guessing the bleeding will stop pretty soon. Then I can fly her to the cave. Karrick can show me the way."

"Well … if you're sure." Marilyn lifted her hand from Carly's wound and moved Bonnie's in its place over the open cut. "Thank you, Carly," Marilyn whispered. "You saved my husband and maybe all of Second Eden."

"You're …" Carly licked her lips. "You're welcome."

Warm moisture oozed over Bonnie's fingers. Blood. Too much blood. Maybe Ashley's healing maneuver hadn't helped as much as they had hoped.

Marilyn retrieved the pot and stood close to Bonnie, her jaw firm. "When we get Jared transformed into Clefspeare, our omega dragon will show that pretender a thing or two."

"That's the spirit." Bonnie offered the best smile she could muster. "How's our dragon sprout doing?"

"He seems fine. In fact, he's grown a little bit. He has a head now, so I suppose he's at the kappa stage."

They gazed at each other for a moment. Bonnie read her eyes—worried yet reaching out for confidence. "Mom, when Clefspeare regenerates, would you tell him something for me?"

"Sure. What?"

"Tell him that Arramos is murdering children. Tell him that Shelly and Mark were gunned down like dogs in the street.

Their blood cries out for justice. Hold nothing back. It's true that vengeance belongs to the Lord, but I believe Clefspeare will be God's instrument to deliver vengeance, to bring wrath against those who would harm the innocent."

Marilyn nodded. "I will. Count on it."

After Karrick picked up a bundle of wood with his forelegs, he latched on to Ashley's belt with a rear claw and flew over the front wall. Marilyn, Thomas, and Mariel walked through a gap on the left side, Marilyn carrying Jared's pot.

Again, silence descended. Although ice continued falling in swirling sheets, Bonnie and Carly sat close enough to the fire to keep the crystals from piling up on their bodies.

"Well, my friend, it's just you and me." As Bonnie shifted to get a better angle for applying pressure, Carly grimaced. "Oh. Sorry."

"It's all right." Carly stifled a moan. "You can't help it."

Bonnie wrapped a wing around her again. "Are you still feeling scared?"

Carly nodded. "Pretty much."

"I don't think anyone will come through the portal. Sapphira would die before she'd let that happen." Bonnie glanced at the fire. The flames had ebbed, allowing a pocket of cold air to envelop them. Yet, she couldn't get up and rebuild the pyramid of logs. "Besides, the fire's dying down. She might not even be able to open it."

"That's not what I'm scared about."

Bonnie glanced at the blood pouring from Carly's wound in spite of the pressure and the tourniquet. The lesions on her face had become every bit as raw and deep as Oscar's. She wasn't immune to the curse. Her eternal soul might really be in great danger. "Are you scared of dying?"

She pressed her lips together and nodded again.

Bonnie drew her closer with her wing. "You read about my visit to Heaven in my letters, but would it help if I tell you about it again?"

A new grimace tightened Carly's features. She breathed out a quiet "Sure."

"Okay." Her free hand now feeling cold compared to the blood-covered one, Bonnie lifted it toward the fire. What would be the best way to describe Heaven this time? What did Carly need to see in her mind's eye? A glimpse of Jesus in glory? Or maybe something more personal.

As the fire died further and a chill descended, Bonnie breathed a silent prayer for help. When her mind settled, she took a deep breath and began. "Once upon a time, two lonely little girls met on a school bus. They both loved Tigger and good stories and strawberry ice cream, so they became fast friends. They also loved their parents, but something terrible happened. One girl's father let a dragon slayer kill her mother. The other girl's parents let the blossom of their love die on a withering vine. The first girl had to run for her life in a driving snowstorm. The second girl was sent away with a ragged duffle bag, a Tigger blanket, and a broken heart.

"They were both put on a train to a faraway town, leaving behind the tragedies that destroyed their beloved homes. But what lay ahead at their mysterious destinations? They had no idea. Fear of that unknown brought shivers. Would it be better there? Worse? And going alone made it feel like running through a dark tunnel with no light at the end."

Fighting against a shiver, Bonnie sneaked a glance at Carly. Although pale as a bed sheet, her eyes seemed alert. Bonnie took another deep breath before continuing. "Then the two girls met again. Both were riding the same train! Now comforted by being together, they took heart. This chance meeting, this coincidental rejoining of hands, had to mean something. Someone was watching over them. Someone cared.

"When they reached separate destinations, they both entered foster homes, one because she was in search of a family who would understand her genetic gifts, though they felt more like freakish birth defects, and the other because the grandmother who was supposed to take care of her in this new town had died unexpectedly.

"The first girl found herself in the midst of fantastic but dangerous adventures, while the second suffered the throes of loneliness, finding no one to love the cast-off daughter of a broken home. The first girl died and went to Heaven. The second girl lived in Hell. The first girl walked on streets of gold. She conversed with angels. She luxuriated in the arms of the savior of the world. The second girl walked streets of darkness with no one to talk to, no one to hold her. She walked alone."

Carly's respiration grew shallow and rasping. Each breath came out in a tiny puff of white vapor. Bonnie pressed harder on the wound. More blood poured. Tears in her eyes, she continued again, laboring to keep her voice in check. "The first girl rose from the dead and brought news to the world that a better place exists, a place of rest from all labors, the end of the path of suffering, a city of light that never sees a sunset. The second girl felt in her heart that her own city of light had to exist somewhere. So, following the summons of a prophet, she set out on a journey and arrived at a home where she hoped to find peace and purpose, and maybe even her beloved friend from the bus and the train.

"She took up residence in this home of love and embarked on a new path that merged with that of her childhood friend. Although many trials and difficulties followed, at least she was using her computer talents and training for a good purpose. People loved her.

They looked to her for help. She was instrumental in saving lives. She made a difference."

Carly leaned her head against Bonnie and shivered hard. "She . . . made a difference."

"Yes, Carly, she definitely did." Bonnie swallowed through a lump in her throat. "Now a new shadow has crossed the path, and the horizon is dark. The two friends sit together once again, this time in a cold cabin on a different train that is barreling toward a city unknown. But is it really unknown? To the second girl, yes. Her ticket has no destination printed on it. This train's final stop is a dark mystery."

Bonnie took Carly's hand—cold and clammy. Carly returned the grasp with a weak grip. "But if the two girls stay together," Bonnie continued, "they will both go to that city of light. They will walk hand in hand on the streets of gold. They will share the savior's embrace. They will live forever."

Carly whispered, faint and wheezing. "How can we … stay together?"

Bonnie rubbed Carly's cold knuckles with a thumb. "The way to keep holding my hand is to reach out for God's hand. Jesus Christ, the son of God, suffered a cruel death on a cross. He died to set you free from all the wrongs you have done. Just forsake those wrongs and embrace faith in him and what he has done for you."

A new shiver rocked Carly's body. Her teeth chattered. "How do I … do that?"

Bonnie forced her own body to stay calm, to fight the cold without trembling. "Confess Jesus as your lord. Believe that God raised him from the dead. When you confess faith, God will put to death the person you were and resurrect you to new life in your heart. And since you will be a new person, you will be issued a new ticket, one with Heaven written as the destination."

Her chattering continued. "You wrote to me about Jesus before … but now you make him sound … so real."

"He is real, Carly. I've seen him with my own eyes." Bonnie compressed Carly's hand. "Will you join me on the train?"

"So … I just … how did you say it?" Carly's trembling subsided. "Forsake my wrongs and have faith?"

"Exactly. It's really all about love—loving God and other people."

"I do feel love." As Carly's trembling returned, she squeezed Bonnie's hand. "I really do."

"I know you do. God loves you. And if you love God, you'll follow him on a new path that will lead to Heaven's gates."

Paler than ever, Carly whispered, "So now … I just … confess?"

Bonnie touched Carly's ashen cheek. "Yes, my dear friend. Just say what's on your heart."

"I …" She licked her blue lips. "I confess … that I hurt Adam. … Would you tell him … I'm sorry … sorry for breaking his heart?"

"Of course!" Tears streamed freely. "Of course I will!"

"And … and I confess that … I love …" As she exhaled, her head drooped, and blood stopped flowing from her wound.

"Carly?" Bonnie pressed two fingers on Carly's wrist. No pulse. "Carly!"

Bonnie curled her wing and drew her into an embrace. As Carly's head rested on Bonnie's shoulder, she rocked back and forth. "Oh, Carly! My dear, sweet friend! Why did this happen to . . . to such an innocent lamb!"

Bonnie kissed Carly's cheek and wept. With every cycle of her rocking motion, she took in a breath to try to settle her spasms, but the sobs kept coming, though gentler each time.

After a few more moments, Bonnie's spasms ceased. She ran bloody fingers across Carly's cheek … her smooth cheek, now free of lesions. As a new round of sobs emerged, Bonnie pressed Carly close and continued rocking as she sang. "Just as I am, without one plea, but that thy blood was shed for me, and that thou bidst me come to thee, O Lamb of God, I come. … I come."

Bonnie laid Carly down on the cold stone and stared at her lifeless friend. Cold and gray, Carly stared upward, as if mesmerized by a wondrous sight. Her flawless skin seemed to glow in the dim light.

"What do you see, Carly? Heaven's glory?" Bonnie looked up. The ice had stopped falling. The sky cleared, and a hint of sunshine appeared over the wall.

Her fingers still covered with blood, Bonnie grasped Carly's hand. Interrupted by new trembling sobs, she cried out, "We're on the train. … The city of light is the next stop. … And it's so beautiful, Carly … It's so beautiful." She forced a smile. "When you get there … write to me. … Let me know what you think. … I can't get off the train. … Not yet … But it will come through again. … And I hope you're there to greet me … when I walk down those steps to … to join you in the eternal light of his presence."

Using two fingers, Bonnie closed Carly's eyes, leaving bloody fingerprints on her lids. "Your confession, dear heart, is the most beautiful of all. … I love. … On those words hang all the law and the prophets."

Although Bonnie's sobs eased again, new shivers rocked her body. After retrieving Excalibur, checking the rubellite in the hilt, and sliding the blade behind her belt, she pushed her arms under Carly and picked her up, using her wings to provide a boost. She flew over the wall, but Carly's weight and the buffeting winds forced her to land on the other side.

She folded in her wings and balanced on a sheet of ice that extended downslope to the right, the horizon veiled by the receding storm. To the left, the sheet ended at a mountain. Shallow tracks led from where she stood to a recess within the mountain's base.

Now unhindered by the portal shelter, the frigid wind tore through her clothes. She lowered her head and trudged along the path. Blood dripped from Carly's thigh to the ice, marking a new trail. Numbness edged along Bonnie's fingers and across her hands. Her arms ached. Spasms knotted her calf muscles. When she came within ten paces of the cave, she shouted, "Mom? Karrick? Anyone?"

Marilyn appeared at the cave's arched entry. Her eyes shot open, and she dashed toward Bonnie. When she arrived, she made a cradle with her arms. "Give her to me."

Bonnie transferred Carly to Marilyn's arms. "She's … she's dead."

"I guessed that. I'm sorry." Marilyn gestured with her head. "Karrick's got a good fire started. Hurry on ahead and get warm."

Beating her wings, Bonnie ran along the ice and ducked to enter the cave's low opening. Inside the ten-foot-deep recess, Thomas and Mariel sat cross-legged and warmed their hands over a campfire, Jared's plant wedged between Mariel's legs. Ice-melt water dripped from their hair and clothes and joined a rivulet that ran a foot or so toward the entry. Smoke rose to the low ceiling and streamed outside, drawn by the stiff breeze.

Ashley sat against a side wall as far away from the flames as possible. Although her eyes were closed, her hands fidgeted in her lap.

"Ashley?" Bonnie withdrew Excalibur and leaned it against a wall. "Are you all right?"

Ashley grimaced. "The worst headache in human history is throttling my brain, but I can still read the shouts in your mind." A sad frown added new lines to her brow. "Carly's dead."

"Dead?" Thomas repeated with a gasp. "Oh, dear Lord Jesus. What has become of her soul?"

"Her soul is safe." Bonnie sat next to Thomas and set her hands close to the fire. "I had a chance to talk to her before she died." Her throat tightened. "The lesions on her face disappeared. … I guess … you could say she … she's healed."

Mariel wiped away a tear. "Then we'll see her again someday."

Marilyn trudged in and laid Carly's body a step away from Ashley. "Karrick and Grackle went to gather more wood. They'll return as soon as Karrick rebuilds the portal fire. When they do, I'll make my way to the birthing garden."

"And I'll come with you." Bonnie intertwined her fingers and stretched them in the newfound warmth. It seemed strange to be planning the next move, pushing forward while Carly lay dead so close by. Shouldn't they pay tribute? Sing a song? Say a prayer? Yet, time was of the essence. They had to press on. "There's nothing for me to do here. Karrick can guard Thomas and Mariel and Ashley."

"Can Grackle carry two passengers?" Marilyn asked.

"He did back when they used saddles, but I don't know how recently. It's still windy, so if he gets tired I can lift off and fly for a while."

"It's not far to the garden by air," Ashley said, her eyes still closed. "And Bonnie, I heard your thoughts. While we're waiting for the dragons to return, we'll sing a song for Carly. I know the perfect one."

Bonnie cast a thought toward Ashley. *Amazing Grace?*

Ashley nodded, a smile breaking through. "If you're not tired of it after all the times I sang it in prison."

"Never." Bonnie rose and sat next to Ashley. As they leaned their heads together, Bonnie reached and grasped Carly's lifeless hand. "Let's sing it responsively. We'll start."

"Wait a second." Marilyn sat next to Thomas and held his hand. He, in turn, took Mariel's. "Go ahead."

Bonnie began in a quiet voice. "Amazing Grace, how sweet the sound …"

Ashley joined in, and the two sang together. "That saved a wretch like me."

Thomas led the response, and the two ladies blended in. "I once was lost, but now am found, was blind, but now I see."

Bonnie compressed Carly's hand. Tears erupted, and a sob threatened to break through as she and Ashley continued. "'Twas grace that taught my heart to fear, and grace, my fears relieved."

"How precious did that grace appear the hour I first believed." Thomas rose to his feet. "Join hands," he said. "All together now."

Bonnie climbed to her feet, releasing Carly's hand. It hurt to let her go, but she had to. Someday they would join hands again, and then they would never have to let go. Bonnie helped Ashley rise, and they formed a circle around the fire. With Thomas again leading, they sang, "Through many dangers, toils, and snares, I have already come. 'Tis grace that brought me safe thus far, and grace will lead me home."

15

CHAPTER

Frozen Companions

"Wake up, Matt. I think the storm is over."

Matt opened his eyes. He lay curled on the floor under a window, his arms clutching a pillow. "How long did we sleep?"

"I'm not sure, but it's late afternoon. We'd better get going." Listener buckled her belt, her spyglass and dagger still attached. She walked to the hut's alcove and retrieved earmuffs, a fur-lined coat, gloves, and boots. "I'm glad I saved these from our cold days. They belonged to Angel."

Matt rose to his feet and picked up his boots. "Angel?"

"My mother." She sat at the foot of her bed and slipped on the earmuffs. "Well, Angel is my Second Eden mother. It's a long story. Her abode is now with the Father of Lights."

"You mentioned that Tamara is your birth mother." He sat on the other bed, pushed his feet into his boots, and began tying them. "Where is she?"

"Probably in Peace Village with my sister, Lily, and the others." Listener looked him over. "I'm sorry that I don't have suitable clothes for you. Candle outgrew his cold-weather garments, so he gave them away."

"No problem. I don't get cold easily." He eyed the shutters. "So is that noise still bothering you?"

"Only in a residual manner. I'm not sure if it's real or if I have suffered damage that's causing a hum in my ears." She put her boots on and began tying the laces. "We have to check on the others. Karrick is supposed to be with them, so they should be warm for the time being, but we will need to construct a bonfire. Elam and Sapphira are gone, Dr. Conner is likely frantically trying to keep his patients from freezing, and although Tamara is wise, her slow tongue is a handicap. Candle and the other men are hard workers, but they lack leadership skills. And, of course, Valiant is dead. My people look to me for guidance, so I'm concerned that they'll be like sheep without a shepherd."

Matt finished tying his boots. "Aren't there any men like Valiant in Second Eden?"

"That is an exceedingly high standard." Focusing on her laces, she smiled. "But now that you're here, I know of one."

Heat surged into Matt's cheeks. "That's … um … nice of you to say."

"I would never tell a falsehood." She rose, put on the coat, and pinched his sleeve. "I'm concerned about you staying warm. The journey to Peace Village is longer than the one between the storm center and here."

"I'll manage. Like I said, I—"

"Don't get cold easily." Listener tied the coat's belt. "If you do get too cold, we can take turns wearing the coat and gloves. They'll be somewhat tight on you but certainly better than getting frostbite." She set a metallic wafer in his hand. "A tooth transmitter, in case we get separated. I mentioned that our tower controls them. I already have one installed."

"Good idea." Matt slid the wafer between two molars. "I've used one before."

"Then you know how they work." Listener touched her jaw. "Two taps to turn it on."

"I remember. I'll turn it on if we get separated. The buzzing sensation gets annoying."

"I understand." She pulled on a pair of gloves, opened the shutters, and climbed through the window. "Let's go."

Matt followed. Once they stood in the gap between the hut and the wall of ice, he boosted her to the top. She reached down, grasped both of his wrists, and hauled him upward while he pushed his feet against the wall. Her tight grip stung, but it felt amazing at the same time. Her strength was incredible.

When he made it to the top, he looked up. Only a drizzle of ice fell, and the sun broke through the clouds here and there. As they tried to walk, their feet slid on the oily surface. Listener hooked Matt's arm with hers. "It's worse than before," she said. "We'll need to support each other."

They trudged together, one careful step after another. In the distance, the tops of ice-encrusted trees protruded from the frozen layer. The scenery looked like a charcoal drawing—sooty silhouettes on a background of ash.

Matt waved a hand toward the trees. "It looks like the lava didn't get to all the forested areas."

Listener shook her head. "That's a higher elevation. After destroying our villages, the lava channeled back to the river and followed its course."

A squall brought more ice pellets raining down in hefty gusts. At the edge of the forest, a branch cracked and fell against its trunk.

Like dominoes toppling, more branches dropped and filled the breeze with wind-blown snaps and pops.

Matt inhaled through his nose. The odor of garlic tinged the air. "I still smell the potion."

"So do I," Listener said as they labored up a rise. "At least it hasn't affected us yet."

"No obvious effect." He kicked through a mound of oily crystals. "It might be a slow-acting poison."

She squinted. "Matt, I need to talk to you about something."

"Sounds serious."

"It is." Listener inhaled a deep breath. "Now that I have no companion, many things have changed inside me. I feel so different."

"In a good way?"

"Most of the time, but I also feel regrets about the past. Whenever I was tempted to do something wrong, my companion would flash a warning, and I would cast away the temptation. Now I see what a weak condition that is. My companion was a crutch." Her feet slid out from under her, but Matt tightened his grip on her arm and kept her from falling. She smiled thankfully. "Maybe I still need a crutch … physically, at least."

"So when you lost it temporarily back at the chasm, what did it feel like?"

"Oh, Matt, those hours are the source of my fiercest regrets. I felt like a rudderless boat set adrift. I treated your father like a stranger, even though he was like a father to me when I was young. I even shot a man in cold blood."

"Didn't you say that he threatened to shoot you?"

"I did say that." She tightened her grip on Matt's arm and looked him in the eye. "I lied."

Lied? Matt forced his voice to stay calm. "Why?"

As she looked again at the path ahead, her voice animated and rose in volume. "I don't know! Anger? Revenge? The reaction of a hot-blooded fool? I just don't know! If I had lied in Second Eden, I could have been punished by stoning or banishment, and my companion would have perished, but not so on Earth. My lie had no consequences except to burden my conscience with a millstone that I couldn't shake loose."

"So losing your companion was like losing your moral compass."

"Exactly, but only while on Earth. In Second Eden I was able to do good things without being prodded by my companion. And now I never need prodding. Doing what's right just flows from within me."

"So let me guess. You want to go back to Earth to test yourself."

Listener nodded. "I want to know if the good within me can stand up to the corruption of that place. I want to be a woman who is not forced to follow a path that is chosen by her external influences."

"I can't blame you for that. That's true freedom."

"And I especially want to apologize to your father. Since my real father is dead, I want Billy to take his place. I want our relationship to be like old times." She returned her gaze to Matt. "Do you think he'd forgive me and be like my father again?"

Matt shivered. Was the cold air finally getting to him? More likely the passing idea that his father could become Listener's father-in-law and fulfill her wishes, but that was just a fantasy. "Of course he would. I don't think he has a vindictive bone in his body."

"I agree. I just wanted some affirmation."

"You have nothing to worry about."

"There is something I am worried about." She stopped and took her gloves off. "Are you sure you're warm?" She covered his hands with her own and began rubbing. "Your fingers are freezing!"

"My inner furnace runs on food. I guess I didn't get enough." Dark oily water dripped from her hair and down both cheeks.

In spite of a mask of filth and a new cap of frozen ash, a radiant glow shone from within. "I'll be all right."

"Here." She began sliding her gloves over his hands. "Wear these for a while."

He pulled away. "Thanks for the thought, but you need them more than I do. My furnace will kick in soon."

Without another word, she put her gloves back on, hooked his arm, and resumed their march at a faster speed.

Matt copied her rapid gait. "Did I say something wrong?"

"Matt, chivalry is usually a beautiful expression of gentlemanly character, but not when it is impractical or causes harm." Listener kept her stare straight ahead. "I do wish to continue our stimulating conversation, but now is not the time."

"If you say so." Matt eyed her face in profile—stoic and calm. She didn't seem angry or irritated, but she certainly got her message across.

For the next several minutes, they trudged over the gray terrain, most of the time without any new precipitation falling. They slid now and then, but their hooked arms helped maintain balance. After negotiating a slippery rise, they stopped at the crest. A new squall began. Wind and swirling ice buffeted their bodies.

Ahead, the slope eased into level ground. A circular depression about fifty feet wide had been carved out of the ice, too deep to see the bottom, though flashes of orange light made it clear that a fire blazed below.

Listener unfastened her spyglass and raised it to her eye. "I see flames but nothing else unusual. … Wait. … A man. No. More than one." She refastened the spyglass, released Matt, and slid down the hill as if skiing. "Come on!"

Matt followed and joined her at the edge of the depression. Here, the wall sloped sharply, about a ten-foot drop. At the center of the depression, five men surrounded a wood fire. All five lay or sat motionless in tall, lush grass exposed by melting ice.

"I'm going in." Listener dropped to her bottom and slid down the depression's slope. Matt did the same. When their slide ended at the grassy area, she knelt next to a man lying on his stomach, his arms tucked underneath. Two others lay in a similar position, and two sat hunched over, covering something in their hands. No one moved.

"What are these men doing?" Matt asked.

"Protecting their companions." Listener shifted toward a seated man—dark-skinned with frozen dreadlocks. "Candle!" She pried open his fingers and withdrew his egg-shaped companion. "What happened?"

Candle looked at her blankly. An icicle hung from his nose, and tiny crystals clung to his lashes.

She rubbed a thumb along the companion's surface. Coated with ash, it lacked the usual glow.

Matt leaned closer. "Is it dead?"

"I don't know." She enfolded the companion in her coat. "They're usually warm to the touch, but this one is like ice."

"I'll get another." Matt pried a companion loose from a prostrate man and rubbed it with both hands. The companion was cold and slick, and the oily residue wouldn't come off. "Whatever this stuff is, it's stuck like glue."

Listener rose and set her hands on her hips. "These men were probably out gathering wood for the others in the huts, and their companions iced over, which weakened them. Then they started a fire to keep from freezing, and the fire melted the ice down to grass level."

Matt pushed the companion back into the man's grasp. "How're we going to get them out of here?"

"One at a time." She pointed to the edge of the depression. "You can boost me out of this hole and then lift one of the men up to me. I'll take him to the huts and come back for another."

Matt imagined the process. Listener had already proven herself strong enough to lift a man, and she could slide him on the ice the rest of the way. "Do you have medical help there?"

"I'm sure Dr. Conner had to ground the mobile hospital somewhere, so he probably isn't far." Listener restored Candle's companion to his grasp and pointed at another man. "Let's take Steadfast. When he recovers, he'll be a good medical aide."

"First let me see if my healing gift will help. Then maybe they can walk home." Matt set his hands on Candle's cheeks—stiff and chapped. As he concentrated on transmitting healing energy, new ice shards pelted the grass. A cold breeze buffeted Matt's face and raised a new shiver. Seconds later, Candle's limbs locked, and his body rocked in spasms.

"He's having a seizure!" Listener pulled Matt's hands away, cupped Candle's jaw, and looked into his mouth. "Just leave him alone for a minute. He's not biting his tongue, so he should be all right."

Matt looked at his hands. What had gone wrong? Maybe his fingers were too cold, and the effect of his touch had somehow reversed.

After another moment, Candle's spasms stopped, his body relaxed, and he resumed a normal breathing pattern.

Listener pulled Matt's arm. "Help me get Steadfast."

After they carried Steadfast to the edge of the depression, Listener ran up the slope, slipping and sliding back a couple of times before digging in and clawing her way to the top. She then lay on her stomach and reached down. "Slide him up as far as you can."

Matt laid Steadfast on his back and pushed the soles of his boots. As he dug in and shoved Steadfast up the slope, the ice covering his body and clothes kept him from bending. Soon, his shoulders drew within range of Listener's hands. She grabbed his coat and hauled him the rest of the way up.

"Keep them warm!" she called as she turned and disappeared from sight. A pair of gloves sailed down in the wake of her voice. It seemed that Listener wasn't taking no for an answer.

Matt put the gloves on, hurried back to Candle, and knelt next to him. The falling ice had diminished to a gentle drizzling of tiny pellets, making it easier to brush grimy fragments from his face. Head-high flames crackled at the center of the circle and lent warmth to the task.

He set his ear close to Candle's mouth. He was breathing, but barely. After transferring Listener's gloves to Candle's hands, Matt rose to his feet. The ice storm had stopped completely, though cold air continued swirling in the bowl.

Looking in the direction Listener had gone, he monitored his danger sensor. A vague feeling of unease registered. With Second Edeners suffering and their companions freezing, it was no wonder. Yet, the sensation emanated from the village. Could it be real or just a phantom generated by concern for Listener? Or maybe the feeling had been there all along, hovering below the noticeable level.

He paced in front of the fire. Waiting felt foolish. Every minute could cost lives. Yet abandoning the plan based on background danger signals felt like giving in to fear.

As he continued pacing, the fire burned on, and the surrounding ice retreated. Grass sprouted in the newly exposed areas and grew an inch in a matter of seconds. One of the men fell to his back. His fingers loosened, and his companion rolled from his hand to the ground, dark and covered with soot.

Matt scooped up the companion and brought it close to the flames. As residual water dripped from its surface, he scratched the soot with a thumbnail but couldn't make a dent.

Kneeling, Matt set his ear on the man's chest. No heartbeat. No breathing. His face was already gray. Maybe he had been dead for a while.

He hurried to another man, knelt, and checked his vital signs. Again, nothing. He leaped to a third man and lifted his arm—already stiff, no need to search for signs of life. Candle was the only one still alive.

The sense of danger surged … nearby … closing in. Matt swiveled in place. Just a few steps away, grass poked through the remaining ice crystals along with gray stems that morphed into crawling vines. As green leaves sprouted, the vines slithered over the third corpse and crept up Matt's legs.

He shot to his feet, snapping the vines. They thickened and covered the dead body in seconds. The odor of ammonia tinged the air, pungent and choking. More vines sprang up and slinked over the other men, as if the warming ground had sounded a wake-up call.

Matt broke the vines around Candle and dragged him away from the fire to an area still covered by ice. When he returned, the vines had completely engulfed the others. They grew thicker and thicker every second.

He walked over the vines and stopped at one of the men. Balancing on top of the woody network, he thrust his hands under a vine and jerked upward, but it wouldn't budge. A green shoot crawled up and around his leg in a tight coil. He fell backwards and rolled to the edge of the fire. The vines crept toward him, but when they drew to within inches of his toes, the ends shriveled and turned back, apparently thwarted by the heat.

Matt vaulted up and ran to where Candle still lay, a foot or two from the growing mass. New vines broke through the edges of the ice and slithered. Only seconds remained before they would take over the entire area.

After hoisting Candle over his shoulder, Matt backed toward the depression's boundary. Climbing up the icy slope while carrying Candle might be impossible, but he had to try.

He turned and kicked a toe of his boot into the wall, then, with one arm around Candle's legs, he clawed at the ice and vaulted himself up a few inches. The foothold broke, sending them both tumbling and rolling to within inches of the encroaching vines.

Matt scrambled to his feet and shouted toward the village. "Listener! Where are you?" The words echoed, fading with each repetition.

Again and again he shouted. The vines drew closer, looking like an army of green serpents. Finally, a feminine voice filtered in from above. "Matt?"

He looked toward the source of the call. No one was in sight. "Down here!"

A slender brunette appeared at the lip of the depression, her hands at the edge as she looked down. Her face, pale and narrow, seemed kind and concerned. "I am … Tamara."

Matt heaved Candle over his shoulder again. "Did Listener send you?"

Tamara nodded. "She needs you." She pivoted and looked back. "Trouble in village."

"What kind of trouble?"

Her lips formed a tight line. "Hard to … explain."

"Never mind. I just have to get out of here." Matt edged away from the vines. They had now covered nearly everything with a tangle of foliage at least four feet high. Only the central fire and a narrow swath of ice at the depression's perimeter remained unaffected.

Tamara reached down. "Can you … lift Candle?"

Matt mentally measured the distance. Heat from the fire had melted the ice on Candle's body, making him more limber, so pushing him that far would be impossible. And Tamara didn't look half as strong as Listener. "I doubt it. And I tried climbing. I can't get a foothold."

"Soon … much easier."

"What do you mean?"

She pointed. "They help … you climb."

Matt looked back. A vine crawled over the thinning ice and wrapped around his ankle. He jerked away, again snapping the wood. More vines slithered around his feet. With Candle over a shoulder, he high stepped in place to stay on top of the growing mass.

As the network grew and his stationary march continued, he slowly elevated. When he rose high enough, Tamara grabbed Candle's wrists and pulled while Matt pushed until they hoisted him out of the depression.

Using the vines as a springboard, Matt vaulted to the lip and slid across the ice. When his momentum eased, he hurried to Tamara, who now knelt beside Candle and blew on his clutched companion. Wearing only a long dark skirt and a thin sweater, she had to be cold.

"Let's get him to the village." Matt again hoisted Candle over his shoulder and looked at Tamara. "If you'll lead the way."

"Of course." She wrapped her sweater tightly and trudged ahead over the ash-embedded ice. "This way."

Matt stayed close behind. With every step, his legs ached, the danger sensation increased, and Candle seemed to grow heavier. Images of carrying Lauren's corpse came to mind—her limp body, her pallid face, her blue lips. Where was she now? Was Sir Barlow keeping her safe? Yet, how could he keep a dead person safe?

His focus on Tamara, he struggled up a ridge, slickened by gray ice. Candle's weight helped his shoes break through and gain traction, but the burden made his legs tremble.

Tamara grasped his wrist and pulled. "Almost there!" Puffing, she jerked with extra force and heaved Matt to the crest.

As in the other village, at least a dozen roofs protruded from the expansive sheet of gray. Smoke rose from exposed pipes on most of the icy tops.

"Come!" She hurried to a nearby hut, more than half buried in ice, and touched its gray-topped roof. "Listener … is here."

Matt jogged the rest of the way, laid Candle next to the gap between the ice and the hut, then hopped down and looked through the window. Listener knelt in the midst of several reclining Second Edeners—two men, three women, and five children. Her coat lay over two toddlers as they rested across the room from the fire. One of the children, perhaps a teenager, had white hair that reached his shoulders.

Listener held a companion in her hand and stroked it as she leaned close to a fire burning within a hearth in the wall. Matt whispered, "Listener. It's me, Matt. I brought Candle."

She set the companion down on a woman's chest and tiptoed around the bodies. As she drew closer, tears in her eyes became evident as well as wet ashes embedded in her swaying pigtails and soot smeared across her cheeks. She reached her arms through the window and grasped his hands. "Come in! Come in!"

"Just a second." He looked up. Tamara stood at the edge of the gap. "Can you guide Candle down here?"

"Yes." She moved out of sight for a moment. Candle's feet slowly slid into the gap. Matt grabbed his ankles and guided him the rest of the way.

Listener reached through and pulled Candle while Matt pushed. After a few moments, Matt and Tamara made their way inside and laid Candle near the fire. Shivering, Matt stayed close to the flames and warmed his hands.

Listener picked up a wicker basket from the floor. "Here." She set it close to Matt. "Eat as many as you can. We have to stoke that furnace."

"Thanks." From a pyramid of sandwich wraps, he selected the two on top. Each consisted of white-meat paste enclosed in a dark green leaf. He took a hearty bite from one and chewed. The leaf crunched easily, and the paste tasted like fish in buttery cream.

"Where are the other men?" Listener set a jar of water at Matt's side.

He swallowed quickly and washed the bite down with water. "Well …" He glanced at Tamara. She bit her lip hard, her eyes red. Obviously she wouldn't want to tell the story. "They're dead. I don't know what got them first, the cold or the lack of a functioning companion."

A tear tracked down Listener's cheek, but she kept a straight face. "More heroes from my people."

Matt hurriedly finished both wraps as well as the water while Listener and Tamara checked on each companion and tried to clean off the sooty residue, but to no avail.

"No one has seen Dr. Conner," Listener said as she scrubbed a companion with a soft bristle brush. "The mobile hospital might be buried in ice. At least the plane has an engine to keep everyone warm, and maybe the Second Edeners who were working as medical assistants were able to keep their companions safe."

"I'm sure they're fine." Matt crouched near a small boy. A dark, soot-encrusted companion sat on his chest. "What happened here in the village?"

"This storm was meant to neutralize us in several ways." Listener joined him in a crouch. "First, the ice paralyzes the companions. Second, the noise keeps me from thinking straight, though that threat has diminished. Third, my mother … Tamara … told me that a vapor in the wind weakened Karrick. He reported that it is thicker near the ground, so he and Grackle left to seek refuge at a higher elevation where the agent might be less concentrated. They were both suffering greatly, so escaping was their only hope of survival."

She nodded toward the hut's southern wall. "We have a portal location in the higher elevations. In emergency situations, we're supposed to light a fire there that makes it easier for Sapphira to open from the Earth side, so I asked one of our men to do that before I went to Abaddon's Lair. When Karrick left, he said he would check on the fire, but as of a couple of hours ago, Tamara couldn't see any smoke, so Mardon's storm must have extinguished it. In theory, Sapphira should be able to open it without our fire, but we need to make sure. I have a feeling that Mardon's devilry consists of more than simply putting the fire out with ice."

"Like what?" Matt asked. "The noise?"

Listener nodded. "I doubt that the noise element was aimed at me specifically." Her face took on a determined aspect. "I want that fire burning. We need our warriors to return. If Ashley is among them, maybe she can figure out a way to clean the film off the companions and revive them. I've tried everything I can think of."

"So that's why you sent Tamara. You were busy trying to save lives." Matt touched an infant girl's limp hand. "Good decision."

"That's my sister, Lily. She isn't fading as quickly as the others, so I am encouraged about her." Listener gestured toward Steadfast, stretched out near the door. "I was hoping he would work with me to try to revive the others, but he never regained consciousness."

Matt touched the white-haired boy's arm. "What happened to him? I don't see a companion."

"Zohar is an Oracle of Fire, not a Second Edener. Something in the air is affecting him, but I'm not sure what. I know Mardon once concocted an agent that weakened Acacia, so I'm guessing this is his work." Listener clenched her teeth. "He's behind every plague. Who can tell what other evils he included in the storm?"

"Man-eating vines," Matt said.

"Man-eating ..." Listener blinked. "What?"

"Vines." Matt nodded in the direction of the depression. "Vines sprouted and grew at an incredible rate. They swallowed the dead men and might've swallowed Candle and me if Tamara hadn't helped us climb out of that place."

Listener rubbed Tamara's back. "Mother, thank you for saving their lives."

"Yes, thank you." Matt plucked a chunk of ice from his sleeve and examined the dark fragments within. "I'm wondering if something in the ice acted like a super fertilizer."

"Volcanic ash?" Listener ran a finger across Matt's cheek and sniffed the tip, now smeared with soot. She wrinkled her nose. "Ammonia. I smelled it earlier. It's used in fertilizers, and we can be sure Mardon knows how to enhance it."

"But why vines?"

"We used to have a grape vineyard in that spot. I suppose some dormant plants sprouted and grew with abandon. The grass also sprang up unusually fast."

"Then wouldn't any plant grow in the same way? If we melt the ice so the ash could get down into the soil, wouldn't any plant take off?"

"I assume so." Listener half closed an eye. "What are you thinking?"

"Just trying to figure out what Mardon's up to. He created a storm designed to kill everyone here, but why the fertilizer?"

"To resurrect someone in the birthing garden? His mother, maybe?"

"Not likely. She's scattered to the four winds, literally." Matt furrowed his brow. "Has the garden ever produced someone evil?"

Listener nodded. "Mardon once planted a seed that eventually produced Devin. The sprout was obviously of evil origin—black and orange without any green—but circumstances wouldn't allow us to destroy it. Unfortunately, the garden doesn't know if it's growing someone from Abaddon's Lair or from a demon seed, but we should be able to identify an evil plant without a problem."

"Abaddon's Lair." Matt tapped a finger on his thigh. Images of that place returned to mind—the table, the book, the two statues. What happened to the second one? "We're assuming that everyone who comes from the lair is good, right?"

"Right. I don't think the Father of Lights would bring them back otherwise." Listener gave a confirming nod. "I perceive your line of thinking, and I agree. The other statue in Abaddon's Lair likely held someone who would be an ally to us, perhaps Eagle if I interpreted Lauren's musing correctly, so Mardon's fertilizer was not meant to resurrect that soul. He had another purpose in mind, but perhaps we can turn his scheme against him."

"Would the person in the statue come up as a baby or as he was when he died?"

"It's hard to be sure. The garden has produced adults—Timothy, Bonnie, and Sapphira. In any case, the garden plants are probably buried in ice. In the past, the leaves have offered protection from the elements, but we always cleared away any snow that fell."

"So the babies might be freezing."

"I've been thinking about that. Now that you know the way, you can go and make sure they're all right. While you're there, you can see what is growing, whether enemy or ally."

"Me? What about you?"

Listener shook her head. "I have to look after my people in this hut and in the other huts. Nine out of ten are unconscious, so I have to force-feed them if necessary." She grasped Matt's arm. "You are wise and strong. I'm sure you can free the plants from the ice."

"But you know a lot more about the garden than I do. I'm not even sure I can find it, especially with everything covered by dark ice."

Tamara raised a hand. "I stay. … I take care … of people."

"There. See?" Matt compressed Tamara's shoulder. "After seeing her haul Candle and me out of that crazy vine trap, I'm sure she can handle it. Besides, like you said, nearly everyone's unconscious, so her speech impediment isn't a problem. Since she's the only other one around without a companion, she's perfect for the job."

Listener picked up a small jar of water that had a bent straw protruding at the top. "Are you sure, Mother? It's a lot of work."

"I am … sure." She let a smile break through. "Winston says … I take … cow by horns."

Listener laughed. "Sir Barlow is right. They will all be in capable hands."

"Super." Matt scanned the hut. Might they have a blowtorch around? "We need something to melt the ice so we can get the fertilizer to seep into the soil like it did at the vineyard. If Eagle is really there, we want to speed up his resurrection."

"I can melt it," Zohar murmured, his eyes still closed.

"Zohar?" Listener slid her hand into his. "You're too weak. You can't even walk."

"I started the fires in the huts." His eyes opened. "Just get me to the garden. I'll melt the ice. I'm physically weak, but I can still create flames."

"It's downhill most of the way," Matt said. "We just need something he can slide on."

Listener looked up. "Ashley fashioned a signal-receiving dish that is no longer in use. I think it will slide quite well."

Zohar pushed to a sitting position. "Let me make sure I can still generate fire." He opened his hand and stared at his palm.

A fiery ball blossomed and quickly swelled. He then blew on the flame, and it vanished in a puff of smoke. He smiled at Listener and Matt in turn. "I can do it."

"We'd better be ready for a lengthy journey, just in case." Listener rose, opened a nearby closet door, and rummaged within. "We'll take whatever food and water we have left in our basket. We have more in other huts. Even if we could clean and melt that ice, I'm not about to drink it."

Matt grasped Zohar's wrist. "Let's see if you can stand." He pulled the young man to his feet easily. Short and thin, he couldn't weigh more than a hundred pounds.

Zohar wobbled for a moment before steadying. "The whole world is spinning."

"I have something for dizziness." The new voice came from the window. A man began climbing through, his face veiled by his arms and a black pliable satchel.

"Dr. Conner!" Listener bolted to the window and took the bag while he climbed the rest of the way. "Where is the hospital? How are the others?"

"The hospital's about a mile from here, and there it will stay until the ice melts." He brushed dark crystals from his coat. "Irene is well enough to take charge there, and Pearl, Onyx, and Windor are helping with the patients. Everyone stayed inside during the storm, so no one was affected by it. I stopped at another hut and saw what happened to the companions. The only conscious person there told me I would find you here."

"Do you have any idea how to revive the companions?" Listener asked.

Dr. Conner shook his head. "It's a mystery. I tried alcohol and diluted ammonia, but they didn't work. I thought it best to look for you to get the details."

"There's a lot to tell." Listener quickly updated Dr. Conner with the information she had, including the need to hurry to the birthing garden. He seemed to put the details together without any trouble.

"Fascinating story." He withdrew a small brown bottle from his medical bag and gave it to Zohar. "Take a few drops. It should alleviate the dizziness, at least for a couple of hours."

After packing supplies in a knapsack, Listener hugged Tamara. "I love you, Mother. I wish we could spend more time together."

"And I … love you." Tamara kissed Listener's cheek. "I see you … soon."

After saying good-bye to Dr. Conner, Matt, Listener, and Zohar climbed through the window, found the signal dish in a nearby hut, and set it on the ice. Matt helped Zohar sit on the dish and gave it a test slide. It moved quite well.

Listener checked the spyglass at her belt, then set her hands on the back of the makeshift sled. "Together?"

"Sure." Matt placed his hands next to hers, dug into the ice with his boots, and shoved. Again, the sled moved easily. With the ice now melting, pits and exposed rocks might slow them down. Still, they would press on, no matter what.

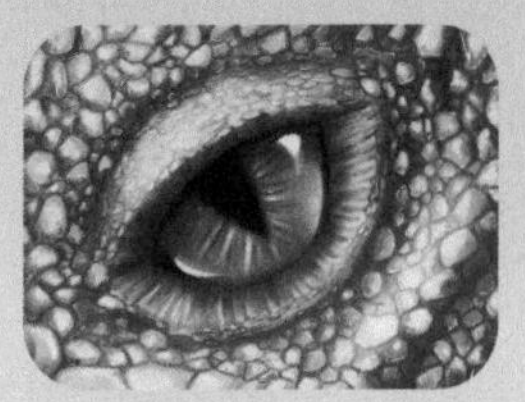

16

CHAPTER

The Third Puzzle Piece

Lauren let out a long sigh. "So when I embraced the tree of life, I became an Oracle of Fire. I think I was one of spirit then, but now I'm like Sapphira. I can create real fire with my hands, or at least I could until we came to this place."

Lauren halted her tale. She and Sir Barlow had engaged in back-and-forth storytelling for what seemed like hours, but in this realm of darkness with only a glowing blue yoke for light, who could tell how much time had passed?

She prodded his arm. "I can't think of any more stories. Do you want to go again?"

"My voice is spent," Sir Barlow said. "But I was right about your tales. They are fascinating indeed."

"Yours are more fascinating. When you talked about battling Goliath back-to-back with Edward, I felt like I was there." She

stifled a laugh. "Especially when you got caught in Goliath's tail, and later you had to walk home in your underwear."

"Feel free to laugh, Miss. It is certainly funny now, but I assure you that I was not amused at the time." The warm yoke lifted. Sir Barlow's grunts returned, and his voice came from higher up. "Dawn does not seem to be approaching, and my backside is nearly frozen, so I suggest a new course of action. Since you have temporarily lost your new gift, we will have to rely on our native skills."

"You mean building a fire? What would you use?"

"I have nothing with which to kindle a flame. I meant that we would have to use common sense. Every world needs light of some kind. We simply have to find it, or allow it to find us. We will call for help."

"I suppose you're right." Lauren rose and joined him. When he handed her the yoke, she hugged it close. The warm wood felt soothing in the frigid air. "Go ahead."

Sir Barlow cleared his throat and shouted, "This is Sir Winston Barlow." At each pause, his words echoed from afar. "I am here on a holy quest sanctioned by the almighty God to find the life reservoir. In my company is a powerful Oracle of Fire, whom I have been assigned to protect from harm to life and limb, and we seek a light to guide us on the path to complete our sacred duty."

When the echoes faded, a new voice followed—male and mirthful. "You and the Oracle are welcome here, Sir Barlow, but there is no need to sound like a script from a medieval theatre production."

Sir Barlow laughed. "Now that's a voice from long ages ago."

"Who is it?" Lauren asked.

"In these lands of imposters, I want to make sure before I divulge his identity." Sir Barlow called out, "Greetings! In order to facilitate a safe concourse, I would like to request a password of sorts. If you are who I think you are, then you will know the answer to my question. When Sir Devin said to King Arthur, 'Your faith resides in coats of scales while you snub your nose at your own kind,' what was your response?"

A laugh echoed in the darkness. "Sire, a man who breathes rumors of treachery had better back his words with more evidence than his own hot air."

Sir Barlow clapped his hands. "I secretly applauded your answer on that cold, wet day, and now I do so without stealth."

"Even though I am the one who sent you into that candlestone for fifteen centuries?" The man laughed again. "Come. I will send a glowbat to guide your way."

A light fluttered in the distance and drew closer. As it neared, wings took shape, and the light cast a flickering glow on a floor of shining ice. The glowbat reversed course over their heads and flew in the direction it had come.

Sir Barlow pulled on Lauren's hand. "The ice is harder now. We musn't keep Merlin waiting."

"Merlin?" Lauren hurried to keep up with Sir Barlow and the glowbat. "The king's counselor in your stories?"

"Correct. Now that we are about to meet him, I should have told you more about his tales."

The glow slid forward on the ice. Along the path, stalagmites protruded from the ground here and there. Lauren eyed one as she passed. This place looked like a cavern somewhere in the frozen North.

Ahead, pinpoints of light appeared well above the ground. Their glow painted a dim column of radiance that surrounded a bearded man. Wearing a red cloak, he leaned on a long staff with a dim light of its own at the top.

When they arrived, Merlin welcomed Sir Barlow with a brief embrace. He lowered himself to one knee, grasped Lauren's hand,

and gazed at her from under a wizened brow. "Welcome, Karen, now known as Lauren. I congratulate you on completing the puzzle and arriving at the life reservoir."

Lauren locked on his eyes—deep and ancient. Answering this wise, old man without sounding like a dumb kid felt out of reach, especially since the puzzle seemed to come together on its own. "Thank you, Merlin. I hope to learn more about these mysteries and how to apply the reservoir so that it will benefit those who need it."

With help from his staff, Merlin rose. "I know only a little about the mysteries, so we will have to merge what we have learned." He touched the yoke. "What is this?"

Lauren lifted it closer to him. "I found it in the first realm. It helped me get into the second one, so I think it's part of Jade's puzzle." When he set his staff against a stalagmite and took the yoke, she went on to explain her discovery of her father in the pool as well as details about his computer glasses, the ravens, and the polluting sludge. She added a summary of Tamiel's deception, how he disguised himself as Micaela and escaped to Second Eden, and finished with the mystery of her own acquiring of fire-creating power and the subsequent loss of it upon entering this realm.

"Mysterious indeed." Merlin ran a finger along the yoke's wooden surface. "I agree that this is one of Jade's devices. I was curious because it is essential that I examine any foreign objects that enter this realm. It is a holy place, and I cannot allow any contaminants to corrupt its purity."

"Then maybe you should look at the glasses." Lauren slid them from her pocket. "Sir Barlow says the computer screen was showing … well … porn, I assume."

"Indeed, lass," Sir Barlow said. "Filthy, to be sure. That's why I threw them away."

Lauren dangled the glasses from her fingertips. "Micaela … I mean, Tamiel, gave the glasses back to me. I forgot all about them."

Merlin took the glasses. "Obviously Tamiel wanted to make sure you brought them in here." He dropped the glasses to the icy floor and stomped on them with a boot.

The glasses flashed with light. Hairy spiders with glowing legs skittered out in all directions. The size of tarantulas, they melted furrows in the ice as they hurried toward the stalagmites.

"Kill them!" Merlin shouted as he chased one of the spiders. "Follow their paths!"

Sir Barlow hurried after a spider. Lauren dropped to her knees and traced one of the furrows toward a stalagmite, but the path stopped abruptly. She called out, "The path ended!"

"As did this one." Sir Barlow snorted. "I should have smashed them in the other realm."

Lauren climbed to her feet. "It's not your fault, Sir Barlow. I was the one who should've—"

"Look!" Sir Barlow pointed at the glasses. Another spider squeezed out of the broken frame and expanded like a balloon. With a body the size of a soccer ball and legs that covered a span of five feet, it scrambled away. Sir Barlow leaped after it, but he slid across the ice and smacked his knee against a stalagmite. Standing on one foot, he stared into the darkness. "There is no catching it now."

Merlin shook his head sadly. "The spiders appear to have heat-generation ability that they can turn on and off. We will have to stay close to the reservoir and watch for them." He reached into a cloak pocket and withdrew a red egg-shaped orb. "Follow me, and I will tell you more about this place." He turned and walked away. "And bring the yoke."

Lauren picked up the yoke and walked side by side with Sir Barlow. Grief weighed down her mind. Why hadn't she thought about the glasses? After Tamiel's deception became clear, she should have gone over everything he did. Forgetting the glasses was stupid.

"I know what you're thinking, Miss," Sir Barlow said. "Remember what you promised about kicking yourself."

"Keep reminding me. I have an active kicking foot."

When Merlin stopped, he sat on a flat rock and balanced the red orb on his knee. "We are in sight of the reservoir, which I will describe soon, but first I want to tell you about this ovulum. It is a viewing port to Earth and Second Eden. If you look closely, you will see Sapphira. She has just returned to Earth from a portal jump to Second Eden, and a medic is tending to her wound."

Lauren peered into the ovulum. Deep inside, a rectangle showed Sapphira as she lay on a field of grass, her eyes open. A man knelt next to her with a needle and thread in hand. She seemed alert and in relatively little pain.

"And on this side ..." Merlin turned the ovulum over. "You will see your twin brother and Listener in Second Eden. They seem to be quite safe."

Lauren looked into the egg again. Matt and Listener bent over a disk of some sort, pushing Zohar across a gray sheet of ice. Listener's hand touched Matt's arm at times as they shifted direction. They seemed friendly ... quite friendly.

"Interesting," Sir Barlow said as he peered alongside Lauren. "Perhaps Listener has changed her mind."

"About what?" Lauren asked.

"She once announced her readiness to accept a suitor, but after Valiant died, she altered her stand. Her affection toward Matt makes me wonder if she has altered it again."

"Why would Valiant's death make a difference?"

"I suspect that her role as default leader of Second Eden gave her a low view of the remaining males there. None of them *stepped up*, you might say. She told me, 'I will not be led around on a donkey by a man whose strengths are limited to the pulling of a rope.'" He gestured with his hands. "You see, in Second Eden a suitor leads—"

"I figured that out." Lauren gazed at Listener's face—steady, certain, unflinching. "She seems … intense."

"On the exterior, yes, but her heart is as soft and tender as they come. Trust me on that."

"I have no reason not to trust you." Lauren eyed the gray ice. "I saw that storm while I was there. What caused it? That device Semiramis planted?"

"Correct," Merlin said. "The storm created great havoc, but since my view into that world is small, I cannot determine all the damage it has done."

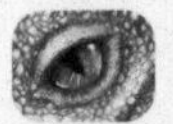

"Where are Matt and Listener going?"

"It is difficult to hear their conversation in full, but I gather that they hope to go to the birthing garden to save the plant-enclosed infants from the ice."

Lauren leaned over and tried to view the opposite side of the ovulum. "Can we see what happens to Sapphira?"

"Her journey could entrance us for hours, but we have our own business to attend to." Merlin set the ovulum in Sir Barlow's hands. "While we talk and watch for the spiders, we will trust our good knight to monitor the events and raise an alarm if something significant occurs."

"I will be glad to." Sir Barlow lifted the ovulum close to his face. "I performed a similar duty when Lauren's father carried a belt camera through the circles of seven." He turned the egg over and looked at the other side. "Though keeping track of two worlds at once is likely to make me dizzy."

"You will adjust." Merlin rose from the rock and let out a shrill whistle. A horde of glowbats launched from the ceiling, flew to a point about twenty paces away, and fluttered in a circle over a span of ice about a hundred feet wide. "That is the life reservoir. Come, I will explain while I show it to you."

Merlin set his hand under Lauren's elbow and guided her to his right. When they arrived at the reservoir's edge, he pushed the bottom end of his staff into the ice. Light rose from the entry point and followed the staff upward to the top. Pale yellow radiance poured from a gem wedged in the three-pronged end.

He pulled the staff out and sighed. "Many streams of life energy have recently entered, but it is not yet filled. According to those who sent me here, the reservoir should not be opened until it is full, which is why the spiders could cause a great deal of trouble. Since they are able to generate heat, perhaps they were sent here to melt the ice and release the energy prematurely. I assume they will stay in hiding and crawl closer when they suspect that we are not watching, so we must remain vigilant. I assume we can crush the little spiders, but I am not sure about the largest one."

"I'll be watching." Lauren leaned closer to the staff and examined the marble-sized gem at the top. "Is that a candlestone?"

"It is."

"Then why don't I feel—"

"Weak?" Merlin brushed the bottom end of his staff against his cloak. "One of many mysteries to explain." He set the forked end in her palm. "Your passage into this realm stripped away many of your powers—your super hearing, your mind reading, and your new ability to create fire. But it also removed your draconic weakness, so you are able to coexist with this dragons' bane."

Lauren absorbed the words, but too many thoughts raced around. Catching them one at a time would have to do. "What is needed to fill the reservoir?"

"The sacred pool contains energy that fuels resurrection power." Merlin set the butt end of the staff on the ground and propped himself against it. "About two thousand years ago the reservoir was filled to overflowing by the sacrifice of Jesus Christ, and that energy provided spiritual resurrection for all of his followers in that time and in the future. It was pumped out and distributed to every point in the world, and it remains available to this day. Now the reservoir contains energy from other sacrificial sources—your mother, your father, Makaidos, and others. One by one, their sacrificial energy poured into the reservoir where it is being saved for physical resurrections and restorations."

Lauren looked at the frozen pool. "When I was in Abaddon's Lair, Abaddon was complaining about everyone associated with my mother getting resurrected, but I never heard a reason for it happening."

"Ah, yes, that mystery is great. You see, your mother is a key figure in God's redemptive plans. She is not as exalted as the Son of God by any means, but she has played a critical role." Merlin held Lauren's elbow again. "Let me explain by illustration. Step carefully now." They slid together out over the ice. A few crackling noises rose from the surface, but it seemed strong enough. When they reached the center of the glowbats' orbit, he touched the ice with his staff. "Look down and tell me what you see."

Lauren peered through the ice. Vapors swirled like windblown fog. At the front of each stream, a face faded in and out of view. "I see foggy streams with faces."

"Where are they going?"

"Nowhere. They're just kind of blowing in circles."

"And they will continue to do so until you release the energy. What you cannot perceive is that their rate of movement is slowly decelerating. You see, this energy needs to be stirred up on occasion or else it will stagnate and become useless. Its power comes from its living flow. A sacrifice adds more energy, and a resurrection draws energy out again.

"As you might know, an inflow combined with an outlet keeps a pool from stagnating. Your mother's death created a huge influx of energy, and her resurrection drained some of it, because every resurrection requires sacrificial energy from this pool. The same kind of influx and outflow occurred with the deaths and resurrections of your father, your grandmother, Makaidos, and a few others. God chose people who have been influenced by your mother because of the tremendous amount of sacrificial love that flows within them."

"So," Lauren said, "to summarize, deaths and resurrections kept the energy active."

"Exactly. After the resurrection of Christ and before your mother's death, Abaddon had no need to stir the soup, if you will, because he was not storing sacrificial energy at the time. Then several years before your mother was born, due to the approaching end of the age, the command came from on high to begin the collection. Quite a number of martyrs died after her death, thereby sustaining the filling of the pool."

"So my mother was the first stirring spoon, the first resurrection since it started filling."

"And several followed, as I mentioned." Merlin led her back toward the edge of the reservoir. "And since the enemy has been seeking a way to destroy this energy source, I was assigned to seal it with ice and protect it from intruders, which have now invaded the realm. Yet, their efforts will be for naught when the reservoir fills and you deliver its energy for the purpose for which God designed it."

When they reached the edge, Lauren spread out her hands. "How do I do that? Thaw the ice? I can't create fire here."

Merlin cocked his head. "Have you not unraveled that mystery? Your presence indicates that you properly solved the riddles."

"I kind of stumbled into everything. I'm here, but that's about all I know."

He stroked his beard. "That is unfortunate."

"You mean you don't know what I'm supposed to do?"

"I am merely the guardian of this realm. I was told that someone would come to release the reservoir's energy, but I was not told the method. I assumed that you would know."

Lauren winced. "I'm sorry. I don't."

Merlin set a hand on her shoulder. "Quickly, then. Add to your earlier tales and tell me everything else you have seen. We will try to solve the puzzle together."

"Okay." For the next few minutes, Lauren told more about the events in the other two portals. As she described the stagnant pool, the weak trees, and the voices, Merlin asked several questions about the details—the odors, the exact words the voices uttered, and consistency of the sludge that polluted the pool, but he didn't bother to give reasons for his questions. When she told of the second realm, he asked only whether or not all three pools were similar, and he seemed unsurprised that they appeared to be identical in shape and size.

When she finished, she let out a sigh. "And you already know the story about Tamiel posing as Micaela."

Merlin propped his chin with his hand. "Did Tamiel personally kill your friend?"

Lauren nodded. "With a car bomb. He looked exactly like her, but if I had just asked him questions only Micaela would know how to answer, I would have figured it out."

"Allay your concern about that. You had no reason to be suspicious. In these realms of the dead and new life, it is quite reasonable to accept the idea that Micaela was resurrected." Merlin's eyes flickered with anger. "Tamiel is crafty beyond what most can imagine. He is able to impersonate anyone he has killed, and that skill has far-reaching potential for deceit. Long ago, he impersonated Seraphina in order to deceive Joran. It seems that he is up to his old tricks."

"Okay. That makes me feel a little better."

"Back to the pools." Merlin tapped his staff on the ice. "One is of water, one is of blood, and one is of spiritual energy. The first one was corrupted, which confused and poisoned people, but now you have cleansed it. You also cleansed the second one when the life-giving water mixed with the blood, which swept up the bones and released more energy. The third one—"

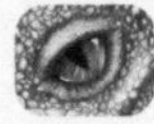

"Merlin!" Sir Barlow called, walking toward them with the ovulum. "I hereby raise an alarm."

17

CHAPTER

The Birthing Garden

Matt and Listener pushed Zohar's sled past the final hut in Founder's Village and let him slide down a gentle slope. Matt straightened and blew warm breath on his cold hands. As numbness melted into tingles, pain throbbed in his fingertips.

Listener stretched her back. "Almost there. We can do it."

"Yep. We'll make it." Matt inhaled a cleansing breath. Although the precipitation had stopped, cold wind blew foul-smelling air. A pale sun shone through thin haze, a welcome change from the cloudy skies.

Listener shivered. "Let's get going again. Pushing keeps me warm."

"Agreed. Except for my hands." Matt walked with her down the slope. Since she left her coat behind, she had only a close-fitting, long-sleeved tunic over loose trousers, as well as boots. Earlier, she expressed relief that her sensitive hearing had returned, though a background hum continued, like a bow constantly running across the strings of a double bass.

After another minute of pushing the sled, they stopped in front of the portal window leading to the tree room, a few paces from the birthing garden. Matt glanced through the window. The tree of life burned on, blocking a view of the portal leading to Jade's sanctum, but there was no time to search, at least not now.

Listener crouched and set a finger on the ice. "The edge of the garden should be about here."

Matt crouched with her. After breaking the crust with a fist, he dug down through ashy slush and tossed handfuls to the side. "I noticed three plants before the storm started." Vapor blew out with his words. "We'd better find them all."

"Three sounds right. I'm not sure how spread out they were."

"One was near this spot. The other two were farther out. I don't recall the exact locations."

Starting at the point where Matt was digging, Listener kicked through the ice and drew a line. "I'm marking the garden borders the best I can remember. I might have to dig down a bit to be sure. I just have to be careful to avoid Emerald's grave. She was Valiant's Eve, and he buried her here. I suppose he hoped she would resurrect."

Zohar climbed slowly to his feet. "I will begin the melting process as soon as the boundaries become clear."

"How are you feeling?" Matt asked. "Any dizziness?"

"Not much. The medicine is helping."

"Good to hear." Matt continued digging until he reached solid ground, then began clearing a space. A footprint appeared on the dark lava soil, the toes outlined clearly, though now white instead of red. He brushed away more ice and found another print, also white and clearly defined. Somehow the ice had altered the color.

"Lauren," he whispered into the air. "Where are you now?"

"What?" Listener looked back and touched her ear. "I heard you say something, Matt, but that hum is still in the way."

"Just mentioning Lauren, wondering where she is." He straightened and looked again at the portal window. "While you two are getting ready, I'll check real quick to see if I can find her and Sir Barlow."

"Sure. It'll be a couple of minutes." Listener continued kicking through the ice. "Give a shout if you need help."

"Will do." Matt stepped down into the tree room, skirted the tree, and looked through the portal on the opposite wall. Inside the sanctum, the central column pulsed, now with white light instead of red. A white beam struck the surrounding wall on the right, and another radiated toward him. Why another color change from red to white? Might this portal be passable now?

He touched the plane with a fingertip. It jolted his hand, making him jerk back. He stifled a yelp and sucked on the burned tip. No. Still the same. Yet, the absence of Lauren and Sir Barlow could mean that they had entered the portal to the right. They were probably safe and still on the move.

Matt pivoted, strode around the tree, and stopped at the Second Eden portal. Listener was rounding the final corner as she continued plowing a line through the ice. The footprints he had uncovered were visible a few feet beyond the window. He lifted his own foot and pictured Lauren taking those fateful steps onto the lava field. What had possessed her to walk on scalding ground? Love? Definitely. A death wish? Maybe. That girl would give her life for someone else in a heartbeat.

He heaved a sigh. She already had given her life. She was dead, a ghost on a mission. A tear welled in his eye. He quickly brushed it away. Strong. He had to stay strong for Listener and the Second Edeners. His own journey had to continue without hesitation. He leaped back into Second Eden and hurried to Zohar's side. "Are you ready?"

Zohar nodded, a hand extended. A ball of fire swirled in his palm and filled it from edge to edge. "I have been testing my power. I think I will have no trouble as long as I can hold out physically."

"If you need me to prop you up, just say the word."

Listener arrived and joined her line in the ice to the starting point. Her final push scattered ice over Lauren's footprints. "That should do it." She walked four steps into the garden, crouched, and waved her hand over a spot. "I think one of the plants was growing right about here."

"I need to get closer," Zohar said, "to ensure precision with my fire. I want to avoid accidentally hurting the plant."

"I'll help you." Matt hooked his arm with Zohar's and guided him to the spot.

Zohar knelt and set his palm close to the ice. His brow furrowed, and his white hair dropped like a curtain in front of his face. A ball of flames blossomed in the gap between his palm and the ice. Soon, a depression formed that spread steadily outward in a widening circle.

A slurry of water and ash pooled. As the depression sank, the water sank with it and seeped into exposed ground, leaving a film of gray ash on the darker soil. When the expanding circle revealed a splotch of green, Listener slid into the depression and brushed melting ice away from a thick stalk and two upright leaves about the size of her hands, posed in the usual praying position.

"I've got it." Her hands trembled. "This one sprouted right after the lava overrode the area. It'll be quite a while before it's ready to give birth."

"Maybe the fertilizer will speed it up," Matt said.

"I hope not too much. We haven't conducted the lottery to choose parents, and no Adam and Eve couples are able to take care of a baby right now." Her face seemed to glow in the brightening sunlight. "If you and I were an Adam and Eve, we would be the only healthy candidates. That would be an exciting challenge, don't you think?"

Warmth filtered into Matt's cheeks. "Yeah. Exciting's a good word."

Listener's smile widened, no sign that her allusion to marriage might or might not be a real hope in her mind. "Zohar," she said. "Come. Let's clear the area."

With Matt's help, Zohar eased down the sloping ice to ground level. He knelt again and concentrated his fire on the ice immediately around the plant. Soon, he had cleared a three-foot-wide circle.

Listener laid a hand on one of the praying leaves and set her ear close. After several seconds, her lower lip trembled. "I ..." She swallowed. "I don't hear anything. No heartbeat. No stirring."

"But your hearing's impaired," Matt said. "Maybe it's all right."

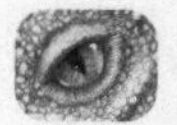

"Let's hope so." Listener rose, her cheeks red. "Zohar, please warm the leaves directly, but don't let the flames get too close."

"Of course." Zohar stepped toward the plant, but his legs gave way. Matt caught him and helped him sit. "That's good," Zohar said. "I can reach it from here."

While Zohar cupped his fiery hands near the leaves, Matt and Listener stood side by side. The soil around the stalk absorbed water and ash, making the area spongy, but the plant showed no signs of change.

"What could be different?" Matt asked. "Between here and the vineyard, I mean."

"I have no idea." Listener folded her hands at her waist, her smile tight. "We must have faith. The Father of Lights wouldn't raise children from the dead only to let them perish in Mardon's ice storm. These wombs are sacred."

Matt let her words sink in. They raised images of the abortion clinic—the dead baby in the bucket—wrapped in a plastic bag and left to rot. "In our world, babies die in the womb all the time. They get sliced to pieces and thrown away with the garbage."

Listener stared into the sky, as if seeing something only her eyes could detect. "This isn't your world, Matt. This is Second Eden. A second chance. A new hope for a better life. Your world hasn't infected ours with its corruption, at least not in a lasting way."

"I wonder if my world is still worth saving. We sure don't deserve it."

Listener turned toward him, her eyes bright and sharp. "Did you deserve saving, Matt?"

The question stabbed like a dagger. He broke eye contact and stuffed a hand into his pocket. "Definitely not."

Listener laid a hand on his cheek and forced him to look at her. "Matt, don't be ashamed. Your transformation is to be celebrated. And now I know how it feels. As I told you earlier, when my companion darkened on your world, I felt lost, without a guide. Void of pity or compassion, I shot a man, not caring for his life and soul. Afterward, guilt overwhelmed me. I begged for forgiveness, but I found no solace for my heavy heart. I asked my companion how to find mercy, but she didn't know. Companions are not equipped to deal with corrupted souls, and such my soul had become. But while we were in Abaddon's Lair, I read a story in the resurrection book, the story of the greatest of all resurrections."

Matt dared not look away. Her eyes were like fiery magnets. "So that's what you were reading. I'm sorry I interrupted."

"No. It's fine. I finished it." Listener grasped his wrist. "I had heard the story of Jesus before. It didn't apply to me then, since I had never offended the Father of Lights. But this time the story shone light into my darkened soul. Then when the waters of resurrection flooded the chamber, they washed over my soul as well. My companion transformed into a shining beacon and penetrated my bosom, straight to my heart. At first, I thought it was just a vision. It took a while for the reality to set in."

Tears sparkled in her eyes. "Matt, I was born anew, and I like this condition better than that of my first birth. Now the light shines within instead of hovering around me like a foreign satellite. The Father of Lights speaks to my heart instead of to my ears. I am a new kind of Listener, one of spirit, closer to the Father of Lights than ever before."

Matt drank in her beautiful words. She was so real, so honest. No girl on Earth ever spoke with such sincerity. "Something like that happened to me. Religion just didn't click. But when my mother told me about faith, it was different, like God spoke through her. Then when I stopped hating Darcy, it all came together. I never had a companion like you did, but I feel different. Like you said, it's a lot better this way."

"Matt, I can't tell you how happy I am to hear that. Maybe now you and I can—"

"I don't think it's working," Zohar said as he turned toward Matt and Listener.

"Let me check." Listener leaned close to the plant again. "I still hear nothing."

Matt resisted the urge to heave a sigh. It sounded like Listener was about to say something really important, but that conversation would have to wait. "Let me think." He looked toward the vineyard and mentally reconstructed the elements—soil, water from ice melt, and fertilizing ash. What were they missing?

Well beyond the vineyard, a plume of dark smoke rose in front of a mountain. Matt pointed. "It looks like a fire."

Listener nodded. "That's the portal area. I saw it earlier. It was burning when we left Peace Village. I asked Karrick to check on it, remember?"

"I remember." Matt imagined ice melting at the base of the rising cloud. That picture raised reminders of the fire in the vineyard—burning logs that crackled on the newly exposed soil. He snapped his fingers. "That's it!"

"What's it?"

"Heat. The vines grew when the fire added heat to the soil. Zohar warmed the plant but not the soil itself."

"I will give it a try." Zohar created a ball of fire in each hand and spilled the flames over the dirt around the stem.

Water sizzled and popped. The smell of ammonia rose and stung Matt's eyes. He rubbed the pain away. If the heat worked, they might have quite an eruption to deal with.

"Let's play it safe." He took hold of Listener's wrist on one side and Zohar's on the other and guided them back.

Within seconds, the plant stretched upward, and the stalk thickened. The praying leaves opened, but no baby appeared, only a round object that looked like a brown gourd.

Matt looked at Listener. "Has that ever happened before?"

"No." Her brow furrowed tightly. "Never."

As the plant grew taller, the stalk split in two, like a tree with twin trunks. The praying leaves stretched out to the side and curled up like scrolls. Knobs with fingerlike appendages grew at the ends. The gourd, now a foot higher than Matt's head, sprouted hair, and humanlike facial features took shape at the front.

"This person is huge." Matt pulled them farther back. "We should be ready to get out of here."

"No," Zohar said. "It's Mendallah! I have known her for centuries, and she will help us. She is a giant."

"A giant?" Matt stepped closer again. The lower part of one trunk bent at a joint and uprooted, revealing a dark bare foot, then the other trunk did the same. Above where the trunks joined, the main stalk took on the curves and muscular bulges of a powerful woman. Tiny leaves sprouted all across the stalk and the prayer leaves, then immediately transformed into pieces of cloth that stitched themselves together into a sleeved tunic that reached to her elbows. Trousers formed as well, covering her legs down to her knees.

A few seconds later, the former plant looked like a storybook giant, a female version with sepia skin and long hair. After fluttering her eyelids, she spoke with a quiet voice—deep, though feminine. "Zohar? Is that you?"

Zohar nodded and reached up with both hands. "My friend!"

Mendallah picked him up and embraced him. About nine feet tall, she looked like a weight-lifting mom hugging a toddler. After the two exchanged kisses, she set him down and glanced from side to side. "Where am I? How did I get here?"

Listener took Mendallah's hand, her head below Mendallah's shoulders. "It's a long story."

For the next few minutes, Matt, Listener, and Zohar took turns telling Mendallah about the events that had taken place in recent times until she seemed satisfied with the account, though no one knew how she had died. Zohar guessed that the green ovulum, with himself and Mendallah trapped inside, met its demise during one of the many battles.

"So ..." Listener swept an arm across the garden. "Let's get to work clearing the rest of the ice. The babies need warmth, or perhaps we will uncover another ally."

"I doubt it," Matt said. "There's only one statue unaccounted for, so it must have held Mendallah's soul."

Listener shook her head. "Mendallah's plant was already here when we saw the statue in Abaddon's Lair. I don't see how it could have held her soul."

"Good point." Matt stooped and dug a hand into the ice. "Let's get to work."

"When we warm the soil, the plants might give birth, so we have to stay here." Listener turned toward her village. "We can get blankets from my hut to take care of the babies. With our portal beacon burning, maybe Elam and Sapphira will be back soon, and we can get them up to date when they arrive."

Mendallah raised a hand. "If I may offer a suggestion, leave the melting to Zohar and me. I will carry him around the garden. The two of you will then be free to travel to the mountain portal to welcome Elam and Sapphira. It is urgent that you inform them of the situation as soon as possible. The plight of the Second Edeners is of utmost importance."

"I like that idea," Matt said. "It's the best use of our resources."

Listener rubbed Mendallah's forearm. "We accept your offer. We'll leave the food and water with you and Zohar." She turned toward Matt. "We'll pick up some weapons at our cache in the enclave. We have to be ready with firepower in case the portal opens to hostile forces."

He gave her a smile. "I like the way you think."

"The way I think?" Her face flushing, she bowed her head. "Thank you. That is the kindest compliment I could ever hope for."

"You're welcome." New warmth rose into Matt's cheeks. The compliment was meant to be a casual quip, yet she took it to heart, which was fine. She really did think in a cool way. "Just to explain, planning to get weapons means you want to be prepared, and you're not afraid of guns. I like that. Most girls are scared of them."

One of Listener's eyebrows lifted. "There is no need to sweeten fresh water, Matt Bannister."

"Sweeten …" He cocked his head. "What do you mean?"

"It is an idiom we have here, but if I explain it, it would lose some of its value."

"Okay. I'll work on it." The warmth spread to Matt's ears. "Ready to go?"

"Ready." Listener slid her hand into his. They exited the garden and looked toward the higher elevations to the south. Ahead lay miles and miles of ice—a dirty sheet that might conceal a hundred holes or other snares. Still hand in hand, they trudged across the frozen expanse through Founder's Village and its ice-covered huts.

A sense of danger boiled in Matt's gut. He scanned the evening sky. Nothing out there so far, but soon it would become too dark to watch for approaching enemies. As they walked by a hut, he leaned to look around it. Again, nothing.

When they passed the final hut, someone called from behind. "Listener! Matt!"

They turned. A man ran from the direction of the birthing garden. Dressed in Second Eden garb and wearing a sword in a belt scabbard, he looked familiar.

Listener gasped. "Valiant?"

An alarm?" Merlin held a hand under Sir Barlow's and looked into the ovulum. "What do you see?"

"Someone has joined Matt and Listener. The display is small, but he looks like Valiant."

Lauren peered at the image. "But Valiant is dead. Could the birthing garden have resurrected him?"

Merlin ran a hand through his beard. "Not unless he was in the lair before Abaddon departed."

"Abaddon kept souls inside statues, and there was one statue left in the lair." Lauren fingered the medallion through her shirt. "I thought it held Eagle's soul."

"What gave you that impression?"

Lauren lifted one of the necklaces, revealing Eagle's medallion. "He gave this to me." She turned it to its inscription side and read it out loud. "My gift to you. My life. It is all I have to give." As tears welled, she lowered the medallion. "Eagle took my place diving into Mount Elijah. He was sacrificial. Couldn't God use his resurrection to stir the life reservoir?"

"My understanding is that Valiant was also sacrificial, so we need to consider the possibility that you are mistaken." Merlin looked at her with piercing eyes. "Considering the medallion's message, is it possible that emotions are playing into your conclusions?"

"Well ... I ..." She exhaled and nodded. "Yes, it's possible."

"Good, but do not yet throw away your idea. Who are we to assume that God has only one way to work his resurrection miracles?" Merlin pointed at Lauren's neck. "When you lifted the medallion, I caught a glimpse of something else. What was it?"

"A couple of things." She lifted the chain again and exposed the attached key ring. The key shimmered for a moment and disappeared. With another finger, she lifted a beaded necklace. "My mother wore this when she resurrected, and the key opened the seventh door."

Merlin drew his finger close. "May I?"

When she nodded, he slid his finger under the necklace. "I know this story. These beads came from Shiloh's plant in the sixth circle. They created a regeneracy dome around your mother, energized by Excalibur's beam. And the key ..." He pinched it between thumb and index finger, making it visible. "I'm not sure what the key can do. I will have to ponder it."

"Can the beads do anything now?"

"Almost certainly. In fact, they might be the very reason you were called to come to this place. Yet, since I am not sure, we might have to make a few educated guesses." Merlin released the key, sat on the icy floor, and patted the space at his side. "Join me for a brainstorming session."

Lauren settled next to him in a cross-legged pose. "I'm ready."

"Then let us begin. Brainstorming is best accomplished when we toss ideas back and forth without taking time to ponder deeply. If my idea lacks merit, you tell me why or else build upon it to make a better idea, and I will do the same for you. Remember, respond quickly. No need to even take a breath. This is not philosophical chess."

"Okay." Cold filtered through Lauren's pants. Now would be a good time to wear the yoke, but getting it would delay this step. She shifted to a crouch. "Let's do it."

"Very well. You start."

"Me?" She shrugged. "Okay, I'll try." She touched the chain that held the key. "Matt told me that the key to the seventh door is a combination of six other keys. They represent virtues."

"A key made of virtues should be able to unlock many doors. Perhaps a way of escape?"

"And the three of us want to escape this realm."

"But we cannot escape yet," Merlin said. "We must first release the life energy to its proper place."

"Where is the proper place?"

"I do not yet know. I am merely the guardian, not the one who releases the energy. That was supposed to be you."

"Okay, okay. But what *can* release it?"

"Since the reservoir is sealed by ice, I assume a great deal of warmth will be necessary."

Lauren lifted the necklace. "What about the beads? You mentioned a …" She squinted. "A regeneracy dome?"

"Correct. The dome is a method to release energy for restoration and resurrection, but we need an energizing source such as an Oracle's fire or Excalibur's beam. They are not available."

"Then we make one of them available. We bring someone in here who has Excalibur."

"You are a Listener. Perhaps you can hear someone respond if you shout through the portal barrier, but I don't think anyone can hear you."

"Well … I could … I could …" She slapped her hand against the floor. "I could dream about someone!"

Merlin inhaled to reply, then cocked his head. "Dream about someone?"

"Right. I talked to Jade in my dream. Maybe I could talk to someone else."

"A fascinating idea. Run with it. Don't stop. Just let your thoughts roll."

Lauren gestured with her hands. "I can talk to people while I'm dreaming, people who happen to be in the dream realm, but I won't know who'll be there at any given time. I could … um … I could go to sleep … maybe at the same time the person who has Excalibur goes to sleep. And then I could tell him how to get here."

"But coordinating sleep time with that person would be nearly impossible. And how do you know that a sleeping person would also enter that realm, especially the person who is carrying the great sword?"

"If I can enter that realm, maybe someone else with my power can do the same. My mother is a dream oracle. Maybe I can contact her or another oracle like Sapphira. One of them is bound to know something about where Excalibur is. And even if they don't, we have to warn someone that Tamiel is in Second Eden and let them know that we're trapped here."

"There is still the sleep timing issue. You cannot know when either one of them is sleeping."

Sir Barlow cleared his throat. "If I may interject, we will soon know exactly when *someone* is sleeping."

Lauren lifted her brow. "What do you mean?"

"Look." He brought the ovulum close. "Evening is coming upon Second Eden. I suspect that Matt and Listener will have to sleep soon. When they do, Lauren can enter the dream world and see if one of them is there."

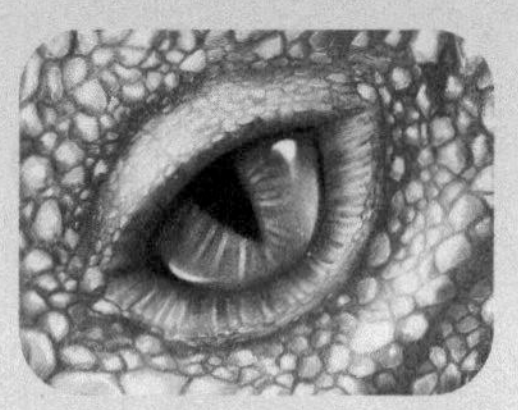

18

CHAPTER

A Stalker

Valiant halted a few steps away. His muscular biceps rippled in his tunic sleeves as he carried a leather duffle bag under an arm. He gave Matt and Listener a solemn head bow. "The garden resurrected me. The white-haired lad and the giantess told me about the recent events here and that you two went this way. I noticed that you left a number of tracks, so I followed."

Listener sprang to him and wrapped her arms around his waist, her head against his chest. "I'm so glad you're here! Second Eden needs you. I've been trying to keep everything in order, but Mardon's ice storm has wreaked havoc. It put out the fire at the emergency portal, and worst of all, it's freezing the companions, covering them with soot that won't wash off." She stepped back and scanned the area around his head. "Where is your companion?"

"I resurrected without it." Valiant's eyes darted as he searched around Listener's head. "Where is yours?"

"It disappeared when Abaddon's Lair flooded, but that's a long story." She bounced on her toes like an excited little girl. "Now I feel so alive. Free. Filled to the brim."

"And I the same way. It is a miraculous filling, indeed." Valiant bowed his head toward Matt. "It is good to see you again, young man. I am grateful for the courage you displayed when I was shot."

As Matt bowed his head in return, the danger sensation soared. "It was my pleasure, sir." He looked again at the sky, then at the surrounding field of ice, but nothing dangerous appeared.

Valiant glanced from side to side. "Where is Eagle? Has he been affected by the plague on the companions?"

Listener gave Matt a mournful look. "Well ..."

Valiant's brow arched up. "Is something wrong?"

"It's like this," Matt said as he took a step forward. "Eagle sacrificed himself to save the original anthrozils. He died a hero, just like you did."

"Eagle is dead?" Valiant's eyes sparkled with tears.

Listener folded her hands tightly. "But we're praying that he will rise from the birthing garden."

Matt concealed a cringe. There was only one statue left in Abaddon's Lair. It must have held Valiant's soul, but reminding her of that would just bring her down. "We can hope for a miracle, but right now we're heading to the portal to see what we can do to help Elam and the others come through. We're thinking maybe Ashley can figure out a way to rescue the companions."

Valiant crouched with his head low and stared at the ground. A sob sent a spasm through his body. He inhaled deeply and spoke with a higher pitch. "I apologize for my expression of grief. Kindly give me a moment."

"Of course." Matt looked at Listener. She returned the look with a wrinkled brow. Something was bothering her, but this was not the time to ask.

After a few seconds, Valiant straightened and scanned the southern horizon, his eyes red. "A fire is burning."

"Karrick relit the portal fire." Matt laid a hand on his stomach. "We should get going. I'm sensing danger, something close and deadly."

"By all means." Valiant drew his sword. "Lead the way, and I will guard your backs."

Listener looked at the hilt. "Where did you get that sword? It is not your usual one."

"I found it." Valiant reached into the leather bag, withdrew a white garment, and shook it out. "I heard someone walking behind one of the huts. When I investigated, the person was gone but left this sword and cloak."

Matt ran a finger along the cloak's sleeve. "It feels like the same material in the one I had, like it has a flame-retardant coating. Maybe it'll come in handy for portal passages."

"Perhaps." Valiant pushed the cloak back into the bag. "If danger is lurking, we should make haste."

Matt reached for Listener's hand, but she drew back and began a brisk march. He caught up and kept pace. "Is something wrong?" he whispered.

She glanced back and whispered in return, her words nearly swallowed by the sound of boots crunching ice. "Not while Valiant is watching."

"Is holding hands against the rules here?"

"Only for widows. But I can't explain. Not yet. Just trust me."

"If you say so." They walked on in silence except for the continued crunching at their feet. Matt searched for what might be causing the danger alert. Nothing appeared in the expanse of grayness except Valiant who continued at their pace twenty or so steps behind. Valiant's eyes scanned this way, then that, obviously wary of a lurking presence.

When they reached the top of a rise, Listener halted and breathed in short gasps.

Matt stopped with her. "Do you need to rest?"

She looked back at Valiant. He still marched with his sword drawn. "We should hurry." She broke into a trot down the other side.

Matt caught up and kept pace. To the rear, Valiant jogged evenly, apparently unconcerned that Listener had taken off without warning. "Is something wrong?" Matt asked. "Did you hear something?"

"I'm not sure." Her face aimed straight ahead.

"Is that background hum still in the way?"

She narrowed her eyes. "No. It's gone." Soon, she stopped and set her hands on her knees. "Give me a moment."

Matt looked back yet again. Valiant was now about fifty paces behind but steadily catching up. "Are you feeling sick? You usually don't get tired so easily."

"Shhh. Let me listen." She cast a furtive glance at Valiant. When he came within twenty paces, she nodded. "Let's go."

As they marched, Listener focused straight ahead once more, her brow tight, her lips firm. "Do you still sense danger?" she asked.

"Yeah. Behind us. I'm not sure how far."

"When we stop, I hear footsteps well beyond Valiant. Someone or something is following us."

"I didn't see anything, but with the ridges and valleys, I could have missed something. Valiant's watching, too, so whatever it is, it must be good at hiding."

"This is true." Without slowing, Listener swiveled her head and squinted at Valiant. "I'm concerned about him. He is not one to stay so far behind."

"He just resurrected. Maybe he needs time to adjust, you know, get his legs going again."

"Maybe." Listener picked up the pace, seemingly no longer fatigued. When they approached Peace Village, Tamara was walking between two of the ice-encrusted huts, a bundle of firewood in her arms.

"Mother!" Listener called, waving. "Wait!"

Tamara stopped, her expression somber. When they arrived, Matt took the firewood from her. "Where is Dr. Conner?" he asked.

Tamara pointed at a nearby hut, a larger one than the others. "I take … wood to him." As her gaze drifted toward Valiant, her eyes widened. "He is … alive?"

"Resurrected in the birthing garden," Matt said.

Valiant joined them and slid his sword away. "Greetings, Tamara." Compassion flavored his tone. "Have you made any progress with thawing the companions?"

Tamara shook her head. "One woman … died. … Two more … soon."

"The danger's spiking," Matt said as he looked past Valiant toward the path they had traversed. "I still don't see anything."

Listener touched a thin log in Matt's bundle. "While you're taking the wood, Valiant and I will go to the weapons cache and bring a couple of rifles back for Dr. Conner. It's not far."

"That's fine, but at least leave the sword with me. Whatever's stalking us might show up."

"Your concern is valid." Valiant drew the sword and slid the blade behind Matt's belt. "We will return soon."

Listener tapped twice on Matt's jaw and whispered, "Be listening." She and Valiant jogged in the direction of the portal, Listener leading the way.

Matt ran his tongue along his molars. A slight buzz tingled. As he listened, a vague whisper came through, Valiant's voice, too distant to decipher. Then Listener responded. "Perhaps we should be silent for a while. I am trying to listen for signs of the person who is stalking us." Only the crunching of boots on ice followed.

Matt scanned the area again. The danger sensation had faded somewhat, but it still remained elevated. He nodded at Tamara. "You'd better stick close to me."

"Come this way." Tamara lifted her skirt and trudged toward the hut.

Matt followed her to the far side of the hut where a trench had been dug down to the door, making entry easier.

Once inside, Tamara walked straight to a little boy lying near the opposite wall. From door to wall, the span was about thirty feet in this spacious community hut.

Dr. Conner sat near a hearth at an adjacent wall. He used a wooden spoon to stir the contents of a small black pot propped by a stack of rocks over a pile of orange embers. "Welcome back." He nodded toward the side of the hearth. "Set the pile there. I'll rebuild the fire when this elixir is ready."

Matt lowered the bundle to the hearth's brick surface. A dozen or more Second Edeners lay on the floor, mostly women and children. After brushing his hands together and moving the sword to a comfortable position, he crouched close to Dr. Conner and whispered, "How are they doing?

"Not good." Dr. Conner kept his voice low as well. "For the most part, the children are faring better than the adults, but that's like saying bronchitis is better than pneumonia. They are all spiraling downward at an alarming rate."

Matt peered into the pot. Flecks of green swirled at the top of the dark liquid. "What are you cooking?"

"A brew of herbs that helped the anthrozils. I have no hope that it will cure a companionless Second Edener, but it might boost their resilience for a while. What we really need is a solvent that will clean the companions and revive them, but I don't have the necessary chemicals available."

"How much time do you think they have?"

"Hard to say, but my guess is that we have hours instead of days, maybe even minutes for some." Dr. Conner removed the pot and transferred new wood to the fireplace. Tiny firelets crept over the edges of the kindling and swelled into flames. "The anthrozils were closer to death than the Second Edeners are, and they survived in spite of the odds against them. I'm not giving up."

"We have some good news. Valiant is here. The birthing garden resurrected him, and he's as healthy as a horse. He doesn't have a companion, so he's not vulnerable."

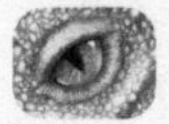

Dr. Conner sniffed the brew. "No companion? How strange."

"Right, but Listener doesn't have one, either. You see—"

"Wait." Dr. Conner's voice grew animated. "I need a blood sample from one of them. I don't care which one."

"What are you looking for? Antibodies of some kind?"

"Maybe. Something is allowing them to thrive without a companion. I just hope I can spot the reason in time. I compared my own blood to the Second Edeners', but the genetic markers are too different. Listener and Valiant are bound to line up much better."

"I'm sure they'll both be willing." Matt rose and walked toward the door. "I'll tell them. Then we're going to the portal to see if we can get Ashley here quicker. If anyone can come up with a cleaning solvent, she can."

"I have no doubt about that."

"I've been sensing danger ever since we left the garden, so Valiant and Listener are bringing weapons." Matt grasped the hilt of the sword. "Can you handle a rifle? I think they'll have AK-forty-sevens."

"I can. Listener trained all the men. She made sure we were decent marksmen. Tamara can handle one, too." Dr. Conner winked at her. "Can't you?"

As Tamara mopped the boy's forehead with a cloth, she smiled, her cheeks red. "Good enough to … not shoot myself."

Matt looked around the room and counted—two men, six women, and six children lying on floor mats in various poses, all with closed eyes and pale faces. Of course, he could stay and try to use his healing gifts, but his hands were still quite cold. He might make the situation worse. "I'll see if Listener and Valiant are back."

Dr. Conner lowered a ladle into the pot. "I'll be here or close by."

Matt strode out the door and walked back to the point he had last seen Listener and Valiant. The sun, now near its setting horizon, shone on the expanse of dirty ice. The light allowed a good view of three sets of footprints from the birthing garden as well as two leading to the higher elevations. He focused on the danger sensation. It had diminished by about half, though it still hovered high enough to keep the alarm ringing.

Matt set a finger on his jaw. "Listener? Are you and Valiant on your way back?"

No one responded. Even the crunching of ice had ceased. Yet, the tingle in his teeth continued, proving that his transmitter still functioned.

After a few seconds, the crunching sound returned, along with Listener's voice. "Valiant, do you remember when I was little and in surgery? My life hung by a thread. Billy told me that you led our people in prayer. When I heard that story, it filled my heart with joy, the idea that you and our people cared so much for me."

Valiant's voice came through, but again the words were too indistinct to understand.

"Since I wasn't there," Listener continued, "I never heard what you said in prayer, so I was wondering if you remember your words. Such a prayer of faith should be memorialized."

Again Valiant answered in an unintelligible way.

"I understand. It was more than fifteen years ago. But if the words do come back to you, please write them down."

Matt pondered Listener's probing questions. Had she turned off her transmitter and then turned it back on so he could listen in? Was she testing Valiant for some reason?

Listener and Valiant appeared in the distance. Each carried two rifles strapped to their shoulders as they retraced their path from the cache. As they approached with a quick march, Matt's danger meter rose. He drew the sword and searched a line of trees in the distance. Several evergreens had shaken off their icy coats, exposing their needled boughs. Any one of them would be a good place for a predator to hide.

Matt tapped his jaw to turn off the transmitter and focused on Valiant. Why did it seem that the danger elevated whenever he was near? Was it real, or had Listener's earlier concerns about him affected the danger meter? Either way, it seemed clear from her questions that her wariness had not yet eased.

When they arrived, Listener pushed a rifle into Matt's free hand. "Someone followed us all the way to the cache and back. I caught fleeting glimpses of a man rushing from tree to tree, but we were in too much of a hurry to flush him out. He stayed well away."

"Well, he's close by again. I sense the danger." Matt concealed a sigh of relief. That explained the reason the danger spiked whenever Valiant was near. The stalker was real and tracking him step-by-step.

Matt handed the sword to Valiant and looked the rifle over—a vintage AK47. "How many of these do you have?"

"Just one more in the cache," Listener said, "but we have handguns, grenades, and many swords and shields there."

"Aren't you worried that whoever's following us can get the weapons? He must have seen where you got them."

Listener shook her head. "The door is strong, and it has a coded lock that only a few of us know. Ashley devised a sophisticated system that tracks and records all entries."

"That should work." Matt gestured with the rifle toward the community hut. "Dr. Conner wants blood samples from you. He's going to compare your genetic markers to the sick Second Edeners'."

"From both of us?" Valiant asked as he slid the sword back to its sheath.

"He said one of you, but it can't hurt to get two samples."

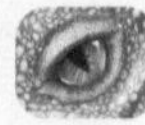

Listener started toward the hut. "Let's go."

"Wait!" Valiant's eyes narrowed as he scanned the distant trees. "I saw someone."

"Where?" Listener joined him and looked in the same direction. "I hear only falling ice."

"The movement has ceased." Valiant gave Listener his spare rifle and lowered his voice to a whisper. "You provide the blood sample. I think I see where the stalker is hiding." He marched off, his gaze fixed on a spot in the forest.

Listener prodded Matt's shoulder. "Go with him. I'll give blood and a rifle to Dr. Conner, then join you."

Clutching the rifle, Matt ran until he caught up with Valiant. As they soft-stepped side by side, Matt stared into the forest. Heavy coats of dark ice still covered the lower parts of the trees, bending the boughs. A breeze shook the higher branches and cast off ice in a curtain of sparkling gray. The crunching cascade masked their own footfalls. The danger alarm blared at a screaming pitch. Yet, no one moved in the forest. Valiant's senses were probably keener than his own. It was best to rely on him.

Valiant marched past the front line of trees and plunged into a dense area, dark and quiet except for the occasional splatter of falling shards. After pushing aside a broken branch filled with icy needles, he halted, raised a finger to his lips, and concentrated on the branches above.

Matt looked toward the village. The huts were now out of sight. Would Listener be able to find them here?

The danger sensation boiled to an explosive level. Matt slid his finger over the trigger. Whoever was out here wouldn't attack two armed men, would he? Valiant kept his rifle strapped to his shoulder, not exactly a ready position, but warning him verbally might spook their stalker.

Valiant slowly withdrew his sword. The metal barely made a *snick* as the blade cleared the sheath.

Matt sidled closer to him and looked into the branches. Nothing appeared besides ice-encrusted wood and greenery. The danger alarm strangled his throat and nearly cut off his air supply. The stalker had to be almost within reach.

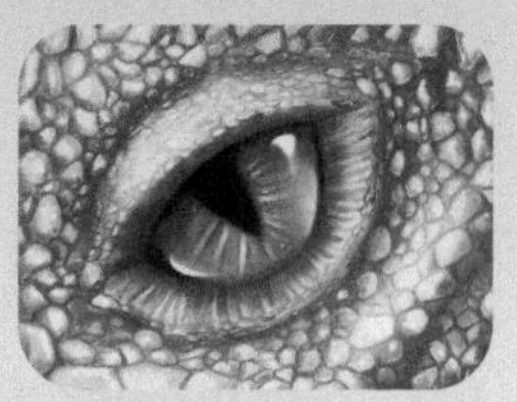

19

CHAPTER

Night Watches

Bonnie walked up Grackle's tail and settled behind Marilyn on his back. His scales radiated heat, a welcome contrast to the cold breeze. After shifting Excalibur at her belt to make sure it wouldn't stab her scaly steed, she wrapped her arms around Marilyn, careful to avoid the potted plant in her hands. "We're ready!"

Grackle flapped his wings. At first, nothing happened, then he grunted and flapped harder. Bonnie opened her own wings and gave them a flutter, canceling her weight's effect on the aging dragon. Grackle lifted into the air. As he struggled to ascend, Bonnie continued flapping and elevated herself an inch or so above his body. It was best to stay close to her seat, both for the warmth and to be ready to catch Marilyn in case of a spill.

The ground drew away—gray expanses with green trees protruding in the forests that the lava hadn't destroyed. The sun sank toward the horizon, half of the disk now blocked by a distant mountain.

Nightfall would soon arrive. They had to hurry. After being absent from Second Eden for so many years, finding the right place to plant Clefspeare might be difficult in the dark, and Marilyn certainly didn't know where to go. That left a wordless dragon as their only source of help. Still, he was a huge blessing. Since sooty ice covered everything in sight, they would need his guidance to find the garden.

Also, decreasing light would hamper another effort—watching for people on the ground. Mardon still lurked somewhere, and the darkness would veil his presence. Not only that, they hoped to spot some Second Edeners who could help with their task of planting Clefspeare at the garden. With the gray-on-gray backdrop covering everything, that hope seemed like a pipe dream.

Soon, they passed over a dense forest. Although ice coated the lower parts of the trees, the upper boughs had shaken free of the shackles. Ahead and to the left, a collection of dark lumps came into view. Bonnie pointed that way. "Probably Peace Village."

Marilyn turned her head. "Do you see anyone?"

"No. It looks deserted." Something moved in the corner of her eye. She looked down into the forest, but the frozen floor zipped by in sporadic gaps between the boughs. No sign of people. It was probably just the trees shedding ice.

Bonnie shifted forward again. Apparently the storm had forced everyone inside, and Mardon could easily hide in the trees. Conducting a search would be futile. They had to move on.

Wings beat over Matt's head. He looked up. Above the tree branches, a blur of purple flashed by, too fast to distinguish. "Did you see that?"

"Just a vague flash of color. The limbs blocked my view." Valiant pointed at a small clearing a few feet away. "Perhaps we can get a better look from there."

"I'll go." His finger ready to pull the trigger, Matt took a cautious step forward. The danger alarm squealed, but not from the trees. It seemed to come from—

"Matt!" Listener called from far away. "Valiant!"

Matt spun toward her voice. Valiant turned with him, both hands on the hilt of his sword. Silence had been shattered. No use staying quiet now. "Over here!" Matt called.

Listener pushed aside a bushy branch. With her rifle poised at her hip, she scanned the area. "Did you hear the wings?"

"We did," Valiant said. "Wings would explain our pursuer's ability to elude us so easily."

Matt checked the danger level. It had subsided quite a bit, though it still hovered at a high plateau. "Well, it won't be easy to find him now."

"Agreed," Valiant said. "We should go straight to the portal. There is no need to tarry here."

"What about your blood sample?" Matt asked.

Listener waved a hand. "Dr. Conner said not to worry about it. My sample will do, at least for now."

They walked single file through the forest, Listener at the front. When they broke into the clear, they hiked abreast up a gentle incline. All along the way, the danger sense stayed fairly constant, no sharp spikes.

Listener nudged Matt with an elbow and touched her jaw.

He nodded and tapped his jaw twice. The tingle returned, and the surrounding noises echoed within his mouth, an odd sensation, but he could adjust.

After a few minutes, they came to a wall of rock with a small opening—an arch that looked like a cave entrance with ice in front of the lower two-thirds. Recessed within the cave, the top of a wooden door stood visible above the accumulated ice. It appeared to be sturdy, as Listener had mentioned.

"I assume that's the weapons cache," Matt said.

"It is." Listener narrowed her eyes. "That's strange."

"Is something wrong?"

"Stay here." She lowered herself to her stomach, belly-crawled over the ice, and rolled down to the cave's floor level, out of sight. A step or two past the arch, the door rattled hard. Then it swung open. A moment later, it closed again. A duffle bag popped up from the gap and slid a foot or so down the ice. Listener hoisted herself up, grabbed the bag, and walked back, her stare moving, as if following something.

"What troubles you?" Valiant asked.

"A set of footprints. They aren't ours. And the last rifle is missing, along with some ammunition." She set the bag down and opened it. "I brought three extra magazines. We might need them."

After they each picked up a rifle magazine and stowed it in a pocket, Matt eyed the cache's entry. "Any sign someone forced the door open?"

Listener shook her head. "Ashley's system says that someone entered the correct code a few moments after Valiant and I left."

"How many people know the code?"

"Just Valiant, Dr. Conner, and I. Everyone else is incapacitated or dead—Steadfast, Eagle, and Candle."

"And I was with Dr. Conner," Matt said.

Valiant looked toward the birthing garden. "I assume the giantess and the white-haired boy have no access."

"Correct." Listener ejected her rifle's ammo magazine, checked it, and shoved it back into place with a loud snap. "We just have to be ready. I'll be listening for any signs that we're being followed again."

After Matt and Valiant checked their ammo, Matt nodded. "Let's go."

The trio jogged side by side up a gentle slope. Since the sun had melted the surface layer, their feet penetrated dirty slush and gained good traction in the remnant ash. As before, the sense of danger never wavered. Their stalker was somehow keeping pace, but if he really did have wings, eluding him might be impossible.

Ahead, the plume of smoke rose beyond a ridge, maybe a mile away. As the exertion created warmth, sweat pooled under Matt's shirt. Listener no longer shivered, though the air stayed chilly as it swirled down from mountain peaks that loomed ahead and at each side.

At times, she called for a halt, listened for the stalker, and looked around with her spyglass, but she found nothing. Whoever it was probably halted every time they did.

When they reached the crest of the ridge, Listener pointed down the next slope. "The portal is behind that wall." The slope led to a brick-and-mortar wall, about ten feet high and eighty feet long. It arced in front of an indentation in a mountain—a bite out of the towering cliff—leaving a two-foot-wide gap at each end, probably access points for the enclosed area. Smoke billowed from behind the wall and shot into the sky. "We built it to block the wind, but we didn't include a ceiling. Otherwise smoke would accumulate."

"If ice snuffed the fire," Valiant said, "relighting it did not open the portal. The flames merely keep it open if it is already in that state."

"That's true, Valiant, but this storm had unusual properties besides ice." Listener touched her ear. "It made a horrific noise that only I could hear, obviously something that Mardon included in the storm. I know what a functioning portal sounds like, so I hope to listen to this one for a … a healthy heartbeat, I suppose. Even if the fire is unable to open the portal for our warriors, perhaps it will make the portal easier for them to open."

"A reasonable course to take." Valiant spread a hand toward the portal wall. "Kindly lead the way."

Listener gave him a hard look. "You want me to enter first?"

"I realize that this is not our custom, but you are more fully informed than I am." Valiant pointed at her rifle. "You have a weapon. There is no need for alarm."

"If you say so." Listener inhaled deeply and let the air out in a stream of vapor. Spreading her arms, she skied down the slope and stopped her momentum by bracing against the wall. Matt copied her moves, then Valiant did the same.

Keeping a hand on the wall, Listener followed the curve to the right for about ten paces until she reached one of the gaps. After looking back briefly, she walked through. "Watch your step," she called back. "The ice melted near the fire, so there's a drop."

Matt followed her through the gap. Once inside, he slid down a slope to bare rock in a circular depression, perhaps forty feet in diameter. A stack of wood blazed near the wall's center with a few sticks of kindling sitting in a pile at the far side of the fire.

"Two sets of dragon tracks." Listener pointed at claw marks in the ice near the kindling. "Both Karrick and Grackle have been here." She stooped and set a finger on a scorch mark that drew a black zigzag line across the rocky floor, maybe ten feet long.

"A burn?" Matt asked as he approached.

She nodded. "But even dragon fire isn't hot enough to scorch rock like this."

Valiant joined them. "What have you found?"

"A burn mark." She touched a pool of red at the end of the line and rubbed her thumb and finger together. "And a lot of blood. It's sticky. Probably less than a couple of hours old."

"Dragon blood?" Matt grasped Listener's wrist and helped her rise.

When she stood upright, she immediately slid her hand away. "Considering the claw marks, that stands to reason."

Matt pretended not to notice the recoil. Why was she avoiding the slightest touch now?

"Speaking of blood ..." Valiant nodded toward the gap they had entered. "I noticed a trail of blood on the ice outside. Once you discern whether or not the portal is functional, we can follow the trail."

"I'll listen to it now." Standing several paces away from the stack of burning logs, Listener faced the flickering light and the man-made wall behind it. She waved a hand in a circular motion. "The portal is right about here—maybe three feet off the ground. If you need to find it later, just step off five feet from the compass painted on the mountain wall behind me."

A log fell down the stack. The fire surged briefly and sent a blast of scalding air across their bodies. Listener stared at the flames. "The high-pitched static I usually hear around portals is coming through. I don't hear anything from the Earth side, though." She unfastened her spyglass, expanded it, and aimed it at the portal as she looked through the eyepiece. "I see a field of grass and two men huddled over something, but their backs are facing me." After a few seconds, she collapsed the spyglass and hooked it to her belt. "The portal is here, but it's not open."

"The fire has cleared most of the ice," Valiant said, "so perhaps Sapphira will be able to open it. Only time will tell."

Matt looked at the compass that had been painted in red at the center of the mountain wall. "Why a compass?"

"It's a symbol of destinations." Listener walked to the wall, rose to tiptoes, and touched the northern point, the southern one at her knees. "North represents Heaven, so we always head in that direction." She then shifted her finger clockwise from point to point. "The rest represent the six days of creation plus a day of rest. Your father drew something similar for us years ago, so I copied it here to mark the new portal. That was before we built the wall. Now it's easy to find."

Valiant looked at the sky. "Nightfall is upon us. Are you two tired?"

"Exhausted." Listener stretched her arms and yawned. "Aren't you, Matt?"

Matt read her expression. Her eyes said to play along. "Definitely." He copied her stretching arms and let out a yawn.

Valiant laughed. "You two should sleep while I stand guard. It might take a while for Sapphira and her company to come."

"I was hoping you would watch for Karrick," Listener said. "He can tell us about the burn mark and the blood, but I don't think you'll be able to see him from in here."

"You raise a good point. Once you two are settled, I will step outside and watch for him. Perhaps I will also follow the trail of blood, though it will be difficult when it becomes fully dark." Valiant picked up one of the larger logs and tossed it onto the portal fire.

Listener sat on a dry spot on the rocky ground about five paces from the flames and just a few steps from the wall gap they had not entered. "This should be close enough to stay warm." She set her rifle down and pointed at the fire. "Matt, I'm sure you can find a good place on the other side."

"Yeah. Sure." Matt gave the portal flames a wide berth and settled on a spot several paces from the crackling logs, closer to the opposite entry gap. He, the burning logs, and Listener made an uneven line parallel to the wall, though he was able to see her as he looked across the front of the fire.

When he laid his rifle down, she cupped a hand to her ear, then pulled her hand down and lay curled on her side. She closed her eyes but kept a finger on her jaw.

Matt lay in the same position. The cupped ear probably meant that she was ready to converse. "What's going on?" he said, his volume low enough to keep Valiant from hearing. "We slept quite a bit."

Her eyes still closed, she covered her mouth. "I am speaking as quietly as possible. Can you hear me?"

Her voice came through the tooth transmitter. He covered his own mouth and whispered in return. "Yes."

"What does your danger sense tell you?"

"The level is about the same. Something's close. If the stalker has wings, maybe he's perched right outside. Why?"

"Let's wait for Valiant to leave. Pretend to sleep."

Matt closed his eyes to a narrow slit. Valiant used a long stick to arrange a new log on the fire. As he grimaced at the heat, light from the flames illuminated his square-jawed face. With evening now settling into nightfall, the fire would soon become their only source of light but plenty bright enough to see Listener.

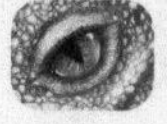

Matt again spoke in a whisper. "I think he'll leave soon."

"Yes. He will."

"Do you think he'll follow the trail of blood he mentioned?"

"No."

"Why not?"

"Shhh."

Valiant stepped back from the fire and drew his sword. He crouched next to Listener and leaned close as if checking to see if she had gone to sleep. His blade glimmering in the firelight, he set his ear in front of her face, then rose and marched out of the portal area through the gap closer to her.

The moment he left, Listener climbed to her feet and skulked toward Matt, her back bent low and her eyes darting between the two entry gaps. She dropped to her knees at his side and clasped his hand in both of hers. "I'm so sorry I treated you that way," she whispered. "I didn't want him to think we were romantically involved."

"Are we? … I mean, why not?"

"If an enemy perceives that two people are inclined toward each other, he can use a threat to one to persuade the other to do whatever he wishes."

"So you think the stalker has been watching us for any sign of romance?"

"Not the stalker. Valiant."

"Valiant? I noticed that you've acted suspicious about him. What makes you think he's an enemy?"

"He's acting strangely. For a while I attributed his behavior to the recent resurrection. He wasn't quite himself. But whenever I asked him about old memories, he always had an excuse for not remembering, and I have never seen him allow a woman to enter a blind chamber without checking its safety first."

"So you think he's been causing my danger alarms? He's someone else in disguise?"

"No disguise is that good. When I laid my head on his chest, I smelled Valiant's smell. I heard his heartbeat, slower than most. It thrums with a unique series of sounds."

"But who could corrupt Valiant? And if he means us harm, he could've easily killed me in the forest a while back. What possible reason could he have for coming all the way here when he could have killed us at any time?"

"Those are questions I have been asking myself, but I cannot answer them. That's why I suggested sleeping far apart. While you sleep, I will stay awake with my rifle ready. We don't know which entry he will use when he returns. If he attacks you, I can shoot him. If he attacks me, I will scream, and you will be able to wake up before he can get to you."

"No. Let me stay awake while you sleep. I'm a trained soldier, and—"

"And I'm not?"

"Right. I'm sorry. I just—"

"Want to protect me. I know. And I like that." She kissed his cheek. "You sleep. He will not be able to sneak up on me. I can hear him walking on the ice even from here."

"I'll try, but I'm not sure I'll be able to."

"You will. Our nap wasn't nearly long enough to counter what you endured in the abyss." She tapped his jaw twice. The transmitter's tingle ceased. "That should help. Don't worry. I'll wake you up soon."

"Real soon." Matt looked toward the gap at the end of the wall. "Why do you think he won't follow the blood trail?"

"The true Valiant would follow it, and that would be fine. If Karrick or Grackle is bleeding, Valiant would help him. If a corrupt Valiant intends to harm us, I don't think he will venture far since he doesn't know how long we will sleep."

"I can't argue with that, but if a dragon is really hurt, maybe you and I should look for him."

"We can. After we see what Valiant will do." She released his hand, rose, and backed away, again glancing at the exit gap. When she returned to her spot on the other side of the fire, she resumed her sleeping position and closed her eyes.

Matt closed his as well, then opened them a slit again. The fire blazed. In the growing darkness, reflected flames danced on the walls. At the compass, the flickering images pointed in the northerly directions—first northwest, then northeast, then due north, then all three at once. They looked like bouncing needles, as if a nearby magnet had skewed the compass readings.

Hot air streamed into his eyes. He closed them to allow moisture to return. In his mind, a negative image of the compass remained, pulsing as the needle shifted from direction to direction. After two revolutions, it stopped on North and stayed there. Soon, consciousness faded away.

As Grackle descended, Bonnie looked down. Another collection of frozen huts breezed by, probably Founder's Village. Ahead, a hulking form stood in the midst of dark soil, a huge silhouette framed by a nearby campfire. She leaned to get a better look. That had to be the birthing garden. Could Yereq have risen from the dead?

The moment Grackle landed at the edge of the garden, Bonnie beat her wings, lifted Marilyn, and flew her down. "I think that might be Yereq!" As soon as her feet touched the ground, she broke into a wing-aided sprint. "Yereq! Is that you?"

The shadowy figure held up a hand. "No. I am Mendallah."

Her heart sinking, Bonnie slowed and walked the rest of the way. As she drew near, Mendallah's feminine form and long hair became obvious in the firelight. "I'm sorry. I thought you might be someone I knew."

"Your mistake is understandable." Mendallah picked up a burning stick and held it close to a small birthing plant. Orange light glimmered on one of the praying leaves. "I have heard about Yereq, and I am honored that you would assume that I am that heroic man." She chuckled. "Even though I am a woman."

"Sorry again. It's getting pretty dark." Bonnie extended her hand. "I'm Bonnie Bannister."

Mendallah wrapped her huge hand around Bonnie's and shook it. "I deduced that. Not many women have dragon wings. They are lovely to behold."

"Thank you." Bonnie knelt and touched one of the leaves. "This plant is still young. It won't release the baby for a few weeks."

"They grow quickly now. It was little more than a sprout when we found it. I am watching it while Zohar cares for the babies who were born here recently. He is a male Oracle of Fire and is in one of the huts." She waved the burning stick across the garden. "He melted the ice to expose the plants, but we found only two infant-bearing plants besides this one. Another transformed into a human who was much older than infancy. He left quickly to follow Matt and Listener."

Bonnie held her breath. "Matt? My son?"

"Yes. Matt Bannister. He is—"

"Bonnie?" Marilyn called as she tiptoed across the garden. "Is it really Yereq?"

"No, but Matt and Listener were here!" Bonnie looked at Mendallah. "And what about Lauren, my daughter? Was Matt carrying her?"

Mendallah shook her head. "The two were alone. They made no mention of Lauren."

"None at all? Matt said nothing about resurrecting his sister from the dead?"

"I apologize for my ignorance. I was also recently resurrected from this soil, so my knowledge is limited to the past few hours and the stories I have been told. I am sure Zohar knows more. I can go to him and—"

"No." Bonnie waved a hand. "I can't do anything about it now anyway. We have work to do."

After Bonnie introduced Marilyn and Mendallah and provided a summary of what they needed to do, the giantess told her own story in brief, how she and Zohar were rescued by Joran, stayed in an ovulum for years, somehow died, and then resurrected. She also gave more details about the person who resurrected wearing Second Eden garb and followed Matt and Listener.

When Mendallah finished, Marilyn set the pot on the ground and patted the top of the plant's head. "This is my husband, Jared, soon to be Clefspeare."

Bonnie leaned closer. The firelight illuminated a tiny mouth at the front of the plant's head. Now about six inches tall, its omicron stage had come, but at this rate it would take days or weeks for it to grow into its omega stage, a full-grown dragon.

"Mendallah," Marilyn said, "do you know if any particular place in the garden is more fertile than others?"

"I sprouted not far from here, and it took less than a minute for me to grow. If the soil can produce someone as big as I am, perhaps it can feed a dragon's growth."

Marilyn picked up the pot. "Show me."

Mendallah led them to a place near the edge of the garden, only steps from where Grackle waited, now barely visible in the twilight. She knelt again and patted a disturbed spot in the soil. "Here."

Grackle blew a sharp whistle. Bonnie looked his way. "Is someone coming?"

He bobbed his head and whistled several short spurts.

"I doubt that he detects Zohar," Mendallah said. "He would not leave infants unattended, nor would he bring them out into the cold."

They all stared into the darkness beyond Grackle. A chilly breeze blew past. Ice crunched, but not with the cadence of footsteps, more likely trees or huts shedding the storm's debris.

Arramos will attack with something far more sinister than brute force."

Marilyn slid closer to her. "True. I'm a brute force kind of person myself, but in all the chaos back at the football field, I lost the gun I was using."

"While you wait here," Mendallah said, "I will watch the other plant. Call me if I am needed."

Bonnie nodded. "Sure thing, Mendallah. Thank you."

When the giantess had walked out of sight, Marilyn picked up the firebrand and set it closer to the plant, though not close enough to risk burning it. "I want to see every change while Jared goes through the stages. He's at omicron. Upsilon is next. Mardon said that's when they uproot the spawn and set it in a growth chamber, but he thinks if the growth is fast enough, he will uproot himself and become a full omega without a chamber."

"Since it took Mendallah less than a minute to grow, shouldn't we be seeing growth in Clefspeare by now?"

"Maybe." Marilyn folded her hands in her lap. "Who knows? Maybe dragons are different."

"For once it would be good to see Mardon. We never figured out the extra information he's holding back."

"I hate to say this, but I agree. He's had time to get here, even on foot."

Bonnie heaved a sigh. Her breath streamed out in a thin white vapor. The air seemed colder, but the fire would keep them from freezing. If not, she could wrap herself and Marilyn in her wings. "Are you cold?"

"I'm fine." She caressed one of the plant's leaflets. "How's your song doing?"

"Tired. Flat. Barely a hum. Singing for Carly helped, but thinking about her being gone really hurts."

Marilyn punched the air with a fist. "Then it's a good time to rev it up."

"Amazing Grace again?"

Marilyn shook her head. "Let's shift gears."

"Okay. What?"

"I think you can guess."

"Psalm one-thirty-nine?"

Marilyn nodded. "But not the condensed version. I need the original tonight. Every word of it."

"Will you sing it with me?"

"Of course. Maybe I'll even add a descant here and there."

"That's the spirit." Bonnie cleared her throat and began. "Whither shall I go from thy spirit? Or whither shall I flee from thy presence?"

Marilyn joined in on the next phrase, and they sang together.

"If I ascend up into heaven, thou art there. If I make my bed in hell, behold, thou art there." Bonnie gave her wings a gentle flap. "If I take the wings of the morning, and dwell in the uttermost parts of the sea, even there shall thy hand lead me, and thy right hand shall hold me."

While Marilyn sang a lovely descant, Bonnie picked up the firebrand, lifted it high, and continued. "If I say, surely the darkness shall cover me, even the night shall be light about me. Yea, the darkness hideth not from thee; but the night shineth as the day."

They clasped hands and finished together, slowing the melody and stretching out the final words. "The darkness and the light are both alike to thee."

20

CHAPTER

Dream Oracles

"Now look again." Sir Barlow pointed at the ovulum. "Matt and Listener have bedded down."

Lauren peered into the red interior and focused on the tiny viewing screen near the center. Matt lay on the ground several steps from a bonfire. On the opposite side of the fire, Listener had curled on her side with her eyes closed. Walls surrounded the area, though dim light shining from above indicated that this chamber lacked a ceiling.

Sir Barlow drew the ovulum back. "If Lauren could tell them of our need for Excalibur, they could find it for us and bring it here."

"It would certainly come in handy," Merlin said as he held his staff with both hands, his eyes wary as he focused on the stalagmites. "We could kill those spiders easily if they ever show their ugly little heads."

"What do you think they're waiting for?" Lauren asked.

"For us to waver in our diligence." Merlin leaned against his staff. "But back to finding Excalibur. Our earlier question remains. If Lauren were to enter the dream realm, would either Matt or Listener be there?"

"Matt is my twin," Lauren said. "Maybe we both inherited my mother's gift."

"An intriguing proposal." Merlin pushed against his staff and straightened. "It is worth an attempt. We have no other solution to employ. Yet, you have not proven that your dreaming gift is functional here. You lost your other powers."

"True, but I have to try." Lauren picked up the yoke, hugged it close to her chest, and lay on her side. The cold floor knifed through her shirt and raised a shiver. The warm yoke helped but not much. "This won't be easy."

"Here." Merlin shed his cloak and spread it on the floor. "It is lined with an excellent insulator."

"Thank you." She shifted over to the cloak and pulled the edges around her body until it wrapped her in a tight cocoon. "That's much better."

The moment she closed her eyes, something tapped her shoulder. "Lauren?"

She opened her eyes. "Yes?"

Merlin knelt close and whispered, "Do you not pray before you go to sleep? The psalmist said, 'I will lay me down in peace and sleep, for thou, Lord, makes me dwell in safety.'"

"Um … sure." Heat surged into her ears. "I just—"

"Do not be ashamed, daughter of the light. Very few have battled the storms you have faced."

"That's no excuse. I'll pray."

Merlin patted her shoulder. "If you wish, I will pray for you. I am a bard, and I will be the psalmist for your slumber. First I will relate a story, and then I will shift to a prayer."

Memories flooded Lauren's mind—her home in Nashville, her foster mother's gentle kisses, and sweet lullabies. She smiled. "You'll sing me to sleep?"

"It will be my pleasure, and perhaps our good knight will hum along. The melody is quite easy."

Sir Barlow cleared his throat. "I will certainly try. I have been told that my baritone harmonies are soothing to sleeping babes."

"Excellent." Merlin clapped his hands and rubbed them together. "Now close your eyes, Lauren, and ponder the words. Absorb them. Let the melody carry you away to that realm of alternate reality as you call to Matt. The urgency is great, but you must relax and trust the one who gave you this oracle's gift."

Lauren closed her eyes and again pulled the cloak tight against her body. Merlin began humming at a high register, a simple tune that sounded like Brahms' Lullaby. Sir Barlow joined in with a hum of his own, lower and rougher, but it blended beautifully.

Merlin added words to match the melody.

Awake at night, I search my room;
Awash in tears, I sense the gloom.
The stroke of twelve, the devil's hour,
The bells declare Satanic power.

A chime for darkness, two for fears,
Three for tyrants' tortured years;
The tones recount the hurts, the lies,
The tears of grief from captive eyes.

The twelfth leaves echoes strewn about,
Like shattered glass reflecting doubt.
I listen while the echoes fade,
And silence starts a new charade.

Lauren floated on a dark cloud that drifted low above a stretch of pavement. In the light of a hazy moon a platoon of soldiers in dark uniforms herded a hundred or more children into a line of cargo planes. One little girl tripped and fell. As she cried, a soldier kicked her in the stomach, then jerked her up by the hair and threw her back into the crowd. An older boy caught the girl and helped her walk into the rear compartment of the lead airplane. As they climbed in, the boy's angry scowl drilled into the brutal soldier.

Lauren wept. What could she do but cry and pray for these tortured little lambs? They were so far away ... beyond her reach.

I cry, I weep, I can't pretend
This darkest night will ever end.
The morn is but a twisted dream;
O wake me now before I scream.

In sweat I rise to break the curse;
I chant my oaths in rhyme and verse,
Then step outside expecting blight,
That nightmare's threats had come to light.

The dawn breaks red, a scarlet mask;
It drinks horizon's bloody flask
And spills the red upon the field,
Exposing devils once concealed.

Lauren's cloud drifted over a suburban neighborhood. The sun dawned red in the eastern sky and painted scarlet streaks across brick-and-siding houses bordering a crooked street. Several adults stood on the pavement, one woman holding a little boy. A huge black vulture swooped and grabbed the boy. Moments later, it dropped him, and a winged woman caught him.

Leaning over the edge of the cloud, Lauren tried to get a better look. The winged woman had to be her mother, though from this distance her face was indistinct.

After a flurry of events, a man in a yellow uniform shot the boy and the woman holding him, and the two crumpled in a bloody pool.

Lauren clenched a fist. The murderer! How could he be so cold? So cruel?

She clasped her hands, barely able to catch her breath. *Dear God! Oh, dear God! Someone has to stop this madness!*

Then Satan's armies line the skies,
Remove the mask, and shed disguise;
Deception ends when swords unsheathe,
When sheep reveal their wolven teeth.

A flash of light from yonder hill
Portends an army brighter still;
A steed of white upon the crest
Transports the lightning east to west.

Then thunder booms a gallop beat,
A call to battle, no retreat;
A thousand horses, men, and swords
Stampede the darkness, pierce the horde.

The winged woman wielded a sword. A laser beam shot from the tip, and she swung it at the murderer. When the beam sliced through his head, he disintegrated, and his uniform dropped empty to the street.

More vultures gathered and chased the remaining adults to a jet on a highway. After a battle that again included the sword's beam and gunfire, the people escaped in the jet and flew away from the rising crimson sun.

Lauren followed the jet's course. They had Excalibur. But where were they going in the jet?

With a kick, Lauren urged the cloud forward. She had to follow and ask for Excalibur. As her scales tingled, Merlin's voice strengthened and coursed through her mind. Her own thoughts mixed into the melody and built up inside like a pressure cooker ready to burst. Words begged to spring forth. She opened her mouth and sang them with all her heart.

O God of wonder, God of love,
I need a guide from gates above;
Empower me to find my twin
To gain the sword, our vict'ry win.

O plant my feet on solid ground,
Where help for rescue can be found;
Assign an angel to my side
To walk with me, to be my guide.

The children need a saving hand
To guard their lives from Satan's land.
We'll shatter ice and make pain cease;
We'll raise the souls and grant them peace.

The words died away. Darkness swept across the sky. The cloud descended, tipped at an angle, and rolled Lauren off to her knees on a cold surface. A cloak fell over her back and slid to the ground at her side.

Bracing against the frigid ground with her hands, she grabbed the cloak and pushed to a standing position. She looked at the cloak's white material. This wasn't Merlin's. It looked like the one Tamiel stole.

She put the cloak on and wrapped it close. Flames ignited to her right and illuminated the area. A red dragon blew fire on a stack of wood. With each blow, he gasped and panted before shooting another stream of fire. A purple dragon sat on its haunches on the other side of the fire. Its wings and ears drooped. It seemed that both had just arrived from an exhausting journey.

Lauren eyed them closely—probably Karrick and Grackle. Dirty ice coated the ground and the surrounding walls, though, as the view in the ovulum had indicated, no ceiling capped this odd chamber. As the fire melted the ice, dripping soot crawled along a painting on one wall—a red compass.

Soon, the fire caught hold and grew into an inferno. The red dragon collapsed, its neck over a pile of wood. Grackle skittered around the fire and used his snout to nudge Karrick's head. Karrick snorted but stayed unconscious.

The fire burned on. More ice melted. The floor sank, and the logs and dragons sank with it. After several minutes, a second fire flashed and vanished. People appeared out of nowhere as if birthed from the new flames. A winged woman fell to the ground, a sword in her grasp. Two other women supported an elderly man between them. Yet another woman dropped to hands and knees as if injured. Finally, a fifth woman, white-haired and petite, stood upright where the flames had erupted.

Lauren called out, "Sapphira!" As she looked around, she identified as many of the others as she could. "Mom, Grandma Bannister, Ashley, Mariel, and Thomas." Lauren leaned close to the injured woman. She was unfamiliar. Her tight grimace indicated that she was in a lot of pain.

"Mom, are you all right?" Lauren reached, but her hand passed through Mom's shoulder. Lauren stepped back. They weren't in the dream realm, so she could only watch and listen. Yet, Mom did have a sword. Might it be Excalibur? If so, that solved one puzzle. Now to figure out how to get her to bring it to the life reservoir.

As if moving at hyper speed, the arrivals zipped around, talking to the dragons and each other. Mom pointed a sword at the ground. Light shot into Ashley, who now embraced the injured woman. Everything moved so quickly, it was hard to tell what was going on.

After another flurry of activity, the dragons and most of the arrivals departed, leaving Mom and the injured woman alone. Mom wrapped a wing around her. They talked for quite a while, their speech muted and garbled. Finally, Mom picked her up and flew with her over a wall.

Lauren took a step to follow, but her feet slipped on the ice. She pushed forward, but no matter how hard she tried, she couldn't get any traction.

Nearby, the fire burned on, though not as vibrantly as before. This looked like the place where Matt lay, so maybe the realm of dreams had been showing scenes from the past, much faster than real time. Soon her dream would bring about the present hour. Matt would come with Listener, and he would sleep.

Lauren pulled the cloak close once more and sat on the ground. The lullaby's melody returned to mind. As she hummed along, she let out a satisfied sigh. Whether or not Matt would be able to communicate in his dreams lay in God's hands, and in that truth, she could rest. The God who gave her the power of an oracle would see this journey through to the end.

Matt lay with his eyes closed. In his mind, an image formed—a young woman standing nearby. As the fire cast her shadow over him, she appeared to be ghostlike, without color or facial features.

He tried to open his eyes and urge himself awake. When they opened, he looked at her, but had he opened his real eyes? It seemed impossible to be sure.

White hair brushed her shoulders, covered by an equally white cloak. Unearthly sapphire irises sparkled around her pupils. Might she be Sapphira? This person was taller, but who else had white hair and eyes so brilliant?

He whispered, "Sapphira?"

"No, Matt." She drifted close and crouched. "Do you recognize me now?"

The voice, soft and lovely, gave her away. "Lauren?"

"Yes!" She rose as if able to float to a standing position. "Sir Barlow said my appearance has changed, but I wasn't sure how I would look in a dream."

"A dream? What do you mean?"

She spread her arms. "I am a dream oracle, and I prayed that I would find someone in my dreams who could help me. I found the life reservoir, but I need Excalibur to melt the ice over the reservoir so we can release its energy. I think Mom has it, and I saw her here earlier, but I don't know where she went. We have to let her know how to find me."

"Okay." Matt looked past her. The fire and Listener were still there, so he hadn't moved to a new location. "How can we find you?"

"Go to Jade's sanctum. Once you get there, look for the only remaining white beam besides the one to the tree portal. You'll need protection to get through." She pinched her cloak's sleeve. "I'm not sure why I'm wearing this in my dream. This is the fireproof cloak you carried me in, but it turned white, then Tamiel stole it from me. And that brings up my next message. Tamiel is alive, and he's loose on Second Eden. I think he might want to get to the life reservoir."

"Tamiel?" Matt pictured the winged demon flying over Second Eden, a dark suit over his scarecrow-like frame. "That explains a lot. We've been thinking that someone with wings has been stalking us. I sensed the danger all the way from the birthing garden to the portal here. Valiant found a cloak that was left behind by the stalker, so it looks like we recovered the stolen one."

"Then you can use it to get into Jade's sanctum." She scanned the portal area. "I saw Valiant through an ovulum. Where is he now?"

"He's on the other side of the wall watching for Karrick." Matt looked at Listener again as she continued pretending to be asleep. "I wonder why Listener's not paying attention. She hears everything."

"She can't hear us." Lauren set her hands in a circular frame. "Stay focused, Matt. You're sleeping, and this is a dream. We can speak to each other because we are both dream oracles. You need to know that Sapphira brought several people through the portal, including Mom and Grandmother Bannister, but Sapphira returned to Earth, probably to bring more people here."

"So the portal's functional. That's good news."

"Yes. Now be sure to remember my requests. We need Excalibur. We need to escape from the life reservoir realm. You need the cloak to get here. And beware of Tamiel. He is the craftiest demon ever to walk on any world. He can take the form of anyone he has killed. If my friend Micaela shows up, she is really Tamiel. He killed her with a car bomb."

Matt pressed his lips together. "And Tamiel killed Valiant. I saw it. I was there."

Lauren's sapphire eyes flashed. "Then Valiant might be Tamiel in disguise."

Matt replayed Valiant's presentation of the cloak in the duffle bag. No one saw where he got it or the sword. "It adds up, except for the *why* question. Why didn't he kill Listener and me on the way to the portal? Why did he follow us for so long?"

"Followed you?"

Matt nodded. "He stayed behind, I assumed to protect us from a rear assault by whoever we thought was stalking us. Then he let Listener enter the portal area before ..." Another image of Valiant came to mind, waving a hand toward the portal wall as he invited Listener to enter first. As Listener said, doing so was against his principles. There could be only one reason for his action.

Matt whispered, "Valiant didn't know where the portal was."

"*Should* he have known?"

"He was a leader here. He had to know."

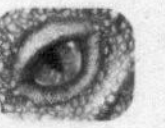

"Which means he let you two live because he wanted to find it. Once he kills you, he can take your place. Then he can deceive anyone without people questioning his resurrection."

"But why? What does he plan to do?"

"Like I said, he might be trying to get to the life reservoir, but first he probably wants to make sure the portal opens for Arramos. He might also be planning to destroy a plant that Grandmother Bannister is carrying. She hopes to put it in the birthing garden to grow a dragon."

"Grow a dragon?" Matt laughed under his breath. "Okay, now I believe this is really a dream. It just took a crazy turn."

"It *is* a dream, but I'm telling you the truth. You need to wake up before Tamiel kills you two in your sleep."

"Listener's not really asleep." Matt gestured toward her. "She has a gun, and she knows how to use it."

"But you have to let Listener know so you can destroy that demon now. If he's standing outside this area, you can sneak up on him while he's not expecting it."

"Okay. Okay. I'll try to wake up." Matt closed his eyes, then opened them again. Lauren still stood there, her body framed by firelight. "I must really be tired. I can't seem to—"

"Matt!" Lauren lifted her hands and screamed. "Matt! He's coming! Wake up!"

"I'm trying!" He closed his eyes once more and snapped them open again. Lauren still stood there, her arms raised and her cloak's sleeves falling past her elbows, though now her hair was no longer white.

A gunshot rang out. A hole tore through Lauren's chest and left a bloody gap. She wobbled, and her eyes rolled upward. Another gunshot echoed the first. A second hole appeared. Dark blood oozed from the wound, and a sword clanked on the floor.

Matt stared at his rifle on the ground, his limbs petrified. They wouldn't budge. Was this still a dream?

A black youth ran in from the wall's closer entry with a Glock aimed at Lauren's back. He fired three more times. The bullets ripped through her body and cracked against a wall, leaving more gaping exit wounds in her chest. She remained standing, her face frozen in shock.

Matt screamed. "No!" He jumped up and staggered for his rifle, but before he could grab it, the youth snatched the sword and sliced the blade through Lauren's neck. Her head toppled off and thudded on the ground. Her body crumpled in a heap next to her head.

Matt grabbed the rifle. The youth lunged at him and latched onto the barrel with both hands. "Matt!" he grunted. "Stop fighting!" He shoved Matt back and spread out his arms. "Look at me! I am Eagle! We met at the waterfall."

Gasping for breath, Matt pointed the rifle at him and screamed, "You killed Lauren! You killed my sister!"

Eagle raised his hands. "No! That wasn't Lauren. It was a shape-shifter. I saw it transform from Valiant into Lauren."

"Transform?"

He nodded. "In an instant."

Matt closed in, set the barrel against Eagle's forehead, and growled, "How do I know that you're not lying to me? How do I know you're not Tamiel disguised as Eagle?"

As Eagle met Matt's stare, his expression stayed rock solid. "I do not know how to prove my words. I only recently resurrected, and I cannot guess how long I have been dead."

Lauren's words returned to Matt's mind. *He can take the form of anyone he has killed.* His throat clamped shut as he squeezed out, "She told me … you jumped into …"

"Mount Elijah." Eagle nodded. "My hope was to save her life."

Matt breathed a whispered, "Tamiel didn't kill you, but he did kill Lauren."

Eagle turned toward Listener. His mouth dropped open. "Listener! She's bleeding!"

"What?" Matt spun toward her. She lay on the ground in a pool of blood. "Listener!" He dropped the rifle, ran to her side, and turned her to her back. Blood saturated her shirt from the hem up to her ribs. He pinched the shirt and slid it up. A three-inch-long vertical gash dug into her skin just below her ribcage. She coughed hard and breathed in gurgling spasms. "Hang on, Listener. Hang on." He laid a hand over the gash. "Come on, healing touch. Don't fail me now."

Eagle knelt next to him and spoke quickly. "I resurrected from the garden and followed you. When I saw Valiant, I noticed that he trailed you and Listener, which is not like him at all. I knew he was dead and that I was the last statue, but I suppose you have no idea what I mean."

"No. I understand. Go on."

"I was suspicious, so I followed."

"But I never saw you." Matt pushed a finger into Listener's wound and probed for depth. Blood warmed his skin. "How could you track us without being seen?"

"I am called Eagle for a reason. I can see details from far away, even in darkness."

"Keep going."

"When you entered the forest, I rushed to the weapons cache and took a rifle and a handgun. I stayed out of sight and watched the three of you enter the portal chamber. At that point, you two were armed, so I thought you would be fine. Then, I noticed a trail of blood and followed it to a cave where I found Ashley and Karrick and an elderly couple, Thomas and Mariel. As soon as I told Ashley what was going on, she asked me to help her get close so she could read Valiant's mind. I carried her to the cave entrance—"

"Carried her?"

Eagle nodded again. "She is very weak from two healings."

Matt pushed a second finger into the gash. How deep could this wound be? "I know how that weakness feels."

"From where we stood, we could see Valiant in the twilight. She said she couldn't read his thoughts, but she could sense murder in his heart. That was all I needed to know. I didn't want Karrick to investigate with me, because he would be too loud. So I gave Mariel the rifle, kept the handgun, and crept as close to Valiant as I dared, hoping he couldn't hear my footsteps on the ice. Then, he pulled a cloak from a bag, put it on, and transformed into Lauren. I suppose Listener didn't defend herself because she thought Lauren had come, not realizing that she would attack."

"The cloak!" Matt scanned the ground. "Where is it?"

Eagle gestured toward Tamiel's headless form. "It's still on the body."

"And you said Karrick's in the cave?"

"He was there moments ago. He had just reignited the portal flames before you arrived, but he returned to the cave to protect Ashley and the others."

"Good. Perfect. The cloak is fireproof, so Karrick can heat my body without burning me. His fire will soup up my healing powers."

"Then I will go to the cave and—"

"Wait. Did you see my mother anywhere? She might have Excalibur. Then I wouldn't need the cloak."

Eagle shook his head. "Ashley told me your mother and your grandmother flew on Grackle to the birthing garden. They have a plant that is supposed to grow into Clefspeare. They hope he will battle and defeat Arramos, though they are unsure about the planting procedure. It seems that Mardon has critical information in that regard. He is lurking about somewhere in Second Eden, so they hope he will eventually come to the garden."

"And Excalibur?"

"Your mother has it, and I hear that she is now quite the expert with it."

"Okay. We'll go with what we have. Drape the cloak over me. Then get Karrick."

"Fools!" Tamiel stood upright, wobbly but intact as he adjusted his head onto his neck, his thin fingers in his dark curly hair. He stood beyond the fire at the spot where Matt had been sleeping. "Bullets and swords cannot kill me."

Eagle snatched up the rifle and aimed it at him. "I swear by my father's name if you take a step closer I will rip your body to pieces with a hail of bullets."

"I will not step closer. Your conversation has given me the information I need." He wrapped the cloak tightly and hobbled toward the gap closer to him.

"Stop him!" Matt shouted. "We need that cloak!"

Eagle dropped the rifle, ran to Tamiel, and grabbed the cloak. As Tamiel tried to jerk away, Eagle set his feet and pulled. The material ripped, leaving a long swatch in Tamiel's hand.

Eagle threw the cloak toward Matt and scooped up the rifle. Wings sprouted from Tamiel's back. He beat them furiously and flew toward the top of the wall.

Eagle fired. A bullet ripped through Tamiel's arm, but he flew on. As Eagle fired again and again, Tamiel accelerated and faded into the darkness.

Huffing, Eagle snatched the cloak from the ground, most of it intact, and walked toward Matt. "Will this suffice?"

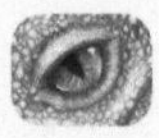

Matt nodded. "It should be plenty."

Listener's back arched. As she groaned, the flow of blood spiked.

Matt reached with his free hand. "Give me the Glock, take the rifle, and get Karrick. Hurry!"

Eagle picked up both guns, pushed the Glock into Matt's hand, and dropped the cloak at his side. "I will return soon." He rushed out of the portal enclosure.

Taking a deep breath, Matt tried to slow his racing heart as he set the gun down and added a second hand to the wound massage. Listener breathed in short gasps. Blood warmed his fingers. Tamiel intended a fatal blow, so he likely struck deep and hard, maybe slicing through an organ. If not for the healing touch, she would probably be dead already.

The flames cast undulating light over his hands. How long ago had he healed Darcy with these blood-covered fingers? Hours?

Days? Just before the healing, love flowed in a warming flood as the last particles of icy hatred melted away. An enemy became a sister, a beloved friend. Love ignited his gift, and new healing power supercharged his hands.

And now he needed that power again. Using the cloak and dragon fire would probably work, but it would bring a crippling side effect—weakness that might last for hours. Tamiel was probably on his way to the birthing garden. He could show up as Lauren, and Mom wouldn't suspect him. Someone needed to be there to warn her of his deceit. Eagle could do it, but Eagle was supposed to be dead. Hearing the truth from her own son would be better.

Tears blurring his vision, he looked up. A few stars twinkled in the dark sky, veiled now and then by the fire's rising smoke. "God …" He cleared his throat. "I need help. You taught me how to love. Well, Mom and Darcy taught me, but I know it came from you. I feel like a little kid with a big gun. The healing worked for them, but I think I kind of stumbled across the trigger. And now I need it to work again. But how do I do it? How do I find the trigger?"

As he gazed at Listener's travailing face, Mom's words returned. *Reject hate and embrace love—love for God, love for others, especially for …* He finished with a whisper. "For Darcy."

He blinked through increasing tears. Mom loved enough to talk about love, to break through a barrier, to shatter chains forged by silence. Love is squelched by thoughts that never become words, by feelings that never flow to the heart of another, by truth that never rides the air in passionate voice.

Sniffing, Matt gazed again at Listener. Maybe her gifted ears could take in his words even while unconscious. Even if not, he had to give voice to love. "Listener, I don't know how to say this except to just blurt it out. … I love you. I'm not even sure what that means. Several things, I guess. At first, I just admired your warrior spirit. Most girls I know think about their hair and clothes, superficial stuff that doesn't matter, but you think about defending those who can't defend themselves. I saw for myself how much you love your family—your adoptive mother, your sister, your brother. I witnessed your fierce loyalty to those who depend on you for survival."

Listener's grimace tightened. Her lips moved as if trying to form words, but only a stuttering groan spilled from her tortured body.

"Shhh. It's going to be all right." Matt bit his lip hard. She was in so much pain! She needed endurance … confidence … a word of assurance. "You're a leader, a champion. Even while Second Eden's villages burned and so many threw their hands up in confusion, you took charge and restored order. When faced with the destruction of a lair that held darkness and death, you marched in with your head held high. You believed in the impossible, that a worthless statue held a priceless soul."

As he took in a deep breath, a tear dripped and fell on Listener's skin, mixing with her blood. "Even though you couldn't possibly gain anything, you risked your life again and again. You nearly drowned, you almost froze, you endured a squealing storm, you marched across miles of ice … for what? For someone else. Always for someone else. And now you lie here near death, your blood pouring out for the sake of another."

Matt swallowed through a tight knot in his throat. "Listener, love like yours is so rare. I want to love like you do. I need to watch how you do it, to witness your ways. I want to show you the same kind of love, to return it with all my heart. I want to be with you forever. But … but if you die …"

Listener gasped. A spasm tightened her abdominal muscles, pinching Matt's fingers within the wound. The blood grew hot. Flesh burned, raising a foul odor.

He slowly withdrew his fingers. With every millimeter of movement, Listener cringed. She cried out, "Oh, it burns! It burns!"

As Matt's fingertips passed across the interior tissues, they sealed, as if cauterized by his touch. "Shhh … It's going to be all right."

Matt pulled his fingers out and massaged the cut, spreading blood over the gash. The red liquid sizzled with tiny bubbles. Smoke rose from the wound. With every passing second, the cut shrank. Soon, only blood remained visible as it bubbled in a shallow pool. Matt wiped it away. The wound had sealed, leaving a thin white scar.

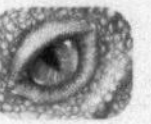

Listener's eyes opened. "Matt?"

"Yes!" He reached a hand toward her cheek, but when wet blood on his palm came into view, he drew it back. "Are you all right?"

As she sat up slowly, she winced. She enfolded his hands in hers, apparently not caring about the blood. "What happened?"

"You got stabbed, so I—"

"Stabbed!" Her eyes shot open. "Lauren stabbed me! She came here, so I thought she—"

"Shhh. Everything's all right. It wasn't Lauren. It was Tamiel in disguise."

She blinked. "Tamiel?"

"He was disguised as Valiant, then as Lauren. He can impersonate anyone he's killed." Matt looked toward the top of the wall. "He's gone, and he didn't do any more damage. But he will if we don't get to the birthing garden before he does. Since he can fly, we have to hurry."

She tilted her head. "I hear wings. Is he still close?"

"That's probably Karrick. Eagle went to get him for us."

Her voice spiked. "Eagle's here? He's alive?"

"Very much so. Tamiel was about to kill me, and Eagle saved my life."

Accompanied by a gust of wind, Karrick flew over the wall, Eagle riding his back. When Karrick landed, the breeze from his wing beats fanned the portal flames.

Eagle jumped down and stared at Listener. "You're healed? How did—"

"Eagle!" She struggled to her feet and limped into his arms. "You resurrected! You *were* the soul in the statue!"

"Yes. I was—"

"Wait." Matt picked up the cloak and put it on. The ragged-edged bottom portion covered his legs down to his knees. "Let's tell our stories on the way." He turned to Karrick. "Can you carry us to the birthing garden? My mother and grandmother went there on Grackle to restore Clefspeare, and Tamiel is on his way to stop them."

"I can fly that far with three, but who will stay to protect those in the cave? Ashley is still very weak."

Eagle raised a hand. "I will. They have a rifle, but I wouldn't want the elderly lady to have to defend everyone for long."

"Good. Thanks." Matt retrieved the Glock and slid it into his pants pocket. "Let's hope this is enough for us."

"May the Father of Lights guide your path." Eagle hugged Matt and Listener in turn, then exited through a gap in the wall.

When he departed, a log near the top of the fire tumbled down the side. The flames diminished, now barely more than a campfire.

"Should one of us stay to keep the fire going?" Listener asked as she checked the spyglass at her belt. "Is the portal open now?"

Matt shook his head. "I walked where it's supposed to be, and nothing happened. But it is functional. Sapphira already sent people through, so maybe she doesn't need the fire anymore."

Listener patted an empty sheath on her belt. "My dagger is gone."

"Tamiel probably took it."

"Most likely." Listener snapped the sheath's fastener. "Let's go."

Karrick lowered his head to the ground. "Feel free to mount."

Matt and Listener climbed up Karrick's neck. With every step, Listener cringed, a hand pressed against her wound. When they settled with Matt in front, Karrick beat his wings, vaulted upward, and sailed over the wall into the cold darkness.

Holding to one of the dragon's spines, Matt stared into the cold headwind. With nightfall nearly complete, trying to see anything might be hopeless. They would have to count on Karrick's senses and memory to get them to the garden in time.

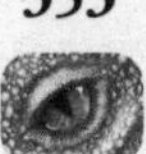

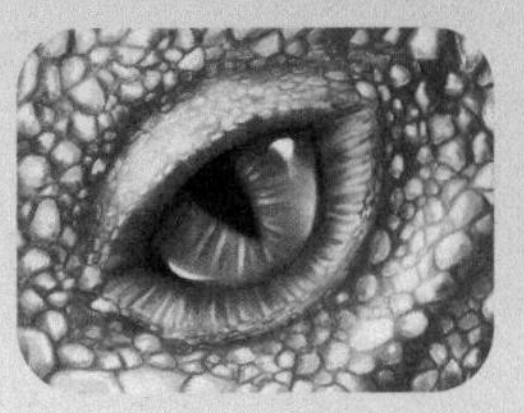

21

CHAPTER

Sleepwalking

Lauren stomped on a flaming spider and ground it under her heel. Sparks and smoke flew, and a foul odor assaulted her nose. Nearby, Merlin and Sir Barlow each crunched a spider underfoot. The three of them had already killed at least a dozen, and now it seemed that the rest of the arachnid army had retreated to the shadows and stalagmites.

Using his staff for support, Merlin sank to the ground at the edge of the life reservoir and shook his head. "I fear that attack was merely a test to see how well we could defend the pool."

"Agreed." Sir Barlow sat on a rock and swiped a sleeve across his brow. "Their captain stayed hidden, so it was definitely a scouting mission. That monster won't be so easy to stomp."

Lauren walked to Merlin's side and scanned the reservoir. "Did the spiders do any damage?"

"Not much." Merlin ran a finger across an indentation in the surface of the pool. "I saw only one on the reservoir itself. It was

able to melt an inch of ice in only a moment, so I assume all of them together could liquefy the surface quickly."

Lauren spotted a spider's dead body a foot or so away from Merlin's finger. "So they'll be back."

"Without a doubt. They don't know when the reservoir will become full, and neither do we for that matter, so they likely won't risk waiting for much longer."

Sir Barlow picked up the ovulum. "Shall we go back to watching our friends? Their activities might provide a clue with regard to the filling."

"Go ahead." Merlin grasped his staff and, with Lauren's help, rose to his feet. "I want to take another reading."

When Lauren joined Sir Barlow, she leaned around his shoulder and looked at the ovulum in his cupped hands. Within the sphere, the red-framed viewing window showed Matt and Listener flying on a dragon, heading away from the Second Eden portal and its dwindling fire.

She turned to Merlin. He held his staff over the reservoir's surface and stared at the top. The light emanating from the candlestone had brightened, but it still looked rather yellowish. "Uh … Merlin?"

"Feel free to call me by my name. I require no formalities." He pulled the staff from the ice. "Even after the addition of Carl Foley's and Carly's energy, we are still far short. It will take a major infusion to fill the reservoir."

Lauren imagined the faces beneath the ice—flowing and swirling in their endless dance. "How many more deaths are needed?"

"Impossible to guess. It depends on the magnitude of sacrificial love the person expresses in death as well as during life. For example, the death of Christ could fill the reservoir by itself, and the death of a long-term missionary would provide a great infusion, while others might provide a minuscule fraction of that amount."

Lauren blew warm air on her chilled fingers. "What about children like those Arramos is killing? Since they're innocent, don't they contribute a lot?"

"It is not merely innocence or purity that creates this energy. The biggest factors are length of service, depth of suffering, and willingness. With the children, it might take hundreds of deaths."

"Hundreds?"

"Again, I don't know. This is untested ground." Merlin walked toward her. "I apologize for the tangent. What was your original question?"

Lauren refocused on the ovulum. "I'm wondering about the portal. No one's left on the Second Eden side. What good would it do for Sapphira to open it now? Clefspeare isn't there to come through, and no one can tell her where everyone is."

"Indeed," Sir Barlow said as he drew his nose close to the ovulum. "Militarily speaking, the Earth-side portal has become a vulnerability, not an asset. Opening it can only provide a way for Arramos to send his forces into the land."

"Well spoken." Merlin stood next to Lauren and looked over her shoulder at the ovulum. "Such is the way with portals. They are merely doors that allow both good and evil to pass through. Without guards at the gates, you might as well tear down the fortifying walls."

"Matt couldn't leave anyone to guard the portal," Lauren said. "They barely survived, and they had emergencies to take care of."

"I am not criticizing their decision to leave. I am merely pontificating a principle."

"Alliteration." Lauren smiled. "You remind me of a friend."

Merlin chuckled. "Abaddon, I assume."

She nodded. "Do you know where he is?"

"He and his horde have been exacting punishment upon evildoers in many regions, which is why the Earth has not suffered a cataclysmic war. Everyone is too busy trying to survive or trying to die to escape the wrath. In any case, Abaddon has a role in our business at hand, as does Enoch. I don't expect them to tarry long."

"Okay, well, back to the portal. Like Sir Barlow said, it's a vulnerability." She nodded toward Jade's sanctum. "All of the portals are controlled from that room, right? Can't we do something there to prevent Arramos from getting to Second Eden?"

Merlin twirled his beard with a finger. "An Oracle of Fire can move a portal from either side, but it would take a monumental amount of energy. If Sapphira were in good health, she could move the portal to exit at the birthing garden, but in her current condition, that seems doubtful. I don't see how she could maintain the massive firestorm that the task would require. The distance is too great."

Lauren pointed at herself. "Can't I move a portal? There has to be a reason God made me an Oracle of Fire."

Merlin lifted a finger. "Ah! A brilliant notion. Perhaps you have provided the third puzzle piece."

"What puzzle piece?"

"You said it yourself. Think, my dear! You are right on the cusp!"

"I said …" Lauren mentally replayed her words. "God made me an Oracle of Fire."

Merlin lifted his brow. "And that means?"

The sequence of events flashed through her mind—the first realm's filthy water and how she diverted the sludge's flow, which cleared the water so she could find the yoke that allowed entry to the second realm; the second realm's field of bones and how her delivery of life-giving water resurrected the energy and cleansed the pool; the third realm's icy darkness, though nothing she had done here fit into the puzzle, at least not yet. Still, each step changed her, gave her a heartbeat, fire, then resurrection.

She looked at Merlin and spoke with confidence. "The reservoir's puzzle isn't a series of physical obstacles. It's a sequence of events that transformed me. The final portal wouldn't have opened unless I had become an Oracle of Fire."

"My thoughts exactly. A villain would be unable to complete the path, because he has neither the purity nor the holy impulse or selflessness to do so."

"So can I do something about the portal to Second Eden? Is that my final step? I might be an Oracle of Fire, but I don't seem to have that power here."

Merlin began pacing, pressing his staff against the ground with every step of his right foot. "That I am not certain about. Only Jade would know whether or not you are able to manipulate the portals."

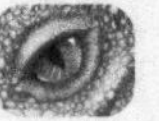

Lauren exhaled heavily. "So I have to dream again to ask her."

Still pacing, Merlin raised a finger. "And if you are successful in locating Jade, you will also have to visit Sapphira in her dreams to let her know what to do."

"But when will Sapphira sleep? She seems tireless."

Sir Barlow cleared his throat. "Pardon my intrusion, but my perception is that Sapphira stayed awake throughout her surgery. Considering what she has suffered, I suspect that she will have to sleep soon. She is extraordinary, to be sure, but she is still human."

Lauren peeked at the ovulum. Two men knelt next to Sapphira, their bodies blocking a view of their work. Only her white hair was visible, scattered on the green turf. "So we watch and wait."

Merlin halted. "I suggest that you go ahead and sleep. See if you can find Jade and then Sapphira. If it appears that Sapphira is going to stay awake for some time to come, then we will awaken you in half an hour."

"All right, but I already slept awhile. Maybe if you sing again, I can go to sleep. It sounded like your story wasn't finished."

"True, my dear." Merlin laid his cloak on the ice and rolled up part of it as a pillow. "Lie here, and Sir Barlow and I will caress your ears with more of the tale."

Lauren curled up on the cloak and closed her eyes. Merlin's gentle humming tenor drifted in, undergirded by Sir Barlow's baritone, though a rasp hampered his voice, likely the result of his long stay in the cold air.

The war has come to end all wars
To pull the shades, to close the doors;
The Alpha to Omega scroll
From first to last will never roll.

As light and darkness storm and clash,
As swords collide and soldiers thrash,
The nightmare pounds within my brain
Of tyrants' tortures, children's chains.

And then draws near the steed of white;
The rider stares, his eyes alight.
With crimson hand he holds a blade,
In letters gold, my name inlaid.

Lauren let the lyrics draw a mental picture—lightning flashes, battles on a darkened field, children being led in chains to a lions' den.

On an old stone table, a parchment covered with ancient runes rolled up and crumbled to dust. Then a valiant warrior riding a magnificent white horse appeared out of nowhere and galloped close. When the horse stopped within reach, it shook its head, and its mane scattered across its muscular neck. The warrior drew a sword from a silver scabbard and showed her its blade.

She focused on the shining metal. What would her name look like in gold? Yet, when the etching clarified, it spelled out a different name—*Sapphira Adi.* This song wasn't about herself at all; it was the tale of a different oracle, the greatest Oracle of Fire the world had ever known.

To heed this rider's wordless plea,
To grasp the sword he forged for me,
Means bloody loss and painful death,
This day to take my final breath.

I clutch the hilt, my fears asunder;
My battle cry resounds like thunder,
To break the chains, to shatter bonds
Till freedom's trumpet call responds.

Like a shadow torn from its moorings, Sapphira stepped out of Lauren's body and grasped the sword. The blade erupted with fire. She held it high and waved it in a circle.

"Lauren?"

Lauren turned toward the voice. A few paces away, Jade stood next to the stone table. Everything else faded into oblivion. "Jade!" Lauren closed the gap with three gliding steps. "I was hoping to find you here."

"It seems that I have found you." Jade crossed her four arms over her chest, her voice less girlish than usual. "I know what you seek, and the cost of securing it is likely higher than you can bear. The sacrifice is too great."

"How do you know? I'm willing to sacrifice a lot."

"Is that so?" Jade curled a finger and walked away from the table. "Come with me."

Lauren followed. They passed through a dark corridor and entered an icy realm. Merlin and Sir Barlow stood near her sleeping form, both watching the stalagmites for more emerging spiders.

Jade stopped at the portal leading to her sanctum. "Fear not. We are able to pass in the dream world." She walked through and approached the sanctum's central column. Lauren hopped across the plane and joined her.

Jade spread two of her hands over the column. Its light cast a pulsing shadow of her on the wall. "When I first planned the security of the life reservoir, I knew that someday I would have to create a portal leading to where the reservoir's energy would be needed. Now that Clefspeare has been planted in the birthing garden, we are ready to provide energy, and the garden will be able to restore life beyond its previous limits." She walked to the portal they had just come through and set a hand on the surface. "In order to send the life energy to the garden, it will be up to you to move this portal there."

Lauren joined her at the portal. "How do I do that?"

"My understanding is that you have seen Sapphira perform this feat." Jade used another hand to comb through Lauren's hair.

Lauren expected a recoil impulse from the intimate touch of a stranger, but instead instinct drew her closer to this exotic woman. "I saw her move a portal, if that's what you mean."

"Then you do the same."

"I'm sure it's a lot easier said than done."

"Indeed." Jade drew her hand back. "Everything worth doing is, and every student of great achievements needs guidance, which I will provide, and you will instruct Sapphira regarding something that she has never accomplished. A new portal must be created along with a conjunction. Since I no longer exist in the physical realm, those tasks will be up to you."

"But I have no idea how to do either one."

"Of course not. I must instruct you." She nodded toward Lauren's pants. "Do you still have the gem?"

Lauren touched her pocket. "Yes. At least, the last I checked. It should still be in my real body's pocket."

"Then you will be able to perform the task." Jade returned to the central column. "Hold the gem's light close to the heart of the sanctum and look into each hole until you see Sapphira. When you find her, ignite the hole with your fire. That will destroy her portal's exit point to Second Eden. Then you must create a new portal with an exit point here in the sanctum. The heart will begin the process by sending a beam to the reflective wall."

Jade walked to the wall and set her hands on the surface at the four corners of an imaginary square. "At that location, you will open a viewing screen so that Sapphira will see this sanctum from her portal, and she will be able to carry her portal flames here. You will have to use two hands at a time, but it will work as long as the gemstone is shining on the wall. For your convenience, I put a hole through the top of the gem so that you can easily add it to the chain you already have. This will allow you to keep your hands free while you work."

Lauren touched the chain around her neck. "That doesn't sound too hard."

"Ah! But it is merely the beginning. Creating the conjunction comes next." Jade stood in front of the portal leading to the reservoir.

"Here you will create a firestorm that will attach to the portal. You do so by making spinning flames, but you create them in a vertically standing ellipse in front of the portal.

"Once the fire has attached to you and the portal, you will each have to create a burst of flames to break the portal free from the wall. Then you will be able to walk and carry the portal with you as if burdened by a flaming knapsack. At the same time, you will see Sapphira approaching with hers. Once you are close enough to each other, lock arms and walk together to the birthing garden."

Jade pointed toward the portal leading to the tree of life. "You will go in that direction and pass through the tree. It will provide you with a burst of energy. Then proceed into Second Eden until you are walking in the garden. Since you will be inside the sanctum, it will seem as if the entire room, including the sanctum's heart, is moving with you, so carrying this place through its own door will appear confusing to your eyes. When you arrive in the garden, face each other and embrace. Then the portals will join so that a person passing through the portal from Earth will step directly into the garden, but only after the portal is opened."

"Okay. I think I understand. How do we open it?"

"Portals that are created in this sanctum can be opened only with life energy. Darcy gave her life to open one that led from here to Abaddon's Lair. She inserted her finger into the sanctum hole associated with that portal. I gave my life to open the portals that formed the puzzle pieces for the life reservoir, but since they are really three doors to various perspectives of the same place, and since the portal to the tree-of-life chamber already existed and was merely reestablished, the openings required only one life.

"In this new case, we will be creating one portal, redirecting another, and joining them as one. Although you might think that we will be using two existing portals, the conjunction will actually re-create both of them anew, so it will take two lives to complete the opening of the conjunction."

Lauren exhaled. "Two more deaths!"

"Two more loving sacrifices." Jade touched the sanctum's heart. "One finger in the hole leading to the reservoir portal, and one finger in the hole leading to Sapphira's portal. Those who sacrifice will donate their life energy to join the two portals."

Lauren imagined two human figures inserting their fingers and shriveling up as their energy drained. She whispered, "So tragic."

"Tragic?" Jade smiled. "Yes, but such sacrifice is also heroic. A martyr's path is not to be followed for the sake of honor, but honor results nonetheless."

"Well, I'm not trying to be a hero." Lauren hid a tight swallow and forced her voice to stay calm. "But I'll volunteer when the time comes."

"I am not surprised." Jade raised a pair of fingers. "But you need two. I wish you good fortune in finding your sacrificial companion."

"Are you sure there's no other way? Can't an Oracle of Fire open any portal without someone dying?"

"Under normal circumstances, yes. When Darcy gave her life, an Oracle could have opened the portal her life energy pierced, but even an Oracle cannot open a conjunction unless it is first opened with life energy."

"Okay. So back to what you said earlier." Lauren pointed at the portal leading to the reservoir realm. "I still have to break free from that chamber. I can't do this conjunction unless I get out. And I can't get out, because I can't create fire in there."

"True. While in that realm, you lack an Oracle's skills. You have only your dreaming gift."

"But why? Is that part of the puzzle?"

"It is, indeed. In every realm you possessed exactly what you needed to complete the step. And now you have one more step to take."

Lauren nodded. "Creating the conjunction. Then I will be able to use fire in that realm."

"I will neither confirm nor deny your conclusion, but I will tell you that escaping from the third realm is a mere formality. Rest assured that your courageous brother will come and set you free. He has a heart like few others. Perhaps he will join you as the second sacrifice."

"No!" Lauren cringed and looked at the floor. "Sorry. I didn't mean to shout."

"I understand. Your brother is close to your heart." Jade touched Lauren's shoulder. "Perhaps Sir Barlow is the best candidate. He indicated his willingness earlier, but Darcy took his place."

"Yes, I heard about that." Lauren refocused on Jade. "Then are we done? Is there anything else I need to know?"

"I have one concern. This kind of conjunction has never been attempted before." Jade returned to the pulsing column and again set a hand on it. "Since the hub of the conjunction will be the sanctum itself, and since it is housed at the theoretical bottom of the abyss, I am unsure how that will manifest in the two worlds. The entire system's stability might be shaken. The result could be dangerous."

"I'll keep that in mind." Lauren looked at the reservoir portal. "I suppose I should go back and try to find Sapphira in the dream realm. She might be asleep by now."

"You may find her quite easily." Jade inserted a finger into one of the holes. "Simply search for her in the way I described earlier.

Locate the hole, ignite it, and go through the portal. Since this is not reality, no one needs to die to open it."

"But will I be able to find Sapphira? Does she have to be a dream oracle for me to visit her dream?"

"Since she is an Oracle of Fire herself, I think you will have no trouble visiting her dream, though you would likely have much more trouble entering the dreams of those who are not gifted."

Lauren gave Jade a thankful nod. "I appreciate all your help. I hope you'll be here when I need you again."

"That is not possible. This is my final opportunity to give you assistance." Jade took Lauren's hands in hers and set two other hands on Lauren's cheeks. "I must go now. You will see me again, but not in this world or on Earth or Second Eden." Jade kissed her on each cheek. "Farewell, brave daughter of God. I will be watching your progress from Heaven's gates."

Jade's body faded until she disappeared, her bright smile the last to vanish.

Lauren's cheeks tingled, as if anointed by sparks. "Good-bye. And thank you." She withdrew the jade stone from her pocket, set it close to the sanctum, and let the aura spread over the holes. "Well, Sapphira, let's see what you're dreaming about."

Standish pulled the final stitch and tied it off. Sapphira winced. When he cut the thread, the pain, more like stinging pressure than the stab of a knife, eased.

"There. That ought to do it." Standish began putting away the medical supplies in a nearby box. "I can't say that it's the best mending job I have ever done, but I think the stitches will hold."

She let out a breath and relaxed her muscles. "Thank you."

"You're quite welcome. I'm just glad that you asked me to more thoroughly examine your ankle first. That injury is far worse.

The splint will help, but you'll eventually need a cast, and even with that, I doubt that you'll be able to put weight on it for weeks."

When she tried to sit up, he set a hand on her shoulder and pushed her back. "Not yet, dear. You need to replenish your blood supply or you might faint. You donated quite a bit to the forty-yard line. Also, I noticed a sizeable lump on your head. You must have fallen somewhere along the way. You might be suffering a mild concussion."

Sapphira felt for the lump. When she opened the portal to go to Second Eden, she had slipped on the ice and fallen hard. At that moment it didn't seem to hurt much, but now it throbbed.

"Are you certain you don't want stronger pain medication?" Standish asked. "The Ibuprofen will not do much to cut the pain you must be feeling."

"No, thank you. I want to stay as lucid as possible."

"Sapphira!"

She lifted her head. Elam ran onto the field at a full gallop. When he arrived, he dropped to his knees and caressed her cheek. "Are you all right?"

"I think so." She looked toward the parking lot, her view blocked by the bleachers. "What's going on out there?"

"We rescued almost all the kids. Gabriel is far down the road taking care of them. They have food and water, so they should be fine."

"Good news, but Arramos will be back soon. He's holding Catherine Foley hostage." She glanced from side to side. Everyone else had left the field except Standish and Edmund who now looked to the east with their rifles in hand. "Where's Walter?"

"At the parking lot. He and Billy and I are planning a way to save Catherine." Elam slid his hands under her. "I'm going to carry you out of here."

"But if I'm gone, Arramos will kill Catherine."

"We've already taken care of that issue." As he straightened, he lifted her into his arms.

The sudden shift tightened the stitches and sent peals of pain roaring through her body. She suppressed a grunt and looked at his tired eyes. "What are you planning to do?"

"I have never kept a secret from you, so I will tell you, though I know you will object." He began walking toward the sideline. "We have a decoy, a brilliant young woman named Jennifer who has volunteered to take your place. She will stand at the portal and create fire by chemical means in a pretense to open the portal. She will then demand Catherine's release or else she will close it."

"Jennifer? Was she the girl who took a picture of me while I was lying on the field?"

Elam nodded. "She was with her mother, Elizabeth."

"I caught a glimpse of them." Sapphira imagined the plan. In her mental scenario, it progressed without a hitch until the time came to escape. "What happens when the exchange is made? How will Catherine and Jennifer get away from Arramos?"

"We are leaving three armed men who will escort them out." Elam pushed the bleachers gate open with his foot and passed through. "Our dragons are slowly coming around, and if their rate of recovery continues, they'll fly away with our remaining allies to the portal at the bottom of the chasm."

"*If* their recovery continues?" She squirmed. "Let me down."

"But your leg."

"I'll manage." She slithered from his grasp until she stood on one foot and leaned against him. Now under a roof at the rear of the bleachers, they were hidden from any potential spies from above. "Elam, this plan is as fragile as foam. When Arramos finds that the portal isn't open, he'll realize he's been had and give chase. He'll kill everyone we leave behind."

"We thought about that. Arramos might not have many allies left. Supposedly there's some sort of apocalypse going on in most of the world, so soldiers, equipment, and war machines are limited. He's already hit us pretty hard, maybe with everything he had, and we survived." Elam firmed his jaw. "But even if he brings a bigger arsenal, Jennifer and the others volunteered. They're willing to take the risk."

"Then I volunteer to stay behind. If the plan falls apart, I'll step in and face Arramos."

"But getting you out of here is the reason for the plan. The point is that Arramos won't force Jennifer to open the portal because she can't do it. But you can. We can't risk that. Maybe he'll return with more children, and he'll threaten them as a way to make you open it. You know how hard it would be to refuse him."

"Compromise, then. If he brings children, demand their release as well and fly them out of here. I'll stay hidden and watch. I'm not about to let a girl risk—"

"Is there a problem?" A white-haired girl strolled toward them from the direction of the parking lot.

Sapphira looked her over. She wore the traditional Second Eden battle uniform, identical to her own down to the rips and stains. Sapphira forced a friendly smile. "I assume you're Jennifer."

"I am." Jennifer extended a hand. "I am honored to meet you. I've read a hundred stories about your courage, sacrifice, and faith. You inspired me in my own faith every time."

"Thank you. It's a pleasure to meet you." Sapphira shook her hand. It felt like reuniting with Acacia. Yet this girl seemed so green, so inexperienced. She didn't wear the face of a girl who suffered under Morgan's cruel whip for untold years. She couldn't know how to deal with pure evil. "I heard about your plan, and I'm impressed with your courage as well."

"It's not really a big deal." Jennifer displayed a palm-sized pouch—clear and filled with liquid. "My flammable fuel. My mother is coming in a minute with a wire arc we built. It's practically invisible. When I set it on fire at the portal, it will look like—"

"Wait!" Sapphira's headache stampeded across her cranium. Thundering hoofbeats hammered at her skull, and her leg and side throbbed as well. "Just stop for a minute." She lowered herself to the ground and leaned her head against Elam's leg.

After taking a deep breath, she gazed up at Jennifer, again attempting an amiable smile. "I'm sorry, but you act like Arramos is a simpleton. I've dealt with Morgan, Mardon, Semiramis, and too many other evil beasts to count. They wouldn't be fooled by this charade, and Arramos is smarter than all of them. And besides, you don't even sound like me."

Jennifer lifted a handheld device and pressed a button. Sapphira's voice emanated. "You don't even sound like me."

Sapphira narrowed her eyes. "What good will that do?"

"I have your voiceprint. My mother will be hiding in the bleachers. When it's time for me to talk to Arramos, she'll type an appropriate response on her computer, which she will send to … " Jennifer turned her collar inside out, revealing a tiny device clipped to the material. "This speaker. We tested it. It's loud, and the sound quality is perfect."

"How will your mother know what to say? Arramos will try to trip you up."

"She's a quick thinker. She'll be fine."

Sapphira shook her head. "No, no, no. You don't understand. Arramos is the devil himself. He invented deception. You might fool him for a while, but he'll ask questions your mother can't possibly answer. Then he'll see through the disguise and kill everyone."

Elam grasped Sapphira's hand. "Do you have a better idea?"

She looked up at him. "Let me hide with Elizabeth. Maybe in the bleachers. I'll tell her how to answer. Obviously I can't open the portal from there, and I'm too crippled to get to it even if I wanted to, so Arramos can't coerce me to open it."

"Do you really think that will work?"

"No. But it's better than the other plan, and I don't think you'll let me stand out there on my own to face Arramos."

Elam shook his head. "You'd keel over in less than a minute, and then it would be too late to replace you. Catherine would be a goner."

"She might be a goner no matter what we do." Sapphira wrapped her arms around Elam's leg and closed her eyes. "I don't think either plan will work, but we don't have much of a choice. Jennifer's our best chance. She has the courage and smarts to keep a level head."

Jennifer's cheeks flushed pink. "Thank you. That means a lot to me."

"It really is a pleasure to meet you." Sapphira lifted a hand.

"The pleasure's all mine." Taking her hand, Jennifer stooped, kissed her cheek, and whispered, "I heard that you danced with Elohim. May his presence guide my every step in this dance with danger."

Sapphira firmed her grasp on Jennifer's hand. "Just let him lead and feel his love."

When Jennifer rose, Elam picked Sapphira up again and carried her to the concession stand embedded in the back wall of the bleachers. After entering a side door to a food storage room, he set her in an old upholstered chair in a corner. "How do you feel now?"

She leaned her head back. "Woozy."

"Adam brought these for you." Elam picked up three water

bottles from a nearby counter, set one at each side of Sapphira, and pushed one into her hand. "Drink as much as you can. You lost a lot of blood."

She twisted off the cap and began drinking.

"I'll come and get you when everything's set up." He stroked her hair. "That water should help you feel better soon."

After draining the bottle, Sapphira looked at an electric analog clock on the wall. It had stopped at 1:45. "How much time do we have before Arramos returns?"

"About twenty minutes." He took the empty bottle. "Drink the other two soon."

As he walked away, she called out, "Elam?"

He pivoted, his brow raised into his scraggly hair. "Yes?"

She reached out a hand and wiggled her fingers, their sign of love.

He did the same.

She smiled in spite of the horrible pain. "Will you stay with me while I do my part of this plan?"

"Definitely." He winked. "I have to make sure you don't hop on one foot out to the portal."

When he exited the room, she lifted a second water bottle and looked at it. Weariness set in, a dizzy sensation that promised relief if only she would allow sleep to hold sway for just a few minutes. She settled back in the chair and closed her eyes. It would be best to relent during this respite. Who could tell when the next opportunity would come?

As she let her mind drift, the feeling of sleep approached, but a pulse of pain in her head chased it away. Each time she tried to doze, new peals of pain erupted, first in her leg, then her side, then her head again, as if demons with mallets took turns pounding on various body parts.

Finally, exhaustion held sway. Sleep arrived. Aware of an oncoming dream, she let it swallow her mind. She walked on the football field, empty of people. Except for a few splotches of red marring the green grass and faded white lines, no one would be able to tell that this had been a field of murder and heartbreak.

Light flashed at the portal site. A young woman walked from its midst, dressed in a dazzling white cloak. Equally white hair adorned her lovely head, and her blue eyes sparkled like sapphires. Still, her striking new features couldn't mask her identity.

Sapphira gave her a curious look. "Lauren? You look ... different. Lovely as ever, though."

"Thank you." Lauren stopped within reach. "You and I are both sleeping, and our dreams have blended together."

"I knew I was dreaming, but how can we both be having the same dream at the same time?"

Lauren touched herself on the chest. "I am a dream oracle, and I am able to enter the dreams of certain other people while we are both dreaming. I have come to tell you what you can do to energize Clefspeare's plant and bring him back to battle Arramos."

"Assuming I believe your blended-dream theory ..." Sapphira nodded. "Go on."

Lauren ran her hands horizontally as if spreading something out. "Clefspeare's plant is now rooted in the soils of the birthing garden, but it is growing much too slowly. If he had grown quickly, he could have flown to the existing portal, but I have seen that your situation here is getting far too dangerous. If it reaches a critical stage, and you need Clefspeare right away, you will have to take this step."

"It might already be critical, and I can't take a step at all. A bullet fractured my lower leg, and I can barely stand."

Lauren covered her mouth. "That's terrible!"

"It's crippling, but my injury provided an advantage. The helicopter pilots who shot me died. Anyone who sheds the blood of an Oracle of Fire dies soon afterward."

"Can you get someone to help you walk? Elam, maybe?"

"Elam will help if he can. Also, a girl named Jennifer has disguised herself as me. She plans to take my place at the portal while Elizabeth, her mother, relays my voice responses through a speaker. I don't like the idea, so I won't mind changing that plan and moving the portal instead."

"Good. We'll see how it goes and maybe make adjustments along the way."

Sapphira narrowed her eyes. "Lauren, I would love to believe that you're alive and that you've come to give me a strategy, but how can I know that this dream is anything more than my wishful thinking?"

"When you wake up, come to the portal and look through it. If you see me in a chamber that has a column of pulsing white light, then you'll know." Lauren withdrew a gemstone from her pocket. Its glow coated her skin in an unearthly green aura. "And I'll have this jade on a chain around my neck."

"That will serve as proof." Sapphira nodded. "Go on. Tell me everything I need to know."

22

CHAPTER

The Battle Begins

Tamiel flew toward a pair of lights flickering on the ground, campfires perhaps. He smirked. How kind of Bonnie to provide a beacon for his arrival. Yet, their reunion would have to wait a few moments. One more detail had to be taken care of.

After visually marking a spot about a hundred paces in front of the garden, he descended and looked around for any movement. As he neared the ground, an ice-covered hut came into view, barely visible in the light of a distant fire. He landed and hid behind it, the sword he had stolen from Lauren at the ready.

"Psst!"

Tamiel looked toward the source of the sound. A man waved from behind a nearby hut. "Tamiel," he hissed. "Over here!"

Tamiel bent low and skulked to the hut. When he arrived, the man's face clarified—disfigured and burn-scarred behind a pair of owl-eye glasses. "Mardon, I am gratified that you kept your promise."

"Of course I did." Mardon clutched a handkerchief tightly. "What gave you the inkling that I might not?"

"I have heard rumors that you possess information that will allow Clefspeare's growth to flourish."

"I have kept that information a secret. The garden needs flames from an Oracle of Fire to grow a dragon, just as Makaidos did when he sprang from the soil. I have listened to their conversations, and they know they need warmth, but they haven't put everything together."

"My understanding is that Makaidos's bones and some kind of verbal call were also necessary as well as a rubellite gemstone."

Mardon gave his head a brief shake. "Not in this case. They were needed because Makaidos was dead. Clefspeare is not. This is a restoration, not a resurrection, though perhaps the bones might speed the process along. Also, Jared's photoreceptors were revived by the parasite I created, so there is no need for a rubellite. In any case, only the Oracle's flames are essential. Acacia is dead, and Sapphira is still on Earth as far as I know. Zohar is here, but he is a naïve boy who can be stopped with relative ease."

"What of the life reservoir? Rumors say that the energy can stimulate Clefspeare's growth, which is why we dispatched agents to try to neutralize the pool before it fills."

"I have no knowledge about the life reservoir. You are on your own in that regard."

"And, of course …" Tamiel touched Mardon's chin with a pointed fingernail. "Someone who hates my master as much as you do would never lie to me."

Mardon stiffened. "I … I have always been completely honest with you. I do hate Arramos, but … but I am keeping my end of the deal."

Tamiel pulled his finger back. "And Arramos will keep his."

Mardon dabbed at his sweaty brow with his handkerchief. "If you would be so kind, tell me your understanding of what his end entails."

"Very well." Tamiel rolled his eyes. "You get Second Eden and Sapphira while Arramos gets Earth, but he will kill anyone who stands in his way, even those with whom you seem to have established friendships."

Mardon folded his handkerchief and slid it into a pocket. "Kill whomever you wish, but make sure that you include Elam. I must have him out of the way."

Tamiel frowned. "Your twisted obsession with Sapphira disturbs even me."

Mardon pulled at the hem of his shirt, though it needed no straightening. "Well … be that as it may, killing Elam was part of the deal."

"Fear not. Elam will die. Arramos has long wanted to assassinate the king of Second Eden."

Mardon raised a finger. "And Arramos stays out of Second Eden. That's the part I'm worried about. I don't trust him at all."

"You need not worry. Since he will own Earth, this frozen wasteland will mean nothing to him."

"Then why is he so adamant about sending his troops here?"

"If my agents in the reservoir realm fail, I must deploy a backup plan, and going through Second Eden is the only way to get to that realm. The portal at the garden provides the last steps on that path, and I cannot get past the final safeguards without military muscle." Tamiel looked toward the garden. "Now back to your role. Do you have the potion?"

"Of course." Mardon withdrew a half-empty vial from an inner pocket. "It will initially cause the plant to grow, but less than a minute later, the plant will convulse and die. While they are watching with joyous wonder at the growth, I will have plenty of time to escape before they realize what is happening. Then when they are despairing over Clefspeare's death, you will be free to fly in and kill them."

Tamiel altered his voice to a skeptical tone. "Suppose, just for the sake of speculation, that the potion fails to work, and a ferocious dragon develops. You will be a hero in their eyes, Clefspeare will battle my master, and, assuming the omega dragon wins, you will get the revenge you have longed for."

Mardon's brow knitted. "You think I will double-cross you."

"I am not willing to take a chance. Clefspeare is too powerful."

Mardon's voice grew anxious. "Watch from here. You will see. If the plant continues growing, you have a sword." He swung an arm as if striking with the sword. "You can cut off its head before it gets too big. Although the plant cannot be torn easily, it will succumb to a blade."

"Oh, yes, the ever-vigilant Bonnie Bannister who now bears Excalibur will allow me to fly in and destroy their final hope, and a quickly developing dragon will refrain from shooting balls of flame at me as I approach." Tamiel chuckled. "I would have better odds surviving Lauren's embrace."

"Then do you have another suggestion?"

"I am glad you asked." Tamiel thrust the sword into Mardon's stomach and twisted the blade.

Mardon's eyes grew big, terrified. He opened his mouth as if to scream, but only a gasp blew out.

Tamiel set his lips next to Mardon's ear and whispered, "I will apply the potion myself. If the dragon continues growing, then I will be close enough to kill them all before they know what hit them."

His eyes filling with tears, Mardon gurgled, "Sapphira ... my love."

"Enjoy your swim in the lake of fire." Tamiel ripped the blade upward through Mardon's heart. "And say hello to your mother for me."

"Sapphira. Everything's ready."

Sapphira opened her eyes. Elam stood next to her, his arms extended. "Jennifer's in place. Billy senses danger, so Arramos is probably on his way. We also have a storm brewing to the east. It looks … well … apocalyptic."

"Apocalyptic? What do you mean?"

"Better if you see it for yourself."

"Just a second." Sapphira picked up one of the remaining bottles, uncapped it, and drank quickly. After she swallowed the final drops and set the empty bottle to the side, she wiped her mouth with a sleeve and nodded. "I'm ready." Her splinted leg aching from foot to knee, she set her other foot on the ground. The chair she had been sleeping in was lower than most. Climbing up might be a challenge.

As she shifted her weight, Elam pulled her to a standing position and lifted her into his arms in a cradle. "How's the pain?"

She looped her arms around his neck. "Pretty awful." She gazed into his still-weary eyes and smiled. "But you're here now, so I'm feeling better already."

He carried her to the passage leading to the field. "Am I a pain-relieving drug?"

"No. It's just that your handsome face is so overwhelming." She put on the voice of a schoolgirl with a juvenile crush. "The pain just runs away and hides."

"The same effect you have on me. My brain goes haywire." He halted and glanced around. "Where were we going?"

"Oh, stop it!" She pulled toward him, kissed his cheek, and whispered into his ear. "To the football field. Just don't look at me, and you'll remember where you're going."

"Right. Got it." He restarted, though at a slower pace. He seemed exhausted, spent, without the usual vigor he had displayed for thousands of years.

When they came within view of the field, boiling clouds drew Sapphira's gaze upward. Farther east, streaks of fire rained on the city skyline. Flaming hailstones assaulted the buildings. Fire blazed on the roofs of some structures, and huge sections had been carved out of others, as if they had been struck by meteors. From the north, a funnel cloud swept toward the city, the central target of the weather's wrath. As Elam had said, it definitely looked apocalyptic.

"Storms around here usually move eastward," Elam said as he slowed even further. "And we're west of the city. We should be all right."

"I don't think there's anything *usual* about this storm, but we can hope."

At the football field, Jennifer stood at the portal plane. From this distance, she looked like a great decoy. Her white hair flowed in the breeze, and her uniform was torn and bloodied in all the right places. Billy and Walter stood nearby, their backs to her, each holding one of the military rifles.

Elizabeth sat on the front-row bleacher seat near the gate leading to the field, a mobile phone resting on her palm. When Elam reached that point, he set Sapphira next to her.

"Greetings. I am Elizabeth Hamilton." She extended a hand. "I am honored to meet the great Sapphira Adi. My daughter has looked up to you and your heroic exploits for years."

Sapphira shook her hand. "The honor is mine. Your daughter's courage will be a model for other girls to emulate for all time."

"Thank you for saying so." Elizabeth handed Sapphira a dark cloak. "You had best cover yourself to conceal your identity. Larry has detected chatter that indicates a five-minute window until aircraft will arrive, but we do not yet know how many will be in the fleet."

Elam sat on Sapphira's other side. "Elizabeth salvaged Larry's core," he said. "His container is shot, but his brain and communications are functioning."

Elizabeth lifted her phone. "And he is communicating with me through texts. He is quite an impressive computer. Unfortunately, I was unable to recover Lois's functions. Her brain is still alive, but I had no time to create an interface to access it."

"You've done a fantastic job." Sapphira covered herself with the cloak from head to toe, leaving a hole for her face. "Arramos will still be able to see us from the field, won't he?"

Elizabeth pointed at a waist-high concrete barrier in front of them. "When the time comes, we'll crouch behind that. I think he will be preoccupied with the scene on the field."

"Okay. Just tell me what to do."

"Jennifer said that you hoped to provide me with responses to Arramos." Elizabeth spoke with a confident voice, her tone authoritative. "We assume that he will arrive with helicopters. They are versatile and deadly. Whether or not he will have more transport planes and children is harder to determine, but we need to be ready for that possibility. I agree with the analysis of others that his forces will be minimized by the ulcerating disease and the chaos that is spreading across the land, but we need to assume they will be formidable and be ready for anything."

"How can we be ready?"

"Adam has an empty airplane for collection and transport. We have no strategy to get the children there, because, as I indicated, we don't know how much manpower Arramos will bring. If they are overpowering, at that point … well …" As Elizabeth looked directly at Sapphira, her voice pitched higher. "We'll just have to hope for someone to be a hero."

Sapphira set a hand on Elizabeth's. "Like your father. I heard that he wrestled a dragon to save many lives."

"He did." Elizabeth sniffed and brushed a tear away. "We might need many heroes today."

Sapphira peered at Jennifer. She stood too far away from the portal. "If Jennifer wants to create a fake portal at the right place, she needs to shift about ten feet to her right."

"Good information. She'll need to move the wire frame for the fire as well." Elizabeth typed into her phone. "I have a shorthand method of communicating with her. The message will transmit to an earpiece she's wearing. When we provide your responses to Arramos, they will enter her ear before they exit through her speaker. That will give her the opportunity to lip-synch the words."

"Perfect." As Jennifer carried the wire frame to the correct position, Sapphira drew a mental picture of a fire at the portal site. Even in the right place, could she align the flames properly? It would be best to show Jennifer exactly where to stand and create a brief fire herself, then she could peek through the portal to see what, if anything, might be going on in Second Eden.

That thought triggered a vague memory. For some reason she *had* to look through that portal. What was the source of the memory? A dream?

More memories flooded in—Lauren's visit during the dream, how the portal was supposed to be moved if the situation became too dangerous, and the signs that would prove that the instructions were real and not merely part of a dream—a pulsing white column and a jade on a chain around Lauren's neck.

"Elam," Sapphira whispered. "I need you to take me to the portal."

"Why?"

"I have to look through it. No time to explain. It'll take just a minute."

"Okay. Let's go." Elam helped Sapphira rise to a one-footed standing position.

Elizabeth looked up at them. "What are you doing?"

"Sapphira needs to go to the portal."

Elizabeth showed Elam her phone's digital clock. "We have less than a minute."

"Choppers!" Billy shouted from the field. "I see two."

Walter pointed with his rifle. "Four! No! Five!"

"The red blotch in the middle must be Arramos!" Billy waved toward the bleachers. "Get low! Stay out of sight!"

Elizabeth slid down to the gap between the bench and the front barrier. "You two had better get low."

"Just a minute." Elam held Sapphira up by the elbow. "If it's important, I'll still take you."

"I'll monitor the situation. Just be ready to take me at a moment's notice."

Elam helped Sapphira sit next to Elizabeth. "The last thing I want to do," Elam said as he sat with them, "is take you to the portal while Arramos is here. Tell me what's going on. Maybe I can come up with an alternative."

"There might not be an alternative." Sapphira spread the cloak over Elam and herself and whispered into his ear. "How are our dragons?"

"Still groggy." His warm breath caressed her cheeks. "They're resting in the parking lot. We decided if we tried to move them, they might be spotted by surveillance aircraft. It's best if everyone thinks they're dead, though Thigocia said she would try to do some healing in a stealthy way. Adam's staying close to them and keeping an eye on the field. If things get really rough, he'll tell them and they'll do what they can. We also have our three knights hiding under a canopy. They'll rush out with their guns if need be."

"Where are Ruth, Shiloh, and Shiloh's son?"

"We sent them to Gabriel. It's best to keep them out of the battle."

Sapphira looked at the approaching helicopters. Aligned in a row, they stayed well apart as their tails wagged in the gusty, changeable wind. "If the dragons can't fight, then this plan can't possibly work. Arramos has too much firepower."

"We already talked this out." He raised fingers in succession. "One, we have to try to save Catherine. Two, we can't just take off and leave the dragons behind. And three, we're willing to die to protect Second Eden. That's why you're here and not out there. They can't open the portal without you."

"I remember all that, and I know we're willing to die, but what if Arramos brings more children, like you mentioned before? I'm not willing to let them die."

"No one wants that to happen." Elam lowered the cloak enough for them both to see the sky. The five helicopters now hovered high over the field as if waiting for an order to land. "Look, I admit the plan is shaky, but it can work."

"*Can work* might not be good enough." Sapphira focused on the helicopters, nearly stationary in spite of the wind. If Excalibur were still available, they would be easy targets for the beam, which meant that they had no fear of it … or they weren't told about it. "Do you think the new arrivals are protected?"

"Impossible to tell without a test." Elam's eyes followed the choppers' slow drift. "They're staying pretty far away. Arramos knows an Oracle of Fire could scorch unprotected pilots if they get too close."

"So if they stay far from Jennifer, it's a good bet they're vulnerable. We'll just have to watch and see."

"Are you planning to cook some chopper pilots?"

Sapphira nodded. "When they land, we'll see if I'm close enough. If not, maybe you can move me into position."

Arramos descended in a glide, Catherine in one of his foreclaws. He landed at the midpoint of the thirty-yard line, about twenty yards from Jennifer, and set Catherine upright, though he kept his claws wrapped around an arm. She stood with a wobbly stance. Blood smeared the side of her pale face.

The five helicopters buzzed over the end zone area, maybe a hundred feet high. Four looked like the others that attacked earlier—missiles loaded underneath. The fifth was much larger with a big door on the side.

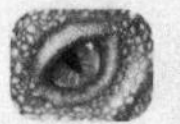

"They're keeping well out of the way," Elam said. "Can you ignite a pilot from here?"

"Not unless I get a really clear shot." Sapphira squinted at the largest helicopter. Might that one be transporting children? If so, she couldn't risk harming the pilot while it was in the air.

"Here is your friend," Arramos shouted, barely audible over the din from the choppers. "Open the portal, and I will release her."

Sapphira whispered to Elizabeth. "Release Catherine first."

Elizabeth typed the message. Within two seconds, Sapphira's voice boomed from Jennifer. "Release Catherine first."

"Do you think you are dealing with a simpleton?" Arramos snorted. "Why should I give up my hostage?"

Billy raised a hand. "Take me as a replacement."

"A replacement?" Arramos extended his neck and looked at Billy long and hard. "An intriguing proposal. You *are* a more valuable asset."

"Then let her go." Billy set his rifle down and marched straight toward Arramos.

Arramos unfurled a wing and touched the ground in front of him. "Lie on your stomach here."

Billy complied. As soon as he settled, Arramos stomped on his back with a rear claw. "Take her." He shoved Catherine. She stumbled forward and sprawled across the turf. Walter rushed to her, helped her rise, and supported her as she walked toward the sideline.

"That was my one gesture of goodwill," Arramos said to Jennifer. "Now open the portal, or I will crush Bannister's spine."

Sapphira whispered to Elizabeth, "First allow Catherine to get to safety."

Elizabeth again typed the message in shorthand. One second later, Sapphira's voice emanated from Jennifer. The conversation between Arramos and Jennifer continued in the same relayed fashion.

"You test my patience," Arramos said, "but I have all the leverage I need. She may go."

Walter opened the bleachers' gate and guided Catherine through. Her pale face and glassy eyes made her look like she might faint at any moment. When they passed by, Walter whispered, "I'll put her in the airplane and be right back."

"Now your friend is safely out of my reach." Arramos extended his neck toward Jennifer, then curled it back as if ready to shoot a blast of fire. "Open the portal immediately."

"Allow my guard to return," Jennifer said with Sapphira's voice.

"Why?" Arramos took a step closer and extended his neck. One eye blinked rapidly. "Has the great Sapphira Adi lost her celebrated courage?"

"Does the great Arramos need helicopters to battle a girl?"

Arramos chuckled. "I see that Morgan's evaluation of your incivility was accurate. It's no wonder she forced you to become a cook for the other underborns. She wanted you out of the way."

Sapphira whispered to Elizabeth, "That's a test. Say, 'Your memory is failing, Arramos. Paili was our cook.'"

Elizabeth typed it in. The response came from Jennifer an instant later.

"A minor error." Arramos huffed a stream of fire. "I detect that you are stalling." He turned his head in every direction, scanning the field and sky. "I noticed that Makaidos and the other dragons appear to be carrion in the parking lot. Are they feigning death? If they dare attack me, we will kill the children we are holding in one of the helicopters."

Sapphira grasped Elizabeth's wrist. "Prove that you have them."

Elizabeth typed the message. Jennifer shouted in Sapphira's voice, "Prove that you have them."

"I expected that challenge." Arramos waved a wing. "You will get your proof."

The transport helicopter drifted toward the center of the field, its tail swinging as it battled the gusts.

Sapphira locked her stare on the pilot. His uniform appeared to be a lighter color, perhaps not one of the protected suits.

Walter ran from the parking lot and stopped at the gate. "What's going on?"

Elam pointed at the chopper. "Arramos said he's going to prove that he's holding children hostage."

"I don't like the sound of that." Walter threw the gate open, sprinted onto the field, and shouted, "Call in Standish!"

Elizabeth set her phone to her ear. "Standish, launch an assault at your first opportunity."

About fifty feet above Jennifer, the rear compartment of the transport helicopter opened. A man in a beige uniform held a small boy's arms. Bound hand and foot, the boy squirmed and thrashed to no avail.

Sapphira whispered, "Oh, dear God. Help him."

The man pushed the boy out. Walter dove and slid on his back under the chopper. The boy landed on Walter's abdomen and bounced hard.

"Elizabeth!" Sapphira hissed. "Type in a shout of *Ignite* and tell Jennifer to point at the helicopter as she mouths it."

While Elizabeth typed in the command, Sapphira pointed at the man in the chopper and whispered, "Ignite!"

The call echoed from Jennifer as she raised a hand. The man's uniform burst into flames. While Arramos watched the burning man, Jennifer lit the fuel in the wire frame and set it ablaze.

As the man fell, Walter rolled out of the way, the boy in his grasp. The moment the man crashed to the ground in a burning heap, Jennifer shouted at Arramos in Sapphira's voice. "The portal is open! Now let us all leave in safety!" With flames seemingly emanating from her body, Jennifer stood with her arms spread, her face stern and rock solid.

Elizabeth whispered to Sapphira, "We prerecorded that one."

Arramos blinked at Jennifer. "You and your guard and the child he rescued are free to go. I will keep the other children and Bannister until my forces have passed safely through the portal."

Sapphira whispered, "That won't work!"

"Wait!" Walter climbed to his feet, the boy limp in his arms. "Release the children and let me take their place as a hostage."

"You are stalling again!" Arramos tromped toward the portal and smacked Walter's shoulder with his tail. Walter skidded across the turf on his back, the boy still locked in his arms.

Now free from the pinning claw, Billy struggled to his feet and staggered toward the portal. Arramos slapped Jennifer with a wing. She stumbled backwards through her arc of flames.

When she righted herself on the other side and began batting flames from her clothes, Arramos roared. "Deceiver! Now the children will die!"

Sapphira clutched Elam's wrist. "Take me to the portal! Now!"

Elizabeth rose to her feet. "I'll summon our dragons."

While Elam carried Sapphira through the gate toward the field, Arramos looked up at the hovering chopper and opened his mouth as if ready to shout a command. Billy ran up his tail, stomped across his back, and looped arms and legs around his neck. He jerked Arramos's head downward, keeping him from speaking.

Standish, Edmund, and Newman rushed from the side of the bleachers. They halted and aimed their rifles at Arramos, but with Billy riding him, they couldn't risk shooting. Edmund handed off his rifle and sprinted toward the struggle.

Arramos thrashed his neck and clawed at Billy, but he hung on with all four limbs and dug his thumbs into Arramos's eyes. The wing claws ripped his shirt and dug bloody lines across his back. At the moment it seemed that Billy might let go, Edmund ran up Arramos's tail and joined in the battle.

Walter hobbled past them, carrying the boy while Jennifer supported him at his side.

The attack helicopters swung into position to shoot at the fleeing group. The two knights turned their rifles toward the choppers and opened fire. Bullets clanked against the metallic skin. A window cracked. One chopper spun away out of control.

Elam and Sapphira met Walter and company at the sideline and stopped. Walter gasped for breath. "Where are you going?"

"The portal," Elam said. "Sapphira has an idea."

"We can't let her open it," Walter said, wheezing as he struggled for breath. "That's the point of the plan."

"I won't let them into Second Eden," Sapphira said. "Trust me."

"Okay, okay, but I'm coming with you." Walter passed the dark-haired little boy to Jennifer. "He's alive but unconscious. Get him out of here."

Jennifer hugged him close and ran off the field.

"Let's go!" Walter led the way toward the portal in a limping trot.

As Sapphira bounced in Elam's arms, she scanned the field. The helicopters regrouped in a line and fired at the knights with their machine guns. Both men fell in place, one motionless while the other writhed.

Sapphira gasped. "Elam! They're down."

"I saw. Should I help them or take you to the portal?"

"To the portal." Tears blurring her vision, she looked again. The helicopters, including the transport, began landing in the end zone.

Walter picked up a rifle and skulked toward the downed knights. "Keep going, Elam! I'll try to cover you!"

"Protect the children first. Sapphira still has her flames." Elam set her down at the portal site on one foot and kicked the smoldering wire frame out of the way. "Okay," he whispered as he steadied her. "Do whatever you have to do."

In a surge of rage, Arramos plunged his claws into Billy's shoulder, tore him away, and slung him toward the sideline. He rolled to a stop near the bleachers. Arramos snapped at Edmund and caught the knight's foot in his jaws. With a huff from his nostrils, Arramos set Edmund's clothes on fire and spat him toward Billy. Billy crawled to him and began batting away the flames.

Heaving deep breaths and snorting sparks and smoke, Arramos glared at Sapphira. "So you allowed a replacement to face me. I am surprised at your lack of courage."

"Silence, dragon!" Sapphira lifted her hands. Flames erupted in both palms. "I will open the portal. Align your forces and get them ready to face what they will encounter in Second Eden."

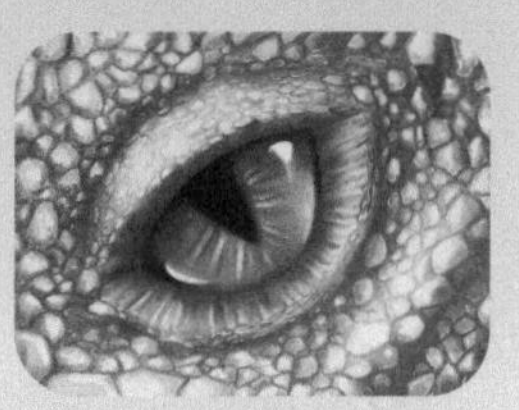

23

CHAPTER

Reunion

Bonnie scanned the garden area. Now that total darkness had fallen, every light seemed to magnify—the nearby fire that warmed Clefspeare's plant, Mendallah's fire at the other plant, and a glow from one of the huts in the village, probably where Zohar was taking care of the babies. If Clefspeare didn't grow in the next few minutes, they would have to summon the male Oracle of Fire.

A fourth light flickered several paces away—obscure, hard to distinguish. Perhaps five feet in height, it looked like a … a flaming tree? "Do you see that?" Bonnie asked, pointing. "Is that a tree?"

Marilyn squinted. "It certainly looks like it."

Rising to her feet, Bonnie whispered, "The tree of life? I knew the portal was around here somewhere, but I didn't know it was open."

Grackle let out a shrill call.

Bonnie looked his way. A man carrying a sword stood a few steps beyond the edge of the garden. Firelight danced over his

disfigured face and shimmered on his glasses. "Good evening, ladies."

"Mardon?" Bonnie asked.

"Yes. I apologize if I frightened you." He displayed a corked glass vial. "I came with the potion Clefspeare needs to grow."

Marilyn rose and stood between the plant and Mardon. "Why do you have a sword?"

"To protect me from beasts in this world."

Marilyn set a fist on her hip. "Where did you get it?"

"As you might be aware, it is a long journey on foot from the portal to here. I stumbled upon a village some distance away where the residents offered me food and this weapon." He raised the sword. "I have not needed it, but it did give me comfort as I traveled."

Marilyn pointed at the ground near his feet. "Leave it there."

"I understand. Of course." Mardon set the sword down. "I have not yet earned your complete trust."

"No kidding." Marilyn stalked to him and extended her hand. "Now give me the potion and leave."

"The potion is yours." He handed her the vial. "But will you kindly grant me the favor of watching the growth? As a scientist who constructed every detail of this mechanism, I greatly wish to witness this miracle."

"As if I care what you wish." Marilyn picked up his sword. "But I'll let you watch from where you are. Just be aware that Bonnie has Excalibur, and she could fry what's left of your face in the blink of an eye."

Bonnie tightened her grip on Excalibur's hilt and made the blade glow.

"Your warning is adequate." Mardon folded his hands at his waist. "I will not move from this spot."

When Marilyn returned to the garden, Bonnie whispered, "Trusting him is like trusting Satan himself."

"I know exactly what you mean."

"But how can we test the potion? Clefspeare isn't growing much without it, and we can't keep waiting. Time is running out on Earth."

"I know. I know." Marilyn gave Mardon a furtive glance. "Mardon knows we can kill him if the potion fails, and he doesn't seem scared at all. Why would he want to stick around if he knows it would do Jared harm?"

"To make sure it succeeds in destroying him?" Bonnie furrowed her brow and stared at Mardon eye to eye. He didn't so much as blink. "He's as cool as a cucumber."

"I know what you mean. He's usually a bundle of nerves."

"And that makes *me* nervous." Bonnie broke eye contact with him and returned her gaze to Marilyn. "Have we ever needed Ashley any more than we do now?"

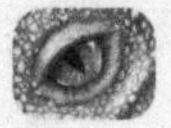

"Not that I can remember." Marilyn let out a heavy sigh. "I guess the decision is mine to make. Jared is my husband. It's his life we're risking."

"And the lives of millions on Earth."

Marilyn held up the vial and stared at the liquid. "We should test it on a different plant to see if it's toxic."

"Good thinking." Bonnie scanned the area. With nearly everything covered by ice, finding a plant in the darkness might be impossible. "I'll look for something. Keep your sword ready."

"Don't worry about me." Marilyn handed her the vial. "Mardon's a coward, and he knows I'd just as soon skewer him as look at him."

"I'll be back as soon as I can." Bonnie summoned Excalibur's glow and let it guide her to the edge of the garden. She peered through the portal window. Leaves from the tree of life lay strewn on the floor, still green and supple looking, at least from this distance.

She touched the blade's tip to the portal plane. No sparks. She pushed a foot through, stepped down into the tree's chamber, and hurried to kneel in front of the tree. After picking up one of the larger leaves, curled and somewhat dry, she pulled the cork from the vial and tipped out a drop on the leaf's surface. The green color deepened, and the curl straightened.

Bonnie exhaled. Good. Mardon was telling the truth.

A sizzle rose from the leaf. It began to shrivel and turn brown.

"Bonnie! Help!"

Dropping the leaf, she jumped up and recorked the vial. In the garden, Marilyn sat on the ground, now twenty feet from Clefspeare's plant. From the direction of the other plant, Mendallah ran closer. Mardon stalked toward Clefspeare, his sword raised.

Bonnie leaped through the portal and ran. Out of nowhere, someone wearing a white cloak hurtled into the garden and bowled Mardon over. The two wrestled and rolled away from the plant, but Mardon took control and set the sword's blade at the attacker's throat. The cloak's hood slid down and revealed his identity, his jaw locked as he swallowed behind Mardon's blade.

Bonnie stopped at the edge of the garden. "Matt!"

Mendallah's thundering footsteps halted within reach of Mardon. "Say the word, Bonnie, and I will throttle him."

"No! He'll kill Matt!" Bonnie raised Excalibur. Its beam shot into the sky. "Let him go, Mardon!"

A deep furrow dug into Mardon's forehead. "First pour the contents of the vial on the plant, throw Excalibur to the side, and call off your clueless giant. Then I will release your son."

Bonnie palmed the vial, hiding it from sight. "If I do what you say, you'll kill him and take off like the coward you are."

"And if you *don't* do what I say in the next ten seconds, I will slit his throat and fertilize your precious plant with his blood."

Marilyn crawled on hands and knees toward Clefspeare.

Mardon shouted, "Stop, woman! I am not bluffing!"

She froze in place and stared, her sparkling eyes fixed on the tiny, vulnerable plant.

"Stand your ground, Bonnie," a woman whispered from close by.

Bonnie turned toward the voice. Listener stood at her side, her brow knitted tightly. "Matt is a warrior and a healer," Listener continued. "You can be aggressive without fear."

"Good point." Bonnie lowered the beam close to Mardon's head. The end burned into the ground behind him, making the soil sizzle. "Let him go right now, or you'll be sparks blowing in the wind."

"Your time is up." When Mardon flexed to strike, Matt thrust his arm out and tried to duck under the blade. The edge swiped against his throat and across his cheek, but he broke free and rolled away.

In a scramble of arms, legs, and flying dirt and blood, Matt and Mardon scrambled toward the plant. Mardon punched Matt in the face and crawled past him. Marilyn ran to the plant and covered it with her curled body. Grackle shot a stream of ice in front of Mardon. Listener threw herself onto the frozen sheet, slid into Mardon's path, and blocked him.

Mendallah lunged, grabbed a handful of Mardon's shirt, and hoisted him into the air. As he flailed, his body transformed. It stretched taller and leaner and grew dark curly hair. She threw him to the ground and stomped on his neck, pinning him in place.

"Tamiel," Bonnie whispered as she shut off Excalibur's beam.

Matt rose, a hand pressed against his throat. "He was in disguise. We found the real Mardon's corpse next to one of the huts.

Karrick is still over there talking to Zohar." Blood leaked between Matt's fingers. "He should be here in a minute."

"Matt!" Listener climbed to her feet and stood next to him. "You're bleeding!" She peeled back a finger and peered at the wound. "I think he cut your jugular!"

He winced. "Then I'd better heal myself fast." As blood dripped from his fingers, he looked at Bonnie. "We have to go through the tree-of-life portal to Jade's sanctum. Lauren's trapped in there, and she said she needs Excalibur. If we don't help her, everyone might die."

Bonnie sucked in a breath. "Lauren's alive!"

"Yes … well … sort of. I can't explain now. We have to get her. And we can pick up leaves from the tree of life to help heal me."

"Of course. We'll—"

The beating of wings announced Karrick's arrival as he landed at the edge of the garden. "What happened here?"

"No time!" Bonnie waved in the mountain portal's direction. "Karrick, fly to the cave and get Ashley. We need a healer for Matt."

Listener blew a shrill whistle. "Grackle, you go with him. Since you have heated scales, you carry Thomas and Mariel. Stop at Peace Village to let Dr. Conner know what's going on. He might want to come, too."

Grackle bobbed his head, and with an explosion of wing beats the two dragons burst into the air.

Matt pointed toward the tree-of-life room. "The portals are this way." He shook the cloak down, trading hands against his throat as the sleeves slid off his arms. When he held the cloak up, blood stained the material around his fingers. "This will protect us when we go through. We'll have to take turns."

"Someone has to stay with Clefspeare," Bonnie said.

Marilyn rose from her protective curl and knelt close to the plant. "I'll stay."

"Then you'll need this." Matt set a handgun at Marilyn's side. "I assume you know how to use it."

"You bet." She picked it up and checked the magazine. "Should be enough."

"Just so you know," Matt said. "Even cutting Tamiel's head off didn't kill him. That's why I tackled him instead of shooting him. Don't take any chances."

Marilyn waved toward the portal. "Just go. Mendallah will keep him underfoot."

With a hand still pressed against his neck, Matt led the way to the tree-of-life portal and leaped inside. Bonnie and Listener followed a step behind. "Keep pressure on your wound," Bonnie called. "I'll get some leaves."

After Bonnie scooped up a handful, making sure to avoid the leaf she used to test the potion, she and Listener skirted the tree and joined Matt at the portal on the other side.

Now wobbling, Matt tried to pull the cloak over himself with one hand, but it slipped from his grasp and slid toward the floor.

"Here." Bonnie held out her handful of leaves. "Let's apply these."

Listener draped the cloak over her head and shoulders. "While you're doing that, I'll test the portal." When she jumped through, sparks flashed around the cloak's edges, and an electrostatic buzz filled the air. She balanced herself on the other side and tossed the cloak back, raising a new splash of sparks. "Whenever you're ready."

"Just a second." Bonnie pressed the leaves against the cut and set Matt's hand over them.

He grimaced, his face ghostly pale. "That stings like crazy."

"You'd better eat a couple."

"I'll try." He allowed her to push two leaves into his mouth.

While he chewed, she picked up the cloak. "We'll go together." The odor of blood mingled with sweat drifted into Bonnie's nostrils. "Just lean on me." She handed Excalibur to him, threw the cloak over them both, and guided him through.

When the usual buzzing noise ceased, Bonnie pulled the cloak away and handed it to Listener. Again Matt wobbled. Bonnie took Excalibur and set a hand on his arm. "Maybe you should sit."

"No … no." He staggered forward and pointed at a vertical column at the center of the room. "See where the white beam leads? I think Lauren's on the other side of that portal."

Bonnie studied the column. A laser-like beam emanated from one side and struck a reflective wall several paces beyond. The light spread out and created a ragged splotch from about knee to head high, its width the same as its height. "So do we just put on the cloak again and jump through?"

"I think so. If we … if we …" Matt dropped to his knees. "I feel sick."

"Nausea?" Bonnie looked at Listener. "Could the leaves have the opposite effect on a healer?"

"Like a clash of two powers?" She shook her head. "I have no idea. I suppose it's possible."

Bonnie peeled Matt's fingers from his wound, brushed the bloody leaves away, and set his hand back in place. "We might have to induce vomiting."

"I'll handle it." Listener grasped Bonnie's wrist. "You have to go. I'll stay with him and watch for Ashley. Toss the cloak back when you get through."

"You're right." Bonnie set a hand on the back of Matt's head and kissed his cheek. "Matt, I love you."

"I love you, too, Mom." He gazed at her with glassy eyes. "Before Darcy died … we … we became friends … and I have faith now." He licked his lips. "I thought you'd … like to know … in case I … don't make it."

"Oh, Matt, I'm so glad you—"

"No more time." He waved at the portal. "Go!"

After kissing Matt again, Bonnie draped the cloak over herself and pushed a covered hand through the portal wall. In a splash of sparks, her hand disappeared. She backed up a few steps, then ran ahead and leaped through.

She broke into a chamber of cold darkness. Her feet slid, but she kept upright and rode out the momentum as she skated along the slick floor. When she stopped, she turned and summoned light from Excalibur, but the blade wouldn't glow. Darkness shrouded everything.

Shivering, she pulled the cloak from her shoulders and tried to look at it, but nothing appeared. She had to throw it back to the others. If Ashley were to arrive at the tree room, she wouldn't be able to get to Matt unless she had the cloak. But how could she throw something to a place she couldn't see?

She shouted into the darkness, "Lauren! It's Mom! Are you here?"

A faint cry drifted from far away. "Mom?" A light flickered in the distance that grew as it approached. Seconds later, a young woman with white hair and shining blue eyes appeared, running on a sheet of ice. A glowing, bat-like creature flew at her side. She spread out her arms and squealed, "Mom!"

Bonnie squinted. "Lauren?"

"Yes!" She set her feet to stop but slid onward, out of control.

Bonnie set the cloak and Excalibur down, caught Lauren with one arm, and spun in place while Lauren orbited her twice in a decelerating slide. When she stopped, they pulled into a tight embrace.

"Lauren!" Bonnie held her close and wept. Her warm, solid body felt like Heaven itself. "Oh, thank God you're alive!"

"I resurrected, and somehow I became an Oracle of Fire like Sapphira." Lauren pushed away. Tears shimmered on her cheeks. "It's a long story, but …" She swiveled her head. "Where's Matt? I thought he'd be with you. I told him how to find me."

"He brought us here, but he's hurt." Bonnie picked up the cloak. "I have to get this through the portal. Ashley will need it when she arrives, but I couldn't see where to throw it."

Lauren took the cloak and put it on. "I'll take it through." She pulled a thin chain, lifted a green stone and medallion from behind her shirt, and let both dangle in the open. "Sapphira and I have some portal-moving work to do. No time to explain."

"Wait!" came a call from the darkness. Another light approached, this one red. Soon, a man appeared in the glow. He carried a red ovulum, but shadows veiled his features.

"That's Sir Barlow," Lauren said. "Merlin is also here, but he's staying at the reservoir to guard against the fire spiders."

"Fire spiders?"

"That's what we call them. They're—"

"Hideous little beasts," Sir Barlow said as he arrived. "We saw in the ovulum that Tamiel wounded Matt. Merlin says that Lauren should return to Jade's sanctum, cover Matt with the cloak, and coat him with fire. That should enhance his healing gift. Bonnie should stay here with Excalibur to help him search for and destroy the spiders. If they attack the life reservoir, all could be lost."

Bonnie picked up Excalibur. Being away from Matt would be torture, but what choice did she have? Merlin knew the situation. She could trust his judgment. "I'll do what I can."

"Don't worry, Mom," Lauren said. "I'll take care of Matt."

Sir Barlow handed Bonnie the ovulum. "This is a viewer. Merlin will explain how it works."

Bonnie held the ovulum in her palm. "You're going, too?"

"Yes. I made a pledge to Lauren that I must fulfill."

At the portal, light from the strange bat illuminated a dim rectangle, though nothing was visible through it. When Lauren raised the cloak high, Sir Barlow bent underneath it. Bonnie guided the cloak's edges over them. With the bottom part missing, it barely covered them, but it looked safe enough. "You're ready."

Without another word, Lauren and Sir Barlow jumped through the portal, raising the usual splash of sparks.

When they disappeared, Bonnie closed her eyes and imagined their next steps. Lauren had to cover Matt, provide fire, and wait to see if the process worked. It might take quite a while to hear news about Matt's recovery.

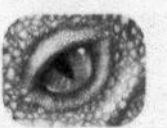

"Follow the glowbat, dear lady." Merlin's low voice sounded like a lion's purr.

The bat flew in the direction Sir Barlow had come. As Bonnie walked that way, a man came into view carrying a staff and wearing a scarlet cloak.

When she arrived, he laid a hand on her shoulder. "You might not remember our first encounter in the candlestone, but—"

"Oh, Merlin. I remember. You encouraged me to sing." She gazed into his deeply set gray eyes. He looked like a bearded Professor Hamilton. "That advice probably saved my life."

"Perhaps we will find time to sing again while we watch what develops." He took the ovulum and held it in a palm where she could see it. "We cannot view Lauren and Matt directly, for my ovulum is unable to penetrate Jade's sanctum, but we can see Sapphira and get a glimpse of Second Eden through her perspective."

"In the meantime ..." Bonnie lifted Excalibur. "I heard you need me to search for fire spiders."

"Yes, they have taken refuge in the shadows. Excalibur's light should be able to chase them from their hiding places."

Bonnie concentrated on the blade and tried to make it glow, but again it stayed dark. "I can't get it to work. The same thing happened when I first entered this place."

"Shhh." Merlin touched the flat of the blade and whispered, "Lauren also lost many of her abilities when she entered this realm. I was hoping you would be able to use Excalibur to open the life reservoir when needed, but that might no longer be an option."

She pushed the hilt into his hand and kept her own voice to a whisper. "Can you make it work?"

"I can try." He lifted the blade high and stared at it for a moment. Again, it stayed dark. "It seems not."

"Then what do we do?"

Merlin handed Excalibur back to Bonnie. "If the fire spiders attack, you, as the better sword warrior, can use the blade to fend them off, which I assume will be more efficient than the stomping method we have used. With regard to the life reservoir, I will explain its purpose, then perhaps you and I can brainstorm a solution to our dilemma."

Bonnie propped the blade against her shoulder. "I'll do my best."

"And speaking of being a warrior, you might also wish to pray about Lauren's torturous dilemma. She has a bitter decision to make that will shake her to the core. Sapphira has a similar dilemma that will torment her godly soul. Should she take the time to move a portal or instead stay and fight to save children's lives? In spite of their best efforts and intentions, Lauren and Sapphira will soon learn that they cannot save everyone."

Bonnie bent to get a better look at the ovulum. "So more people will die?"

"It is inevitable that someone will perish in Jade's sanctum." Merlin lifted the ovulum closer to their eyes. "Let us watch while I explain what Lauren is trying to accomplish."

Standing on one foot with Elam at her side for support, Sapphira waved her arms and stirred flames into the air. The usual fiery cyclone formed overhead and began a slow descent. As always, a sense of sadness washed over, and her eyesight sharpened. A scene beyond the portal clarified—a compass design on a wall. She swiveled her head and looked behind her. Burnt logs and smoking embers lay in a slipshod pyramid—the remains of the fire that had earlier broken the atmospheric static.

Yet, no one was around, not even Lauren. Had the dream really been only a dream?

Sapphira blinked to clear the vision of Second Eden and refocused on the Earth realm. Arramos stood several paces away, his eyes wary. Beyond him, the helicopters had all landed. Thugs dressed as military soldiers guided children down a short ladder from the transport chopper, forming a line that led toward Arramos. They appeared to range from four to eight years old, girls and boys, maybe twenty in all. Some cried as the thugs prodded them with rifles.

To the east, dark clouds drew closer, defying the usual west-to-east movement pattern. Lightning flashed green within the weather front. Thunder boomed. Streaks of fire continued falling over the city in sporadic intervals, like meteors plummeting from the heavens.

Near the bleachers, Billy struggled to his feet. His shirt was little more than shredded ribbons, and blood streamed from claw marks on his back. He helped Edmund rise and brushed the remaining sparks from his clothes.

Walter ran toward Sapphira and called to Billy. "The other knights are dead. Get Edmund out of here and see what you can find out from Adam. I'll cover Sapphira."

"On my way." Billy helped Edmund stagger to the bleachers and cross the passage toward the parking lot. Arramos and the thugs ignored them. They had all the hostages they needed.

Sapphira stalled the portal curtain's descent at head level and searched the sky around the bleachers. Walter's words meant more than he had let on. He wanted Billy to check on Makaidos and the other dragons. Maybe they had delayed their attack because of the presence of child hostages.

When the children gathered within reach of Arramos, he extended his neck toward Sapphira, his head only an arm's length away. "Is the portal open?"

"Almost." Sapphira swirled the cyclone with exaggerated arm movements. "The way this works, I can either surround one of your soldiers with the fire and take him through, thereby protecting him from the portal's boundary, or I can leave the portal open and walk away. The flames will persist for a short time, and the portal will remain open, but it is impossible to say for how long. The trouble is that anyone who passes through without my protective fire will be in danger. You see, the boundary carries a jolt that varies in severity. Some portals cause superficial burns while others cause death. This one feels more severe than most."

"Is a helicopter able to fly through it? Remember, if you lie to me, I will slaughter the children."

"An airplane once flew through a portal without harm, but that portal was exceptionally large. Allow me to check the size of this one." Sapphira blinked and opened her vision to the Second

Eden side. Still the same—a compass design and a dying fire. Lauren's visit must have been a dream after all.

Just as Sapphira made ready to refocus on Earth, the compass flickered. Like a sheet of paper igniting, everything burst into flames and burned away, replaced by a dark void.

Lauren appeared at the center, her body small. Wearing a chain with an attached green gem, she turned and walked away, as if floating in space at a great distance. She set her flaming hands on a flat surface and seemed to be drawing a box on it.

Sapphira dared not speak to her. Arramos would know something was amiss. She blinked away the vision and looked at Arramos. "I need to make the portal bigger. This will take some time."

"Do what you must, but I will kill one child for every minute I think you are delaying, so I suggest that you hurry."

Lauren whipped the cloak from herself and Sir Barlow. Matt lay on the floor two steps away.

Listener pressed a hand against his neck. "He's unconscious." Tear tracks stained her reddened cheeks. "He's fading fast."

"Maybe this will help." Lauren spread the cloak over Matt. "Sir Barlow, as soon as I start my fire, bring him close to me. I have to do both jobs at the same time."

"Right away." Sir Barlow slid his arms under Matt and lifted while Listener kept her hand in place. "Say the word, Miss."

Lauren walked close to the sanctum's heart. As the jade dangling at her chest glowed, she peered into one of the holes, but only darkness lay within. She shifted to a second hole, then a third, both dark. In the fourth hole, something glimmered. She narrowed one eye. An image appeared deep inside. Sapphira stood with flames encircling her head, and a red dragon sat beyond her.

After backing up a step, Lauren pointed at the image and called out, "Ignite."

Sparks sprayed from within the hole, and a beam of light shot out. It streaked across the chamber and drilled into the surrounding wall, making an acute angle with the beam leading to the reservoir portal.

Her hands aflame, Lauren followed the new beam to the wall and set her palms on the surface at two corners of a large square. The beam's contact point at the center expanded toward the corners and created a glowing smudge. When she shifted her hands to the other two corners, the smudge spread out to fill the square.

Sapphira and Elam appeared behind the newly created frame. Fire spun around their heads in a swirling curtain as he helped her walk. Now within inches of the viewing plane, they stopped, seemingly locked in place. Her hands grasping the inner portion of her curtain of fire, she looked straight at Lauren and whispered, "I am ready."

"Okay. I'm going to attach myself to my portal, the one leading to the reservoir." Lauren raised her hands palms up and shouted, "Give me fire!"

A ball of flames blossomed in each hand and traveled up her arms to her shoulders. She stood with her back to the reservoir portal and waved her arms up and down as if making a snow angel with the fire. When the flames adhered to the wall, she shouted, "Engulf!" Fire erupted around her body from head to toe. She vaulted up with a backwards step and embedded herself within the portal plane.

An electrostatic jolt sent a shock wave through her limbs and up her spine. Her back scales tingled like never before. Every sound magnified—her own breathing, Matt's failing heartbeats, Listener's whispered prayers.

Waving her left arm to keep the flames going, she reached out with her right. Everything hurt from head to toe. "Sir Barlow . . ." She spoke between pain-streaked gasps. "Bring Matt. Lean him against me. I'll apply the pressure to his wound."

"Immediately, Miss." Sir Barlow pulled Matt away from Listener, covered his head with the cloak, and propped him up in the portal plane, his feet even with Lauren's, several inches from the sanctum's floor. Sparks flew around the cloak, creating a buzz that pierced her ears with a deafening screech.

When Sir Barlow stepped back, Lauren wrapped an arm around Matt's shoulders and supported him as she tried to reach for his neck, but her hand wouldn't stretch that far. "Matt," she whispered as pain throttled her words, "you have to … try to stand. I can't … put pressure … on your wound."

"I'm …" His arms slid around her waist, and his weight shifted to her hips. "I'm trying."

"Good. Good. That should be enough." She curled her arm over his shoulder and pressed her hand against his neck. With the cloak acting as a buffer between her skin and his, no heat or blood passed through.

She looked to her left. Sapphira and Elam also stood within the wall. Elam grimaced. The pain must have been horrible for him, though Sapphira's flaming shield likely protected him somewhat.

"Sapphira," Lauren called, "let's break the portals from their places. A burst of fire on three."

Sapphira offered a weak nod. "You count."

"All right." Lauren whispered to Matt. "Hang on. The fire will get hot, and I'm going to have to jump."

His arms tightened around her waist. A faint "Do it" reached her ears.

After inhaling deeply, she called out, "One! … Two! … Three!" She willed a surge of flames. An inferno exploded all around and ran along her body and the cloak. She bent her knees and leaped toward the sanctum. An ear-splitting squeal ripped from the wall. She dropped toward the floor in a slow drift, as if parachuting.

When her feet touched down, she leaned forward, flexed her leg muscles, and pushed toward the central column. A force pulled back, like stout ropes attached to every inch of her body.

At the other portal, Sapphira did the same. She and Elam appeared to be carrying a thin door on their backs. Fire and sparks streamed backwards from it, like radiant fingers trying to grasp for reattachment to the wall. Every time Sapphira stepped with one foot, Elam lifted her so she could step with the other.

No longer needing to stir the fire, Lauren clenched a fist and pumped with her arm and legs, desperately trying to keep a hand on Matt's neck as she pulled him along. At times, he pushed with his legs. At others, she had to drag him. Yet, they made progress as they inched toward the sanctum's heart.

When they drew within two paces, Lauren reached out to Sapphira and grabbed her wrist. A blast of sparks flew from their connection. A new laser beam ran along their arms and formed a triangle with the two beams radiating from the sanctum's heart. The doors on their backs expanded and melded into one, and the pulling force from behind slackened.

Lauren took another step forward. The entire chamber, including the heart and the surrounding wall, moved with her at a slight angle, turning toward Sapphira, likely because she hadn't moved at the same time. Pain now easing, Lauren exhaled heavily. "We did it." She took in another breath and nodded toward the tree-of-life portal. "Next we'll go together to the birthing garden."

Sir Barlow cleared his throat. "What do we do, Miss?"

"Let me check on Matt." Lauren angled her head and whispered. "Matt? How are you doing?"

"Better … I think." He set his feet, relieving the pressure of his weight. He pushed her hand away and, with the cloak still on, walked through one of the beams. He staggered forward, but Listener caught him.

Listener stripped the cloak off him and touched his neck, hot as an iron. She jerked her finger back. "He's red hot, but the wound looks better. The bleeding's stopped."

"Great! Wonderful!" Tears welled in Lauren's eyes but quickly dried in the heat. "You three take the cloak and go through the tree-of-life room to the birthing garden. When you see what's going on there, send Sir Barlow back to report to us. We might have need of him."

"To do what?" Matt asked as he swayed in place. "What exactly are you doing?"

Sapphira called out, "No time to explain. Arramos vowed to kill children while I'm here."

"We're going!" Listener spread the cloak over herself and Matt. "Sir Barlow, we'll toss it back to you." She helped Matt hurry to the portal. When they stepped through together, the cloak raised the familiar eruption of sparks.

After they passed the cloak to Sir Barlow and he exited as well, Lauren looked at Sapphira. "Let's go. Together now."

They took a single step at the same time. The horizontal beam radiating across their locked arms bent backwards, then snapped to its original position. The chamber shifted forward with their progress as if pushed by the beam. The sudden jerk sent a jolt through Lauren's arm and into her skull. She winced. Sapphira moaned.

"We'll have to take this slow and easy," Lauren said as she tried to ignore the pain. "Are you with me?"

Sapphira groaned. "We need to … go faster. I'll endure the pain."

Elam scooped Sapphira into his arms. Lauren's hold on her wrist stayed in place. His face awash in sweat, he nodded at Lauren. "We'll go as fast as you can stand it."

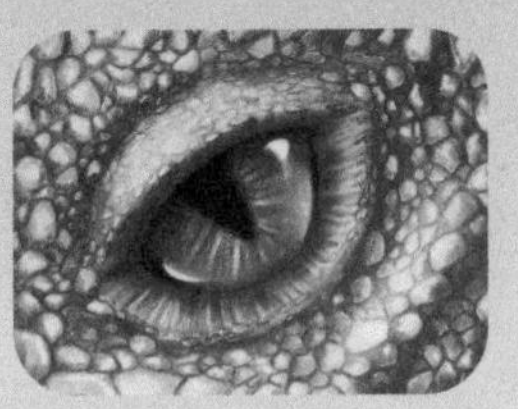

24

CHAPTER

Two Tragedies

Billy limped toward the parking lot, an arm around Edmund as he half dragged the wounded knight at his side. On the lot, Adam and Elizabeth stood next to the three dragons who lay on the pavement, all with their eyes open, though they didn't move a muscle. Adam held a rifle, and another lay near Elizabeth's feet.

When Billy arrived, he helped Edmund down to the pavement. His foot mangled and his leg burned, he would not fight again anytime soon, but he could stay and help guard the dragons.

"Can they get up?" Billy whispered to Adam.

"They can … barely." Adam handed Billy and Edmund each a bottle of water. "I've been giving them updates while they lie here pretending to be dead. We almost attacked a few minutes ago, but then the children showed up. We didn't want to risk getting them hurt, especially since our dragons are so weak."

"Risk doesn't mean anything now. We have to attack. Arramos will—"

Screams erupted from the field. A gunshot rang out, then another, then a rapid barrage, too fast for one gun to shoot. Then, the gunfire stopped.

"Mother!" Jennifer appeared from around the east end of the bleachers and ran toward them in a halting, haphazard line, a hand over her stomach. When she arrived, she coughed and sucked in a wheezing breath. "He … a boy! … A little boy! … Arramos … He …"

"He what?" Elizabeth steadied her with a hand on her elbow. "Breathed fire on him?"

Tears streaming down her flushed cheeks, Jennifer shook her head. "I can't say it!" She let out a raspy wail and looked upward. "Oh, dear God, why? Why?"

Billy grasped Jennifer's wrist. "We heard gunshots. Did you see what happened to Walter?"

"I didn't wait to see." She dropped to hands and knees. "I think I'm going to be sick!"

"I'll check it out." Adam ran in the direction Jennifer had come. Within seconds he disappeared around the corner of the bleachers.

Elizabeth stroked Jennifer's head. "Do what you must to get it out of your system, dear." While Jennifer heaved bile and spittle, Elizabeth pivoted toward Makaidos. "As William said, hang the risk. At least give us your presence on the field as a distraction. That's all I ask."

Makaidos gave her a head bow. "Very well. If we die, we die. It will not be the first time for any of us."

"Jennifer." Elizabeth touched her shoulder. "You have no more time for vomiting. Get in position with the device."

"The device?" Billy asked.

"Our hologram projector." Elizabeth helped Jennifer rise and wiped the corners of her lips with a sleeve. "I assume the images and voiceprints are ready."

Sniffling, Jennifer touched her pants pocket, her voice pitched high. "On my phone. I got some from Arramos and Walter, too. It's easy to transfer them."

"Perfect." Elizabeth picked up the remaining rifle and pushed it into Billy's hands. "It has fifteen rounds. Use them judiciously. Your role will be to make sure no one approaches Jennifer while she works her magic."

"Where will she be?"

"In a helicopter, I hope." Elizabeth clutched his arm. "After you hijack one."

This is what I was afraid of." Merlin stared at the candlestone wedged at the top of his staff. Yellowish light streamed from the gem in a steady beam. "As tragic and callous as it sounds, the child provided very little energy. He was a brave lad, but he died unwillingly and has not known a life of loving sacrifice. And the two knights provided only a little more. We will need a much bigger infusion." His eyes looked tired and sad. "I desperately hope the infusion does not come from a series of child murders."

"I don't think I could take it." Standing several paces away from the reservoir, Bonnie looked into the ovulum, now cradled in her palm as she held Excalibur in her other hand. Although cold air bit into every inch of exposed skin, heat crawled across her body from head to toe. Seeing Arramos kill that child ignited a surge of rage. Such an evil beast! And that poor boy! How many more would Arramos kill?

She exhaled slowly. *Just stay calm.* She had to keep her wits about her. At any moment the spiders might attack. If she could quiet her heart and take the time to pray for Billy and Jennifer, that might help quell any anxiety. Scenes within the ovulum and some explanation from Merlin had introduced Jennifer and her mother as well as some of their plan to hijack a helicopter. It sounded like a long shot, so they needed all the prayer they could—

"Bonnie!" Merlin shouted. "They're coming!"

She set the ovulum down and ran toward him. At least fifty fire-legged spiders the size of tarantulas had formed a semicircle around Merlin. Leading with the sword, she leaped over the line of spiders and swiped the blade through them as she passed. The sharp edge sliced through two bodies and removed their heads.

Bonnie landed, slid on the ice to Merlin, and spun toward the spiders. She held Excalibur in front, while Merlin wielded his staff. The spiders closed in slowly. Their fiery legs melted the ice underneath as they inched along, now within a foot of the edge of the reservoir.

"Hold steady," Merlin whispered. "Our goal is not complicated. We must keep them at bay until the reservoir is filled."

"I could disintegrate them all if I could call up the beam, but it's still not working."

"I think they realize that, which is why I tried to keep that news quiet earlier. Perhaps they feared Lauren while she was here. Now that she is gone, they perceive us to be weak, so their captain sounded the charge."

"Their captain?"

Merlin pointed past the encroaching line. Illuminated by glowbats on the ceiling, a huge spider crawled toward them. Bearing a human head and dragon-like claws, it looked all too familiar.

Bonnie whispered, "The spider in the church."

The spider raised a leg and shouted, "Attack!"

Lauren walked onward, still holding Sapphira's wrist. Carried by Elam, she looked back from time to time, obviously worried about the events on Earth. The sanctum's heart moved a foot or so in front of them, following a beam that painted a portal on the reflective wall and provided access to the tree of life. The curved wall to the left and right stretched beyond the portal as if reaching around to enfold the next room in its grasp.

When they reached the portal, Lauren looked at Elam. "Ready?"

Burn marks ravaged his face along with sooty smears across his scarred lips. "I am ready."

Protected by the flames, they walked through together. The surrounding walls reeled out and encircled the tree-of-life room except for a gap on the far side where the next portal led to Second Eden. Sir Barlow stood beside the tree. He shifted his weight from foot to foot and clasped his hands tightly at his waist.

"All is not well," he said. "Tamiel used his strength to escape Mendallah, but Marilyn's shooting skills discouraged him from attacking Clefspeare's plant. Perhaps bullets cannot kill him, but they produced sufficient pain. He flew away and is probably lurking nearby waiting for an opportunity to strike." He patted a sheathed sword at his hip. "I was able to retrieve this, so he has no weapons that I know of."

"Thank you." Lauren looked him over. He seemed as nervous as a cat. "Are you ready to carry out our plan?"

"I am ready, Miss. My only concern is Tamara. She and I declared our marital intentions to each other, so I hope her disappointment will not cause her too much heartache."

"What plan?" Elam asked.

Lauren heaved a sigh. "I suppose I have to tell you, since you and Sapphira are part of it."

"Hurry," Sapphira said. "Arramos killed one child. He is sure to kill another soon."

Lauren spoke with rapid-fire words. "When we carry the combined portals to the birthing garden, they will no longer be open, so someone has to give his life to open each one by inserting a finger into the hole that the beam comes out of. Since we have two portals, it will require two lives. I plan to provide the life energy for one, and Sir Barlow will provide for the other."

"I volunteered," Sir Barlow added. "I am ready to finish my course."

Lauren gestured with her eyes toward Second Eden. "Go now, Sir Barlow. Thank you for the information."

"My pleasure, Miss." He skirted the tree and disappeared beyond the portal.

Elam whispered to Sapphira, "Are you thinking what I'm thinking?"

"Without a doubt." Sapphira intertwined her fingers with Elam's. "Everyone has to finish the course eventually."

Elam gave Lauren a firm nod. "Around the tree, or through it?"

"Through it." Lauren lifted a foot. "Together."

They marched onward. Elam struggled with each step. When the sanctum's heart passed into the tree, the branches exploded in new flames—an inferno that enveloped Lauren, Elam, and Sapphira.

Intense heat surged across Lauren's skin. Energy swept through her limbs. Elam walked with more vigor, but new marks scarred his face, deep grooves that looked like bleeding wrinkles. Cracks ran along Sapphira's skin, as if the heat had absorbed moisture from her body.

As quickly as the flames had erupted, they died away, and the tree's fire extinguished. A cool breeze drifted in from the Second Eden portal. Lauren lifted a hand to her cheek—still smooth. The tree's flames hadn't affected her as much … yet. "Keep going," she called. "We're almost there."

Clutching a rifle, Billy peered around the corner of the bleachers. Behind him, Jennifer carried a video projector the size of a large book while Adam attached it to her phone with a short cable. As she looked at the phone's screen, her fingers and thumb tapped buttons on each device.

On the field, one of the combat helicopters had parked about ten paces away from Billy's hiding place. A single pilot sat inside with the glass windshield open. The gunner seat behind his was empty. Only a short fence stood as a barrier.

Billy imagined himself charging out and leaping over the fence. The thought brought a scalding sting to the claw marks on his back as well as painful throbs to his broken toes. Still, he could do it. He had to do it.

Adam peeked over Billy's shoulder and whispered, "Do you know how to fly a chopper?"

"I flew a small one once. Nothing like this. Maybe I can get it off the ground, but Walter's the guy who can maneuver it the way we need."

"Then you'll have to hop over everyone and pick him up. I'll cover you when you land."

"Yeah." Billy swallowed. "Sure." He scanned the field past the helicopters. Arramos stood near the center with more than a dozen children lying facedown on the turf. Many squirmed, and some cried, proving that they were still alive. Beyond Arramos, Elam carried Sapphira in the midst of a firestorm. Elam seemed to be walking in place—floating, as if he were marching in zero gravity, the details fuzzy because of the flames.

Walter sat on the ground, a rifle in his lap. Blood streamed from his scalp to his chin and dripped to his legs. He looked around, obviously dazed. A helicopter sat near him, its propellers spinning down. It looked like Walter was on the losing end of the short gun battle they had heard earlier. A rifle against a Cobra wasn't exactly a fair fight.

Billy turned back to Jennifer. "Are you ready?"

"Just … one … second." She pressed a button on the projector. "There. That should do it."

"Okay. Your mother's had time to get in place with the speaker. Let's start step one."

Jennifer sneaked around the corner and climbed the bleachers. Gaps in the side rails kept her in view. When she stopped about halfway up, she aimed the projector at a point near the closer end of the fifty-yard line and pressed a button. An image of Walter appeared on the field near the sideline. His voice boomed from the image. "Dragons! Attack!"

Arramos looked that way. He shouted, "Helicopters! Take flight and find the dragons!"

Billy and Adam ran toward the nearest helicopter and vaulted the fence. Just as the pilot started the propellers, Billy grabbed his arm, jerked him out of the seat, and pulled him to the ground. Adam smacked the pilot in the face with a rifle butt and knocked him out.

"Jennifer! Now!" Billy climbed into the seat. As he had hoped, the three other combat choppers were busy lifting off and searching the sky for dragons, giving Jennifer cover to hustle down with the projector, jump over the fence, and crawl into the rear seat of their helicopter.

As Billy and Jennifer lifted off, Adam ran across the field toward Walter. While the other choppers hovered about a hundred feet above the ground, Billy stayed lower and glided to a point thirty feet over Walter.

Adam arrived at the spot under the chopper and began shooting at Arramos. The bullets pinged off his scales. He reared his head back and blew a blast of fire. Adam leaped and rolled out of the way. Walter lurched in the opposite direction. The fire missed them both and scorched the grass.

Jennifer aimed the video projector out the open windshield. Images of Makaidos, Thigocia, and Roxil appeared at the spot where Walter's image had been. With their heads high and their wings outstretched, they roared, thanks to Elizabeth's nearby speaker.

As the helicopters moved into position to fire at the images, Arramos shouted something that sounded like a command to hold off. Knowing that the dragons wouldn't sit still for an attack, he likely had figured out the ploy, but the buzz of propellers batted his words away.

Two helicopters fired bullets while the third shot a missile. It blasted into the bleachers. A cloud of dust erupted, and debris flew, most of which rained back down over the remains of the bleachers.

Jennifer shut off the projector. "I hope Mother was far enough away."

"She was." Billy drifted lower. The control stick felt stiff, making the movements jerky. "Hang on. We're landing."

They descended and hit the ground with a thud. While Adam attacked Arramos with a new barrage of bullets, Billy leaped out, grabbed Walter, and hoisted him to his feet. Half dragging him, Billy hurried to the pilot's seat. "Can you fly this bucket?"

Walter nodded. "Sure. But my leg took a slug of lead."

Arramos blew a long stream of fire at Adam. The new blast hit him squarely as he tried to dive out of the way. He rolled on the grass, his clothes aflame.

"Up you go!" Billy heaved Walter toward the pilot's seat. Jennifer leaned from the rear and hauled him in. Arramos turned his fiery maw toward the chopper. Billy ran toward Adam, waved his arms, and shouted, "Makaidos! Over here!"

When Arramos looked, Billy dove for Adam and helped him snuff the flames. Walter's helicopter took off and zoomed upward. A missile launched from his chopper and slammed into one of the others. It exploded, sending fire, smoke, and shrapnel flying in every direction.

Billy leaped from Adam, threw himself over a little girl, and covered her as the debris fell. Something sharp slapped his back, but he stayed put and whispered in the girl's ear as she whimpered. "It's all right, sweetheart. I won't let anything hurt you." A few other children cried out, but they stayed put, apparently more frightened of Arramos than the raining debris.

Raising his head, Billy spotted Walter's chopper in the sky. As it whirled into position to aim at Arramos, the other choppers fired their machine guns. Walter dodged the volleys but not before a few bullets clanked into his tail section. With smoke pouring from the tail, he took off toward the storm to the east, and the other choppers gave chase.

Billy lifted himself from the girl and looked at Adam. He lay writhing on the grass, his body charred from the waist down. To the east, boiling clouds loomed, just minutes away. Closer in, the transport helicopter sat empty in the end zone. Perfect. An escape craft for the children. Now if the dragons could cause a distraction—

A roar sounded from the direction of the parking lot. Makaidos flew over the remains of the bleachers, landed on the sideline, and shouted, "Arramos! Hearken to me!"

Right on time! Billy scooped the girl into his arms. "Children! Run! Follow me!"

"Do not move!" Arramos blasted fire over the children. They stayed on their stomachs, trembling.

Billy hurried on. As he limped toward the remaining helicopter, his toes pulsed with pain. She was just one of maybe twenty. Better than none. He glanced back every few seconds to check on the others.

Arramos focused on Makaidos and laughed. "What do you want, former king of the dragons?"

"Cease your murderous ways. Release the children, or—"

"Or what?" Arramos spat a sizzling ball of flames that rolled across the ground, narrowly missing a boy. "You know you cannot defeat me in battle."

"Perhaps not, but maybe the three of us can." Just as Makaidos charged, Thigocia and Roxil flew over the debris and joined him.

Arramos launched toward them. He slammed shoulder to shoulder into Makaidos and whipped a tail at Thigocia in the same motion. Makaidos crashed to the field, nearly landing on Adam. Thigocia flailed her wings and flew backwards for a moment to a spot behind the portal where she fell, smacked her head hard on the ground, and lay motionless.

As Arramos flew a 180 turn, Roxil landed in the midst of the children. "Stay away," she growled. "I will defend these little ones to the death."

"Allow me to serve up that dish." Arramos zoomed toward her. She blasted a ball of fire that glanced off his neck. Leading with claws and teeth, he bowled her over.

As they bit and clawed, Billy lifted the girl into the helicopter and ran toward the battling dragons. Adam crawled that way as well, and Elizabeth sprinted from around the bleachers. Before anyone could arrive, Arramos wrestled Roxil down and pinned her with a rear claw. He snatched a little girl from the turf and held her aloft with a clawed hand around her waist. Her head flopped forward as she appeared to faint. "Stop! All of you! Or else this morsel will meet the same death the boy did!"

Adam collapsed to his stomach. Elizabeth halted and knelt next to him, a hand on his back. Makaidos and Thigocia lay unconscious with their wings splayed. Billy slowed his pace but kept moving with his head low.

The drone of a helicopter's propellers drew near. A silvery blotch flew out of the storm bank and toward the field, free of smoke at its tail section. Billy searched for Walter's chopper. No sign of it. He probably headed into the storm to try to shake off his pursuer. He couldn't last long in that kind of weather, especially with a crippled aircraft.

The helicopter landed on the far sideline. As the props spun down, the pilot opened the windshield and removed his helmet. Open sores covered his cheeks and forehead. "I lost the enemy. He must've crashed. That storm is like a cat-five hurricane."

While Roxil squirmed under Arramos's weight, he turned to the portal and stared at it, as if perplexed. Sapphira stood with a glowing aura around her, deep wrinkles in her face. Her hair, although still white, looked scraggly and dull.

"Sapphira," Arramos shouted, "I do not know what has happened to you, but if you do not report on the size of the portal immediately, I will kill all the children."

Lauren stepped up into Second Eden. At her side, Elam carried Sapphira. As soon as they passed the portal plane, something crackled. To the rear, the tree of life shriveled and vanished, and the portal's edges drew closer and closer to the center until the entire plane collapsed and disappeared. Retreat was now impossible.

The pulsing column hovered in front, and the sanctum's walls stretched out around the birthing garden, both features nebulous, as if hazy images had been superimposed over a clear photograph of Second Eden.

Matt, Listener, Sir Barlow, and Mendallah stood around Marilyn as she knelt behind Clefspeare's plant. Now about a foot tall, its pod looked like a head with triangular ears. Miniature teeth poked out from its tiny mouth, and little claws hung on the ends of its leaflets. Yet, it was still a long way from becoming a dragon who could do battle with Arramos.

Matt and Listener stood side by side with the cloak draped over their shoulders. Matt still looked pale. Blood loss had taken quite a toll.

Marilyn rose and backed away. "Lauren, the others told me what's going on. Is the reservoir full?"

"I don't know, but we don't have time to check. We have to create the combined portal here right away."

"She's right," Sapphira said, her voice gravelly. "Arramos is killing children. We can't wait."

Marilyn gasped. "Sapphira! Your … your skin is … wrinkled. Elam's too."

"Probably temporary." Sapphira slid down from Elam's arms and stood on one foot. "We'll join the portals now."

Lauren, Sapphira, and Elam walked forward until the sanctum's heart hovered near Clefspeare's plant. Lauren turned toward Sapphira, making the portal she carried turn with her. Elam helped Sapphira pivot to face Lauren, then moved out of the way as she stood on one foot, steadied by Lauren's hand.

The triangle of beams flattened into a line that ran toward the sanctum's heart and split into two just before their respective holes. Now the portals faced each other with Lauren and Sapphira separating them as they stood nearly nose to nose.

Lauren wrapped her arms around Sapphira and pulled her closer. The great Oracle of Fire felt thin and frail. Her body trembled.

As they pressed together, their fires and the two portals combined. A painful jolt ripped through Lauren. She gasped and held on. In an enormous splash of sparks, the surrounding flames flared out and died away, leaving a pulsing white aura around their bodies.

When Lauren released Sapphira and drew back, the beams from the sanctum's heart disappeared, though the holes where they originated still glowed. The joined portal shimmered and flashed. The moment the light dimmed, Sapphira disappeared from Lauren's view.

A door-like rectangle, at least thirty feet high and ten feet wide, radiated white light from its extremities and stood with a vertical edge facing the sanctum's heart. Through the portal, only darkness appeared. This side led to the realm of the life reservoir.

Lauren walked to the door's edge and peered around it. Sapphira looked through the portal from her side. "This one is functioning," she said. "I see Arramos. He has a little girl in his claws. Billy is close by. He's hurt. His shirt is torn to shreds. I also see a helicopter, probably the one Arramos wants to send through here."

A deep voice reverberated from somewhere beyond the portal. "Sapphira, I do not know what has happened to you, but if you do not report on the size of the portal immediately, I will kill all the children."

Steadied by Elam, Sapphira leaned close to the door and shouted, "The portal is of sufficient size. Allow me a few moments to expand the opening to the boundaries. When I am finished, you will be able to see it for yourself."

Arramos growled. "Perhaps the cries of this child will motivate you to hurry."

"I will work as quickly as I can." Sapphira backed away from the portal, again helped by Elam. "Arramos is not bluffing. We have to hurry."

Lauren nodded. "First we have to open the portal from each side." She reached toward the sanctum's heart. "Sir Barlow? As we agreed?"

"Of course, Miss." Sir Barlow walked toward the sanctum's column, a finger raised. "Someone please send my love to Tamara."

"Wait!" Elam called. "Pay heed to us. Our time is short."

Everyone stared, seemingly frozen by his command. As he guided Sapphira to the sanctum's heart, their wrinkles deepened, and their bodies withered. When they stopped next to the sanctum's glowing holes, Sapphira looked at Sir Barlow and spoke with a rasping voice. "Kind and courageous knight, thank you for your sacrificial heart." She turned to Lauren. "Gracious saint of God, it is with great pleasure and perfect confidence that I pass my mantle to you. Second Eden will always need an Oracle of Fire."

Elam and Sapphira stood face-to-face, wiggled their fingers, and intertwined them to form a clasp. Gazing at each other with tender smiles, they each extended a finger and inserted it into one of the holes.

They both stiffened. Pain flashed across their faces. They took a deep breath and slowly exhaled. Their bodies shrank and crumbled with the respiration, contented smiles on their lips as they dissolved. Seconds later, only two piles of clothing remained. Silence descended. Everyone stood with mouths agape.

Lauren dropped to her knees and picked up Sapphira's battle tunic—warm and moist. She pressed the material against her face and wept into it. Elam and Sapphira, king and queen of Second Eden, were dead.

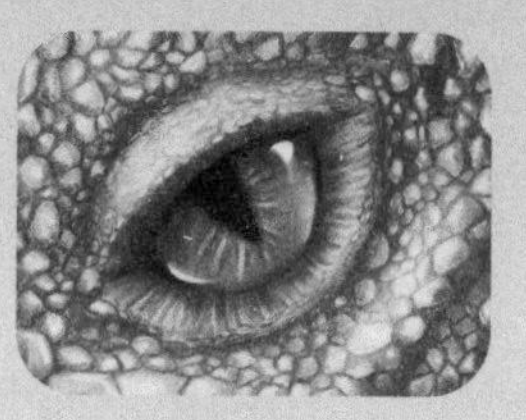

25

CHAPTER

Life Energy

Now at the edge of the reservoir, the spiders pushed their heated legs into the ice. Hissing vapor rose from the contact points. Bonnie lunged and swung Excalibur at the closest spider. The blade sliced through its body and cleaved it in two. Merlin hacked with his staff and crushed the head of another.

Bonnie slid along the line of spiders and swept the blade though them. Severed heads and legs flew. Merlin walked down the line in the other direction and smacked more spiders one by one.

The arachnid captain leaped on Bonnie's back and began throwing thick strands of stinging silk around her face. Crying out in pain, she twisted, grabbed one of his legs, and slung him off. He crashed to the ice and slid closer to Merlin.

The strands burned into Bonnie's forehead and cheeks. Her vision blurred, and the ground seemed to sway. While she tore the strands, the captain righted himself and called out, "Hurry and melt the ice while the warrior is disabled!"

Merlin helped Bonnie strip the remaining strands away. "Are you all right?"

The stinging persisted, and the icy floor still seemed unsteady. "Not yet." She strode on trembling legs to the captain, swung the sword, and sliced through his neck. His head dropped and rolled to her feet with his humanlike face up, his eyes open and vacant. "That should help."

"Good." Merlin pointed at the attacking spiders. A new swarm of at least thirty approached from the shadows. "We have a long way to go."

Lauren scooped up a handful of the remains of Elam and Sapphira—sparkling dust particles that dwindled and disappeared in a matter of seconds. She covered her face with her hands and cried out, "Oh, Sapphira! Elam! What have you done?"

Matt knelt at her side and pulled her close. "They gave their lives hoping to save others."

"But did they save anyone?" She gazed into his eyes—weary and bloodshot. "Was their sacrifice enough?"

Everyone looked at Clefspeare's plant, now almost three feet tall with a thick stalk and twin leaflets that resembled dragon wings. His toothy mouth opened and closed, as if chewing. Two eyelets blinked, and his ears twitched, but no perceptible growth ensued.

Marilyn ran a hand along the stalk. "We should call Zohar. His fire warming the soil is the only difference between Mendallah's rapid growth and Jared's slowness. We were thinking that trying to grow a dragon might be different, so I put Makaidos's bone under his roots, but it hasn't helped."

"I can warm the soil." Lauren raised a fireball in a palm. "But we'd better make sure there aren't any other missing elements. Who was here when Makaidos resurrected?"

Sir Barlow raised a hand. "I think I am the only one, though I did not personally view the resurrection itself because I was engaged in battle at the time. I heard an account, and the details are fuzzy now, but I am quite sure that Makaidos's bones were on the surface, not under the soil."

"That's good to know." Lauren raised her other hand and summoned a second fireball. "Let's unearth the bone and lay it on the surface. And please hurry."

Marilyn pushed her fingers into the ground and probed. After a few seconds, she withdrew the bone and laid it near the stalk. "Done."

When Lauren set her fireballs on the soil, strange noises emanated from the joined portal—hissing and cries of pain. The reservoir! The cries sounded like her mother's.

"Get Zohar! I have to go!" Lauren created a halo of fire around her body and ran through the side of the combined portal leading to the reservoir. As always, the portal sizzled, but at least it was open. The sacrifices of Sapphira and Elam had worked.

Surrounded by darkness, she lifted a hand. Now that she had completed the conjunction, could she create fire here?

She whispered, "Give me light."

A ball of flames erupted on her palm and spread its flickering glow all around. She exhaled. Finally! The puzzle was finished!

Careful not to slip, she hurried toward the reservoir. The hissing sounds increased. Ahead, light from the glowbats appeared. Mom and Merlin stood on the surface of the pool. Mom swung Excalibur at approaching spiders while Merlin battled them with his staff. Rising vapor veiled their movements, though it seemed clear that they were growing tired. With so many spiders attacking, the reservoir's defenders couldn't last much longer.

Lauren waded into the swarm. She spread her arms and shouted, "Ignite!" A wave of fire rolled across the spiders and set them ablaze. As they burned, she ran on top of their flaming bodies, her heat-resistant soles protecting her.

When she joined Mom and Merlin, Mom lowered Excalibur and gave her a one-armed hug. "Thank you!"

"Excellent timing," Merlin said as he kicked a smoldering spider from the ice. "What news do you bring?"

Lauren looked toward Second Eden, though darkness veiled the exit window. "Sapphira and Elam died to open two joined portals."

Mom gasped but said nothing.

"How long ago?" Merlin asked.

"Just a couple of minutes."

Merlin exhaled, sending out a stream of vapor that joined a fog hovering over the ice. "We shall see if their act provided the desired result. Their energy should arrive within moments."

Lauren called for a new fireball in her palm. When it appeared, she showed it to Merlin. "I have my Oracle powers. Should I get ready to open the reservoir with my fire?"

"Without a doubt." Merlin used a finger to lift the beaded necklace at Lauren's neck. "Good. You still have it."

"What do I do?"

"Stand at the center of the pool." Merlin transferred Excalibur from Bonnie's hand to Lauren's. "I suspect that you will also be able to use this now."

When Lauren wrapped her fingers around the hilt, the blade began to glow.

"Excellent. You will create a regeneracy dome. Your necklace should produce colorful sparks that will enhance the process. If we can somehow collect them at the end of the procedure, they might be useful for future resurrection purposes."

"Got it … I think." As Lauren slid her bare feet over the surface, she gripped the sword's hilt with both hands. Tiny jagged lines in the ice marked her trail and raised a tinkling crackle. She stopped at the center. Below, mists with vaporous faces swirled as if stirred by a frenzied spoon. The expressions seemed agitated, anxious, as if they felt that something big, something monumental, was about to happen.

"Turn on the beam," Merlin called. "We need to make sure you're ready when the infusion comes."

Lauren stared at the glowing blade. "How?"

"Wait." Mom slid out and joined her. With one hand over Lauren's, she whispered, "Concentrate on your connection with the sword, and you'll feel a source of your own energy inside. Mentally guide the energy to the connection point, and the beam should appear. To create a dome, just wave the sword in a circle over your head like Sapphira does when she creates a portal."

Lauren nodded. "I'll try."

"I'm sure you can do it." Mom hurried back to the edge of the reservoir.

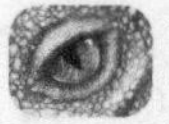

A tremor raced along the ice. The top layer cracked around Lauren's feet. New jagged lines raced across the reservoir in a weblike network. The surface swelled, and the energy vapors below boiled as if blown and twisted by a tornado.

"Merlin!" Lauren called as she spread her feet to maintain balance. "The ice is breaking up!"

"Hold on!" Standing at the edge, Merlin plunged the end of his staff into the ice. Radiance shot up the wood and flashed through the candlestone. White light filled the chamber with brilliance. "The infusion is massive! Create the dome!"

"Here goes!" Lauren tightened her grip and concentrated on the hilt. As Mom had said, energy flowed within. When she sent it into the sword, a beam shot upward and drilled into the rocky ceiling. As she began the stirring motion, the beads on her necklace glimmered. The beam spread out above, and radiance spilled all around as if following the outline of a bowl.

A tiny white ray shot from the dome and struck the necklace's blue bead. It reflected as a blue stream and bounced off another spot on the surrounding shield, then ricocheted from place to place at lightning speeds. More white rays emerged and collided with other beads to make new bouncing streams. Soon, dozens of colors zipped back and forth at hundreds of angles to create a matrix of shimmering hues.

As the colors bounced off the reservoir's surface, they made glowing pinpricks in the ice, though when they glanced off Lauren's skin, the pain was no more than a minor sting. Soon the ice began taking on a multicolored radiance of its own, and the pinpricks joined to create divots that deepened into depressions and thinned the surface.

Merlin shouted, "Now douse the beam and use your fire to melt the ice!"

She lowered the sword. When Excalibur's light blinked off, the radiance rained to the ice and lingered there in dancing sparks. She created a fireball and threw it down. The colorful particles joined with the fire. The blended radiance crawled along the ice and ate away at the frozen plane. "It's getting thinner!"

Merlin pulled the candlestone from the staff and tossed it to her. "Absorb the color remnants and get ready to escape!"

She caught the gem with her free hand and slid Excalibur across the ice to her mother. The gem burned in her grasp. Had this vulnerability returned along with her gifts? Groaning at the pain, she crouched and ran the stone along the cracked surface. It swept up the radiant particles like a vacuum cleaner. As the stone swallowed each spark, the chamber dimmed. Only the light from the glowbats remained.

"Throw the candlestone to me!" Mom called. "I'm immune!"

Lauren tossed the gem. Mom caught it, pushed it into a pocket, and slid Excalibur behind her belt.

The pool swelled further. More cracks raced along the surface. Radiant vapors spewed from vent holes and melted the surrounding ice, as if the mists had absorbed superheated light. More tremors shook the entire room.

Lauren straightened and spread her arms to keep from falling. "It's about to blow!"

Merlin scooped up the ovulum and set it in his cloak pocket. "Get off the ice!"

Mom spread her wings and grabbed Merlin from behind with both arms. "Hurry!"

"I'm coming!" Just as Lauren set a foot to run, the surface exploded. The force threw her forward with a tsunami of ice, hot mist, and water surging close behind. She landed on her feet and ran, her bare feet providing good traction.

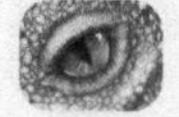

Mom flew with Merlin at Lauren's side. "The energy is heading toward the portal!" Merlin called as he dangled from Mom's arms. "The only escape is to fly right through it!"

The roar and crackling of the surge closed in. Mom beat her wings harder. "Lauren has fire, but I can't protect us from the jolt!"

"Let the wave overtake us as we go through and pray we don't get electrocuted!"

"Get ready for a swim!" Ahead, the portal window came into view, illuminated by the radiant vapors in the pursuing wave. Just as they were about to zoom through, Mom folded her wings around Merlin and shouted, "Duck!"

Lauren created a new fire shield and leaped. Water and sizzling mist rolled over them and sent her barreling through the portal. She tumbled in a somersault through the wave until she found her footing and battled to stand upright.

Her head and torso broke through the surface. Now in Second Eden, she stood waist deep in the flow of water and mist. Mom and Merlin joined her, both dripping wet.

The rush flooded the garden. Marilyn scooped up the bone, grasped the plant's stalk, and held it upright against the surge. As she knelt, water rose to her chest, and vapor slithered around her face. She gritted her teeth and clenched her eyes shut as she gasped, "What's … what's happening?"

Matt and Listener sloshed to Lauren and company. "Are you all right?" Matt asked as he steadied Merlin.

"Fine. Fine." Merlin squeezed water from his cloak's saturated sleeve. "But I am far too old for body surfing."

Her hair dripping and wet clothes clinging to her lean frame, Mom shook her wings and cast off droplets. "Did it work?" She turned toward Marilyn and the plant. "Is Clefspeare growing?"

The flow now spreading over the entire garden, Marilyn released the stalk. "Maybe. I felt him vibrating." She rose to her feet and wobbled as she clutched something in her hand. "I feel … different."

Sir Barlow rushed to her in a series of hefty splashes and grasped her arm. "I have you. Just lean on me."

As she shifted her weight toward him, she opened her hand, revealing Makaidos's bone. A white aura pulsed around it. "It's so strange. I'm tingling all over."

"Look!" Listener pointed at Clefspeare's plant. The stalk vibrated, and the winglike leaflets stretched.

"While we are waiting for the omega dragon, I must address an important issue." Merlin strode to the pulsing column, using his staff for support. "This is the center of all portal accesses. It should not be here in Second Eden."

Lauren splashed toward him and scanned the garden area. Mendallah was missing. She must have gone to the village to get Zohar.

When Lauren joined Merlin, she looked at the pulsing heart. "What does it mean?"

"It means that we are standing in a cross-dimensional field. In moments, it will snap back into place. I cannot predict the result." Merlin turned toward the dual portal. "I assume the other side leads to Earth. We should go there at once."

"Shouldn't we wait for Clefspeare to grow so he can come with us?"

A frown tightened Merlin's face. "We have already waited far too long. Arramos will not delay in carrying out his threats."

"I'll see what I can do about that." Lauren faced the Earth-bound portal, created a fiery shield around herself, and walked into the plane. As the boundary sizzled, she peered into the Earth dimension. A dark cloud roiled in the sky. Rain and fiery hail fell over several children who lay trembling on the ground. One combat helicopter had landed on the field, a second descended, and a larger helicopter sat farther away. A girl leaned out of its open door until a pair of young hands pulled her back in.

Closer to the portal, Arramos stood on a swath of scorched grass with a dragon pinned under his rear claw. He no longer held a girl in his grasp. Nearby, Dad and two other adults used their bodies to shield children from the catastrophic weather. Obviously a lot had taken place on Earth during the past several minutes. Dad and the others had likely battled to keep Arramos from carrying out his threats and managed to get some of the children to the distant helicopter.

"Well, Sapphira," Arramos said as he blinked an oozing eye. "I have waited with the utmost patience. What is the status of the portal?"

Lauren glanced down. Most of her body was still on the Second Eden side. Arramos could see only her head. She cleared her throat and tried to imitate Sapphira's silky voice. "The portal is completely open, and a large object is able to pass. Release the children."

"When the helicopter has safely traveled through." Arramos waved a wing. The engine of the closer helicopter roared to life, and its propellers began spinning. Dad looked up. Lauren followed his line of sight but couldn't find what he had spotted.

The helicopter lifted off. Lauren swiveled her head and peered into Second Eden. Clefspeare continued growing. His head pod, still as green as grass, swelled to the size of a volleyball, and his leaflets stretched out into full-fledged dragon wings. His single stalk split into two thick trunks, and his body expanded in every direction, including a skinny protrusion that morphed into a spiny tail. The surface divided into scales from the tip of the elongating snout to the end of the tail.

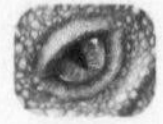

Lauren swiveled again. The helicopter hovered several feet ahead, apparently ready to fly through. The front edges of the spinning blades eased closer and closer.

Swallowing hard, Lauren turned again. Clefspeare's green stalks uprooted and stomped down, now dragon's rear feet. As his claws dug into the soil, white radiance raced along the scales. His wings shook. His tail whipped upward and thumped against the ground. Finally, as the radiance ran toward his head, his neck stretched out, and the energy seemed to explode through his mouth in a ground-shaking roar.

The dragon, as white as pearls, beat his wings and shouted, "I am Clefspeare! And I have returned!"

Marilyn wrapped her arms around his foreleg, then leaped back and shook her hands. "You're scalding hot!"

The sanctum's heart erupted with bright light. Radiance shot from every hole. The ground quaked and shook Lauren from her stance. She stumbled backwards until she could regain her balance and set her feet.

"The portal structure is unstable," Merlin called as he leaned against his staff. "We had better go to Earth while we can."

Something exploded beyond the portal. Metal fragments flew into Second Eden and scattered across the water-covered ground.

"Clefspeare!" Merlin shouted. "The reservoir's energy is now your armor. It should protect you! Fly through the portal! Lauren will create a shield so the rest of us can follow!"

Marilyn called out, "Clefspeare! Arramos murdered Carl and Shelly and countless children in cold blood. Hold nothing back." She slapped him on the flank. "Go! Be our omega dragon!"

Billy arched his body over a fallen girl and boy. They heaved rapid breaths, apparently still conscious. Elizabeth and Adam shielded other children in the same way, though Adam's legs had been scorched in a fiery battle against Arramos as they kept him from killing children while waiting for news from the portal. They had managed to send most of the little ones to the transport helicopter, and only these few remained on the field—too scared to run.

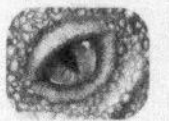

The head of a white-haired girl appeared at the portal while the rest of her body stayed hidden behind a wall of fire. Billy studied her features. She looked a lot like Sapphira, but the hair couldn't mask her identity—Lauren.

A surge of relief swelled in Billy's heart. There she was … his precious daughter … back from the dead, but would Arramos fall for this disguise? Maybe his failing eyesight would help the cause.

Arramos looked at Lauren and blinked rapidly. "Well, Sapphira. I have waited with the utmost patience. What is the status of the portal?"

Lauren glanced around before answering. "The portal is completely open, and a large object is able to pass. Release the children."

"When the helicopter has safely traveled through." Arramos waved toward the first grounded helicopter with a wing. The pilot started the engine and set the propellers in motion. Another engine hummed somewhere above, nearly drowned out by the storm.

Billy looked up. A third helicopter dipped below the clouds, then shot back into hiding. He squelched any reaction. That had to be Walter.

The first helicopter lifted off the ground and moved into position in front of the portal. As it drifted closer, Lauren stared at the approaching blades.

Billy whispered, "No, Lauren. Don't sacrifice yourself."

The pilot slowed the chopper to a pause. The front of the blades barely touched the portal plane. Sparks flew, but the blades remained intact. With a roar of engines, the helicopter backed away as if making ready to surge and burst through.

Billy rose. It was do-or-die time. He couldn't let that helicopter through no matter what.

Just as he set his feet to dash toward the chopper, it exploded. Shrapnel flew everywhere. He dove for the children and covered them. Again, sharp objects pierced his back and raked across his skin. With each scrape, he grimaced at the excruciating pain.

When the flying debris settled, Billy looked up once more. Walter's helicopter spun in the buffeting wind, and smoke continued streaming from its tail. He seemed to be trying to get into position to shoot at the final enemy helicopter or maybe at Arramos, but the storm slapped him around with water, hail, and gusts.

The other helicopter took flight and shot at Walter's with its machine guns. A few bullets glanced off the frame, but the storm tossed the attacker as well.

Arramos shifted his rear claw from Roxil's neck to her belly and shouted, "Now she dies!"

Sparks exploded at the portal. A white dragon burst out, plowed into Arramos, and bowled him over. The attacking dragon's tail smacked Arramos full in the face and drove him back. As Arramos regained his balance, he called out to the sky, "Drones! Come to my aid! The time has arrived!" With the battle paused, Roxil dragged her body across the rain-slickened grass toward Makaidos.

Billy peered at the white dragon's face. Clefspeare! His father had finally come! But why was he white?

Arramos lunged at Clefspeare, and the two dragons clashed again—clawing, biting, and whipping tails. Growls and screeches pierced the rain-swept air.

"Hang on, Dad!" Billy scrambled to his feet. Adam rose to his knees and tossed his rifle. When Billy caught it, Adam shouted, "You're in better shape to use it than I am."

Elizabeth picked up one of the children. "I'll take the rest to the transport!"

Billy helped Elizabeth form a chain of connected hands, then she and the children dashed together across the field toward the helicopter.

A new burst of fire erupted at the portal, a cyclonic swirl of flames in the shape of a wide cylinder. The flames sizzled in the downpour and vanished, revealing Lauren, Matt, Listener, Marilyn, Sir Barlow, and a man in a red cloak carrying a staff.

Billy blinked away rain droplets to clear his vision. The cloaked man looked a lot like Professor Hamilton. Could he be … Merlin?

Wielding a sword, Sir Barlow ran to the dragon battle and set his feet as if looking for a chance to jump into the fray. Arramos swung around and slapped him away with his tail. Sir Barlow sailed to the sideline and rolled to the remains of the bleachers. Lauren and Marilyn sprinted to him and knelt at his side.

"Clefspeare," Merlin called through the swirling storm, "we are expecting a dimensional rift, but I have no idea what it will do."

He waved his staff. "Matt, work on Thigocia first. She can help with healing the other two."

Matt, Bonnie, and Listener rushed to Thigocia where she lay to the west of the portal. Matt spread his body over her head, while Listener stayed close, a white garment wrapped around her waist.

Arramos vaulted into the sky. Clefspeare gave chase, latched onto his tail, and slung him through the air. Arramos spread out his wings and banked back toward Clefspeare. Their eyebeams flashing, the two dragons blasted fire at each other. The flames deflected off their scales, and they collided shoulder to shoulder. Both dragons veered away and circled back for another clash.

While the dragons fought and two flying helicopters battled the weather, Bonnie backed away from Matt and summoned Excalibur's beam.

"Bonnie!" Billy limped toward her, the rifle in hand. "Did you remove the rubellite?"

"Got it in my pocket." She plunged the beam into the ground. A streak of radiance shot along the turf and drilled into Matt. He stiffened. Twin lights shot from his eyes and into a deep wound in Thigocia's face.

An explosion from above rocked the field. Chunks of metal rained down at the end zone on the west side. Walter's helicopter, now the only one in the sky, flew eastward and hovered over the portal. The gale-force wind slapped it time and again, but he kept it in place. He appeared to be maneuvering into position to get a missile shot at Arramos, but the danger of hitting Clefspeare was too high.

Bonnie shut off the beam and rested the sword's tip on the ground. "I think that should be enough."

Matt slowly peeled himself away from Thigocia. Listener helped him walk back a few steps. She pushed him to a seated position, caught rainwater, and splashed it into his face. Thigocia rose and shuffled toward Makaidos and Roxil, flapping her wings to provide lift.

Shrieks blistered the air. A mass of churning blackness descended from the clouds—drones. Billy aimed his rifle at the swarm and edged closer to Bonnie. "We've got drones!"

"I'm on it!" Bonnie raised the sword and whipped the beam skyward. The swarm scattered and swooped toward the ground.

Lauren and Marilyn helped Sir Barlow rise. He lumbered toward the transport helicopter, a hand on his bleeding head. "I will guard the children!"

"You'll need a pilot." Marilyn caught up with him and held his arm as they hurried.

Lauren ran toward Billy and threw fireballs at the descending drones, but the wind and rain blew the balls apart. Billy breathed flames at the attackers. When the flames sizzled and died, he fired the rifle again and again. Hitting the randomly flying creatures in such a windstorm seemed impossible.

The transport helicopter took off. A few drones flew after it, but it quickly zoomed out of reach.

Bonnie waved Excalibur back and forth. The beam struck a few drones, disintegrating them and delaying a mass attack. One drone flew into the portal plane. The protective field zapped it and sent it somersaulting backwards, its wings on fire.

Billy limped to Bonnie's side. Every inch of his body ached as he gasped for breath. "If you get tired … I'll take over."

Wet hair clung to her face as she searched for another target. "I'm fine. Maybe you can—"

A blast of white light ripped through the portal. A winged man burst out in the midst of the blast and rolled over the wet grass, extinguishing flames on his dark suit. White cloth covering his head and hands, he leaped up, tore the material away, and shouted toward the sky. "Attack now! Show courage! I will deal with Excalibur!"

"Tamiel!" Lauren stalked toward him. "I'll take care of him!"

Tamiel thrust his arms toward her. Raindrops scattered in front of a pressure wave that rocketed from his hands. It struck Lauren in the chest, knocked her down, and sent her skidding backwards across the saturated turf.

Billy blasted fire at Tamiel. The ground quaked. Billy staggered back, and Tamiel fell to his side.

A hole opened in the ground on the west side of the portal and expanded toward Matt and Listener. Billy shouted, "Matt! Watch out behind you!"

Matt leaped up and turned. The ground crumbled at Listener's feet. He grabbed for her wrist but missed. She toppled backwards and plunged into the void. Without a second's hesitation, he dove headfirst after her.

"Matt!" Bonnie dropped Excalibur, beat her wings, and surged toward the hole. A huge drone slammed into her chest and knocked her to the ground.

"Do not kill her!" Arramos shouted from the sky. "Just neutralize her!"

Billy scooped up Excalibur, summoned the beam, and ripped it through the drone. It burst into flames and exploded in sizzling globs of dark goo.

Clefspeare collided with Arramos again and drove him to the ground near the portal. There the two dragons wrestled with beating wings, gouging claws, and snapping teeth.

As Billy slashed through and disintegrated drones, he glanced at the other battles. Makaidos, Thigocia, and Roxil sat on their haunches and shot streams of fire at the flying horde. Closer to the portal, Lauren and Tamiel stood five paces apart and stared at each other as they sidestepped in a standoff circle, Tamiel with a dagger in his grip. Flames radiated around Lauren. Although they sizzled in the driving rain, they kept the drones away.

While Billy continued battling next to Bonnie, she rose to her feet and whispered, "Let's go!" Their heads low, they hurried to the side of the hole and looked down. Far in the depths, a white light pulsed. Swirling wind shot up and mixed with the falling rain.

A screeching drone attacked from above. Billy sliced through its midsection with Excalibur's blade, cleaving it in two. With a wave of the sword's beam over his head, he created a protective dome.

Sucking in quick breaths, he looked again into the dark shaft. "The abyss? Did it move here from the seventh door?"

"I think so." Bonnie's voice shattered as she spoke. "The sanctum's heart … was about right here … in Second Eden. Merlin said …" She shook water from her wings. "Never mind. I have to fly down there and save them."

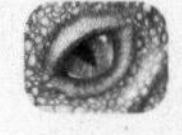

"But the wind! Gabriel couldn't fly in it. Even Roxil wasn't strong enough."

"Matt is our son! And every second counts!" Bonnie took Excalibur and shut off the beam and the dome. She stretched out her wings and leaped over the hole, but a blast of air blew her upward. A drone crashed into her side and sent her barreling into Billy. Their cheeks banged together, and Billy slammed onto the turf, smacking the back of his head.

He blinked at the driving rain. Dozens of dark-winged monsters flew in a swirl, barely visible against the clouds. A drone landed on his chest and exposed its dripping fangs. Billy commanded his arm to swat it away, but the muscles wouldn't respond.

The drone sank its fangs deep into his neck. A blade whipped by and sliced the drone in half. Bonnie shouted from somewhere, her call frantic. Billy opened his mouth to answer, but a pit of darkness engulfed his vision, and everything faded away.

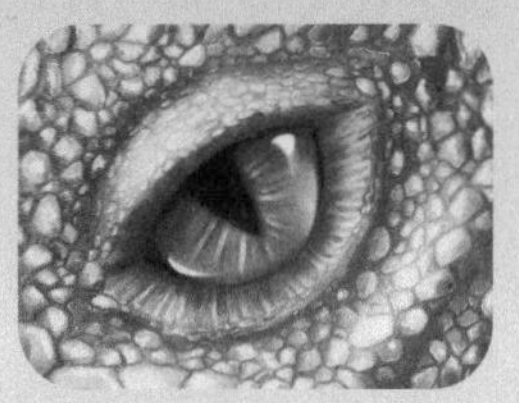

26

CHAPTER

The Abyss

Matt dove into the hole and knifed through a surge of rising wind. Illuminated by white light from below, Listener fell with her limbs splayed. Her horizontal position increased the striking surface for the upwelling air and slowed her plunge. The wind slapped her against one side of the surrounding wall, then whipped her to the other.

After several seconds, Matt, still in a vertical dive, fell to her level, shifted his body to horizontal to slow his descent, and caught her in his arms. As they fell together, protrusions dropped open from the wall's surface, like short drawbridges falling into place, making pathways leading to shallow recesses. Holding one arm around Listener's waist, Matt spread his other arm and legs to make their bodies into a sail.

The updraft slowed them further, but the swirling breeze sent them toward another collision. Just as they neared the wall, a rocky

drawbridge opened below. Matt pulled Listener and himself into a standing position and struck it with his feet, bending his knees to absorb the impact.

Pain shot into his heels, through his legs, and up his spine. When Listener's feet hit the protrusion, she cried out, then stifled herself.

Matt's knees buckled, and he dropped to his bottom. Again the impact sent a shock wave to his skull that jolted his brain.

After taking a moment to clear the fog, he whispered to Listener who now sat in his lap, his arm around her waist. "Are you hurt?" The cyclonic wind snatched his words away, but Listener wouldn't miss them.

She grimaced. "I think I broke my ankle."

"Just now?"

"No. When I slammed into the wall a few seconds ago." Listener rolled off his lap and knelt facing him. "Are you all right?"

Matt touched the wound on his neck. "This still hurts, and healing Thigocia took a lot out of me, but I don't think the landing injured anything. The wind slowed us down quite a bit. Otherwise I might have broken my legs. Or worse."

"I know. What you did was amazing. I thought we were both goners."

"Same here." Matt stretched out the tightness in his back. "Maybe we still are."

"Don't lose your confidence now." Listener looked up, terrible pain still evident in her eyes. "We must have fallen a thousand feet. I lost my spyglass when I slammed into the wall, so I can't look to see what's going on up there."

Matt followed her line of sight. Dim light shone through the hole's opening far above. Large raindrops fell down the center of the swirling wind. Smaller droplets were probably swept upward where they combined with others until they were heavy enough to fall through the less-turbulent center. "I don't think anyone can fly down through that wind. We'll have to climb."

"How? The wall is sheer."

Matt tapped his foot on the rock beneath them. "These protrusions jut out all over the place. They stay for a little while and then close again. This one's staying put because of our weight. I got a lot of experience while I was carrying Lauren's body."

"So you're hoping to climb up to one above us?" Listener scanned the abyss's cylindrical enclosure until her gaze stopped at the recess their drawbridge had been concealing before it opened. "Is that a tunnel?"

Matt peered inside. The shallow cave led to a bare wall. "Just a hole. It doesn't lead anywhere. Darcy and I found a tunnel behind one of those drawbridge rocks, so maybe we'll find another behind a different one."

Listener looked up again. "How can you know where and when a drawbridge is going to drop down?"

"You can't. You just have to watch and wait." Matt locked his gaze upward. After about twenty seconds, a protrusion dropped down four feet to their right and eight feet above. He could jump and reach it, and Listener probably could if not for her ankle, but reality squashed that possibility. Only two options came to mind—climbing to the top by himself and looking for a rope, or trying to carry her.

A mental image of hauling Lauren down this same abyss returned. That task was so grueling. And this time he would have to climb up. But if he went by himself, what would happen to Listener? Obviously drones wouldn't fly down this far, but would she be safe sitting here? Would her weight be enough to keep the drawbridge in place?

"I'm going to check something." Matt rose, leaped to the protrusion above, and grabbed the ledge with both hands. The bridge below began lifting. Listener slid toward the shallow cave. She pivoted and pushed with her good foot to get closer to the end, but her efforts did nothing to slow the rise.

Matt swung his legs back and dropped. His feet struck the angled drawbridge and slid toward Listener. The shift threw him off balance. Teetering, he flailed his arms. Listener lunged, wrapped her arms around his waist, and threw him down to the protrusion's surface. As the drawbridge rumbled back to its open position, she lay sprawled over his chest and let out a groaning whisper. "Let's not try that again."

"No argument from me." Matt helped her lift off his body and settle on her knees. "Thanks for saving me."

She winced as she smiled. "My pleasure."

"More damage to your ankle?"

"I don't think so. It's just a constant throb."

He nodded toward the recess, a cave deep enough to hold at least two people. "If I climb up, you could stay in there. You'll be fine until I can find a rope and harness."

"But what if it doesn't open when you come looking for me? How can you be sure it will ever open again?"

"I can't be sure." He crouched low. "All right. Get on my back."

"On your back? You can't possibly climb with that much weight."

"If I can climb this wall carrying a dead person I love, I can certainly do it with a living person I love." He gestured toward his back with a thumb. "Just trust me and get on."

The sound of rushing wind reigned for a moment, then Listener squeaked, "Matt?" She brushed tears from her cheeks. "Matt … I trust you … but …"

"But what?"

"Never mind." She crawled over him and straddled his back. "At least we'll be together, no matter what happens."

"We'll have to work together to survive this." When he rose, she wrapped her arms around his neck but kept pressure off his throat. "We're going to jump and try to ride the updraft like we did before. Maybe it will give us a boost."

"So we jump spread eagle to increase our surface area."

"Right, but I have no idea how much lift we'll get, so …" Matt heaved a sigh. "If we drop another thousand feet, we'll just start over."

Tightening her leg embrace around him, she leaned over his shoulder and pressed her cheek against his. "I'm ready. Let me know if there's any way I can help."

"Just play it by ear. Do whatever you can to help me climb." Matt raised his arms and leaped. The wind helped but not much. His forearms slapped over the protrusion and caught hold. As Listener's weight dragged him down, he pulled upward. A spasm knotted one bicep. His hands cramped, and tremors shook his already-weakened body. He growled under his breath, "Giving up … is not an option!"

"Let's do this." Listener shifted on his back, grabbed the ledge with both hands, and released him. Now dangling on her own, she shouted, "Swing up! Then help me!"

Matt fought off the pain and swung his legs to the protrusion. After bracing on his knees, he grabbed Listener's wrists and hauled her to the top of the ledge. When they stood together, they embraced, Listener balancing on one foot. Wind swept through Matt's clothes and cooled his sweaty body.

He looked up. The opening at the top didn't seem any closer, still far, far away. That painful ordeal was just one step. How many more would they have to climb? And would each step be within reach?

Listener sat with her legs extended. "Rest, Matt." She grasped his hand and pulled. "We have time. Who knows? Maybe someone will rescue us."

"With that battle going on up there?" Matt lowered himself to a cross-legged position. "Did you see all the drones?"

"I saw them." She took his hand in hers and looked at the wall of the abyss. She stayed quiet for almost a minute before saying, "Thank you."

Matt lifted his brow. "For what?"

"For what?" Listener turned toward him, her expression incredulous. "Are you serious?"

"Uh … sure. I mean …" He cocked his head. "Why wouldn't I be?"

"Matt, are you really so blind to your own courage and chivalry?" She glanced upward briefly. "The Father of Lights as my witness, you've been doing nothing but risking your life for me at every turn. You saved me from drowning, you carried me through a freakish ice storm, you slept by a cold window instead of in a comfortable bed, you stayed at my side every possible moment while we trudged through a land covered by ice, you gave your bodily energy to heal my stab wound, and then …" She laughed under her breath, though tears streamed down her cheeks. "Then you dove headfirst into a bottomless pit. Bottomless! The great abyss itself!"

She grasped his wrist. "Matt, you didn't hesitate. You didn't for one second think about what might happen to you. You cared only about me. You were ready to die to save me, even though you had no idea how you could do it."

"Well …" Matt slid his wrist away and regrasped her hand. "Is that so strange? You're worth dying for."

Listener lifted his hand and kissed his knuckles, then looked into his eyes. "The last time I kissed a man's knuckles …" She licked her dry, cracking lips. "It was Timothy. I was hoping to sacrifice myself, but he died for me instead. He took away my corrupted companion and gave me the ability to speak. And now God used your sacrifices to take away my other companion and give me the ability to hear the voice of God. You didn't die for me, but you were willing to." She laid a palm on his chest. "When I was that little girl who wanted to die, I learned how to measure a man's heart. Your willingness to sacrifice proves that yours is as big as Earth or Second Eden."

He let her beautiful words sink in. Without a doubt, she was the most amazing girl he had ever met. "Thank you, Listener. And I think you're—"

"No." She set a finger to his lips. "No reciprocation. Just enjoy the gift of heartfelt words." She pulled the Cracker-Jacks ring from his pinky and slid it onto her ring finger. After gazing at it for a moment, she set her hand on top of his. "I trust that you understand my gesture."

He looked at the ring—Darcy's, left behind when she gave her life in Jade's sanctum. Now it was a symbol of sacrifice, passed on from the giver to the receiver, cheap tin representing pure gold. It meant *I am willing to die for you.*

Matt whispered, "I understand."

A drawbridge opened above, this step a somewhat bigger leap than the previous one.

"Well …" Listener angled her head and looked at the new protrusion. "Shall we try for it?"

Matt shifted closer to her. "Let's have a look at the break."

She pulled up a pant cuff, revealing a swollen, bruised ankle. "It's pretty bad."

"And the pain?"

"Excruciating." She offered a pain-streaked smile. "But I'm getting used to that."

"We'll rest. We have to get stronger for the next step." He ran a finger lightly over the bruise. "When I get some strength back, I'll try my healing touch."

"And if that doesn't work?"

Matt pulled the pant cuff back down. "The battle up there can't last forever. Someone will eventually find us. We'll just hope that a friend finds us first."

Bonnie swung Excalibur and slashed at the drone on Billy's chest. The blade sliced the scaly buzzard in half and left the head and upper body still clinging to Billy's neck. Using the tip of the blade, she pried its jaws loose and slung its limp corpse away.

As more drones flew toward them, Bonnie summoned the beam and created a protective dome over herself and Billy. The attackers slammed against it, sizzled for a moment, and flew away screeching. She set a finger on Billy's neck and felt for a pulse. It thrummed erratically. At least he was alive, but for how long?

Near the middle of the field, Clefspeare and Arramos continued clawing, biting, and thrashing. Arramos's movements seemed slower now. Maybe the battle was finally nearing an end.

A few steps from the dragons, Merlin swung his staff this way and that, smacking drone after drone. At least fifty of the dark monsters covered Makaidos, Thigocia, and Roxil. In their weakened states, they could no longer do battle. Only their scales protected them now.

Closer to Bonnie, Adam lay on the ground, covered with several black beasts, his head and feet the only parts in view. Lauren, shielded by her own dome of fire, ran to him, ignited the drones, and kicked the flaming bodies away one by one.

Now free from any threat by Lauren, Tamiel called out, "Allies of Arramos! To his aid! Attack the white dragon as a group! He cannot fight all of you at once!"

Arramos appeared next to Tamiel and shouted to the drones, "No! I am here! That battle between me and the white dragon is an illusion. It is being staged to lure you to your doom!"

Whipping blades drew Bonnie's gaze upward. A helicopter hovered about fifty feet overhead. Walter sat in the front, and a young woman with white hair perched on the rear seat, leaning out and pointing some kind of device at the ground. She had to be Jennifer.

"Our real enemy is the helicopter!" the new Arramos continued. "It is preparing to shoot all of you! Attack it immediately!"

As the drones beat their wings and rose, Tamiel shouted, "Very well! Destroy the helicopter! Then return for further orders!"

Jennifer jerked herself inside and closed the hatch. The new Arramos vanished, but the dark horde didn't seem to notice. As the helicopter backed away over a nearby forest, its machine guns ripped into them with a spray of bullets. Scales flew. Black goo splattered. Drone corpses dropped to the ground by the dozens.

When the shooting ceased, the remaining enemy attackers swarmed the fuselage and beat at the windows with claws and wings. The helicopter spun and flew away with the horde still clinging.

With the drones temporarily out of the way, Bonnie shut off Excalibur. She felt Billy's neck again—hot and clammy, but the pulse thrummed on. Lauren dragged Adam close. Bonnie embraced her. Warmth radiated from Lauren's skin and clothes. "The girl in the helicopter is Jennifer," Lauren whispered. "She's disguised as Sapphira."

Bonnie nodded. "I saw Jennifer and her mother in the ovulum."

As growls and roars from the dragon battle continued, Lauren pulled away from Bonnie. Tears flowed down cheeks and chin. "All three of our dragons are down again, and the man I dragged over here is alive, but he has bites all over."

"His name is Adam, an old friend." Bonnie glanced at the trio of dragons lying in deepening puddles of water and blood. "We need a healer, but Matt dove into the abyss—"

"I saw." Lauren's eyes closed, but tears seeped out. "Go and see about him. I'll check the portal. Ashley might be at the birthing garden by now. Maybe we can get some of our wounded out of here."

Just as Bonnie turned to fly, a loud roar made her stop. At midfield, Clefspeare rammed Arramos into the ground and raked claws across his belly's vulnerable spot. Dark blood spewed and spilled to the ground. Arramos flailed to free himself, but Clefspeare clamped down on his neck with a rear claw and pinned him.

"Cease fighting!" Clefspeare gasped for breath. "You are defeated!"

As rain continued falling in torrents, Arramos growled. "My horde will return, and they will bring greater numbers. And even if you kill this body, you cannot kill me. I am Lucifer, the most magnificent of all the angels. I will escape this borrowed shell and live on."

Merlin walked toward Clefspeare, blood smeared across his bearded face. He withdrew the ovulum from a cloak pocket and spoke toward it. "Conquest has been accomplished." He inhaled a tight, wheezing breath. "If you have finished with your other business, come to the portal site as soon as you can."

Bonnie flew toward the abyss. No time to ask Merlin about who might be coming. When she arrived, she slid Excalibur behind her belt. As before, wind surged forth in a powerful, swirling updraft that sent water droplets flying out as quickly as they dropped in.

Below, the white strobe still pulsed. She leaned over and squinted. Here and there, rocky projections lowered from the wall, like drawbridges on hinges, while others lifted to a closed position. Could Matt or Listener have fallen onto one of them? Billy had mentioned that these projections led to recesses in the wall. Maybe they could have survived the plunge.

She straightened and took in a deep breath. It was a long shot, but she had to give it a try. "Lord," she whispered, "catch me in your loving hands." After collapsing her wings as tightly as possible, she leaped in. The wind caught her body and slowed her fall to a fluttering swirl, as if she were a leaf twirling toward the ground.

As she descended, the flat of Excalibur's blade whipped against her leg. She reached and held it in place. With each spin around the cylinder, she drew closer and closer to the wall. She extended a wing now and then to turn back toward the center of the spiral.

Within seconds, dizziness took over. She collided with the wall and bounced off. Pain shot into her shoulder. She shook her head hard to clear the fog. Another collision like that might knock her out cold.

Edging closer to the perimeter again, she spread her wings fully, turned her body, and struck the wall with her feet. After pushing off, she battled the wind by opening and closing her wings in short bursts. Every time she opened them, the updraft surged into the canopies and sent a ripping sensation through her mainstays, but being able to control the plunge made the pain worthwhile.

Soon, two figures came into view below as they sat on a protrusion. One of them stood and held out his arms. "Mom! Over here!"

Bonnie guided her body that way, folded in her wings, and collided with him. The force sent him sprawling backwards, and they tumbled together into the recess.

"Gotta stop the bridge from closing." Matt disentangled himself from her and crawled out to the protrusion, now at a slight angle. When he joined Listener at the far end, it lowered into place once more.

Listener extended a hand. "Can you come out here?"

"I think so." Bonnie shuffled on hands and knees, Excalibur dragging on the stone. When she drew close, she sat in a triangle with them, Matt to her left and Listener to her right. Wind whistled all around, lifting Bonnie's wings. Pain from the movement made her wince.

Listener touched one of the canopies. "You have tiny rips all over the place."

"I feel every one of them." Bonnie looked at Matt and Listener in turn. "Are you two all right?"

"Exhausted." Matt nodded toward Listener's leg. "We think her ankle's broken. I tried healing it a minute ago, but I'm out of gas."

"We climbed up here from another one of these drawbridges," Listener said, "but the next higher one is farther up. Besides, it's closed now, and it hasn't opened in a while."

"I could carry you." Bonnie tested her wings. Each flap ignited a new peal of pain. "Well, maybe one at a time from bridge to bridge."

Matt shook his head. "Not with the pain you're in. Even if you could carry us that far, it would take forever. You'd be exhausted before the second bridge. And the person left behind would get stuck behind the protrusion when it closes."

"You're probably right." Bonnie rose. As her legs straightened, Excalibur's point again dragged on the stone. She withdrew the sword, summoned the blade's glow, and gazed at the battling dragons etched in the metal. "Let's see if we can come up with another way to escape."

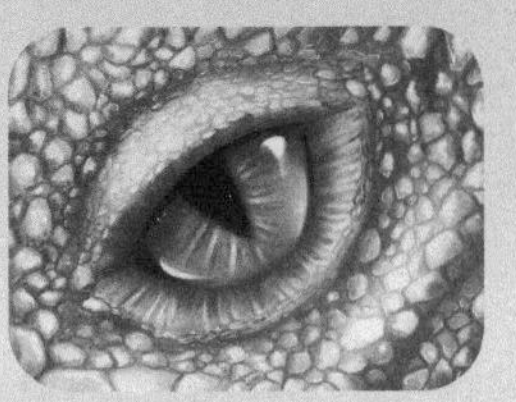

27

CHAPTER

An Oracle's Blood

Lauren trudged across the wet, muddy field toward the portal. Rain continued falling, though now a heavy drizzle instead of a downpour. They needed a healer, and Ashley was the only one left, but would she be at the birthing garden yet? Since Dad and Adam had been bitten by drones, they might not last much longer. And what about Mom? Could she somehow fly out of the abyss?

As Lauren passed Clefspeare, he shifted his weight on Arramos. The conquered dragon bled from a belly wound, obviously too weak to protest. Clefspeare and Merlin spoke in low whispers. Their buzzing conversation penetrated the persistent wind and entered Lauren's sensitive ears.

"I need to find Marilyn," Clefspeare said.

Merlin patted his scaly white neck. "Patience, my friend. We have one more step to accomplish."

"Should I attempt to capture Tamiel?"

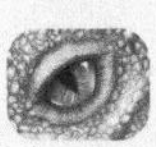

Merlin shook his head. "He would simply fly away, and we cannot afford to have you chase him in air pursuit. You must keep Arramos down."

Lauren tuned out the conversation and focused straight ahead. At the portal, Tamiel pushed his arm through the plane, but it stayed in the Earth realm. As she drew close, he glared at her. Fangs descended over his lower lip, his wings expanded, and he brandished a serrated dagger. "If you have come to kill me, I will not be easy to catch this time."

Lauren ignited a fireball in each palm. As they crackled in the drizzling rain, she raised one in a throwing stance. "Just back off."

"By all means." Tamiel sidestepped a few paces away and gestured toward the portal with his blade. "Be my guest."

Lauren dropped the fireballs and halted in front of the portal. A sense of sadness crept in, and her vision altered. Every detail in Tamiel's face clarified. His pupils dilated, and the corner of his lip twitched, belying his cocksure words. Her back scales tingled like an electric jolt. Tamiel's thoughts streamed in, delivered with a virulent bite. *Enjoy your moment of victory. It will not last long.*

She shook the invading thoughts away and focused on the portal. With Tamiel near, opening it for passage was too risky, but maybe a peek into Second Eden would be safe. She waved her arms and created a wall of flames. As she concentrated on the dividing plane, the birthing garden came into view.

Mendallah carried a burning torch that illuminated the area. Zohar stood nearby, a blanket-wrapped infant in his arms, but there was no sign of Ashley, Eagle, Dr. Conner, or the two dragons. No healer was available yet.

A series of loud whistles drilled into Lauren's ears. She extinguished the flames and spun. Tamiel looked skyward, two fingers at the edges of his mouth as the whistles continued in shrill warbles.

"He's calling the drones!" Lauren shouted.

Keeping a rear claw on Arramos, Clefspeare launched a fireball that splashed against Tamiel. The flames dispersed in the driving rain, and his wet clothes merely smoldered.

"As long as Arramos lives, I will live, unless Lauren touches me. And you know what will happen if she dares to take that step." Tamiel backpedaled and stretched out his wings. "I shall return with my allies."

"No!" Lauren lunged at him. He swiped at her with his dagger. The blade sliced across her left palm. When she recoiled, he leaped into the air and flew over the field's perimeter fence. Soon, he soared above a nearby wooded area and faded into the veil of rain.

Her palm stinging, Lauren eyed the woods. That was the same direction Walter had taken the helicopter. She looked at the wound, a gash from the base of her thumb to her pinky, not deep but painful. Blood trickled to the heel of her hand and mixed with the falling rain. It probably wouldn't need stitches.

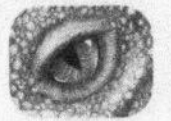

The squish of feet on wet turf entered her ears. A woman slogged across the field toward the portal, her head low. When she arrived, she stopped at Lauren's side and extended a hand. "Elizabeth Hamilton."

"So you're Jennifer's mother." Lauren shook her hand. "I'm Lauren Bannister."

"You look different from the photograph I have seen." Elizabeth gestured toward Dad and Adam. "They're both still alive, but Adam is near death." She looked toward the woods in the direction Walter's helicopter had fled. "My understanding is that you are a Listener. Do you hear anything out there? I'm concerned about my daughter."

"I'll check." Lauren trained her ears in that direction. Rain pelted leaves, and wind brushed against branches—way too much background noise. She tried to tune it out and focus on anything unusual.

After a few moments, a steady cadence of rustling noises emanated from the trees. "Someone walking, I think." Two figures trudged out, their bodies caked with mud from head to toe. The shorter of the two supported the taller with a shoulder. Once in the clear, they picked up their pace, mud dripping as the rain washed it away. By the time they arrived, their identities became clear—Walter and Jennifer.

Elizabeth grasped Lauren's arm. "They survived!"

After helping each other climb over the perimeter fence, Walter limped onto the field while Jennifer held his arm. When they stopped near the portal, Walter shook his head hard and slung mud into the air. "That's an escape I don't want to try again."

"Brilliant!" Jennifer clenched a fist. "It was the coolest escape ever!"

Elizabeth embraced her. "How in the world did you do it?"

Jennifer drew back and looked at Walter. "Piece of cake."

"A piece of concrete cake." Walter set his hand in a horizontal position. "We were hovering over a bog. While Jennifer unloaded the machine guns into the drones, I programmed the autopilot. I guess everyone was occupied with watching the drones getting blown to bits or maybe you'd have seen us open the hatch and jump into the bog. The chopper flew away on its own, and those freaks chased it just like we hoped."

Jennifer punched Walter's arm. "This guy is the king of crazy. I mean, who else would come up with an insane idea like that? And it worked!"

"I got the idea from when Billy, Gabriel, Ashley, and I jumped from a helicopter to escape Tamiel's goons. Bogs are great cushions, but that's the last one for me." Walter peeled a dirty leaf from his cheek. "I hope."

Elizabeth ran trembling hands through Jennifer's mud-streaked hair. "And no more jumping out of helicopters for you, young lady." A smile broke through. "Unless, of course, you're being chased by drones again. Then we'll make an exception."

Walter brushed mud from his clothes and looked around. "So what happened here? Where is everyone?"

Lauren grasped his wrist. "First, let's check the abyss." As she led him at a limping pace toward the gaping hole, she summarized the recent happenings in rapid-fire fashion. By the time they reached the edge, she had finished the tale.

Walter pursed his lips. "So we have no healer, but we can escape to Second Eden before Tamiel gets back. We'll have to round up our wounded. Now that the drones are gone, I think Marilyn will be back soon. She'll want to check on Jared."

"We'll signal the helicopter!" Elizabeth called as she and Jennifer ran toward the remains of the bleachers.

Lauren looked down into the abyss. No sign of Mom, Matt, or Listener. Walter clasped her shoulder. "Don't give up hope. Remember who's down there. Your mother is a warrior's warrior."

Sniffing, Lauren nodded. "So are Matt and Listener."

"Come on." Walter pulled on her arm. "Let's check on Billy and Adam."

As Lauren sloshed alongside Walter, it seemed that the abyss pulled her back. With the possibility that her mother, Matt, and Listener needed her help, how could she turn away?

When they arrived, Walter checked Billy's vitals while Lauren knelt next to Adam. After brushing away rainwater that had pooled in his eye sockets, she set a finger on his neck next to a pair of fang marks. No pulse.

Barely able to avoid squeaking, she breathed out, "Adam's dead."

Walter's shoulders slumped. "God help us."

Lauren slid her hand into his. "How's my dad?"

He lifted his fingers from Billy's throat. "Pulse is weak. He's hanging in there. … Barely."

The buzz of propellers cut through the storm. The transport helicopter descended, swaying back and forth in the wind. When it landed about twenty yards away, Walter grabbed Billy's arms and hoisted him over his shoulder. "Let's gather everyone to the chopper. We'll fly through the portal, maybe rig up something to haul the dragons."

Elizabeth and Jennifer ran back onto the field and joined Lauren. When Lauren told them the bad news about Adam, they stood and stared at him. Rain fell over their already-saturated forms. After a silent moment, Elizabeth bent over and grasped Adam's wrists. "Jennifer and I will transport him to the helicopter. Perhaps you can see if our dragons are ambulatory." Jennifer grabbed Adam's ankles, and the two carried him away.

Lauren walked to the three dragons, her bare feet slowed by water and mud. She leaned close to each motionless dragon and listened for breathing, but the whipping wind, splashing rain, and the transport chopper overwhelmed all other sounds. The blades kept whirring even while Walter and Sir Barlow hoisted Dad and Adam into the passenger compartment.

"They are here!" Merlin called as he pointed at the sky.

A black dragon descended toward the field, a bearded rider on its back. Lauren breathed a whispered, "Abaddon!"

As Abaddon circled overhead, he dropped thick chains from his rear claws. They splashed down next to Clefspeare and Arramos. When Abaddon landed, his rider waved. "Hail, Merlin!"

Merlin returned the wave. "Hail, Enoch!"

Enoch slid down from Abaddon's back and walked gingerly to Merlin. "That was a ride I will not recommend to others. It was a nightmare."

"A necessary nightmare." Abaddon sneezed twin streams of sparks. When he recovered, he turned toward Arramos. "It seems that Satan now sings scales of a sober sort."

"Indeed." Enoch withdrew a massive padlock from a tunic pocket. "Let us proceed with our appointed duty."

Merlin looked toward the forest. "Yes, the horde of darkness will return soon."

Abaddon picked up one end of the chain and tossed it over Arramos's body. With help from Clefspeare, Merlin, and Enoch, he bound Arramos from tail to snout and set the padlock to fasten the ends of the chain together.

"What are you going to do with him?" Lauren asked.

Abaddon picked up the chain with a foreclaw. "Hurl him headlong into an abyss of adversity."

"But he has wings. Won't he get out when he heals?"

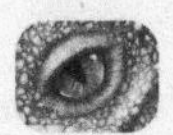

Enoch shook the chain. "Not after Abaddon seals the top." He gestured toward the abyss. "Let us go."

With Merlin and Enoch leading the way, Abaddon dragged Arramos through the mud while Clefspeare walked alongside and kept a close watch on the conquered dragon.

Lauren caught up with Merlin and Enoch. "You can't seal the abyss yet. My mother, Matt, and Listener are down there. We need to rescue them."

"I know," Enoch said. "Merlin told me while we were binding Arramos." They stopped at the edge of the abyss. "Bonnie is the only one who has a chance to return, and even her chances are slim. The wind is a monstrous enemy of anything winged."

Abaddon dropped the chain. "We will wait. Bonnie Bannister has overcome obstacles of mightier magnitude."

"You're right." Merlin leaned against his staff. "But I have no doubt that Tamiel will be anxious to save his master. He will return soon with his horde."

Lauren looked down. Warm wind blew her hair back and dried her eyes. She blinked, then squinted. The rock projections Matt had mentioned lowered and rose, but they proved to be the only movements below.

Walter hobbled to her side. "What's the status?"

Lauren whispered, "We're waiting to see if my ..." She stifled an emerging sob. "My mother, my brother, and Listener—"

"I get the picture. They can't throw Satan in the rabbit hole until our bunnies pop out."

Lauren forced a smile. Walter was trying hard to lighten the mood. "But I don't see them. Just those rocks that fall down and come back up."

Walter peered into the hole. "Yeah. Your father called them drawbridges. They do look sort of like that."

Lauren gazed at him. Clotted blood marked a deep scratch from his ear to the bridge of his nose, and blood soaked the lower portion of a pant leg. "How is Dad doing now?"

"Not good. We can't wait much longer. We have to get him and the dragons through the portal."

"But the dragons are too—"

"Back!" Walter grabbed Lauren's arm and pulled her away from the edge of the abyss. "Everyone stand back!"

A laser beam shot up through the hole and into the clouds. It waved in a small circle for a moment, then disappeared.

Walter smiled. "I saw something flash. I guessed Excalibur's beam might be coming."

"So my mother must be all right." Lauren leaned close to the edge again and strained to pierce the darkness with her vision. A cry filtered into her ears. Seconds later, a scream erupted from the pit. Mom burst out with her wings fully spread and her hands clutching something tightly. The wind threw her to the ground, and she rolled over and over, her tattered and torn wings flopping in the mud. She stopped on her side with her mouth in a dirty puddle.

Lauren ran to her and turned her face up. "Mom! Are you all right?"

She blinked at Lauren and whispered, "I made it."

"Yes! Yes! You did!" Lauren wiped mud from her lips. "Did you see Matt and Listener?"

Slowly loosening her fingers, Mom opened her hands, revealing Merlin's candlestone. As pain shot through Lauren's body, she grimaced.

"Sorry." Mom closed her hand around the gem. "Matt and Listener are in here." She swallowed, and her whisper diminished. "We have to take it to Ashley. She can get them out."

Lauren looked at her mother's belt. It held no sword. "Where is Excalibur?"

"Gone. I dropped it. I'm sorry. I just couldn't hold on while I was—"

"It's okay. It's fine." Lauren blocked the rain with a hand to keep it out of her mother's eyes. "You and Matt and Listener survived. That's all I care about."

Walter splashed to them and knelt in the mud. "Bonnie, first of all, Billy's hanging in there. We put him in the transport helicopter."

"Good. Thank you."

"And second …" He grinned. "You've dropped Excalibur before. Haven't you?"

She smiled weakly. "I thought you might mention that."

"I didn't want to disappoint you." Walter grasped her wrist. "Want to try to get up?"

"Yes. Thank you."

"Lauren," Enoch called from the abyss. "We need you."

"Coming." Lauren sloshed to him. "What can I do?"

Enoch touched her medallion necklace. Lifting the chain, he drew the nearly invisible key over her head. "I need this to seal Arramos inside."

"Is it the key to the abyss?"

"Actually, *I* am the ultimate key. This key to the seventh door enables me to do what I must now do." Enoch nodded at Abaddon. "Throw him in."

Abaddon beat his wings, latched on to the chains with his rear claws, and lifted Arramos over the abyss. Still bleeding from the belly wound, he dangled within the tight bonds.

"Stop!" Tamiel descended from the sky and landed in front of Lauren. Paler than ever, he wobbled from side to side. His scalp was visible through gaps in his hair, and deep wrinkles pinched his face. He glared at Lauren with bleeding black eyes. "I suspect that you touched me at some point, but I fail to understand why I am deteriorating and you are not." He pointed upward. "Release my master and tell me what you did to me, or I will unleash my horde upon you all."

While Abaddon settled to the ground with Arramos, everyone looked up. A mass of winged beasts approached from about a hundred yards away. They would arrive in seconds.

Lauren stealthily looked at her palm. As blood trickled from the gash, Sapphira's words returned to mind. *Anyone who sheds the blood of an Oracle of Fire dies soon afterward.*

"Answer me!" Tamiel lifted his hand. "Or I will touch you and wrap you in the coils of death with me."

Lauren aimed her palms at him. "I have a better idea. I'll send you to the hellfire that spawned you." She shouted, "Inferno!"

Tamiel's hair burst into flames. Lauren grabbed Merlin's staff and thrust it into Tamiel's chest. He toppled into the hole and plummeted out of sight.

"Quick!" Lauren said to Abaddon. "Drop Arramos on top of Tamiel, or he might fly out."

Abaddon launched again, lifted Arramos, and released him into the abyss. Abaddon landed at the side and blasted a stream of fire around the top of the pit. The edges collapsed into concentric circular stairs that descended and met several feet below the surface.

Lauren looked up. The drones flew in a circle almost directly above. Their erratic flights made them appear confused, perhaps because of Tamiel's sudden disappearance. The delay might not last long.

"We must make haste." Enoch extended his hand. "Merlin. The ovulum."

When Merlin handed over the ovulum, Enoch hurried down the stairs, stood at the center, and looked to the sky. "Father above, I have served you for thousands of years, and how I have longed to enter your presence." He lifted the key to the seventh door. "You have bestowed upon me the seven virtues represented in this key, and in your ultimate wisdom, you will use it to usher me to your throne."

Lauren chewed on her lip. Maybe this formality was necessary, but with venomous drones circling above, the pomp felt like rearranging furniture while the house was burning down.

Red lightning streaked across the sky, followed by a ground-shaking rumble of thunder. "Red is the color of humility." Enoch set the ovulum at the very center and knelt with his hands on the orb, the key in his grasp. "So now I kneel before you and these witnesses. Do what you must to seal the enemy of souls in this abyss and take me home to be with you. Here at the sunset of days, fulfill the final prophecies and be the lightning that comes from the East and flashes into the West."

A white lightning bolt streaked from the clouds and blasted into Enoch. Lauren and the others fell backwards in the shock wave. Above, the drones scattered in every direction.

When Lauren scrambled back to the edge, Enoch was gone. A transparent shimmer ran along the top of the stairway from edge to edge. With each drop of rain, a color appeared where it fell, and the color followed the droplet as it sizzled and danced toward the edge of the shield as if pushed along by an electrostatic impulse. Thousands of drops raised thousands of dots of color—red, blue, green, yellow, and more.

Lauren's legs buckled. She dropped to her knees and stared at the beautiful yet tragic site. Enoch! Why? So much death. So much sorrow. *When will it all end?*

"The drones are regrouping," Clefspeare growled. "I think they will delay no longer."

Using Merlin's staff, Lauren forced herself to rise. She had no choice. It was time to fight once more.

As Merlin looked at the sky, his expression sagged. "We have insufficient weapons. Two dragons and an Oracle of Fire against perhaps hundreds of drones."

Walter pointed skyward. "They're coming."

The mass descended with claws extended and fangs exposed.

"It's time to fight!" Walter picked up a rifle that dripped with muddy water and stood next to Lauren and her mother. "Give us cover!"

While Clefspeare and Abaddon blasted fire at the approaching beasts, Lauren tossed the staff to Merlin and created a shield of swirling flames around herself, Mom, and Walter. Big gaps appeared in the swirls. She pushed harder to make more flames, but the gaps expanded to reveal more and more of the world outside her shield.

Walter aimed at the winged beasts and pulled the trigger, but the rifle jammed. "Merlin!" Walter shouted. "Take cover with us!"

Merlin ducked low and ran. A drone crashed claws first into his shoulders and knocked him flat. The drones flocked over him like vultures.

"Merlin!" Mom cried.

She took a step toward him, but Walter pulled her back. "Not yet. Let the dragons thin them out first."

Clefspeare shot a stream of fire at the drones atop Merlin, setting them ablaze. Abaddon blew flames all around and incinerated dozens of the slower attackers.

"Now!" Walter shouted.

Lauren extinguished the shield. Mom and Walter ran to Merlin. While Mom checked on him, Walter used his rifle as a bat and smacked drones away. Lauren joined in and pointed at one beast after another, igniting them with fire, but the flames seemed smaller with each burst.

A drone rushed past Walter's swing, pounced on Mom, and bit her shoulder. Walter jerked it away and stomped on its head, but too late. Mom fell to the side and lay over Merlin.

"Mom!" Lauren straddled her and Merlin and created a new fire shield, but it had more gaps than the previous one. Still, it was enough to keep the beasts at bay for now.

The battle raged on. At the transport helicopter, the whirring blades kept most of the drones at bay. Sir Barlow stood near its door and hacked with his sword at any attackers that made it past the propeller. A huge drone rode Clefspeare's head and gouged at his eyes. Another did the same to Abaddon. More drones swarmed both dragons, pulling away from their attack on Lauren and Walter.

Walter stormed toward the battle, his fists tight.

"No!" Lauren doused her fire shield, ran to Walter, and pulled him back. "It's no use. They'll just kill you."

"I have never given up in a fight," he growled. "I'm not about to—"

A shout and a trumpet blast filled the heavens. From the east, the clouds parted, giving way to brilliant light. In the midst of the shining divide, a white horse galloped across the sky, its rider bright and blinding as they drew near.

The drones flew to the west like shadows fleeing the sun.

Walter let out a whoop. "It's Dikaios!"

The white horse looked his way and gave a brief nod of acknowledgment.

Now able to see past the brilliance, Lauren focused on the rider. He had eyes like flames and wore a robe that seemed to drip blood. A string of foreign words emblazoned the material.

"You are safe now," Dikaios said. "My master and I will pursue the horde and give them what they deserve."

The rider bowed his head toward Walter and Lauren. Although his lips didn't move, whispered words trickled into Lauren's ears. "Well done, my friends. All will be well, and I will see you again."

Dikaios galloped away and rose into the air as his rider pointed toward the west.

Walter scooped up Lauren's mother and set his ear close to her mouth. "She's breathing."

"Thank God." Lauren looked to the west. The light of the rider still shone in the distance. "Thank you for everything."

Abaddon set his snout next to Merlin and sniffed. "The primeval prophet has passed and has hastened to Heaven's halls." He grasped Merlin's cloak with his claws and spread his wings. "My mission is no more, so I bid you good-bye." With a flapping burst, he leaped up and flew away with Merlin.

"Good-bye, Abaddon," Lauren whispered as she watched him ascend. "Good-bye, Merlin."

Clefspeare splashed closer. Although the rain had stopped, deep puddles covered the entire field. He looked up. "Master Merlin?"

"He's gone." Lauren stroked Clefspeare's neck scales—smooth and wet. "Were you and Merlin close friends?"

"Very close." Clefspeare blinked through tears. "Yet I cannot tarry to grieve. We should all escape to Second Eden immediately. I sense danger of a magnitude that I have never experienced before. Wrath. Pure and righteous. I cannot say if anyone in its path will be spared."

Lauren nodded. "I'll open the portal. Please gather everyone, including the children and whoever is taking care of them."

"Consider it done." Clefspeare flew toward the parking lot.

Walter walked alongside Lauren, her mother in his arms. When they reached the portal, Lauren waved her hands over her head and created the usual fiery vortex. Within seconds, her vision penetrated the plane. Ashley paced back and forth just a few steps away while Eagle stood nearby, his arms crossed over his chest. At least a dozen torches protruded from the ground and lit up the garden where a hundred plants had sprouted. The praying leaves already bulged with new Second Edeners.

Air rushed into Lauren's lungs. What a beautiful sight! But where had the babies come from? Had the souls of the children murdered on Earth gone directly to the garden?

She looked at Walter and gave him a tired smile. "Ashley's there. I can take you and my mother and return for the others. But I'll have to bring Ashley back with me to heal people until they're, as Elizabeth put it, ambulatory. We have to move fast."

Walter gave her a nod. "Sounds perfect. Beam us home."

"Our new home." Lauren lowered the flaming curtain, blocking her view of Earth's ravaged landscape. "Let's see what it has in store for us."

Matt stood with Listener in the candlestone's shadowy chamber. Colorful sparks of light floated around like multicolored fireflies flitting about. Their own bodies glowed with white light, though not enough to illuminate this place beyond a shade of dark gray.

When they first entered, Matt's energy form had been vague and filled with static, but after heeding his mother's advice to stay perfectly calm, the static settled, and his limbs and fingers took shape.

Listener, her own glowing form clear, sat on the crystalline floor. She patted the space next to her. "It's a good time to talk, don't you think?"

"I don't see why not." He settled to the spot. "What about?"

"About you and me." She smiled. "If that's not too forward."

"Not at all. I prefer being open about everything."

She pulled her legs up, wrapped her arms around her knees, and gazed at the twinkling colors. "I hope you will forgive me."

"Forgive you? For what?"

"Because I have been … how do you say it on Earth? Dragging your heart around?"

Matt let out a soft laugh. "I guess that's one way of putting it. But how do you think you've been doing that?"

She looked straight at him. "I am familiar with the differences between our cultures, and I realize that my affectionate ways have been alluring to you as well as confusing, especially when I suddenly became aloof from time to time."

"Well …" He ran a fingertip across the glassy floor. "I did feel like you were sending mixed signals."

"That was my fault. I should have known better than to show such affection, considering that I was not open to accepting a suitor, especially one from Earth who would misinterpret my touches as being something other than casual and nonromantic in nature."

"Okay …" Matt swallowed. The static in his hands returned. He had to calm down, but this conversation wasn't going in the direction he had hoped. "I understand, and I forgive you. I guess … I guess I don't mind just being friends. You could be like a sister."

"A sister?" She laid her glowing hand on his cheek. The sensation sent a tingle throughout his nebulous body. "That is an option I do not wish to consider, Matt Bannister."

"What? What do you mean?"

"We are now of truth the same, followers of the Messiah. We possess the same spirit, so we are compatible in every way." She slid her hand into his. "If it pleases you, I would like to pursue a courtship arrangement with you."

"But you said—"

"I said I *was* not open to accepting a suitor, because I didn't believe that any man I knew could be strong and sacrificial enough, but after watching you all these hours, I changed my mind. You are the greatest hero I have ever seen. So … again … if it pleases you—"

"It definitely pleases me!" New static ran through Matt's energy. "You're the most amazing girl I can imagine."

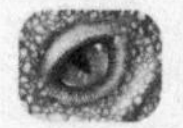

She gave him an appreciative nod. "Thank you, kind sir."

"But what about our age difference? You're what? Thirty?"

"Does it matter? Biologically we differ only by a few months at the most. It is not an issue."

"Well … that might be true … but I'm not sure I can live up to your perception of me. I mean, a hero? That's quite a—"

"Don't underestimate yourself. I have watched you, the way you respect your mother, even though you met her a scant few days ago; the way you love Lauren, barely more than a stranger to you, yet you risked life and limb to carry her dead body down an abyss with little hope of success; and especially your willingness to forgive Darcy, forgetting her cruelty and torture."

Listener tightened her grip on his hand. "Matt, the way you treat each of these women lets me know that you will honor and cherish me. Men like you are as rare as red diamonds. I would be a fool to turn aside and maintain my isolation, to be a loner who spurns romantic partnership. That's why I am directly asking for you to consider me as a potential Eve."

"You mean … as a wife?" Matt shook his head. "But I'm so young. I'm not even seventeen yet."

"I'm sure your parents will be glad to oversee our relationship and guard against emotional upheavals. You are the son of Billy and Bonnie Bannister. You have their blood coursing through your veins. You have their ideals implanted in your mind, so you are far more mature than any calendar indicates." Glittering tears of energy spilled from her eyes. "And you love me, Matt. You know you do. It's time to break down your walls of fear forever."

Matt drank in her sincerity. At that moment it seemed that every blockade he had erected around his heart gave way and crumbled. "Listener, I do love you. And … and I accept your request. How could I turn down a wonderful girl like you?"

Smiling broadly, she caressed his cheek again. "And how could I not ask for the companionship of a man with a heart as beautiful as yours?"

They sat in silence, holding hands as they looked up at a tiny speck of light high above, their entry channel into the candlestone. Now they just had to wait for Ashley to draw them from this refuge. And she would. It seemed that hope had blossomed, and love had painted the night sky with dazzling colors.

Matt leaned his head against Listener's. Everything would work out, as long as they stayed together.

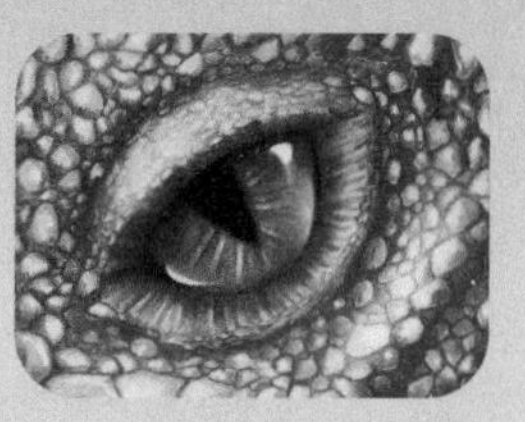

28

CHAPTER

The New Forever

Billy lay on something soft. Darkness filled every corner of his vision. Were his eyes closed? Yes, they had to be. He tried to open them, but they stayed shut.

Something sharp stung his arm, then the pain quickly eased. A muffled feminine voice bounced around, warped and indistinct. Then a new voice drifted by, this one male. A hum followed the notes of a somber melody. A skillful tenor added words and crooned in time with a familiar meter.

> I charge to red horizon's stocks,
> Upend the gates, destroy the locks,
> And free the captives young and old
> To flee unbound from Satan's hold.

A scale, a tooth, a dragon wing,
Appear above, the twilight's king.
Then blade meets claws, our wrath collides;
My skin spews red, his scales divide.

A holy power actuates;
His head and body separate.
The king of darkness falls and dies
Then thund'rous hoofbeats fill the skies

The king of light from Calvary
With sword in hand rides cavalry;
Amidst a shout and trumpet calls
The devil's army folds and falls.

Alas my fractures leave me there
To merely stand in awestruck stare.
I give my blood and final gasp
And fall into the reaper's grasp.

The vultures feast; corruption creeps;
Yet I am but a man asleep.
The bell then tolls the twelve of noon;
Again I count within my swoon.

A chime for daylight, two for cheers,
Three for heroes through the years.
The bells of truth destroy the lies,
And wipe the tears from joyous eyes.

The twelfth sounds loud and ever strong
And calls to gather countless throngs.
Then hushes reign, I hear aloft
The children's voices whisper soft.

Fresh trumpets blare the dawn's commands;
I wake to see a thousand hands,
The children lifting me from death,
Their songs infusing kindled breath.

Our bodies elevate with ease;
With wings of gold we sail the breeze
From vistas high and wide we view
Uplifted hands; a world made new.

We join the throng to dance and sing,
To celebrate our risen king.
The clock has stopped, no more to chime,
At peace until the end of time.

When the song ended, Billy's eyelids loosened. He opened them and looked around. He lay in a bed in a familiar room. Artwork scrawled on notebook paper covered the walls, attached by yellowed tape. This was his old bedroom back when he was fourteen.

He lifted a hand. The last time he had awakened in an unexpected place, tape covered his rubellite ring, but now his finger was bare. Had he lost the ring somewhere? All memories seemed fogged.

"Ah! William! You're awake."

Billy turned his head toward the voice. Professor Hamilton sat in a straight-back chair, his legs crossed and his hands folded on his lap. Wearing khaki pants and a white button-down shirt, he looked ready to teach class back at Castlewood Middle School. "Prof? What's going on?"

"If you are wondering about a ring, no one bears a rubellite now. Everyone is considered equal, and there will be no draconic symbols to separate us." He uncrossed his legs and leaned closer. "I am not surprised that you are disoriented. You have been through quite an ordeal."

"An ordeal is right." Blinking, he looked at the sheet that covered his body. "I battled demons. I fought side by side with dragons. I rode on the back of the devil himself and tried to gouge out his eyes."

"Yes, I listened as you vocalized your nightmares and watched as you thrashed with your bed coverings. During those fitful weeks, we gave you medication to calm you down, but it rarely worked."

"Then was it all a dream? The dragons? Arramos? Second Eden?"

Professor Hamilton huffed. "Of course not. You fought against the forces of evil for twenty years. I was referring to your dreams of late. You have been in a coma for four months, and your righteous battles continued in your mind as you slept."

"Then you must be ..." Billy narrowed his eyes. "Dead?"

"Far from it. You will soon learn that the definitions of life and death have drastically altered since you were on Earth."

"Earth?" Billy glanced at one of the drawings—a dragon battling a knight in armor. It certainly looked like one of his childhood sketches. "You mean we're not on Earth now?"

Prof waved a hand. "That is a realm that you need no longer concern yourself about. All portals there have been closed forever, God is doing what he will with those who remain, and you have been granted rest from your labors." He rose from his chair. "We can go now if you're feeling up to it."

Billy mentally probed his body. "I'm just groggy, and my throat's really sore."

"The sore throat is from a nasogastric feeding tube, and the grogginess will soon clear up. We had to use some conventional medical methods, because our healers were unable to counter the drones' venom, so your body is still flushing it out. Bonnie was also bitten, and her recovery followed a similar course."

"Mardon created a serum. Couldn't you have used that?"

"Good question. Ashley was suspicious of Mardon's character, so she first injected the serum into a lab rat. Although the rat improved remarkably for a short time, it died the next day. She called the problem a time-bomb component and said that Adam would have died from it if not for the fact that the drones killed his mortal body."

Billy's throat tightened. "Adam is dead?"

"As I said, the definitions of life and death have changed, as you will soon learn." He extended a hand. "Would you like to get up and test your legs?"

"Sure, but where's Bonnie?"

Prof nodded toward Billy's bed. "During her months in a coma, she was at your side. She awakened last week and feels perfectly well now. Her wings mended nicely, thanks to Ashley and a local woman who is familiar with such matters. Ashley has been caring for both of you and expected you to wake up today, so only an hour ago she removed your tubes and monitors to make you ready and to clear this room of medical equipment."

Billy gestured toward a drawing on the wall. "If Earth is closed to us, how did my room get here?"

"I asked for this room to be constructed and decorated in this manner so you would wake up to familiar surroundings." Lifting his brow, the professor looked around. "It is quite good, if I do say so myself."

"It is good, Prof. Thanks for doing that." Billy grasped his wrist and pulled to a standing position. The sheet slid away, revealing beige linen pants, a loose medieval-style shirt, and bare feet. He wiggled his toes. They all worked, even the two that had been broken.

When he tried to take a step, a calf muscle gave way. Prof caught his arm and held him up. "Ashley was worried about muscle atrophy. She and Walter took turns exercising your limbs, but it seems that the effort was not enough. You will have to walk carefully until they can get you the proper physical therapy."

Billy lifted and lowered each leg. They felt pretty shaky. "Did Bonnie have the same trouble?"

"Certainly, but she has wings to give her lift. Ashley exercised those as well as her arms and legs."

Billy took another step, easing into it this time. The muscles stayed firm, though the bare skin against the floor felt somewhat tender. "Do I have shoes somewhere?"

"Shoes are unnecessary in this world, though we can provide them if you prefer." He nodded toward the bedroom door. "Shall we?"

"Definitely."

The professor grasped the doorknob and gestured with an arm. "Lead the way. Your friends long to see you, not me."

"My friends?" When Prof opened the door, sunshine poured in. As Billy's eyes adjusted, he walked out onto velvety grass.

A breeze wafted by, the temperature perfect. Against a background of lush trees, at least fifty people swarmed around picnic tables that stood about twenty steps away.

A woman shouted, "Billy's here!"

Everyone turned toward him. Bonnie burst out of the crowd and flew to him, her wings full and flawless. She landed in front of him in a trot, threw her arms around his neck, and kissed him. When she drew back, her eyes danced with excitement. "How are you feeling?"

He looked her over. Braided hair ran along each side of her head and joined at the back. Wearing a silky pale blue blouse with flowing long sleeves, a royal-blue skirt that swept her calves, and a form-fitting black vest embroidered with roses on the front, she looked fabulous. "Now that you're here … perfect."

"Wait till you see who else is here!" She grasped his hand and led the way across the cool, spongy turf.

Billy looked back. The professor closed the door to a small house and followed, though now his face looked younger, and his skin seemed to glow. Elizabeth and Jennifer joined him. One hugged him at each side as he smiled and spread his arms around them.

As Billy and Bonnie drew close to the tables, familiar faces came into focus. Walter stepped out and gave him a hug with a pat on the back. "It's about time you woke up. I've been working my gluteus maximus off while you slept."

Billy laughed. "Then get some super glue and ask Ashley to put it back on."

"Very funny." Walter pulled away and held Billy's shoulders, a twinkle in his eye. "I made a special sandwich for you. It has a hot dog, a hamburger patty, baked beans, coleslaw, and potato chips. I'm sure you remember."

"How could I forget?"

Ashley stepped forward out of the crowd. "And here it is!" One hand held a sturdy plate with a triple-stacked sandwich on top. Her other hand lay over her slightly rounded belly.

As she caressed the bump, the realization crashed into Billy's brain. "When is the baby due?"

"Five months." Ashley looked at her abdomen. "Since I'm so big already, we're hoping for twins. I think I'm detecting two sets of brain waves in there."

Billy hugged her and whispered into her ear. "Blessings to you, Ashley. Thank you for everything. You are truly amazing." He kissed her cheek and drew back. Tears spilled from his eyes, but he didn't bother to brush them away.

Ashley set the plate down on a table and dabbed Billy's cheeks with a cloth napkin. "Thank you for being my husband's best friend. Without you and Bonnie, I never would have met him … or God."

"You're welcome. Walter is the best."

"Billy …" Bonnie hooked her arm around his and looked into his eyes. "Something very important happened while we were unconscious. They wanted to get our permission, but no one knew how long we would be out."

"Our permission? Sounds serious."

"It is, and I'll let them tell you about it." She turned him toward the left. Matt walked up, a rope in hand as he led a donkey. Listener rode sidesaddle on its back, her bare feet exposed below a long, flower-printed skirt and ivory petticoat. Daisies and miniature roses threaded through her pigtails, and floral lace trimmed the edges of her frilly blouse. She looked stunning.

Darcy stood next to the donkey and stroked its neck, her smile as bright as her bodily glow. Wearing a flowing white gown trimmed with blue, she offered a shallow curtsy but said nothing.

Billy gave her a nod. A blend of sorrow and joy for this courageous young woman swelled his heart. Apparently she had died during the journey but now lived in the embrace of Paradise.

Lauren joined the group on foot. She wore dark pants and a matching short-sleeved polo that made her white hair and bright smile more radiant than ever. She held hands with a dark-skinned male youth to her left and an unfamiliar glowing girl to her right.

Billy studied the male youth's chiseled face and shining eyes. He looked like Derrick, the blind boy from the underground lab in Montana, but this young man obviously had no trouble seeing.

Matt, dressed in cargo pants and a black polo, walked up to Billy, hugged him warmly, then drew back. "Dad, since you and Mom were in a coma, I asked someone else for permission to engage in courtship, so Listener and I are hoping you don't mind—"

"No, no, it's all right. I'm thrilled." Billy trembled. His two beautiful children had grown so quickly. They looked far wiser than their years. "But since you were leading Listener on a donkey, doesn't that mean—"

"We're betrothed." Listener slid down from the donkey and ran to Billy. She kissed him on the cheek and embraced him with strong arms. "I'm so sorry about how I treated you the last time we were together." She pulled away. Tears sparkled in her eyes. "I have since been transformed, and God has washed away my sins in the waters of resurrection. I hope you will forgive me and be like a father to me again."

"Without hesitation." As his own tears welled, he kissed her forehead. "Being a father to you is a great honor."

Her smile as wide as an ocean, she removed a daisy from her hair and pushed the stem into his shirt pocket. "In Second Eden, we see no reason to delay commitments. Although I said we are betrothed, we have been waiting for you to wake up before speaking our official betrothal vows."

"Assuming you approve," Matt added. "We hope to marry when you and Mom think we're ready."

Billy tightened his own arm lock with Bonnie. "I approve with all my heart."

"As do I," Bonnie said as she caressed Listener's cheek.

Lauren approached hand in hand with the Derrick look-alike. "Dad, this is Eagle. He saved my life by diving into a volcano in my place, and he resurrected in the birthing garden."

Eagle lowered to a knee and looked up at Billy. "Lauren and I received permission to spend more time with each other, but now I am asking for your permission to continue. Our desire is to become better acquainted so we can learn if we are a compatible couple."

"Since Lauren approves, you have my permission." Billy grasped his wrist and pulled him up. "Thank you for saving her life."

"You are quite welcome, sir."

Billy looked past Lauren and Eagle at the glowing girl. "Who is the young lady you were with?"

Lauren glanced back. "My friend Micaela. She died in a car bomb planted by Tamiel. She lives in Heaven now, and she's here for the celebration. So is my foster mother."

"This day is getting better every minute." Billy's smile grew so wide it hurt his cheeks. It seemed that a thousand questions poured through his mind, so he grabbed the first one. "Who was the person you guys went to for permission?"

Walter laughed. "The senior officer, of course."

Another couple stepped forward from the crowd, a burly, bearded man and a petite woman—Sir Barlow and Tamara. "That would be me," Sir Barlow said. "How could I refuse? They are far more mature than most teenagers." He smoothed out his immaculately clean beige tunic. "Besides, Tamara and I married without your permission, so it seemed consistent to—"

"Wait, wait." Billy held up a hand. "Why would you need my permission to marry?"

"Because in Second Eden all officers must receive permission to marry from someone of higher rank. I had no one to ask, since I held the highest rank until you and Bonnie revived."

"Rank? What rank do you think Bonnie and I hold?"

Tamara slid her arm around Sir Barlow's. "He is teasing you by holding back information until the last moment. He is an actor playing a dramatic role."

"Tamara!" Billy drew his head back. "Your speech! It's perfect!"

She smiled, her face now fuller, complete with rosy cheeks. "When the reservoir released its energy, everyone here was healed, including the Second Edeners who had not yet died from the storm's blight. Their companions dissolved, and they had no need of them any longer. Like Listener, they felt the voice of God within. The original anthrozils were healed completely as well. Dr. Conner found something in Listener's blood that helped him keep them alive until the reservoir opened. That energy evaporated before you and Bonnie arrived, but it lasted long enough for those who were already here."

"That's all great. Miraculous, even. But what about the rank thing?"

"A picture is worth a thousand words," Sir Barlow said as he stepped aside.

From the midst of the crowd, a glowing couple walked into view—Elam and Sapphira. Her hair as white as sparkling snow and eyes bluer than ever, Sapphira smiled. "It is Coronation Day.

Elam and I have gone on to Heaven's glory, but we and several others have been allowed to come to the crowning of the new king and queen of Second Eden—Billy and Bonnie Bannister."

"That's what this feast is all about," Elam added. "Walter thought it appropriate to provide humble foods in a rustic setting, and soon we will walk to the venue for the coronation. A special guest will officiate the proceedings, but that person's identity will remain a secret until the time comes. Your parents will be there as well, and all four of them are preparing a surprise."

Bonnie drew close and whispered into Billy's ear. "Just accept graciously. I tried for days to get them to change their minds. It's not happening."

"Thank you." Billy bowed his head. "We'll do our best."

"Good!" Walter patted him on the shoulder. "Now walk around and mingle. People are dying to talk to you. In fact, a lot of them are already dead. They're the ones glowing like the moon. And Joran and Selah are going to sing and play the lyre, so have fun." Walter gestured toward the forest. "Take a look."

Just inside the tree line, Joran and Selah each held a lyre, strumming the strings as if practicing for a performance. They, like many others, glowed.

Billy and Bonnie walked into the crowd. They shook hands, enjoyed embraces, and shared laughter. They concentrated on greeting the glowing guests first. They would have plenty of time to talk to the others after the ceremony.

Karen told her favorite Walter joke, a silly story about a fish that played golf. Acacia recalled a time when she and Billy sat alone at the shore of an underground lake and talked about her life as a slave in Morgan's mines. Adam and Carly approached together. Adam reminisced about using a lighter in the restroom to try to set off the fire alarm, but a puff of dragon breath really did it. Carly and Bonnie exchanged tear-filled hugs and recounted their first meeting on a bus.

Billy and Bonnie chatted with Merlin, Enoch, Yereq, King Arthur, Flint, Angel, Valiant, Standish and the other deceased knights, Joseph of Arimathea, and Ashley's grandfather. With each person, they shared stories that brought back memories both light and heavy. In this joy-filled reunion, it seemed that even the darkest memories carried no heartache.

During the meal, Billy and Bonnie sat at a long table with Matt, Listener, Lauren, Eagle, Professor Hamilton, Elizabeth, Jennifer, Thomas, and Mariel. At nearby tables sat Sir Patrick, Ruth, their son, Walter and Ashley, Carl and Catherine Foley, Shelly and her family, Shiloh and Gabriel and their kids, Mendallah, Zohar, Edmund, Naamah, Stacy, Rebecca, and Monique.

Billy let out a delighted sigh. The gathering was too good to be true. When Walter began telling funny stories, everyone laughed and felt at ease as they munched on ginger sticks, blister beans, and berry bread—traditional Second Eden fare.

Billy took only a few bites of the sandwich Walter had made, laughing more than eating, and Bonnie munched on her favorite sandwich, a roll stuffed with turkey breast, lettuce, black olives, and honey mustard. Her own laughter spasms sent a dollop of mustard into her nose instead of her mouth.

Joran and Selah walked to and fro in the midst of the tables. Their lyres and voices melded together in flawless harmonies as they sang of past adventures—the plane crash in the Otter Creek Wilderness; imprisonment in the candlestone; dark journeys in the circles of seven; battles against demons after a mysterious rain; Walter's visit to the lake of fire; dangers in Second Eden against the Nephilim; the great battle at the gates of Heaven versus evil warriors from the past; fifteen years in prison for Billy, Bonnie, and Ashley as well as their escape; Mount Elijah's eruption and the disease that ravaged the anthrozils; the mysterious encounters at the seven doors and a wild helicopter ride with Tamiel's goons; and finally the most recent battle against Arramos that concluded with Clefspeare's triumph.

As the stories bounced about, Billy looked around. He inhaled the aromas and let the laughter and excited chatter soak in. It was all so wonderful! But something was missing. With the exception of Listener and Eagle, the only living humans were from Earth. "Bonnie, where are the Second Edeners? And the dragons?"

Bonnie swallowed the last bite of her sandwich. "I heard that the dragons are preparing something special, and the Second Edeners and some others ate before we did and reset the tables with plates and utensils."

"Why would they eat before—"

A trumpet blared from somewhere in the forest. A man bellowed with the tone of a kingdom crier. "It is time to gather for the crowning of the king and queen of Second Eden! Follow the path to Heaven's Tower."

As people rose from the tables' benches, Billy turned to Bonnie. "Heaven's Tower?"

"I heard about it, but I haven't seen it. They're revealing it to mortals today." They joined the crowd as they funneled onto a narrow path leading into the forest. "The Tower of Babel was mankind's vain attempt to reach God. With this new tower, God has provided access between Heaven and Second Eden. The citizens of Heaven can visit us whenever they please, though we can't go from here to there until we die."

Billy looked ahead in the line. Walter and Ashley walked with Walter's folks and Ashley's grandfather, all laughing as they stepped with a lively gait. "So Prof and Walter's dad and sister and others might be visiting us frequently?"

"I don't know how often they'll come, but it's a comfort to know that they can."

"Definitely. I have no idea about how to be a king. Getting advice from Elam will help a lot."

"And Sapphira for me. I would've missed her terribly. We spent four years in Abaddon's Lair with Joan of Arc."

"Right. Joan." Billy looked for a glowing blonde in the line of people but found none. "Have you seen her? I'm not sure what she looks like other than what you've told me."

"I haven't seen her. Most of Heaven's visitors arrived about an hour ago. Maybe she's not coming."

Ahead, the trees thinned out, and the path led to a grassy meadow three times the size of a football field. It sloped gently upward to a ridge with a flat-topped knoll at the center, big enough for a couple of dragons to stand on.

Blankets lay spread out here and there across the grass. Babies played on them, some on their backs, others cuddled in the arms of fathers, mothers, and older siblings—the surviving Second Edeners.

Billy smiled. No wonder they chose to eat first. The babies probably couldn't wait for the comatose guest to awaken. Also, other children frolicked in the grass, some faces familiar—the children they rescued from the airplanes and transport helicopter.

A few Second Edeners stood and guided the new arrivals to open spaces on the meadow, though they kept the area around the stage clear. When Billy and Bonnie stepped out of the forest, Cliffside met them and bowed from the waist, his body glowing brightly. He offered a trembling smile, tears in his eyes. "I have the great honor of escorting you to your places." He turned around and curled an arm at each side. "If you are ready."

Billy took Cliffside's left arm, and Bonnie took his right. As they walked across the grass, the people who were already seated began to rise. Some moved their blankets out of the way to create an aisle. Those closer stood first, followed by those farther away, as if drawn to their feet by the approaching trio.

Billy forced his weak legs to stay steady. This show of honor and respect seemed strange. What had he and Bonnie done to deserve all this? Bonnie looked relaxed as she smiled and waved a wing at the staring children.

A dark-skinned father held an oriental girl and used his fingers to make her wave back at Bonnie. The girl, wearing a frilly pink dress, just stared. A female Latino teenager hiked a diapered white baby higher on her shoulder and smiled. A tear trickled down her cheek as she mouthed, "Thank you."

"Thank you?" Billy repeated to Bonnie.

"Walter told the story about our battle against Arramos and how we kept him out of Second Eden. The story got around. You can figure out the rest."

"Walter told the story." Billy nodded. "That explains everything. I guess he kind of embellished it a bit."

"Oh, he told the truth. He just did it with a dramatic flair, and the story kind of grew on its own after that."

When they reached the open area in front of the knoll, Cliffside stopped and released their arms. He turned toward them and bowed. "Stand here, please, and face the people."

Billy and Bonnie pivoted. Cliffside walked along the aisle, his arms swinging as if he had just heard wonderful news. The people kept their eyes fixed forward. Smiles grew. Children swayed, as if dancing. Anticipation thickened.

Sapphira Adi appeared in the aisle. Her hands folded at her waist, she walked forward and sang with a sweet alto.

While trapped in Hades, hope adrift,
I watched a saint forgive a fraud.
She cast her cares to God's embrace
And leaned on shoulders strong and broad.

I ran to bridge o'er lava deep,
Set cross to flame, and cried aloud,
Jehova-Yasha, make me die
And cause your grace to be my shroud.

Then raise me up to holy light,
The corpse of Mara leave behind;
Sapphira Adi, I will be,
An Oracle who once was blind.

When she reached the front, she set her glowing hands in Bonnie's. "Now I have walked the streets of gold." She rose to tiptoes and kissed Bonnie's cheek. Her brilliant blue eyes glittering, she smiled. "Thank you for showing me the way."

Bonnie kissed her in return. "And thank you for being my everlasting friend."

A male voice sounded from the knoll. "Everyone pay heed!"

Billy and Bonnie turned. Elam stood at the top of the knoll and shouted, "All dragons gather now."

The sound of rustling and beating wings filled the air. A multitude of dragons flew from the forest, one white, some red, and some tawny, some of them glowing. They landed in the cleared area in front of the knoll and settled to their haunches.

As Elam rattled off their names, the dragons bowed their heads. "Shachar, Zera, Hilidan, Makaidos, Thigocia, Goliath, Roxil, Clefspeare, Hartanna, Legossi, and Firedda."

"My dad and your mom are here," Billy whispered. "But I didn't think she'd be in dragon form."

As Sapphira walked to the front of the knoll, she raised a fireball in her palm and waved it across the dragons, scattering sparks over them. "Welcome, friends. Not all dragons are here. Some, of course, chose the way of darkness, while others are here in their human forms."

Elam stepped down and joined Sapphira. A light flashed at the top of the knoll and shimmered, starting at ground level and shooting skyward until it disappeared. Another shimmer ran down. It looked like a glowing elevator car shooting through a narrow crystalline shaft.

"I assume that's Heaven's Tower," Billy whispered. "Very cool."

Bonnie's gaze locked on the sparkling shaft. "So that's how our visitors from Heaven got here."

When the shimmer reached the ground, a transparent door opened. A pulsing white light the size of a large pumpkin drifted out and settled atop the knoll. As it grew in size and brilliance, limbs sprouted along with wings and a long neck, all with reddish scales. Within seconds, it had transformed into a dragon. The color indicated a male, but the light blurred its face. When the shimmer cleared, the face came into focus.

Bonnie gasped. "Arramos!"

"Where is my sword?" Sir Barlow shouted from the crowd. "I knew I should have brought one!"

Arramos laughed. "Peace, friends. It is I, the real Arramos, the first dragon. I had this body long before Satan did. I came in this form to demonstrate a new ability the surviving dragons have been given." As he spread his forelegs, his neck shortened, and his wings shrank. The spines on his head transformed into reddish-brown hair and the foreclaws into hands. Clothes stitched across his body and dressed him in typical Second Eden garb—beige leather tunic and pants with a belt wrapped around his narrow midsection.

Several in the crowd cried out, "Father Abraham!" Others shouted, "The Prophet!"

While everyone clapped hands or thumped tails, Abraham bowed. When he rose, he waved his arms. "You see that I am able to transform whenever I wish, including garments of my choice. The same gift has been granted to the living dragons as well, with the exception of Sorentine, who requested that she stay human forever so she could grow old as Tamara at the same rate as her new husband, Sir Winston Barlow. And Thigocia, who never received a human soul while on Earth, now has one."

At that moment, Makaidos, Thigocia, Clefspeare, Hartanna, Roxil, and Firedda began shrinking. Within seconds they morphed into Timothy, Hannah, Jared, Irene, Abigail, and Dallas. Chatter and laughter broke out everywhere—in the midst of the crowd as well as between the dragons and newly transformed humans.

Billy's heart thumped. Dad stood only a few steps away. Would it break protocol too terribly to run to him and hug him? He exhaled. The hugs would come soon.

He glanced at Bonnie. Her mouth hung partially open, and a tear spilled to her check. Obviously she wanted to leap forward and embrace her mother, who looked young, healthy, and vibrant, in spite of nearly dying only a few months ago.

When Abraham cleared his throat, everyone grew quiet. "Now for a startling revelation. Prepare for news of a wonderful miracle from above." He extended an arm toward the forest. Two more dragons flew toward them, one red and one tawny. Both dipped and swayed in flight, as if unsure of where they were going.

Billy blinked. "They don't look familiar."

"Not to me either." Bonnie narrowed her eyes. "Both are beautiful, though. Not a mark on either of them. Their scales are shiny and flawless."

"And they fly like younglings. Kind of erratic. But they don't look that young."

As they descended toward the knoll, the anthrozils and the other dragons made room. When the duo landed and their wings settled, Abraham called out, "Tell us your names, dragon and dragoness."

The male bowed his head. "My name is Hippocrates."

"And mine is Fidelia." She bowed her head as well.

Their gazes fixed on Billy and Bonnie, they began shrinking and transforming as the others had. Within seconds, Matthew Conner and Marilyn Bannister stood before them.

Bonnie rushed ahead and hugged her father. Irene joined in a three-way embrace. As they laughed and wept together, Billy tried to dash ahead, but tremors shook his weak legs. Jared ran and caught him under his shoulders, then Marilyn slid her arms around them both and drew everyone into a tight hug.

Billy wept. His body shook as he looked into his parents' teary eyes. "What happened? What's going on?"

Marilyn pressed a shaky hand on Billy's cheek and brushed away a tear. "A miracle I prayed for—a combination of water, life energy, birthing soil, and a bone of Makaidos. As soon as I figured out what happened, I told Bonnie's father about it, and it worked for him, too."

"Amazing!" Billy rubbed his mother's back. No sign of wings. "Just … just amazing."

Abraham spread out his arms again. "Let the only tears in Second Eden be tears of joy!" He gestured for the chatter to subside. "Now clear this area except for those who will take part in the crowning."

Billy and Bonnie released their parents and resumed their positions as before, while the anthrozillic humans blended into the audience and the dragons who had not transformed flew toward the back of the crowd. Now only Abraham remained on the knoll. "Billy. Bonnie. Kneel, please."

When they knelt, Abraham called out, "Now you will each choose someone to give you a crown and deliver your blessing. I ask that you choose someone who has ascended to Heaven, for such a person walks with angels and has seen the face of God. He or she can also return to visit you when needed for counsel." He nodded toward Bonnie. "The lady will choose first. If you have not seen the one you wish to deliver the blessing, I will be able to call for that person's presence."

Still on her knees, Bonnie smiled. "That's easy. The warrior with whom I spent four years preparing for battle. My dear friend, Sapphira Adi."

Abraham let out a gentle laugh. "I thought you might name her, but the former queen cannot bless the new one. A proper royal blessing requires the perspective of someone who has never ascended to a throne."

Bonnie looked up at Abraham. "I haven't seen Joan here. Joan of Arc."

"I will call for her." Abraham turned to the crystalline tower and touched the surface. After a few seconds, a shimmer appeared in the sky and descended along the line of the tower. When it reached bottom, a ball of radiance floated out and glided down the knoll. It stopped in front of Bonnie and transformed into a petite blonde woman wearing a simple white dress that flowed loosely from neck to toes, the sleeves reaching past her elbows. Her youthful face's creamy skin glowed.

Bonnie's smile quivered. "Joan!"

"You called for me?" Joan grasped Bonnie's wrists and kissed her cheek. "Mon ami! How am I qualified to deliver your crown and blessing?"

"Your counsel has been a source of wisdom for me ever since our years in Abaddon's Lair."

Joan's French accent flowed in the gentle breeze. "I am gratified that my simple words have borne fruit."

Bonnie bowed her head. "Then, please. Do me the honor."

"Very well." Joan laid her hands on Bonnie's head. "Years ago I told you to speak the truth, live the truth, and be the truth, to never let the faithless ones change any of those three principles. I planted those seeds, others watered them, and God made them grow. It is clear that you are fertile ground, ready to receive wisdom and bear fruit a hundredfold. So I know that only a few words are necessary, and they need to be said only once."

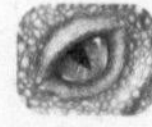

Joan looked at the audience, her eyes shining. "A queen's garments are to be frayed at the knees from prayer and service. Her hands are to be calloused and familiar with bearing the burdens of others. Her feet are to be shod with merciful missions. And her tongue is to be trained to speak messages of peace and goodwill. As you allow these new seeds to sprout and grow, the fruit of wise and noble citizens will follow."

Joan lifted her hands and backed away. Whispers rose from the audience. On each side of Bonnie's head, a streak of white hair ran through her braids to the back.

"Crowns in Second Eden," Abraham said, "contain no gold, no jewels, no signs of wealth or material standing. You will wear a symbol of wisdom, the mark of those who have gained the sagacity that accompanies age and experience." He nodded at Billy. "And your choice?"

"Without a doubt ..." Billy turned his head and called out, "Professor Charles Hamilton."

The professor, still bearing his youthful persona, rose from the last row and ambled forward. As he approached, wrinkles formed on his face, and his dark hair turned gray. When he arrived, he stepped between Billy and the knoll, looked him in the eye, and whispered, “William, I have very little to say that I have not already said to you in the past.”

“Even a little is a lot from you, Professor.” Billy gave him a confirming nod. “I want to hear it.”

“Of course. As you wish.” He laid his hands on Billy’s head and spoke with a resonating voice. “I once told you that God always provides a light that will guide you in the way you should go, no matter how dark it seems. You have journeyed through some of the darkest regions the world has ever produced, and by following the light you have broken through to a new day in which every man, woman, and child has the light dwelling within. Those dark days are over, and light will reign in this realm forevermore, with you, the prophesied returning of King Arthur, finally on the proverbial throne. Yet, even with darkness purged and a crown of wisdom on your head, you must continue to grow in that wisdom. That journey of the faithful ones never ends.”

Professor Hamilton backed away, joined hands with Joan, and ascended the knoll. Billy glanced at Bonnie. She pulled her lips in, as if suppressing a grin, likely indicating that he, too, had gained white streaks in his hair.

Abraham nodded. “Billy and Bonnie. Rise and turn to your people.”

When they rose and turned, Abraham called out, “Citizens of Second Eden, I present to you your new king and queen, Billy and Bonnie Bannister.”

As the people applauded, Billy’s grogginess came back. The rest of the celebration seemed to pass by in a fog. After joy-filled farewells, the visitors from Heaven entered the elevator and zipped up the tower. Billy and Bonnie returned to the picnic tables to help with the cleanup, but everything had already been put away.

After spending some time with their parents, Billy walked with Bonnie to the house he had awakened in, a humble cottage with three bedrooms—one for them, one for Matt, and one for Lauren. In the cozy living room, all four settled on a sofa, each with a mug of hot chocolate as they looked out a picture window at a storm of red, green, and purple lights generated by fireflies.

Bonnie explained that Ashley resurrected dead fireflies using regeneracy sparks she collected when she drew Matt and Listener from the candlestone. Although the sparks had since dissipated, maybe more could be created for future resurrection experiments.

She went on to explain that the revived photoreceptors in the anthrozils allowed them to transform whenever they chose. In the past, the birthing garden was able to give the choice when energized by the bone of Makaidos. Now the power to choose had become permanent.

While Bonnie, Matt, and Lauren chatted and laughed, Billy stayed quiet most of the time. The relaxing atmosphere was heavenly. Matt and Lauren held hands, finally able to enjoy each other's company in peace. Bonnie's wings stayed exposed with no concern about Enforcers. After so much turmoil, it seemed surreal, almost like a dream that might end at any moment.

When Matt and Lauren went to bed, Billy and Bonnie strolled outside. After being in a coma for months, sleeping now seemed less than desirable.

Lantern light shone near the edge of the forest. Hand in hand, they walked toward it. Pegasus and Phoenix shone in the sky at opposite ends of the horizon. Walter and Ashley sat at one of the picnic tables, their faces illuminated by moonlight and the lantern's flickering wick.

Billy and Bonnie sat at the table's other side. "I hope you don't mind company," Billy said.

"Not at all." Ashley stared at a handheld computer. "I'm just checking on updates from Larry and Lois. They're mobile now, like land rovers with wide treads. They're exploring frontier areas—relaying soil samples, air quality, that sort of thing."

"They look like little tanks," Walter said, "but Ashley wouldn't put guns on them, you know, in case of a wolf attack or something."

"They'll be fine." Ashley turned off the computer and slid it out of sight. "Last month we put them in the Valley of Shadows to see if they could find any trace of the shadow people. Nothing. Looks like they're gone forever."

They all sat and watched the lantern's flame. Spider frogs peeped. Crickets chirped. A soft breeze blew. The aroma of gardenias drifted by, a scent that once carried fear but now brought delight. Billy sighed. The peace and tranquility felt good, but something was missing, something important. Might it be … adventure? Purpose?

"By the way …" Walter reached out and flicked Billy's hair. "I like the white streaks, Gramps."

Billy combed with his fingers to straighten the mess. "Because it's dignified?"

"No. Because I get to call you Gramps." Walter nodded toward the cottage. "And with your kids growing up so fast, maybe you'll really be a grandpa soon. I'm guessing three years. Five years tops. Ashley gave Listener a full physical, and her reproductive system looks perfect."

Ashley swatted his arm. "Walter, that's getting way too personal."

"Just sharing the good news." He shrugged. "Anyway, no new birthing plants have sprouted for a while, so it looks like Second Edeners are going to learn a new way to have babies."

"We hope without the pain," Ashley added. "I haven't had even a moment of sickness with my pregnancy, and a pregnant Second Edener has had the same experience, so it looks promising."

"That's good news." Billy shrugged. "Actually, I'm kind of looking forward to being a grandfather. It'll give us something to do."

"Something to do?" Walter's brow knitted. "What do you mean?"

Billy slid a fingernail under a loose sliver on the picnic table's surface. "Well, the ceremony was great—seeing all the people from Heaven, getting crowned, hearing Prof's words and Joan's, but it was kind of anticlimactic."

"How so?"

"Think about it. The party's over. The guests are gone. So what's next? We've been in battles for more than twenty years. And I'm talking hair-raising, sword-clashing, blood-letting, run-like-crazy-till-you-crash battles." Billy pried the sliver loose and tossed it away. "Now they're suddenly over."

"Hey, I'm all for the blood-letting part to be over. I think I've donated at least ten gallons over the years."

"I suppose so." Billy searched for another sliver to peel. "But normal life will feel kind of boring."

"Boring?" Walter laughed under his breath. "Are you kidding me? The adventure's just beginning."

Bonnie tilted her head. "What adventure?"

Ashley reached across the table and took Bonnie's hand. "While you two were recovering, Matt, Listener, Lauren, Eagle, and Sir Barlow explored new territory in Second Eden. The landscape has changed. The natural barriers to travel and expansion have been removed. Challenges await. Frontiers lay before us. It will be far from boring."

"You got that right." Walter set his hands two feet apart. "I saw paw prints this big. It'll be a blast exploring this place and finding what kind of beast planted that print. Not only that, Grackle and I plan to search for his place of birth before he gets too old. The ice-breathing dragons had to come from somewhere, so we hope to find his relatives."

Ashley gathered Walter's hands into her clasp with Bonnie's. "We have a new start in a new world, a world where there is no corruption—no liars, thieves, or murderers. We're surrounded by people we love, people who love us in return. And we have exciting frontiers waiting for us to explore. I can't imagine a better adventure."

Billy joined his hands with the others. "And I can't imagine better friends to share it with."

"Yep." Walter nodded. "It was the four of us way back then, and it's the four of us now. We're still together, no matter how many times you two died."

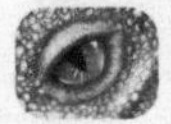

Billy kicked Walter under the table.

"Hey!" Walter grinned. "I guess I shouldn't have worked your legs out so much. They're pretty strong."

"Boys …" Ashley stretched out the word, her own grin wide. "Friends. Remember?"

"Got it." Walter winked. "Friends."

Bonnie leaned close and gestured for the others to join her. When the four heads drew together, she whispered, her voice sounding like a song. "The adventures we have lived through are in the past, phantoms that will live in the memories of those who hear the stories. We hope that what we have done will spark faith, hope, courage, and love in their hearts. But now we have to move on. We have reached the end of a long and harrowing tale. Do new adventures await us? New dangers? New discoveries? Or will we die tomorrow and meet at Heaven's gates?"

She took in a deep breath and tightened their clasp. "I say it doesn't matter. We're friends forever. Nothing will be able to separate us. Not even death. Regardless of what tomorrow brings, our love will last until the end of time."

All four whispered in unison, "Amen."

The **Dragons in our Midst®** and **Oracles of Fire®** collection
by **Bryan Davis**:

RAISING DRAGONS

ISBN-13: 978-089957170-6

The journey begins! Two teens learn of their dragon heritage and flee a deadly slayer who has stalked their ancestors.

THE CANDLESTONE

ISBN-13: 978-089957171-3

Time is running out for Billy as he tries to rescue Bonnie from the Candlestone, a prison that saps their energy.

CIRCLES OF SEVEN

ISBN-13: 978-089957172-0

Billy's final test lies in the heart of Hades, seven circles where he and Bonnie must rescue prisoners and face great dangers.

TEARS OF A DRAGON

ISBN-13: 978-089957173-7

The sorceress Morgan springs a trap designed to enslave the world, and only Billy, Bonnie, and the dragons can stop her.

EYE OF THE ORACLE

ISBN-13: 978-089957870-5

The prequel to *Raising Dragons.* Beginning just before the great flood, this action-packed story relates the tales of the dragons.

ENOCH'S GHOST

ISBN-13: 978-089957871-2

Walter and Ashley travel to worlds where only the power of love and sacrifice can stop the greatest of catastrophes.

LAST OF THE NEPHILIM

ISBN-13: 978-089957872-9

Giants come to Second Eden to prepare for battle against the villagers. Only Dragons and a great sacrifice can stop them.

THE BONES OF MAKAIDOS

ISBN-13: 978-089957874-3

Billy and Bonnie return to help the dragons fight the forces that threaten Heaven itself.

The **Children of the Bard®** collection by Bryan Davis:

SONG OF THE OVULUM

Print ISBN: 978-0-89957-880-4
ePub ISBN: 978-1-61715-107-1
Mobi ISBN: 978-1-61715-043-2

It has been fifteen years since Billy and Bonnie Bannister helped repel the demonic assault on Heaven. The fate of two worlds now rests on the Bannisters' two teenagers.

FROM THE MOUTH OF ELIJAH

Print ISBN: 978-0-89957-881-1
ePub ISBN: 978-1-61715-108-8
Mobi ISBN: 978-1-61715-044-9

In *Song of the Ovulum*, Matt and Lauren set their father, Billy Bannister, free from a demonic captor. Now, Lauren and Billy set out on a journey to find Bonnie.

THE SEVENTH DOOR

Print ISBN: 978-0-89957-882-8
ePub ISBN: 978-1-61715-110-1
Mobi ISBN: 978-1-61715-046-3

An apocalypse approaches, and only Matt Bannister and his mother, Bonnie, can stop it.

OMEGA DRAGON

Print ISBN: 978-0-89957-883-5
ePub ISBN: 978-1-61715-467-6
Mobi ISBN: 978-1-61715-468-3

The epic conclusion to the Children of the Bard and the complete Dragons story world by Bryan Davis.

Published by Living Ink Books, an imprint of AMG Publishers

www.livinginkbooks.com • www.amgpublishers.com • 800-266-4977

THIRD STARLIGHTER

(BOOK 2 IN THE TALES OF STARLIGHT SERIES)

Bryan Davis

Adrian and Marcelle continue their quest to free the human slaves on the dragon planet of Starlight. While sword maiden Marcelle returns to their home planet in search of military aid, Adrian stays on Starlight to find his brother Frederick, hoping to join forces and liberate the slaves through stealth. Both learn that reliance on brute force or ingenuity will not be enough to bring complete freedom to those held in chains.